The Hitman and the Psychic

Jocelyn Drake
with
Colleen Helme

MANETTO BOOKS
COLLEEN HELME

Dedication

To Shelby Nichols
You are the inspiration for this book!
I hope you love it!

DEAR READER...

This book is based on the Shelby Nichols Adventure Series, and two of the main characters, Shelby Nichols and Alejandro Ramos. In the Shelby books, Jackie Manetto has become a romance writer with the pen name of Jocelyn Drake, and she tells Shelby she is writing a book based on her and Ramos.

Naturally, this sparked my imagination and I decided this book needed to be written! For those of you who have been dying for Shelby and Ramos to get together – this book is for you!! YAY! Just FYI - their names have been changed to protect their privacy, along with a few other details.

Also, this is a *spicy romance* written by Jackie, a.k.a. Jocelyn Drake, so if that's not your cup of tea, you have been warned!

I hope you love the book!
XOXO,
~Colleen

Shelby Nichols Adventure Series

Carrots
Fast Money
Lie or Die
Secrets that Kill
Trapped by Revenge
Deep in Death
Crossing Danger
Devious Minds
Hidden Deception
Laced in Lies
Deadly Escape
Marked for Murder
Ghostly Serenade
Dying Wishes
High Stakes Crime
Ties That Bind
Grave Duty
Presumed Dead

Devil in a Black Suit ~ A Ramos Story
A Midsummer Night's Murder ~ A Shelby Nichols Novella
License to Steal ~ A Shelby Nichols Novella

THE HITMAN AND THE PSYCHIC
A Jocelyn Drake/ Jackie Manetto Novel

ACKNOWLEDGEMENTS

I'd like to thank Melissa Gamble for brainstorming and editing this book with me. Your amazing ideas and great feedback have made this book so much better, and given me the confidence to write it!!
You are a rock star!!
XOXO

Also, a big thanks to Kristin Monson for your great edits and making this a better book!! You're the best!

Contents

Chapter 1 1

Chapter 2 9

Chapter 3 19

Chapter 4 31

Chapter 5 53

Chapter 6 63

Chapter 7 73

Chapter 8 83

Chapter 9 103

Chapter 10 117

Chapter 11 125

Chapter 12 137

Chapter 13 157

Chapter 14 167

Chapter 15 179

Chapter 16 187

Chapter 17 193

Chapter 18 203

Chapter 19 213

Chapter 20 237

Chapter 21 255

Chapter 22 271

Chapter 23 283

Chapter 24 303
Chapter 25 311
Chapter 26 329
Chapter 27 335
Chapter 28 341
Chapter 29 349

Chapter 1

Stone

The blast knocked me off my feet, sending me rolling into the wall. Hitting it hard, pain erupted in my arm and head. Heat from the blast grew, and I blinked the disorientation away, knowing I had to get out of there.

Smoke billowed, blocking my way out the door. Coughing, I rushed toward the window across the room, pulling my shirt over my nose. Without a moment to spare, I yanked the window open, and jumped onto the fire escape.

My feet landed on the rickety grating, and the whole thing groaned, threatening to collapse. With every step, it wobbled beneath me, and I hurried faster, knowing I wouldn't survive the forty-foot drop.

At the next landing, the grating groaned, before a crack sounded, followed by a puff of brick dust. Several screws holding the metal to the brick wall pulled loose, sending the staircase into a dangerous slant.

Off balance, I slammed against the stair railing, barely gripping the center pole to swing out over the drop. Adrenaline spiked through my body, giving me strength to swing toward the next landing and let go.

Stretching my arms as far as I could, I managed to catch the railing. As I jerked to a stop, sharp pain spiked through my right arm, but I held on tight. Groaning, I climbed onto the landing, grateful that it held my weight. Holding my arm, I hurried down the remaining stairs and hopped off the landing to the ground.

The closest route to my motorcycle took me under the window, where smoke billowed into the blue sky. Without looking up, I crossed the street and ran down the alley to where my bike waited. Taking a moment to slip on my helmet, I jumped on and started it up in one smooth motion. Cutting a tight U-turn, I headed down the alley in the opposite direction of the explosion and made it onto the street.

Damn, that was close.

About a block away from the building, I caught the wail of approaching sirens, and heaved a sigh as the firetruck sped past me in the opposite direction. I'd been lucky to make it out of there as fast as I had. If not for my sense that something was off, I'd probably be dead.

Hot anger surged through my chest. I'd been set up... again. I couldn't deny it any longer. A low growl curled my upper lip. The bastard had nearly killed me this time. If only I knew who it was.

Vanetti would enjoy saying *I told you so.* I'd convinced myself that he was being paranoid when he said someone was after me. But he'd been right, and I'd nearly gotten killed. My jaw tightened. I should have listened to the old man.

Blood dripped from my elbow, and the sensation of something hot and sticky seeped down my face and into the padding of my helmet. Dammit. This was my favorite helmet, and now I'd have to replace the padding. Could this day get any worse?

I cracked my helmet visor open to get a breath of fresh air. Even after opening all the vents, the aroma of blood, sweat, smoke, and blasting powder overwhelmed me. I'd to have to check every inch of my skin to make sure I hadn't been impaled by anything. Wouldn't that be something? Survive all that crap just to go down from tetanus? I should probably get another shot.

Shaking my head, I turned onto my street, but before I got to my house, my phone started ringing through my helmet-com system. Damn. Now what?

"Call from Vanetti," the voice assistant announced. "Answer it?"

I was tempted to say no, but I didn't have that luxury, so I sent the call through. "Yes?"

"Stone. I need you in my office, now."

I huffed out a breath. "Now's not the best—"

"I don't care what you're doing," Vanetti interrupted. "Drop it and come in. This can't wait."

The line went dead and I groaned. Dammit. Apparently, this day *could* get worse. Shaking my head, I rode past my house and turned back toward the city. Sometimes, being the big boss's right-hand man was a pain in the ass. At least I could clean up and change in my apartment at the office.

It was hard to believe that I'd known Vanetti for ten years now, ever since that fateful day when I'd saved his life. Of course, if not for him, who knew where I would have ended up? He'd taken a chance on a discharged army vet like me, and I owed him everything.

That's why it was hard to believe that someone thought they could take me on. My reputation alone would stop most people from even thinking about it. Whoever it was, they either didn't know me, or they didn't care.

Fifteen minutes later, I pulled into the parking garage of Vitality Ventures, and cut the engine. Stepping onto the elevator, I glanced down at my black t-shirt, and my mouth twisted. I hoped Vanetti didn't need me for anything formal, since I was covered in grime.

Flying debris had even burned a few holes in my shirt. My jeans hadn't fared any better, but at least the blood wasn't dripping from my arm anymore, although it stung like a bitch.

Leaving the elevator, I strode through the high-class lobby. The warm tones, with glass sconce lighting and dark wood molding, gave off an aura of rich luxury, seldom seen in a corporate office. Of course, this wasn't just any office. This company belonged to Quintin Vanetti, the most respected and revered businessman in the city.

I bypassed Vanetti's executive assistant and headed straight to Vanetti's personal office. Without knocking, I pulled the door open and stopped in my tracks.

Whoa. Who the hell was she?

A beautiful woman stood chatting with Vanetti. Average height, with long golden hair that somehow framed a perfectly oval face. Her bright, blue eyes shone like sapphires, darkening as she turned toward me.

Heat flooded through me, and my throat went dry. Damn. Several yards still separated us, but I could almost feel her presence in the space between us.

"What happened to you?" Vanetti's voice snapped me out my trance.

Grimacing, I sent a pointed glance toward the beautiful visitor. Did he really want me to tell him in front of her?

"It's fine, Nate. Spit it out."

Flattening my lips, I stepped into the office, and closed the door behind me. "You were right. It was a trap."

Vanetti's lips turned down. "I told you so. But you wouldn't listen." He shook his head. "It's time we find out who's targeting you and put an end to this. That's why Serenity's here."

He motioned to the woman, and my gaze met hers. Her eyes darkened, and her full lips parted, sending a blast of heat through me.

"Serenity, this is Nathan Stone, my security specialist and bodyguard. He's the one I need your help with." He glanced at me with a raised brow. "Since nothing you've done so far has worked, I've hired Serenity to help you figure out what's going on."

"What?" My eyes widened. "I don't *need* any help... especially from—" I glanced at Serenity. Sure, she was probably amazing in bed, but in a brawl? Could she even shoot a gun? Would she even fight if she were in danger? Most people froze or ran. "—someone like... *her*."

"Someone like *me*?" Serenity's nostrils flared, and a rush of dark pink stained her cheeks.

She had a nice voice, too, even when she was mad. Yeah, I'd offended her, but it hardly mattered. She wasn't cut out to help me in any way, shape, or form, and Vanetti was blind to think she could. If anything, she was a liability that I didn't need.

"Now, Stone." Vanetti held up his hands, but his lips twitched. "You're over-reacting. You've been with me long enough not to question me." His eyes glinted with a dangerous challenge.

I tried not to grind my teeth, but he was right and we both knew it. "So, what's the angle?" I glanced at Serenity.

She crossed her arms tightly over her chest, enhancing the cleavage below the collar of her blouse. Hmm. Nice. Even from here she smelled amazing. Shaking it off, I shifted my stare to the boss. If his plan was to distract me, it was working.

"It's simple, she's perfectly suited to help you, because she's got something you need."

My brows rose. How did he know I'd be attracted to her?

Humor crinkled his eyes, and his lips twisted. "She's a psychic."

"*What?*" I glanced at Serenity in time to see her lips twist in a grimace before she composed her features into something resembling... serenity? With sudden clarity, I stepped close to tower over her. "Are you trying to scam Vanetti? Because let me tell you right now. It won't work. He's not a fool, and neither am I." Dammit, she smelled even better up close.

She jerked back a little before straightening to glare at me, her gaze sparking with blue fire. "I am *not* a scam artist, and if I was, I wouldn't be stupid enough to try it on Mr. Vanetti."

With a huff, Vanetti stepped between us. "Back off, Nate."

I fell back a step and crossed my arms.

"She's not scamming anyone." His eyes narrowed. "She's the real deal, and if you'd give me a moment to explain, you'd see that."

"You believe her?" He *had* to be joking.

He nodded. "Yes... and you would too, if you'd shut up and listen." With a shake of his head, he turned to Serenity.

"I apologize, Ms. Jones. I should have told him what was going on over the phone so he wouldn't be so pig-headed." He looked me up and down. "You're a mess. Go clean up. I'll explain the plan when you come back."

"Fine." I glanced at Serenity, and she glared at me.

Unfortunately, the argument hadn't made her any less attractive. Dammit. Shaking my head, I left the office and stalked to the door at the end of the long hall. Unlocking the door, I opened it into the apartment Vanetti kept for my use. Thankfully, I had everything here that I needed.

My mouth twisted. What the hell was going on? No matter what, I wasn't about to be bamboozled by a beautiful woman. A psychic? Had Vanetti lost his mind?

Chapter 2

Serenity

I took the soda Mr. Vanetti offered me and sat down to wait in his office, while he left to check on Stone, which was the name Mr. Vanetti told me he prefers. After he left, I couldn't help imagining Stone in the shower, naked and dripping wet. Ugh. What was I thinking? I needed to keep my head in the game. Besides, getting involved with a man was the last thing on my to-do list, or any list for that matter.

Letting out a breath, I cracked the soda and took a sip, finally relaxing for the first time since coming here. Taking this job was probably the stupidest thing I'd ever done, but what choice did I have? The pay was too good to pass up, and with my lawyer's fees stacking up, I had to do something.

And now I had to explain my psychic abilities to someone like Nathan Stone? Human-man-God and personification of all things sexy? It would be like trying to convince him that Santa Claus was real. He'd never believe me, and working with him would be pure hell.

Well... maybe not quite pure hell, I'd still get to look at him. Oh, boy. I was in trouble. The moment he'd stepped into the office replayed in my head. He'd come inside like he owned the place, and when his gaze landed on me... a palpable shock hit me in the chest. Tingles had spread through my whole body, and I'd wanted to throw myself at him, and taste those full lips.

I'd never had a reaction that strong in my life, even when I met Brandon. In fact, I hadn't thought something like that was possible... until now. If Stone hadn't been such a jerk, I might not have been able to resist the pull, so maybe it was better this way. He might not necessarily be the enemy, but he certainly *wasn't* a potential lover, in spite of my reaction to him... or maybe even because of it.

If only I didn't have to convince him that my psychic powers were real. Once I proved what I could do, he'd look at me differently. Instead of seeing a normal person, he'd think I was a freak on the crazy side. That heat in his eyes would change to disdain, and a little part of me would die inside. No. I couldn't think that way. His opinion didn't matter. And besides, I didn't want a man in my life.

At least Vanetti didn't seem to mind my abilities. He'd hired me for a simple job a week ago, and I'd come through with flying colors. He was fascinated with my gift, and his acceptance had meant the world to me. That's why I hadn't hesitated to come back for another job.

But he hadn't mentioned that Stone was... well... a living, breathing fulfillment of every woman's deepest desire. Just thinking about him sent heat into my core.

But what if Stone refused to work with me? He hadn't been too happy that I was a psychic. Even proving it to him might not change his mind. Would Vanetti insist on the plan anyway?

Dammit. Why hadn't I thought of that sooner? Now it was too late.

The door opened, and my heart jumped as Vanetti stepped inside, followed by Sexy Stone. Yeah, that's what I was calling him, now.

My insides turned to mush at the sight of him, and I had to hold back a groan. Talk about tall, dark, and handsome. When I'd first seen him, he had dirt and blood on his face, and his hair was a mess. Even then, it had given him a dangerous, but oh-so-sexy vibe that took my breath away.

But now? Holy hell! I could barely swallow. With the distraction of the blood and dirt gone, his dark eyes had depths to them I'd never imagined. His strong jaw seemed even more defined, and his dark hair brushed his forehead in a way that made me want to push it out of his eyes... ugh!

He met my gaze, and I caught a touch of heat in his eyes before a shadow crossed over them, quickly shifting into disdain. Yup... this was not going to go well.

"Let's sit at the table." Vanetti motioned toward the round table in the corner of his elegant office.

Stepping to it, I automatically pulled my pink dust-cloth from my purse so my bare skin wouldn't come in contact with the chair. After pulling it out, I sat down, keeping the cloth in my lap in case I needed it again.

Stone's eyes narrowed, and he leaned forward to peek at the cloth in my hands. He raised an eyebrow. "What's with the hankie?"

His low voice sent a shiver down my spine. I tried to ignore it as I fought back a sarcastic reply. I was a professional, and this was a great opening to explain my 'psychic powers,' so I might as well take it. I cleared my throat and straightened my shoulders.

"My... *ability* manifests through extrasensory perception. It's something called psychometry." I shot him a challenging glance. "Ever heard of it?"

Stone smirked. "I like to know what tricks scam artists use, but this one's new."

Mouth twisting, I glared back but didn't take the bait. "Most people are uneducated when it comes to things like this."

"Why don't you educate me, then?" His voice hardened, but he motioned with his hand to continue.

"Fine." Oh, I wanted to educate him all right... in bed. Focus. "It's simple. When I touch an object, or sometimes, a person, I get some kind of insight about them."

"Such as?"

"Like their history... or something about the person who last came into contact with the object... that sort of thing. Depending on the circumstances, I can get a vision of the past or the future, and how it relates to the object." I kept my tone firm and professional, ignoring the little voice in my head that reminded me how crazy that explanation sounded.

Stone raised his brows. "And... what's the hankie for?"

I grimaced. "Well... I don't like to touch every little thing, so I use it to protect me from sensory overload."

"Right." He nodded, but his lips twisted. "So, touching things tells you something about the object." Huffing, he glanced between Mr. Vanetti and me. "No offense, but how's that supposed to help me? I'm pretty sure touching that bomb today wouldn't have stopped it from going off."

"A *bomb*?" My eyes widened. I cleared my throat and tried to school my face. "Well, no, but I may have gotten something warning me away from it." I didn't add, *without my gloves on.* "But I bet if I went back there now and touched a remnant of it, I'd get something from that." Well, that explained the dirt and blood.

"Really?" Stone leaned forward, dark gaze intense. "Like what?"

"Hopefully, an impression of the person who made it. I might get a vision of them and I'd know what they looked like." I shrugged like it was no big deal. "It could be any number of things that would lead us to them, like their initials, or an address... something like that."

I almost added that my visions weren't always clear, but that wouldn't help my case. Though now that I knew he'd almost been blown up, I wasn't sure I wanted the job.

Dammit; too bad I needed that money. "I'm a licensed private investigator. I have a concealed carry permit, and I know some martial arts, so I can take care of myself."

Stone stared at me for several long moments before shaking his head and turning to Vanetti. "You can't be serious. You want *her* to help me figure out who's after me? And the major qualification is that she's a psychic? How do you know she's not lying?"

That jerk. Glaring, I opened my mouth to retort, but Mr. Vanetti held up a hand.

"Stone... remember that missing contract from about a week ago?"

His brows puckered. "You mean the one the courier lost? You told me you found it."

"That's right, but it was Serenity who found it. Since you were busy at the time, I hired her for the job. She tracked it down in a couple of hours. It was amazing."

"Okay, fine." Stone glanced my way, his eyes tightening. "But this is a lot more complicated than finding a missing document."

Vanetti shrugged. "The principle is the same. Besides, you haven't made much progress on your own."

Mouth tightening, Stone sat back in his chair. "I haven't had enough time to figure it out."

Vanetti's lips thinned. "And the longer it takes, the more likely this guy is to succeed. Like it or not, the clock is ticking. Work with Serenity, and she'll figure it out in no time."

Stone huffed out a breath and crossed his muscular arms across an equally muscular chest. "I don't need a... *psychic* to figure it out." He practically spit out the word.

Vanetti pursed his lips and narrowed his eyes. "But look what happened today. I'm certain she'll find the bastard. She might just save your life."

"No—"

"Wait a minute," I interrupted, glancing between the two men and settling on Vanetti. "I thought I was just helping you figure out who had a grudge against—" I motioned to Stone "—him." I licked my lips. "I know we agreed that I'd be working with him twenty-four seven, but—"

"*Twenty-four seven?*" Stone cut me off, rising to his feet. "Absolutely not."

Vanetti slowly stood, his gaze hard and flinty. My heart froze in my chest, and I shot a wide-eyed glance at Stone. After a couple of tense seconds, he wisely sat back down.

Vanetti's quiet voice cut through the silence. "This isn't negotiable. She's helping you, whether you want it or not."

Stone didn't reply, and I was honestly too scared to say anything either.

"My mind's made up." Vanetti shifted his gaze to me. "You'll be staying with him twenty-four seven like we agreed. Your job is to figure out who's after him, *like we agreed*. Hopefully, you'll manage to keep him from getting killed while you're at it."

I gulped. "But... this is a *lot* more dangerous than I thought."

Nodding, Vanetti sat back down. "I'm aware. It's more dangerous than I realized as well. And I'm sure, since you've met Stone, you might want to back out, but I'll make it worth your while."

I glanced at Stone, who was sitting completely still as if every feature on his face was chiseled from granite. Huh, maybe that's why his name was Stone. His gaze locked on mine, and I knew he'd make my life a living hell if I accepted. Could any amount of money be worth that? Probably not. But I didn't want to get on Vanetti's bad side, either.

"A hundred and fifty grand. That's how much I'll pay you."

I blinked. "What?"

"I'll give you half right now, and the rest when it's over."

I could barely breathe, let alone speak. Licking my lips, I knew I couldn't pass up that much money. Not when it would solve all my problems. "Okay... but what if Stone gets killed? Will I still get paid?"

"Depends on who kills him." Vanetti's mouth twitched. "If it's you, no. If it's someone else... it depends on the circumstances."

My eyebrows shot up. "Seriously?"

Again, a corner of Mr. Vanetti's mouth twitched. "Look, Ms. Jones, I've invested a lot into Nathan here, and if I didn't firmly believe you could help, I wouldn't have hired you."

"And... the whole keep-him-from-getting-killed thing?"

Stone glared at me again.

"Find the culprit, and Nate's safe."

I let out a breath. A hundred and fifty thousand dollars was a lot of money. "Okay, you've got a deal." I'd better not regret this.

"Good."

Vanetti stepped to his desk to write me a check for seventy-five grand. As he wrote it out, I tried to ignore Stone's murderous glare. He jumped from his seat and began prowling back and forth like a caged panther. Was he trying to intimidate me? No way was I going to let that work.

Heat came off him in waves, and I swallowed. This was definitely a mistake. But I could handle it. A few days and I'd be done. All I had to do was find the person who wanted him dead. With my psychometry, that shouldn't take long. In fact, I could figure it out by tomorrow, right?

Vanetti handed me the check, and I examined all those zeros before stuffing it in my purse. I stood and gave him a fist bump instead of shaking his hand. "Thanks Mr. Vanetti, I won't let you down."

"I know. Did you bring everything you need?"

I nodded. "I have a bag in my car."

Vanetti glanced at Stone, and his lips flattened. Stepping to his side, he put his hand on Stone's shoulder. "I have a few things I need you to do, but I want you to spend most of your time finding the son-of-a-bitch who's after you. Why don't you take Serenity to your office and give her the rundown of what you know?"

Stone's jaw was so tight, I worried that his teeth would crack. It surprised me that he didn't start yelling and complaining, but after our chat at the table, he held it all in, only giving Vanetti a curt nod before striding to the door.

I figured he'd just march right out, leaving me in the dust, but, after pulling the door open, he glanced my way. "Coming?"

The danger in his tone sent shivers down my spine. Knowing this wasn't the time to back down, I rose to the challenge and sent him a regal nod. "Of course."

Holding my head high, I followed him out.

Chapter 3

Stone

The door closed behind us and I sent Serenity a glare. "Let's get one thing straight. I don't need anyone to *protect* me."

"Of course you don't, but I've got a job to do, so let's start with a few questions."

"Fine. Go ahead."

I headed down the hall while she quizzed me, but my head pounded, and I hurt in so many places that I didn't know which felt worse. It didn't help that I was stuck with a *psychic* day and night until this was over. What the hell was the old man thinking? She was like a babysitter. I'd never been so humiliated in my life, not even in the army.

The moment Serenity realized the job could be dangerous, I'd hoped she'd refuse, but then Vanetti had to go and offer her a hundred and fifty grand. No one in their right mind would pass that up, so of course, she took it. Dammit.

Still, that didn't change my mind about making her life miserable. In fact, I'd make sure she earned every penny of that money, and I'd enjoy every moment it took.

She'd quit talking, so I glanced her way. Her brows drew together, and her eyes shone with blue fire. "You're not even listening to me."

I raised a brow. "We'll talk in my office. I'm not a fan of airing my personal problems in front of everyone." That may have worked better if there were more people around.

"Oh? You mean *all* the people here?" She gestured to the empty hall. "Yeah, I can see how you'd need more privacy.

Rolling my eyes, I continued to my office. It was at the end of the hall, right next door to my apartment. As I pulled the door open, it was tempting to let the door shut in her face, especially after that snarky remark, but my manners got the better of me, and I held it open for her.

"After you." I motioned her inside, raising an eyebrow and not trying to hide my sarcasm.

Mouth twisting, she slid past me, keeping as much distance between us as possible. For some reason, her distance made my stomach twinge, but I pushed the feeling away. Maybe I could actually get her to quit.

"Well... have a seat." I motioned toward the chair beside my desk. My office was only a quarter the size of Vanetti's, but since I wasn't there much, it hardly mattered.

She glanced around the sparse space. "Where're all the security cameras?"

"In the office down the hall. I'll introduce you to Forrest Slater another time, but he monitors the security cameras, and protects everyone's computers from hackers."

"Oh. So... what do you do all day? Stand around flexing in the mirror?"

I almost snorted. Almost. "Why? Is that what you're hoping to see?" I stood up a little taller and winced as my shoulder and side pulled.

"You okay?" Her voice softened.

"Fine." I sighed, lowering into my chair, hoping I wasn't bleeding all over my shirt. I hadn't had time for more than a cursory glance at my injuries. "Let's cut to the chase." I let out a breath, and met her bright blue gaze. "You don't want to be here, and I don't want you here. So there's no need to pretend that you care, got it?"

"Absolutely." Her jaw tightened, and she glared at me. "I'd hate to waste my energy on caring about someone like *you*."

My stomach twisted, but I shoved the feeling aside. This was what I *wanted*, remember?

She very deliberately sat down in the chair beside my desk, her movements controlled and smooth. "So?" She set her shoulder-bag on the floor. "What do you have to show me?"

I stared Serenity down for a few seconds while I tried to come up with something. I didn't actually have a folder full of suspects or anything. Hell, until today, I hadn't actually accepted that someone was trying to kill me, and I couldn't let her think I was an idiot. "I... uh... just a sec."

I twisted to open the bottom drawer in my filing cabinet, which sent a sharp stabbing pain through my upper back. Ignoring the pain, I pulled the drawer open, blindly searching for something in there to show her. Even an empty folder was better than nothing.

She gasped.

Now what? I ignored her and kept digging.

"Stone... you're bleeding."

"What?" I straightened up. "Where?"

"Your back." She pointed.

I raised my arm to look, only lifting it halfway before hissing in pain, and grabbed my shoulder.

"I think you'd better let me take a look at it. Do you have any bandages in here?"

"What? Now you're a doctor?" Pain always brought out my charming side.

"Would you rather bleed all over your shirt?"

"No." Point taken. The pain in my shoulder faded to a dull ache, and I let out a slow breath. "I have some supplies in my apartment." I shook my head. "It's right next door."

"Great." She sent me an overly cheerful smile, obviously enjoying my pain. "Let's go."

"Fine." I took my time getting up, doing my best to act like nothing was wrong. From her raised eyebrows, I didn't think I'd fooled her.

"Need a hand?" She smirked. I glowered at her, but she just grinned and hurried to the door. "Here, let me get that for you."

Straightening to my full height, I stalked to the door. It might have been more impressive if I could have moved faster. But at least I managed to walk through the door without limping.

"Wow... so what hit you? A mini-nuke? It must have been huge to damage someone as tough as you."

I growled and stepped past her to the apartment door. "You mean you didn't see the fallout?" Unlocking the door, I held it open for her.

"Oh, I'm sure there's plenty of fallout when you're around." She slowly scanned me up and down before raising a brow and sauntering past me, giving me a great view of her perfect little ass. Glancing over her shoulder, she continued. "But I haven't seen it yet."

My stomach jolted and heat rushed through me. Bantering with her brought a crooked grin to my lips. "Am I really bleeding? Or is this your way of getting my shirt off?"

She grinned back, though a flush covered her cheeks. "You're really bleeding."

I raised an eyebrow. "I'm pretty sure you just insinuated that I'm nuclear-level hot."

She rolled her eyes. "Yeah... right." Clearing her throat, she glanced away. "Where did you say the bandages are?"

Mouth pinching, I shook my head and flipped on the lights, illuminating the hallway and kitchen area. "The bathroom's down the hall on the other side of the kitchen... on the left."

What was I thinking? I wasn't here to flirt with the woman. She was here because Vanetti thought she was a psychic who could help me figure out who wanted me dead. Besides that, I'd barely met her, so bringing her into my personal space should have been uncomfortable. But it wasn't. Instead, a thrill went through me to have her here.

On the way to the bathroom, she took her time, glancing into the open kitchen and taking in the white cabinets, granite counter tops, and all the latest appliances.

She stepped to the right, where the short hallway opened into the living room area, with floor-to-ceiling windows on the west side, showing fantastic views overlooking the city.

As she took in the decor, featuring off-white carpet, couches, and furniture, accented by splashes of color and abstract art on the back wall, her breath caught, and her eyes widened.

She paused, looking around. "Wow, this is amazing. You live here?"

"Sometimes. It depends on what Vanetti needs, but yeah... I spend a fair amount of time here."

She glanced my way, her eyes the color of clear, blue water, and I froze. How could anyone have eyes that color? Maybe she wore contacts... yeah... that was it. Fascinated, I took a step closer, just to see if I was right.

Her scent wafted over me, and I breathed in deeply, wanting more. I'd never had a woman in my apartment without sex involved, and having Serenity here stirred my desire. Part of me knew that I wouldn't be satisfied until my lips were on hers and her body was crushed against mine.

Her eyes darkened, like she was thinking the same thing. She even licked her lips. Unable to stop myself, I slowly closed the distance between us, but she cleared her throat and stepped away before I reached her.

"Uh... the bathroom's this way, right?"

As she walked away, I took a deep breath without bothering to answer. Should I give in to this attraction? Did *she* want me to? Was she playing this little game of cat and mouse on purpose? And more importantly, how long would she last before giving in? I'd seen the look in her eyes.

Anticipation flowed over me, and I followed her down the hall to where she waited in the bathroom. She stood on the far side of the room beside the huge walk-in shower, taking her time to examine the jacuzzi bathtub.

"Wow... this is nice... I love the tile. It reminds me of a spa."

A beautiful pattern of sea-green and turquoise tile covered the walls, and the crystal lighting made everything sparkle. Along with the white and sea-green fluffy towels, I could see what she meant. "Do you go to the spa much?"

"Well... no. Actually... I've never been to one, but I'm sure it would look a lot like this... I think it would, anyway."

"Right." I couldn't hold back a smile.

She shook her head and clasped her hands together. "Where are the bandages?"

"You *really* want to bandage me up?" There was just something so *nice* about that. I wasn't used to nice... not really. I was used to sexy and daring and lust. Not *nice*.

"You're hurt. You already told me you didn't want to bleed all over your shirt."

I studied her for a moment, until another blush rose on her cheeks.

"I don't have to." She shrugged. "I'm not trying to invade your personal space."

I smirked. She'd expertly invaded my personal space so well I hadn't even noticed. "No, I appreciate it." I gestured to the white cabinets. "They're in the bottom drawer on the left."

"Right." Nodding, she stepped to the cabinet and opened the drawer, pulling out the plastic crate full of first-aid supplies. After setting it on the counter, she turned to me, all business-like. "Do you want to do this in here or at the kitchen table?"

Again I smirked, but held back my reply. Did she know how that sounded? "Here's fine." I slowly unbuttoned my shirt, keeping my gaze down so she could stare if she wanted to. As I unfastened the last button, I raised my gaze to her face.

Her eyes were glued to my chest and she was chewing on her bottom lip. Her chest heaved like she'd just run a marathon, and her cheeks turned rosy. For a second, I worried that she'd clutch her chest and fall over from a heart-attack.

She raised her gaze to mine, and the desire in her eyes changed the clear blue depths into a stormy hurricane. My heart quickened, and, without taking my gaze from hers, I slowly peeled off my shirt, hearing a small gasp escape her lips.

Her eyes widening, she quickly pointed to my shoulder. "Whoa... your shoulder's bruised. That looks painful." We both knew she was trying to distract herself. A moment later, however, her gaze wandered from the bruise to roam over my chest again.

Her lips parted. "Damn." She swallowed, still staring.

Was she going to start drooling?

Coming to her senses, she snapped her lips shut, and swallowed again before shaking her head. Without meeting my gaze, she motioned with her hand. "Uh... you'd better turn around and let me take a look at your back. That's where the blood was coming from."

A primitive wave of anticipation sent tingles skating over my skin, and I could hardly wait to feel her fingers on my bare back. I turned, closing my eyes as her feather-light touch brushed my skin. It was easy to imagine what her bare breasts would feel like pressed against my back while her hands roamed my chest.

I breathed in her scent, grateful she couldn't see my face... or that I was getting hard under my jeans. Her hands roamed over my back, pausing at the smaller cuts and bruises.

"It looks like you got thrashed pretty good, but I don't think you need stitches on any of these cuts. I'll clean up the biggest one and put some antiseptic on it before I bandage it."

Opening my eyes, I caught her vivid-blue gaze in the mirror. Shit, the mirror. Was it too much to hope she hadn't seen how much I enjoyed her touch? Holding back a groan, I fought the sudden urge to throw self-restraint to the wind and pull her against me.

She was seriously messing with my control. "Fine, just hurry it up." My voice came out gruffer than I intended, but her nearness made me want to know her in all the sexiest ways.

She frowned and got to work, wetting down a piece of gauze and wiping the wound. I held still, leaning over the sink with my head down so she couldn't see my face, while she applied the gel.

Once she'd taped the bandage on, she pulled back. "That should do it."

"Thanks." A little calmer now, I turned to face her, not bothering to reach for my shirt. I wanted to make her feel as crazy as I did. Her eyes darkened, and I couldn't resist teasing her. "See anything else that needs a bandage?" Just as I'd hoped, her gaze roamed over me. Her hand rose to touch my bruised shoulder, and I held my breath in anticipation.

At the last moment, she dropped it to her side and stepped back, flustered and red-faced. "Uh... I'll wait in your office while you put your shirt on."

She'd have to pass me, first, and I wasn't ready to let her go. "Do you think I need an ice-pack for my shoulder?"

"Uh... yeah. That's a good idea." Her brows drew together and she shook her head. "What happened, anyway?"

I raised an eyebrow. "A bomb. Did you think I made that up?"

"No, but how did the bomb get there? How did *you* get there?"

Smirking, I pushed through a burst of pain in my head. There wasn't any reason to keep her in the dark. "A contact messaged me and said he was in trouble, so I went to help."

"And?"

I tilted my head and let out a slow breath. Maybe asking me all these questions while I was half naked was a turn-on for her. Liking that idea, I leaned towards her to see how she'd react. Her eyes widened, but she held her ground.

"He was meeting someone in a condemned office building and told me he needed backup. It wasn't far, so I went."

"And that didn't seem unusual to you?" Her brow quirked.

"Nope." Mouth twisting, I shook my head. "The meeting was supposed to be in an office on the top floor, but when I got there, it was empty." My jaw tightened, intensifying the ache in my head. I needed some pain killers. "I knew something was wrong. I just didn't know how wrong until I heard the ticking. I barely had enough time to duck behind an old desk before the bomb went off."

"Oh my gosh." Her eyes widened. "You're lucky the bomb-maker used a timer."

"No kidding." I grimaced.

"So the blast did all of this?" She gestured to my chest and shoulder.

"Hardly. Let's just say the fire escape was a little rickety."

"Jeez." Her soft lips pursed, drawing my gaze to them. "No wonder you're so beat up." Her fingers skimmed across a bruise on my chest, and my skin rippled under her touch. Gasping, she snatched her hand away. "Sorry.... I was just wondering about broken ribs. I'll go find that ice pack."

As she brushed past me, the place where she'd touched my chest still burned. Whoa, I'd never felt anything like that before. Did she have Icy-Hot on her hands or something? Rubbing the spot, I crossed the hall into my bedroom.

Pulling a fresh shirt out of my closet, it hit me that she'd probably be staying here, in the apartment... with me. Desire rushed over me, and I had to take a few deep breaths to get under control.

That's when I realized she hadn't used a hankie to keep from touching me, or anything else in the bathroom. Had she used it at all since she'd been here? Was it just a ruse for Vanetti?

But that feeling when she'd touched my chest... had she actually seen something about me? Was *that* why it burned? I quickly slipped on my shirt and hurried into the kitchen, rubbing at the spot again.

I found her standing in front of the fridge, holding the ice pack. I waited for her to turn around, but she seemed frozen in place.

"Uh, Serenity?" I took a few steps forward, but she still didn't move. "Are you okay?"

Chapter 4

Serenity

A warm hand on my shoulder jerked me out of the vision. The truck barreling toward me disappeared, leaving Stone standing next to me. I blinked the image away and let out my breath.

His eyes narrowed, and he put his other hand on my shoulder to steady me. "You okay?" For almost the first time, his gaze didn't hold any anger or disdain. If I had to guess, he was genuinely concerned.

My heart squeezed. Clearing my throat, I swallowed and pulled back. "I... uh." I licked my lips, the vision flashing through my mind once more. "Just..." I shook my head and took a deep breath. "When was the last time you used this ice pack?"

His brows drew together as he studied me, some of the cynicism returning to his dark eyes. "Why don't you tell me?"

"Seriously?" I huffed out a breath, but he didn't budge. "Fine. There was a truck. You were on a motorcycle, and it came right at you, like it was trying to hit you. You got out of the way, but your bike slid out from under you." I raised my eyebrows at him. "I think you hurt your leg."

"Wow." Stone's eyes widened an instant before narrowing into a glare. "Wait. Vanetti told you, didn't he?"

"No. Why would he? He only told me that someone had a vendetta against you." I shoved the icepack into his hands and slammed the freezer shut. "I can't see *why*, though," I muttered, stalking to the kitchen island. Jerk.

"What was I wearing? Tell me the color of my helmet."

I spun to face him. "What were you wearing, huh? Are we playing that game, now?"

He met my gaze without flinching, staring me down, challenging me to prove myself. I should have been used to it by now; after all, I did advertise as a psychic. I got it almost every day, but part of me had hoped that Stone would believe me because of Mr. Vanetti. I rubbed my forehead a short breath. "Your helmet was black and red. And you wore a black leather jacket."

His intense, dark eyes narrowed slightly, but he didn't acknowledge my information. "So— what did you see when you touched my chest?"

My eyes widened. "What? Nothing."

He raised a brow. "Liar."

I glared back. "I didn't see anything." But I couldn't hold his gaze, and glanced away, trying to hide the heat rising in my face. Just the memory was enough to send tingles down my spine. Touching his chest had been like touching fire and ice at the same time.

I'd had to use all my willpower to resist running my hands over his skin, hoping to feel that electric shock spread from him into me. What would it be like to peel my shirt off and feel his bare chest against mine? Tingles raced over me again, and I had to rub my hands up and down my arms to push the sensation away.

Needing to change the subject, I concentrated on my vision. "Why don't you tell me about the truck? The driver was obviously trying to kill you. Did you manage to see the person's face?"

His lips turned down and his eyes narrowed. He knew I was sidestepping him, but he let it go. "No. It all happened too fast."

My shoulders sagged with relief. "That makes sense." My gaze landed on his chest, which wasn't too hard since it was right in front of me. His shirt was unbuttoned, and I got a tantalizing view of all that skin.

Without thinking, I raised my hand to touch him, but caught myself just in time. Stepping back, I nearly tripped over my feet. I needed to get out of there. "Uh... we'd better get back to your office so we can find this guy." I motioned toward his chest. "And you need to finish getting dressed."

He smirked. "Why? This is comfortable."

"It's too distract—" I stopped myself just in time. "Never mind." I shook my head and rushed out of his apartment, nearly running to his office. Ugh. This was the worst. What was I thinking? Obviously, I wasn't.

I took my seat beside his desk and waited for him to join me. Hopefully, he wouldn't razz me about my stupid comment. This attraction could *not* go anywhere. Needing to appear totally professional, I sat up straight and tried to look like I knew what I was doing.

He was slower joining me, and I was grateful he'd taken the time to button up his shirt. Of course, now that I'd seen his bruises, it made sense that he was moving slower. He studied me for a long, uncomfortable moment before huffing out a sigh.

"Look." Twisting his lips, he met my gaze. "I don't have any files to show you. I didn't realize what was happening until the bomb went off this morning."

I'd had a feeling that was the case. "Don't worry about it. Why don't we make a list of your enemies? That's a good place to start." Thank goodness he was focusing on the task at hand. Maybe offering to bandage him up hadn't been the best idea. But I'd felt bad for him.

I'd left my shoulder bag on the floor, so I grabbed it and took out my notebook and pencil. I flipped to an empty page and labeled it *Enemies*. "Okay. Let's get started. Can you think of anyone who'd want you dead?"

His brows rose, then his lips twisted into a frown, like he thought it was a stupid question. "Well... yeah." He scratched his neck. "In my line of work, it comes with the territory, but I don't think many of them would go to the trouble. I mean... a bomb is kind of overkill."

"Well, not exactly. It didn't work, so it wasn't actually overkill."

He rolled his eyes and shrugged. "Fine. There's Switchblade... but I think he moved back to Orlando, so probably not. Maybe Brent White's son, Jake... since Brent's... uh... dead. Although I'm not sure Jake would be that upset about it... so maybe not him, either." He huffed out a breath. "This is a waste of time. It's not going to be that obvious."

"It's not a waste. Let's just be more specific. How about this? Do you know anyone who knows how to make a bomb?"

Stone shook his head. "Not that I can think of, but that doesn't mean they couldn't learn if they wanted to."

"Okay. Well... let's try a different approach. Did you make anyone mad recently? Say... within the last six months?"

Stone glanced up at the ceiling before shaking his head. "I've made a lot of people angry, but they'd never come after me. I have a reputation, and they know it wouldn't turn out so well for them."

"Right." I swallowed, grateful I hadn't seen a vision of him beating someone up... or... killing someone. He didn't look like the kind of person to kill people in cold blood, but what did I know? Still, I definitely didn't want to see that. "Then tell me about the times you were nearly killed. Including today, how many are there?"

"Including today... three... no four."

"Okay. Tell me about the first one."

He sat back in his chair. "Sure... but first you have to remember that I didn't think someone was trying to kill me at the time, or I might have done a better job of tracking them down."

I raised a brow. "Sure. I totally get that. So what happened?"

His brows dipped. "The first time is the one you saw, where I barely missed getting hit by that truck. I managed to get out of the way, but my bike slid out from under me. The truck just took off, so I chalked it up to incompetence and forgot about it."

"When was this?"

"A little over a week ago."

My brows rose. "Oh... that recent? Okay. What happened the next time?"

"That was a day later in the parking garage here. I had just parked my car and was walking to the elevators. I heard a car coming up behind me, so I moved to the side. Instead of driving past me, it slowed and waited for me to cross in front of it. When I took a couple of steps, the driver sped up and came right at me."

Stone shook his head. "I managed to dive out of the way, but it was close. By the time I got to my feet, he'd gone around the corner, and I didn't see a plate. The car was a tan, late model sedan, but there was nothing to distinguish it."

"Did you check the security cameras in the garage?"

"Of course I did." His voice hardened. "But the angle didn't show anything more than what I saw."

"Okay." I made a note of it and met his gaze. "So, the first two times they used a vehicle to kill you... uh... I mean... try to kill you. When was the next time?"

He let out a breath. "It was two days ago. I was just leaving the gym and walking down the street to my bike. My buddy yelled at me to watch out, and I ducked into a doorway. This big AC unit comes crashing down from the roof. If not for his warning, it would have hit me for sure."

His lips twisted. "I was so mad that I rushed into the building to see which apartment the unit had fallen from, but no one seemed to know anything. I hurried to the roof and found some scratch marks on the concrete. Whoever put it up there either had help, or they were strong. That's when I first suspected someone was out to get me. I told Vanetti, and he agreed. The bomb this morning was the fourth attempt."

"Okay... so this morning you were lured to the building by a text from a contact?"

"Yeah."

"But it obviously wasn't them, right? So did you talk to your contact afterward?"

"Yeah... I called him while I was cleaning up, and he insisted he hadn't sent it."

I shook my head. "So it was someone pretending to be him?"

"Yes. It was sent from a burner phone, and they used his name."

"Okay... so it's someone who knows your contact *and* your number. I think that could be a good starting point. Who's the contact?"

He shrugged. "His name's Razor, and he's part of the Shadow Serpents gang. But I don't think it's any of them. Razor knows better than to cross me or Vanetti, and so does his gang."

"It wouldn't hurt to talk to him though, right? Maybe I'll pick something up."

"I guess."

"You still don't believe me, do you? Even after I described your accident?" I couldn't blame him *too* much, but it still annoyed me.

"I don't know." He sighed. "Maybe I do, but I don't get how your ability even works. And even if you *could* pick something up, connecting it to me seems like a stretch."

My mouth pinched. "Okay, fine. I get that, and I wish I could explain it better, but that's how my psychometry works. When it isn't connected to the job, I just keep it to myself."

"So you pick up a lot of things?"

"Yes, I do." My teeth clenched. "But, I usually *know* if it's connected."

He raised an eyebrow.

"Ugh." I threw my hands in the air. "So typical. You know what? Mr. Vanetti hired me to figure this out, so that's what I'm going to do, even if I have to visit this snake gang by myself."

"Hang on." He held out a hand. "Don't even *think* about going anywhere without me."

"Why? I get the feeling you'd be happier *alone*, anyways."

His jaw tightened.

It looked like I'd hit a nerve, but I didn't take it back. He'd been a total jerk ever since Mr. Vanetti told him I'd be working with him. "You know, I would *think* someone with a target on their back would be happy to get help."

Mouth twisting, he let out a frustrated grumble. "Fine. But if you really can pick stuff up, then we should start with the bomb. Believe me, you *don't* want to meet the Shadow Serpents. Especially if you call them the 'snake gang' to their faces." He shook his head, obviously disgusted.

I sniffed. "Okay, fine. But we're still going to have to talk to your snake buddies."

Stone rolled his eyes and pushed to his feet. He winced when he stood, but I was done feeling bad for him. Relief to do something constructive washed over me, and I put my notepad back in my purse and slung it across my shoulder. I bit my lips as I followed him out, noting his slight limp. But it wasn't my problem that he'd nearly gotten himself killed today, even though my stomach plunged at the thought.

Stone stepped into his apartment for his leather jacket, and we took the elevator down to the parking garage without saying much. He led the way to his car and popped the trunk. Taking out a motorcycle helmet, he held it toward me. "Here. This should fit you."

I froze. "We're going on a motorcycle?"

"Yeah... unless you're afraid to ride it." He let his hand fall and raised a brow. "Maybe you should touch the bike? It might show you who's after me."

I narrowed my eyes. "I guess it's worth a try." I couldn't quite tell if he was being serious or just goading me.

He moved to the side, allowing me access to the bike. Suddenly nervous that I wouldn't get anything, I ran the fingertips of one hand across the leather seat. Getting nothing, I placed my entire palm over it and still got nothing.

Crap. This was bad. Using both hands, I felt my way to the handlebars. As I wrapped my hands around the grips, a blast of pleasure surged through me. It felt so good that I closed my eyes. I could almost feel the wind blowing through my hair. The sudden vision of a truck swerving into my lane sent a spike of adrenalin through my body, and I jerked my hands away, my breath heaving.

"What was that?" He *almost* sounded concerned.

I bit my lips. "I think I saw the truck that nearly killed you. But this time I got a look at the driver. It's definitely a man, because he had a beard, and he wore a ball cap and dark glasses."

Stone's brows rose. "Okay, that's actually helpful, but still not much to go on." He paused, eyes narrowing. "But I guess if you saw that, then it's possible you might actually pick something up at the bomb site. *If* we're lucky." He shrugged, like it was a long-shot.

"Rude." I glared at him, crossing my arms over my chest.

His brows rose. "What? I didn't mean it in a bad way. It just seems like your visions aren't always crystal clear." His lips twisted. "It kind of sounds like a crap shoot to me, but if you saw the driver, then maybe we can figure it out."

"Of course we can. I wouldn't be doing this if I couldn't."

"All right. Well then, let's go." His brow cleared, and he sent me a nod. "Have you ever ridden a bike before?"

"Uh... no."

He flipped the pegs down on both sides of the bike. "That's where you'll put your feet, and you'll be holding onto me. A motorcycle is a lot like a bicycle, so you need to lean with the bike. Just hold onto me and go with the flow. Got it?"

I barely kept from rolling my eyes. "I'm sure I can handle it."

He met my gaze, and his lips twitched. "Good. And one more thing."

I lifted a brow. "What?"

"Hold on tight. It wouldn't look good for me if you fell off." He snickered, and I barely refrained from smacking him.

He held the spare helmet out to me and I hesitated. If I touched it, would I see a vision of all the other women he'd taken on his bike? It had to be a possibility since he had a helmet that was just the right size for a woman to wear. How was I going to put that on my head and not see something? This was terrible. "Do I need to wear that?"

He glanced at the helmet as if seeing it for the first time. "You're afraid of this?" Understanding dawned, and his eyes narrowed. "You don't want to see who wore it last." He smirked. "Why? You think it belongs to my girlfriend?"

My stomach jolted. "You have a girlfriend?"

He frowned. "Why is that so hard to believe?"

"No reason... I just...you seem too... uh... busy, I guess." I barely managed to keep from saying *arrogant* and *egotistical*, but it was close. Besides that, he'd almost kissed me in his apartment. What kind of guy goes after another woman when he's already seeing someone?

He shook his head, so I reached for the helmet. "Here. Give me that. At least if your girlfriend wants you dead, I can warn you, right?" I grabbed the helmet and braced for the vision of a beautiful woman smiling at him with adoration glowing in her eyes. Nothing. Crap. Now that I'd made such a big deal out of it, I had to say something. "I guess you're in luck."

He smirked. "You didn't see anything, did you?"

I hesitated, but since he'd spot the lie, I had to give in. "No, I didn't. So let's go already."

While he closed the trunk, I tried to slip the helmet on, but it was like stuffing my head into a soup can. It was either going to rip my ears off or pull my hair out in chunks. "Are you sure this will fit me?"

Stone glanced my way and his lips twisted, but he managed to keep a straight face. "Here. Put it on from the back like this." Stone guided me through the process, and I finally had it on my head with my ears still attached.

"You fasten the chin strap on the side."

I felt for it, but couldn't find the snap.

He pushed my hands away. "Here... I'll do it." He fastened the strap together and stepped away. "Leave the visor up until we get going. Then just flip it down."

"Okay."

"After I'm on the bike, step on the peg, here, and swing your leg over the back."

"Sure." I waited while he got on the bike. Ready, he held out his arm for me to grab, and I stepped on the peg. I had to brace both of my hands on his shoulders before I could swing my leg over the seat.

It took me a second to find the peg with my other foot, but once I did, I settled down behind him. Glad to have that part over, I flipped my visor down and carefully placed my hands on the sides of his waist. I wasn't sure how tight I'd need to hold on, but I didn't want to give him the satisfaction of me wrapping my arms around him.

He started off slow, giving me a chance to get used to the bike. After winding through the parking garage, we came to the exit. He stopped to look both ways before crossing the sidewalk to the street, where he stopped again to merge with traffic.

He smoothly pulled out and began to accelerate. I swallowed, and my grip on him tightened. A little thrill of excitement sent butterflies through my stomach, and a grin spread over my face. I liked this... a lot.

Soon, my arms were tightly wrapped around him, and I was molded to his back, my inner thighs touching his legs. I peered over his shoulder to see where we were going and leaned with him around every turn. I didn't know if he was showing off, or if all motorcycle rides were this great, but I was hooked.

Several minutes later, we drove past an old building with yellow crime scene tape across the entrance. The police were still there, along with a fire truck, and I knew we'd never get past them.

That didn't seem to matter to Stone. He drove the bike around the block and parked in an alleyway across the street from the back of the building. After he turned off the engine, I knew I had to get off before him, but I wasn't sure how to do that.

"Stand up on the pegs," he said. "Then swing your leg over."

"Okay." I put my hands on his shoulders for balance and swung my leg over the back of the seat. He held out his arm, and I grabbed onto it before stepping down, grateful I hadn't fallen over.

He slung his leg over the bike a lot more gracefully, and pulled off his helmet. After shoving his hair back from his forehead, he turned to me, and I sucked in a breath. Holy hell... how did he get even more handsome?

His dark brow rose, and I realized I still had my helmet on. Reaching for the snap, I couldn't seem to find it. Taking pity on me, he stepped close and pulled it apart.

"Thanks." I tugged off the helmet and ran a hand through my hair, hoping it didn't look too terrible. He took my helmet and set it on the bike with his before turning my way.

"See that alley at the back of the building?"

"Yeah."

"There's a window on the fourth floor, just above a fire escape on the west side of the building. That's the room with the bomb. I'm hoping some of the debris might have shot out of the window and fallen into the alley. With the police still here, that might be our only way to find something you can touch."

"Oh... okay, let's go." At least the police were on the other side of the building, so we should be okay to walk over there.

We hurried across the street and into the alley. "Where's the window?"

Stone pointed to the fourth floor with the fire escape hanging off to the side.

"You came out that way?"

"Yeah, but the fire escape was still attached when I started down."

"Sheesh! I'm amazed you didn't fall."

"Yeah... it was close." He turned his attention to the debris on the ground. Broken glass, a few bricks, and building material littered the alley.

"So are we looking for wires or something?"

He shook his head. "No... I'll know it when I see it. But if anything stands out, go ahead and pick it up."

I wasn't sure this would work. I needed something a lot more concrete than a piece of the building. But I didn't want Stone to complain that we were wasting our time. We spent several minutes combing through the junk, but nothing looked promising.

I found a piece of metal that could have been from a desk and picked it up. "What do you think this is?"

Stone came to my side and took it from me. "Looks like part of a chair. You get anything from it?"

I wrapped my hand around the metal rod and waited, but, after running my fingers over the entire surface, nothing came to me. "Sorry... I'm not getting anything."

"Try this."

He handed me a piece of wood, but I got nothing from that either. A second later, he picked up a pencil and handed that over. I took it, and got an instant vision of a man holding it between his teeth. It faded away before I could see his face, but I noticed that his bottom teeth were a bit crooked. "I saw something. A man was holding this pencil in his mouth."

"Was it the guy you saw in the truck?"

"Uh... I'm not sure. I only saw his teeth."

He raised a brow. "That's it? Nothing else?"

"No." I almost apologized, but held back. "It's possible he didn't touch anything but the bomb. That would explain why I haven't picked anything up. If I could get inside the room, I might have a better chance."

Stone glanced up at the window, and his lips flattened. "Without the fire escape to get up there, we can't risk it. I guess we could come back after the police are done."

"Yeah... that's a possibility."

"Okay. Then we might as well go."

His tone lacked conviction, and I hated disappointing him. Stone strode to the street, and I followed, more discouraged than I liked to admit. For the first time, I began to doubt myself. What if my abilities weren't enough to figure this out? Stone didn't seem impressed with me, and now I wondered if I'd over-sold myself.

Stopping at the bike, Stone pulled out his phone. "You're sure you want to meet the *Shadow Serpents?*"

I almost smirked at his emphasis on their name, but resisted. "Yes. It's our only real lead."

His lips twisted, but he gave me a nod. "Then I'll need to let Razor know that I'm on my way." He sent a text, and, a few seconds later, his phone chirped. He read it and nodded. "He's at the shop, so we can talk to him."

"Great." I got my helmet on, but still couldn't figure out the strap. I was going to leave it undone, but Stone noticed and snapped it for me. I thought he muttered something under his breath but I couldn't make it out. Had he just compared me to a two-year-old? "Did you say something?"

He met my gaze, his eyes wide and innocent. "Me? No. Not at all." As he turned away, a smile tugged at the corners of his mouth. I chose to ignore it and waited for him to climb onto the bike.

Squashing my frustration, I stepped onto the peg, grabbed his shoulders, and swung my leg over the seat. I started to sit down, got a cramp in my leg, and jerked back up. Could this get any more embarrassing?

His head twisted toward me. "You okay?"

"Uh... yeah... just give me a second." The painful cramp finally went away, and I slowly sat down. Grateful it didn't come back, I slipped my arms around him, and he started up the bike.

Not sure where we were going, I relaxed into the seat and let myself enjoy the ride. We ended up driving to the other side of town, and I realized that riding the motorcycle was perfect. It saved me from the awkwardness of making small talk with a guy who, for all intents and purposes, was forced to be with me and hated my guts. Probably.

It reminded me of my ex and his penchant for ruining my life. His stupid accusation that I owed him for mental abuse was bad enough, but now he was dragging his feet and wouldn't agree to anything. How stupid was that? At least with this job, I'd have enough money to pay my lawyer's fees.

Stone glanced down at my hand, and I realized I'd grabbed hold of his jacket and was clenching it in my fist. I quickly let go and tried to smooth the jacket out, which left me rubbing his side and stomach. I froze, hoping he wouldn't get the wrong message.

A few minutes later, we pulled into a run-down auto-repair shop, where we continued around the lot to the back of the building. Stone slowed the bike in front of a double garage-door opening, where two men were tinkering on a car, and pulled to a stop.

They both glanced up at us, and one of them hurried inside the garage. The other guy crossed his arms and leaned against the side of the car. He wore his long hair in dreadlocks, and a black bandanna was tied around his forehead. His sleeveless tee showed off the tattoos that covered the dark skin on his muscled arms.

Stone held out his hand for me, so I did my best to climb off the bike without falling over. He got off right after I did and pulled his helmet off. After setting it down on the seat, he stepped toward the muscled man. "Hey, Joint, Razor tell you I was coming?"

"Yeah. He'll be ready in a minute." Joint glanced my way and his lips twisted. "Look like your woman needs some help."

Stone glanced over his shoulder to find me struggling with my stupid strap. I'd tried everything to get it unsnapped, but nothing worked. I'd just about given up when Joint nodded at me. Had he just called me Stone's woman? Heat flooded my cheeks. Maybe I should just leave the helmet on.

Stone pursed his lips and stepped my way, tugging on the strap and popping it open. I managed to pull the helmet off, but my hair flopped forward into my face, and I had to shove it back. Damn. This could get worse.

Wanting to be careful about what I touched in this dirty place, I pulled my leather gloves from my purse and put them on. I glanced up and found Stone watching me, a frown on his face. "What?"

"Nothing." He shook his head. "But it seems like you're not doing your job with those on."

"I don't want to pick up every little thing, so I have to protect myself."

Stone shrugged. "Whatever." He turned back to Joint. "So... how's business these days?"

"We keepin' busy."

"Good to hear."

The man who'd run off came back out, stopping beside us. "Razor says to come to his office."

Stone nodded, but his shoulders tensed. He glanced my way, looking at my hands, and spoke under his breath. "Maybe you'd better wait here."

My brows rose. I wasn't about to let him go in there without me. I had a contract to uphold. "I'm sticking with you. Remember? Twenty-four seven? I can take these off anytime, you know."

Stone's mouth twisted, but he didn't argue, so I followed him inside. The garage smelled of oil and grease, and we passed a couple of cars that were on lifts, with men working on them.

Continuing down a hall, Joint led us to a large office, where a man wearing a black tee with several holes in it sat behind a desk. His long, dark hair was tied back and a bushy beard covered his lower face. He held a rag in his hands, and wiped off his dirty fingers.

With our arrival, he motioned toward the chairs in front of his desk. "Hey, Stone. Good to see you in one piece." He looked my way before glancing back to Stone. "What can I do for you?"

Joint stayed at the door, blocking us in, and the other guy sat down behind us. The hairs on the back of my neck rose, but I tried not to show any fear. Besides, Stone could take them all out, right? After his greeting, Razor sat back in his chair like he was a king holding court.

Stone didn't seem fazed by any of this, and his voice had a hard edge to it. "I'm looking for the guy who sent me the text that nearly got me blown up. As you said before, it wasn't you. But it had to be someone who knows we have a working relationship."

Razor set the rag on his desk and leaned toward us. "You think it's one of my men?"

Stone shrugged. "Who else would use your number? That's why I'm here. I'm sure it's not someone loyal to you, but I'm wondering if you have anyone new... say... in the last month or so."

Razor glanced behind us at Joint. "What do you think?"

"We have a couple of newer recruits, but I doubt they'd be dumb enough to go against Stone."

I sat forward. "Do any of them have short hair and a beard?" Glancing at the men around me, I realized they all wore beards, and my eyes bulged. "Uh... and who also wears a ball cap?"

Razor smirked. "Not everyone's here today, but you can talk to the guys out there." He shook his head. "But I don't think it would be any of them." Rubbing his beard, he pursed his lips and met Stone's gaze. "I can't imagine any of my crew setting you up."

Stone nodded. "I get that, but it only takes one."

Razor scowled. "Fine... do what you gotta do. Let me know if you figure it out; that way I'll know how to handle the situation."

He was warning Stone to let him take care of it, and the way Stone grumbled under his breath, I knew he didn't want to do that.

Stone glanced my way. "Anything here you want to touch? Like that rag?" He motioned to the greasy rag sitting on Razor's desk.

"Uh... no." I narrowed my eyes at him so he'd know it wasn't funny.

He shrugged. "Fine." He turned to Razor. "Thanks for your help. We'll go talk to the others." Pivoting, he faced Joint. "I might want to meet your new recruits. When would be a good time for that?"

Joint glanced at Razor for his okay before answering. "Come to the park tonight around eleven. They'll be there then."

"Thanks."

Joint moved aside to let us pass, and we stepped into the garage. Stone leaned close to me and spoke in a low tone. "Feel free to touch anything you want out here."

My lips turned down. "I know how to do my job."

He ignored that and continued around a couple of cars to one on the opposite side. The man working on the engine glanced up, then did a double-take. He grabbed a rag and wiped his hands. "Stone... what are you doing here?"

"Hey, Cash. I'm looking for someone. This morning, I got a text to meet Razor at a condemned office building. But Razor didn't send me the message, so I'm asking around if anyone knows who sent me the text. Was it you?"

"Me? I don't know what you're talking about."

Stone glanced my way and lifted an eyebrow. I knew he wanted me to touch that dirty old rag Cash was holding. Knowing I couldn't put it off forever, I held out my gloved hand.

"Can I see that rag for a minute?"

Cash wrinkled his nose. "This thing?" At my nod, he handed it over.

"Thanks." I took the stinky cloth, but didn't take my glove off.

Stone raised a brow, so I beckoned him a few paces away and lowered my voice. "I'll check it in a minute."

His eyes narrowed. "Why not now?"

"I don't like having an audience. I'll check it before we leave."

He opened his mouth to object, but shook his head instead. "Fine... whatever."

We made the rounds to the other workers, and I picked up two more rags. I kept them in order so I wouldn't get them mixed up, and hoped there weren't many more. I was probably doing this all wrong, but it was too late to change direction now.

Luckily, those were the only men with rags I had to check. Once we got to the bike, I laid them on the seat and pulled off my glove. Stone stood beside me with his arms crossed, and I picked up his impatience.

"Here goes." I touched them in reverse order, since that was easier to remember. The first one showed me an argument between the guy and Joint, but nothing about Stone.

I moved to the second and saw a poker game, and the guy losing all his chips. He was pretty upset, and I wondered if I should warn him. Of course, it could have already happened, so I let it go and picked up the last rag.

At first, nothing came to me. Then I got the impression of Cash holding a phone to his ear. He spoke, but I couldn't hear the words clearly. I closed my eyes and concentrated, finally hearing Cash's words that the guy owed him some money and he'd better pay up before Stone got wind of it.

My eyes flew open. "Cash was talking to someone about paying up before you found out. We'd better get back in there and ask him who he was talking to."

Stone didn't waste any time, and I had to run to catch up with him. Unfortunately, Cash wasn't there anymore. Shaking his head, Stone grabbed a worker's arm. "Is there another way out of here?"

"No. Just the way you came and the main entrance."

We hurried through the building and out the main entrance to the street, but there was no sign of Cash. Frustrated, Stone stormed back inside, straight to Razor's office. "I need to know where Cash lives."

"He's your guy?"

I stepped closer. "Not for sure, but he might know something about it."

Razor huffed out a breath and tapped on his computer. A few seconds later, he found the address and gave it to Stone.

"Thanks. I owe you."

With a small smile on his lips, Razor nodded. "Good to know."

We hurried back to the bike, and Stone had his helmet on and the bike started before I could get my chin strap snapped. He glanced my way and shook his head.

Leaving it undone, I stepped on the peg and managed to sit down before Stone took off. I wanted to tell Stone that Cash probably didn't go to his house, but I just let out a breath and kept my mouth shut.

Chapter 5

Serenity

We arrived at a trailer park on the west end of town. Stone pulled inside and drove through the park until coming to the correct trailer on the end of the street. There was no car parked in front, so it didn't look like Cash was home, but that didn't stop Stone from stepping to the door and knocking. He even peeked inside the window before admitting Cash wasn't there.

I'd remained by the bike, and Stone came back with a scowl on his face. "Do you want to try the rag again? Maybe you'll see where he went?"

"Oh... I left it at the car shop... but I don't usually get more than one vision from an object, so it's no big deal." I shrugged.

"No big deal?" His jaw tightened. "If you'd touched it back when we were standing in front of Cash, we wouldn't have to be here."

"I realize that." I bit back. "But I don't like using my ability in front of people... especially guys like that."

"They wouldn't have cared. Besides, you said you knew what you were doing." He glared.

"I do!" My heart raced and heat flushed my cheeks. "And *you* don't know what would've happened, so back off."

"Fine." He crossed his muscular arms over his chest and threw an angry look at the trailer. "I guess we're back to square one, then."

"Not necessarily," I countered. "I might get something from the trailer. I can try touching the doorknob at least."

Stone's brow relaxed. "Okay."

He followed me to the door, where I touched the knob and waited for a vision, but nothing happened. Frustrated, I twisted the knob and the door popped open. My eyes widened. "I guess he didn't lock it."

Stone's brows rose. Without any hesitation, he pushed the door open and stepped past me into the trailer. Taking a breath, I slipped my glove back on and followed him inside, locking the door behind me. I turned to find the place neat and tidy, which surprised me.

While Stone shuffled through stacks of mail, I wandered into the bedroom, impressed by how clean and uncluttered it was for a guy living alone. It sure made it easier to start touching things, even when I didn't want to.

I knew touching other people's stuff was what I'd signed up for, but that didn't make it easy. Mostly because I always felt a little guilty that I was invading their privacy. Plus, there were some things I just didn't want to see.

But this was my job, so I might as well get used to it. I found some photos on the wall and took a moment to examine them. A young Cash stood with another guy who seemed slightly familiar. Was that our guy? His baby face, without a hint of beard, made it hard to know.

I picked up the picture frame and carried it to Stone. "Does this guy look familiar to you?"

Stone took it from me and his brows dipped. "That's Cash... but I don't know who the other guy is." He glanced my way. "Is this the guy from your vision?"

"No. That's why I asked." I took off my glove and touched the frame, but didn't get any vibes. "Not getting anything." I set the frame down on the kitchen counter and looked around. "I need to touch the right object. Something connected to Cash and this person he was talking on the phone with."

"If the guy came here, would you pick that up?"

"Yeah... I might."

I stepped into the living area and began touching the furniture. Feeling nothing from the couch, I ran my fingers across the pillows, then continued through the room, touching a lamp, the light switch, and the big screen TV. Nothing happened, and I worried that Stone would lose faith in my ability.

I spotted the remote and hurried to pick it up. As soon as I touched it, a vision swam into view. Standing in this exact spot, Cash was holding a phone to his ear and talking. "Hey Johnny. It's been a while. Sure, a drink would be nice. See you then."

The vision faded and I jerked back to myself.

Stone stepped closer. "Did you see something?"

I nodded. "Yes, but I don't know if it's going to help. Cash was talking on his phone to a guy named Johnny. They planned to meet somewhere for drinks. It could have been yesterday, or a while ago. So it's probably already happened. Do you know anyone named Johnny?"

Stone shook his head. "Not that I can think of. I guess we'll have to track Cash down for a talk before we'll know for sure."

"Yeah." I sighed. "Look, I'm sorry I didn't touch the rag to begin with. I messed up."

He huffed out a breath and nodded, then his brows dipped. "Tell me about your vision from the rag again. What exactly did Cash say?"

"He was telling someone to pay up before you got wind of it. Doesn't that sound like Cash set you up for money, and the guy hasn't paid him yet?"

Stone blinked. "Maybe. But it could be something else."

"Like what?"

He shook his head. "There's a weekly poker game that Cash has a penchant for, but he doesn't always have the funds. I told him that he couldn't play without settling his debts first."

"Really?" I shook my head. "You know... I did pick up that one of the other guys lost everything at a poker game. So I guess that could be it, but what if it isn't?"

"We won't know until we talk to Cash."

"So it might not be him at all?" I closed my eyes. "I feel like such an idiot."

Stone sighed. "You know what? It's probably okay that you didn't touch the rag right away. I don't know what I would have done if he'd been right in front of me. So, don't be too hard on yourself." He shrugged. "Like you said, it *could* still be him." But his tone remained skeptical. He sighed again. "I know you think it's connected to me, but maybe you just need more practice to know what's what."

That just made me feel worse. If I couldn't figure out how my ability worked, what the hell was I doing? I wanted to make a name for myself, but this could totally ruin my reputation. Could I be that far off? "No. I'm sure I'm not wrong."

Stone's mouth twisted and his jaw tightened. Since I didn't want him to think I was unreasonable, I continued.

"But, like you said... we won't know for sure until we talk to him. Maybe we can come back later?"

"You mean like after we go back to the building with the bomb?" He heaved a sigh and stalked to the door. "We might as well head back to the office."

He stepped out of the trailer house, holding the door for me, and it was easy to feel his impatience. Did he think I was useless? That this whole thing was a joke? I had to prove that he could trust my abilities. I trusted them... right? But what if I was wrong?

We got to the bike, and I managed to get my helmet on and the strap fastened all on my own. Go me. Stone seemed withdrawn, and I couldn't blame him. I just needed to convince him that I knew what I was doing.

After pulling into the garage at Vitality Ventures, we got on the elevator and I glanced his way, my stomach squirming, but I *had* to say something. "Look, I know you're probably having doubts about me, but I didn't pick those things up by accident. I think there's a connection between you, Cash, and your stalker."

He shrugged. "If you say so."

A surge of frustration pulsed through me, and I opened my mouth to argue, but snapped it shut before I said anything. To be fair to him, the evidence wasn't on my side, and, aside from seeing Stone's near miss on his bike, nothing else had panned out. So where did that leave me?

Stone glanced sideways at me. "Let's be realistic, Serenity. I don't think this is going to work out." My gaze jumped to his, but he glanced away, his lips thinning. "I'm sure it's not your fault, but I don't want to waste time with this. How about we make a deal? Since Vanetti's convinced that I need your help, you can act the part while I figure this out *on my own.*

"You can stay in my apartment, or my office, and do whatever you want. Once I know who it is, you can collect your money, and we'll go our separate ways. Sound good?"

My breath caught. Did he really think I was that useless? "No. That does not sound good. I can't believe you'd even suggest it. Vanetti trusts me, and even if you don't, it doesn't mean I can't figure it out."

"Sure, but finding a missing letter is a lot easier than tracking down a murderer. Touching things isn't getting us very far. In fact." He finally faced me. "Concentrating on that is probably taking us away from making real progress. Face it, I can do this a lot easier on my own."

Anger burned through my chest. "No way. I made a deal with Vanetti, and I'm earning every bit of that money. If that means I'm sticking by your side every minute of the day, then you'll just have to get used to it."

"If that's the way you want it, then fine." He sneered. "Go ahead and touch all the things you want, but I'm going to focus on *actual* detective work."

I shook my head and glared at him. Jerk. "Oh, so you get to do your job, but I don't get to do mine? How the hell am I supposed to help you if you won't let me?"

His lips twisted. "That's not really my problem. I can see that you're trying really hard, and that's great, but I don't see the point in continuing to do something that's not working."

"Not working? We've barely begun. It's been what? Two hours? And now you're giving up? I didn't think you were such a quitter."

His eyes narrowed. "You don't know me, lady. I'm perfectly capable of handling this on my own. I don't know what the hell Vanetti was thinking, but I don't need your help. If anything, you're a distraction, and it's making this—" He cut off, rubbing the back of his neck.

"A distraction? What's that supposed to mean? I'm just as dedicated to finding this guy as you are."

He stepped closer to me, and his nostrils flared. "I work better alone." Pausing, his gaze raked over me, and my heart sped up. His voice rumbled. "You're just too damn—"

The doors slid open, and we glanced up to find Vanetti standing there. Stone stepped away from me, and I straightened, automatically putting a pleasant smile on my face. "Hey there."

Vanetti's brows rose. "You two getting along, okay?"

"Of course. Going down?"

"I was, but since you're both here, I need to talk to you first. Let's go to my office."

Stone motioned for me to go first, and I followed Vanetti through the reception area and down the hall to his office. What was Stone about to say? I'm too damn... what? I wanted to think it was stupid so I could keep arguing with him, but the way his voice had gone all rumbly... and how he'd looked at me. That's not the way you look at someone you think is stupid. Unless it is? No, definitely not.

Vanetti sat behind his desk, and we took the chairs in front. Clasping his hands on his desktop, he gazed between us. "So... are you two having any luck?"

"No," Stone said.

"Yes," I said.

Vanetti's brows rose. "So which is it?"

"We didn't find much at the office where the explosion took place," I spoke up before Stone could answer. "But we found a lead with Razor and his gang. One of the gang members knows something, but he took off before we could question him." I shrugged, leaving out the part where I'd messed up. "But I picked up a name at his trailer house, so we're going to look into that."

Stone glowered at me, but I ignored him. My job wasn't his problem? We'd see about that.

"What's the name?"

"Johnny. Do you know someone with that name who might want to kill Stone?" I raised a brow at Stone. "Because he can't think of anyone."

Again, he glared back, but didn't try to stop me.

Vanetti's brows rose and he shook his head, so I went on. "Also, tonight we're supposed to meet with some of the newest gang members, and the bad guy could be one of them. If he is, we'll wrap it up tonight."

"Hmm. You think it will be that easy?" Vanetti glanced at Stone for confirmation, but Stone just shrugged, his lips flat.

"Anything is possible." I shrugged. "But we won't know until tonight."

Vanetti studied Stone for a long moment before turning back to me and nodding. "Good. I'm glad you're making progress. If it won't be a problem, I need Stone to pay a visit to the club. After that, you're free to go back to your investigation."

Stone raised a brow, his expression clearing a little. "You have a delivery for me?"

"Yes. It shouldn't take long." Vanetti glanced at me. "Could you excuse us for a moment?"

"Oh, sure." I slipped out of the room, leaving the door ajar to wait in the hall. Behind me, I heard chairs shifting before a beep sounded from the safe.

"Here you go. Wes knows you're coming," Vanetti said.

A moment later, Stone strode out the door, walking passed me as if I wasn't there. If I didn't know better, I'd think he was trying to ditch me. Peeking back inside, I sent a quick wave to Mr. Vanetti. "Uh... see ya."

I followed Stone back to the elevators, but kept my mouth shut. He may want to ditch me, but I wasn't going to let him, no matter what his reasons were. After all, it was his life I was trying to save, and I'd do my job. If he ended up dead, it wouldn't be my fault. And, as long as I didn't kill him, I'd still get paid, right?

Chapter 6

Stone

We waited for the elevator to arrive, and, more than anything, I wanted to tell Serenity to stay here, but Vanetti wouldn't let me do that. Still, having her dogging my every step was getting on my nerves. I'd told her she was a distraction, and that was putting it mildly.

Having her so close was messing with me. Since her visions didn't seem to help much, I'd latched onto that as an excuse to stop working together. It had hurt her feelings, but I didn't know what else to do.

Taking her to the shop hadn't been the best idea. The way the guys had looked her over had set my teeth on edge, and I'd wanted to punch each of them in the face.

Then there was the bike. What was I thinking? Having her body molded against mine filled me with pleasure. It brought her close enough that I could still smell her scent, which seemed even more intoxicating than the first time we'd met. Was it possible that her psychic ability included seduction? If I didn't know better, I'd think she'd put a spell on me.

We stepped into the elevator, and I was relieved that she didn't try to talk to me, even though her eyes held anger and enough hurt that I felt like a first-class jerk. That irritated me, so I blew out a breath and filled her in. "If you don't know, Vanetti owns The Comet Club. I take care of security for him, so I'm there a lot. This errand shouldn't take long, so we'll be back soon."

"Oh... sure." Her gaze narrowed. "Hey... maybe your stalker is linked to the club? We didn't include that possibility. What do you think?"

I shook my head. "I have no idea. I wouldn't think so, but I guess it's possible."

"That's good enough for me." Her eyes glinted with determination, and she licked her lips. Warmth spread over me. Damn! I did not need this right now.

The doors opened and we stepped through the garage to my bike. She grabbed her helmet like she was ready to beat it up, and I tried not to smile. She held it over her head and pushed down, but struggled to get it on. I couldn't help smirking. "Need some help?"

"No. I've got this." She finally popped it on and reached for the straps. With her lips pursed, she felt for the snaps and managed to get them clasped together, for a change.

I had to admit I liked helping her, so it disappointed me a little. But, at the same time, I liked seeing her learn so quickly, almost like she really wanted to ride the bike with me.

She also looked insanely sexy in her black pants and ankle boots. The only thing missing was a black leather jacket. Instead, she wore a dark blazer that made her look like a cop. I'd have to tell her to wear something else before our meeting tonight, or she'd scare the boys off. But maybe that wasn't a bad thing, since I didn't really want her around them.

She waited while I settled onto the leather seat. Riding the bike calmed me in a way that nothing else could. On the Triumph, I was in control, and the familiarity comforted me.

Serenity stepped onto the peg and grabbed my shoulders for balance while she slung her leg over the seat. She was getting better at it, and I appreciated how quickly she was stepping into my world, even after our argument. Yes, I was still kind of upset, but that didn't stop me from savoring the moment she put her arms around me. I was in so much trouble.

I needed to shift my focus, so I kicked the stand up, pulled in the clutch and pressed the starter. The bike rumbled to life, and I gave it a few satisfying revs before taking off. Coming to the exit, I sped up the hill just enough to feel her arms tighten around my stomach. It was pure torture... but oh, so sweet.

The ride to The Comet Club went by much too quickly. I pulled around to the back and parked in front of the rear entrance. It was too early for most of the workers, which suited me just fine. But if Serenity was right, which I wasn't going to admit, then we might need to come back at some point.

After we took off our helmets, I opened my mouth to tell her to wait out here, but, at her raised brows, I changed my mind. We stepped to the door and I pulled it open. After ushering her inside, I led the way to Wes's office.

His door was shut, so I knocked before pushing it open. "Hey, Wes."

"Stone." He nodded my way, then his brows rose as he glanced behind me.

"This is Serenity. Vanetti hired her. She's... helping us out for a few days."

Wes jumped to his feet and held out a hand. "Hey, Serenity. I'm Wes. Nice to meet you."

"You too." She smiled and shook his hand with her glove on.

I pulled the pouch from my inner pocket and handed it to him. "That should see you through the next couple of shipments."

"I'm sure it will." Wes opened the safe on the floor behind his desk and tucked the packet away. He took a thumb-drive from the safe and handed it over. "That's for you. Vanetti told me about your problem, so I downloaded all the surveillance from the last week. Maybe you'll see something there that will help."

"Thanks, Wes. I'll take a look."

"Sure."

We stepped back into the hall, and I hesitated. We were already here, so it wouldn't hurt to ask. I glanced her way. "Do you want to go inside the club and see if you pick up anything?"

Her eyes widened. "You mean you trust me to do that, now?"

My jaw tightened. "It's not about trust." My gut twisted. "But we're here. So do you want to or not?"

She shook her head. "You know... one of these days, I'm going to save your life, and you'll have to admit you were wrong. I can't wait."

I snorted. "Yeah, right. More like I'll save *your* life, and you'll be sorry you didn't take my offer to stay out of it."

"Ha! You're on. And... for the record, if you saw some of the things I've seen, you'd never take your gloves off again.

There are some things you do *not* want to know." Shaking her head, she muttered, "I'm definitely never using a public bathroom again."

I barked out a laugh. "Yeah, okay, maybe. I didn't think about *that*, but it would be worth it to know everyone's secrets."

Her brows dipped, and her perfect lips twisted into a soft pucker, making it hard to keep from kissing that disdain right off her face. "Yeah, right. Well, if you're finally ready to give me a chance, then let's start here, in the offices."

"Okay." I stepped down the hall and opened a door to show her the desk filled with monitors and computer equipment. There were six monitors all together, each covering a different part of the club. "This is the surveillance center where I spend a lot of my time."

Her eyes widened. "Wow. Do people know you're watching them?"

"I would think so."

"But isn't that illegal?"

I huffed out a laugh. "It's Vanetti's club. He can do whatever he wants." She frowned, and it occurred to me that she might not know that Vanetti was a mob boss. "It's not illegal. This is an exclusive club. People know what they're getting into when they come here."

"Oh... right."

My brows rose. "Have you ever been here before?" I studied her, suddenly wanting to show her around, and not for the investigation, but just to show off a little.

"Me? Uh... no. I'm not into that sort of thing..." She raised her gloved hands and wiggled her fingers. "...mostly because of this."

"I see. Well, come on. I'll show you the rest." I almost reached for her hand, but resisted the urge at the last minute. We continued down the hall toward a door that opened off the side of the bar inside the club. A worker was re-stocking the bottles of booze, while another guy mopped the floor.

Serenity followed me past the bar to where booths and tables were set up along the outer edges of the hall, with a big wooden dance floor in the middle. Without any people, the space looked big and cavernous.

Special lighting was mounted all along the vaulted ceiling, ready to shine down on the dance floor in strobes of color. But, for now, the place was pretty tame, with golden light pouring from above the wainscoting lining the walls. The club oozed wealth and privilege without being stuffy.

"I thought clubs were supposed to feel sleazy during the day, without all the fancy lights and music, but it's nice here, especially without any people." Serenity glanced around the room before sending me a shrug. "But I guess that's not the point."

Her phone rang, and she quickly pulled it from her purse. Her brows dipped, and she caught my gaze. "Is it okay if I take this?"

I shrugged. "Sure." I knew it wasn't polite to listen, but who said I was polite?

"Hi, Ethan. What's up?" Listening, she paused and her mouth twisted. "Are you kidding me?" Closing her eyes, she sighed. "I can't believe it. He's suing me? For what?" Rubbing her forehead, her lips pinched together. "Seriously?" She let out another frustrated huff. "He has to know I can't give him what he wants. I don't have it. Is there anything else we can do?" Her brows rose. "What? Go to trial? This is unbelievable."

Someone was suing Serenity? It sounded serious, and an unexpected anger flooded my gut. My fists clenched, and I had to consciously relax them. Who would do that to someone like her?

She turned to pace a few steps away, but I could still hear her. "I know... you're right. I'll stay the course. Just let me know when you find out the details, okay? Sure. Thanks."

With her head lowered and her back to me, the pain I'd heard in her voice was etched into every rigid muscle of her body. Anger stirred my stomach. Even though I thought we were wasting time, it wasn't because I thought she was a fake, but because—

She took a deep breath and straightened her spine before turning to face me.

"Is everything okay?" I really wanted to ask who I needed to beat up.

Clearing the gloom from her face, she nodded and tried to smile. "Of course. Just a little bad news, but it's nothing new. I can handle it."

I raised a brow, knowing a lie when I heard it. I was dying to pry, but now didn't seem like the best time, so I let it go. "You want to touch anything while we're here?"

She swallowed. "I don't think it'll help. Let's go back to your office. I'm interested to see what's on the surveillance videos. Maybe I'll see the guy who ran you off the road? That would be good, right?"

"I can't argue with that." Especially since it was what I wanted to do, anyway.

She nodded and took off toward the doors behind the bar. She pulled the door open and nearly collided with one of the workers carrying a box of full of bottles. Luckily, I was close enough to catch the box and avert a disaster.

Serenity's face turned a bright shade of red. "I'm so sorry! I didn't know anyone was there."

I couldn't help razzing her. "Maybe if you took off your gloves, you'd see things like that coming."

She sent me a glare that could have melted the flesh off my bones, and opened her mouth to retort before closing it with a snap. Turning, she strode through the door and down the hall. Dang, I'd really gotten to her. I was only teasing, but she'd taken it wrong, and I'd totally upset her. Talk about bad timing. Shit. Now I felt bad.

I hurried after her, taking long strides to catch up, but even then I only barely made it in time to keep the outer door from smacking me in the face. "Hey, I wasn't trying to be a jerk. I was just—messing with you."

"It's fine." Her mouth twisted.

I raised an eyebrow, but she didn't say anything else, only picked up the helmet and shoved it down over her head, snapping the strap into place with finality.

My breath whooshed out of me, and I shook my head. The sooner we figured out who was after me and she was out of my life, the better. I didn't date women like her, anyway. They usually wanted things like a family, a long-term commitment, a *relationship*, and I wasn't going to give them that. Trying to be with someone like Serenity would only end badly. She was off limits, period.

Still... deep down inside, I couldn't help wondering what it would be like to give in to this electric charge between us. She'd probably hate me in the end, but it just might be worth it.

Who was I kidding? Even if it was worth it, I wasn't sure one night would be enough. What was it about her that intrigued me so much? She was gorgeous, sure, but I'd had plenty of women like that in my life. Serenity was different. She was trying to prove herself, and her vulnerability brought out the protective side of me, which was a huge red flag.

Most women took one look at me and liked what they saw, but I wasn't the type they'd take home to meet their parents. Part of me didn't mind that, but being with Serenity made me wonder what I was missing.

Chapter 7

Serenity

I left Stone in the dust and hurried to his motorcycle, grateful I'd stopped myself from saying something I'd regret. If Ethan hadn't called me right then, Stone's teasing wouldn't have gotten to me.

Stone stepped from the building, his face almost apologetic. "Hey, I wasn't trying to be a jerk. I was just— messing with you."

My heart twisted. "It's fine." I didn't need another man messing with me. I had enough problems with Brandon, I didn't need it from Stone.

He raised an eyebrow, daring me to say more, but I was done. I picked up the helmet and pulled it over my head, snapping the strap into place with satisfaction. At least I was getting better at that. The sooner this case was over, the better.

"Ready to ride?"

At my nod, he slipped on his helmet and mounted the bike. I got on behind him, and the tension melted away. As I wrapped my arms around him, I couldn't believe how comforting it felt to mold my body against his. It was almost like we were made for each other. Or did it feel so good because I was starved for physical contact?

At least I knew it wouldn't last, so nothing that happened would disappoint me. Since that was the case, I might as well hold him close, even if my heart screamed that it was a bad idea.

But what the freak? How could Brandon do this to me? The divorce should have been final six months ago. Now he was suing me for mental cruelty? I held onto Stone a little tighter as he accelerated.

None of this was my fault. Sure, I'd changed after the accident, but I'd been damn lucky to survive. That accident had nearly killed me. In fact, the doctors told me I'd *died* during surgery. The surgeon said they'd tried four times to get my heart started. Another doctor had even called it, but a nurse told them to give it one more try. That last try had saved my life and brought me back from the dead.

I didn't remember dying, but I remembered floating above my body and watching them work on me. I wasn't scared or concerned, I just thought it was weird. Right after that, a bright light completely enveloped me in warmth, taking away all my cares and worries.

The next thing I knew, I opened my eyes to see the nurse hovering over me. She told me I was going to be okay, and I believed her. Later, I woke up in a room with my mom and Brandon watching over me. I told them about the warm light, but they didn't like talking about it, so I never spoke of it again.

Brandon had been so happy that I'd survived, until the visions started. I remembered the exact moment his eyes changed from love to abhorrence... like I'd turned into a monster.

It didn't help that I'd embraced my newfound ability, deciding to actually make a career out of it. I'd always wanted to help people, and now I had this gift. I had to use it. But, for Brandon, that was the last straw.

He hated the idea that I could learn information just by touching someone or something, and fear pushed him over the edge. He couldn't even stand to let me touch *him*, and I finally realized that no amount of begging or talking would ever change that.

I could never go back to who I was before the accident, but he couldn't go forward with who I'd become. I understood that, but why couldn't he agree to the terms of the divorce instead of suing me? I knew it was all about the insurance money, and I'd even agreed to give him some of it, but it wasn't enough. It was never enough.

Sure... he was angry, but claiming I'd ruined his life was ridiculous. He'd done that himself. He just wanted me to suffer, because he claimed I'd made him suffer. It was pointless and discouraging, and the last nine months had been hell.

Before I knew it, we were back at Vanetti's, and I made a pit stop at the restroom before joining Stone in his office. He'd already started the surveillance video, pushing the arrows to make it go faster or slower, depending on what was going on. I sat beside him and watched, only stopping him if I thought I saw someone familiar.

By the time we got done, the work day was over. I'd seen enough to know that the man from my vision wasn't any of the people on the video. But that wasn't the worst of it. For some reason, it had irked me to watch so many women throw themselves at Stone. Didn't anyone have any dignity these days?

Stone put the thumb drive in his desk drawer and slowly stretched, careful of his bruises and sore muscles. I tried not to stare, but couldn't help myself. There was just something about watching him move that mesmerized me.

He caught me staring, and a blush stained my cheeks. "Uh... I may not have picked up anything on the video, but I still think The Comet Club is worth checking out."

"You want to go back?" His brows rose and he studied me for a moment.

"Yeah. Look, I'm sorry I overreacted back there." I didn't like having bad feelings between us, and I wanted Stone to know I could apologize when I was wrong.

"It's not a big deal." One corner of his mouth quirked. "It was probably bad timing on my part. Do... you want to talk about it?"

My eyes widened, and I shook my head. "So, The Comet Club?"

"Sure. We can head over there before we meet the boys at the park tonight." He paused. "But that means you'll have to dress up."

I blinked. "Well... yeah... of course." Did he think I didn't know how to go clubbing? Tightening my jaw, I tamped down my defensiveness before I made things even worse.

"It also wouldn't hurt to lose that jacket. You look too much like a cop."

I glanced down at my clothes, knowing he was right. In fact, I'd dressed like this for that very reason. Not being able to completely suppress my frustration, I couldn't help asking. "Well then, what would *you* suggest?" I wasn't so sure that 'the boys' thinking I was a cop was such a bad thing.

His eyes narrowed, and his assessing gaze flicked over me. I swallowed, and a shiver ran down my spine. In a moment of weakness, I licked my lips, just to see his eyes darken, and boy... did they. "You know what? Don't answer that." I raised my brows. "I'm a professional. I'll wear what I want, even if the snake gang doesn't like it."

Rolling his eyes, he shrugged, wincing a little before he could mask it.

My stomach gave a little squirm. "You okay? That looked like it hurt."

"My shoulder's just a little sore." His voice firmed. "I'm fine."

"Okay. Uh... I brought most everything I thought I would need for a couple of days in my suitcase. It's in my car, but I need to go home and get a dress for the club." I glanced away, unsure how to ask my next question. "So, are we staying here? In your apartment? That wasn't real clear to me."

Stone closed his eyes and exhaled. "I guess that would work. There's a spare room." His gaze met mine. "You'd probably be more comfortable here than at my house?"

"That's true." Even though I wouldn't mind seeing where he lived, going to his house seemed way too intimate for me.

His eyes narrowed. "How about we go to your house for the dress, and pick up something for dinner while we're out. I'm afraid there's not much food in the apartment, and I'm starving."

"I think that will work."

"Good. Let's go."

Taking the elevator to the garage, Stone strode to the bike. He handed me a helmet, and I raised a brow. "Uh... will there be room for the food if we're on the bike?"

His left brow quirked. "Don't you like the bike?"

"I do... I love it—I mean..." I shrugged, hoping he wouldn't read too much into it. "Yeah, it's nice enough."

He grinned but didn't comment on that. "Let's go to your house first, and then we'll figure it out."

I nodded. "Okay." I gave him my address and managed to get on behind him without too much trouble. The ride to my house didn't take long. Stone pulled into the driveway, driving back to park in front of the garage.

After unlocking the back door, I glanced around the kitchen to make sure I hadn't left it in a mess. Relieved that it looked okay, I invited Stone inside.

"It'll just take me a minute to grab my dress." At his nod, I left him to look around while I hurried into my bedroom. Knowing he was in my house and looking at my things made me nervous. I'd been alone for nearly a year, and I hadn't had a man in the house since Brandon left.

I'd done a lot to make this place my own. Getting rid of anything that reminded me of Brandon had been my top priority. Still, I'd been lonely, and having Stone here just reinforced how much I missed being in a relationship with someone special.

I found my red dress and heels. The dress was about the sexiest thing I owned, leaving one shoulder bare and molding to my body, with the tight skirt barely covering my upper thighs. I grabbed a thong and a strapless bra to wear under it, and hesitated. It was skimpy, but thoughts of Brandon and his court battle firmed my resolve.

I was not going to be intimidated by Brandon or any other man. Plus... part of me couldn't wait to see the look on Stone's face when he saw me wearing the dress. I knew it was like picking up a snake and hoping it wouldn't bite me, but I couldn't help it. He probably thought I wasn't the type to dress like this, and I wanted to prove him wrong.

Luckily, the dress wouldn't wrinkle, and I found a small backpack to hold it. On a whim, I took off my boxy blazer and rummaged through my closet for my cute, black leather jacket. I hadn't worn it since before the accident, back when I was more carefree and easygoing.

But it was just the thing to wear on a motorcycle. Plus, I could wear it to the club tonight over my dress. It was late spring, so I knew I needed something to cover my bare skin. Slipping it on, I smiled, pleased that I looked a little more adventurous. At least I'd been smart enough to wear my black ankle boots, and now I totally rocked my new look.

I came out to find Stone studying the photographs that covered my wall. He glanced at me, taking in my leather jacket, and gave me an appreciative nod. I tried not to smile, since his response was exactly what I'd hoped for.

He motioned toward the photos. "You take these?"

I glanced at them, as if seeing them for the first time, and inwardly cringed. "Uh... yeah. Some of them are kind of abstract, so it's okay if you don't like them."

He shook his head. "No. I think they're amazing." He pointed at the tree trunk. "It took me a minute, but I found the face."

"Oh yeah?" My chest warmed. "That's great."

"And this one? Is it a leaf?"

I nodded. "Yup, you got it."

He smiled. "It reminds me of being a kid. My friend used to hold leaves up to the sun just to see the little veins." He twisted his head to the side, quickly pointing at the next photo. "Smoke?"

"Not quite." I smiled. Who would've guessed that the mighty Stone was ever a kid? "That's one of my favorites. It's actually a black and white photo of the mist at the base of a waterfall. I have another one over there that's in color and shows the entire waterfall."

He stepped to where I'd pointed. "Oh, wow... yeah, I can see that now. It's beautiful. Is the waterfall local?"

"Yeah, it is. Just up the canyon." I smiled, enjoying his praise.

"And who's this?" He pointed to a photo of my niece, running down a green hill with her arms spread out and her laughing face tilted to the sky. You could practically hear her laughter through the photo.

"That's Gracie. My niece." That photo always brought a smile to my face. Just the pure joy of my niece was enough to lift me out of a bad mood.

Nodding, he glanced between me and the photo, a smile playing around the corners of his handsome mouth. "I see the resemblance. She's adorable."

I smiled. "Yeah... she is."

He motioned to the wall, brows raised. "These are great. You're really good."

I shook my head, but wasn't able to suppress a blush. "You should see all the ones that didn't turn out. But... thank you. It's a new hobby of mine; it helps with the stress."

"When did you take it up?"

"After the acci— um... about a year ago. I've been too busy to do much lately, but I'm hoping to get out more." I itched to take some photos of him and his motorcycle, but now that I'd seen more of his smile, I really wanted to capture that. There was something about his mouth, something genuine and honest when he smiled. Not that I'd necessarily show the pictures to anyone... they'd be just for me.

Catching myself staring, I rubbed my nose. "Should we go?"

"You got everything?"

"Yeah."

I locked up the house, and climbed on the bike behind Stone, feeling like I belonged there, wearing my black, leather jacket, and ankle boots. Elation rushed over me, and I couldn't help smiling.

On the way back to his apartment, we stopped by a Mexican restaurant. Stone had ordered some food while waiting for me, and it was packed in a sturdy Styrofoam container and ready to go.

He placed it on the back of his motorcycle and fastened it down with a bungee cord. That didn't leave a lot of room for me, but, since it gave me an excuse to plaster myself against him, I couldn't complain. He didn't seem to mind, either, but that was his problem, not mine.

Back at his apartment, he showed me the guest room, and I put my luggage inside and hung up my dress. He was on the phone when I came out, so I set the table and put the food out.

He paced back and forth in the living room, and I tried not to eavesdrop, but I couldn't help listening to his side of the conversation. From his tone, he didn't sound happy, and I heard him say that staying in touch just wasn't working for him. It hit me that he might be having an argument with a woman.

He'd mentioned a girlfriend earlier, but I thought he was bluffing. I knew he wasn't married, but that didn't mean he wasn't in a relationship. Although, from his side of the conversation, it sounded like it was over. For some reason, that brought a smile to my lips. He ended the call and joined me in the kitchen.

"Everything okay?"

He glanced my way before sitting down. "I hope you like Mexican food."

"Yeah, I do." He really should have asked long before now, but obviously, he was deflecting. I let it go.

We ate in silence, but my nerves about going to the club and meeting more snake gang members got the best of me, so I couldn't eat much. "Thanks for dinner. What time do you want to leave for the club?"

He checked his watch. "It's just after seven-thirty. Let's leave in about an hour."

"Okay. After I clear this up, I'm going to settle into my room. Let me know if you need me."

His mouth quirked. "I'll clean up. Go take care of whatever you need to."

Chapter 8

Stone

After clearing away her plate, Serenity hurried into her room to change. I wasn't sure what she'd heard of my conversation with Aubree, but I wasn't about to discuss it with Serenity.

Aubree kept calling me, even though I'd broken it off several weeks ago. She claimed she just wanted to stay friends, and that's why she was keeping in touch, but it was starting to get on my nerves. What had I ever seen in her? Compared to this weird connection with Serenity, Aubree didn't even register on the chart.

It reminded me of Serenity's chat on the phone earlier. It sounded like someone was suing her, and it sounded personal. Maybe that's why she'd taken this job. But what had she done to get sued? Whatever it was, it sounded like the other person was dragging things out.

I wanted to know what was going on. Not that I cared, but if it affected her job with me, it would be good to know. I shook my head, admitting to myself that, even though I didn't want to care, I did.

After putting away our dishes, I slipped into my room and changed into a black dress shirt, making sure my usual shoulder holster and gun were in place before slipping on my black jacket.

A few minutes later, Serenity came out of her room wearing a sexy, red dress that took my breath away. Before I could say a word, she hurried into the bathroom and shut the door. Holy hell. I closed my eyes and let out a sigh. How was I supposed to concentrate on the job with her looking like that? I was going to have to fight off every guy in the club before the night was over.

Taking a deep, calming breath, I stepped into the living room and stood in front of the big window to watch the city lights sparkling on the streets below. The minutes crawled by before she finally came out of the bathroom.

"I'm ready to go."

I spun, and there she was, standing in the doorway and looking even more beautiful than I could have ever imagined. Hot damn. A touch of makeup made her eyes seem bigger. With her red dress and matching red lips, that familiar burn shot to my groin, and I had to work hard to get under control.

I must have made a face, because her eyes widened. Still, her lips twisted with satisfaction, and I held back a groan. Thank God we weren't taking the bike.

"Uh... good." That came out gruffer than I'd intended, but she just nodded. "There's another way out of the apartment. I'll show you." If I could even think straight.

"Great. Let me grab my jacket and purse." She hurried into her room and came out wearing her black leather jacket, with a small purse slung over her shoulder.

"It's this way." I nodded down the hallway, and she followed me into the laundry room and to the door at the back. Even the scent of her perfume was intoxicating. "I only use this door after hours, or if I don't want anyone in the office to know I'm here."

"I'll bet that comes in handy." Was that a hint of amusement?

My lips quirked up. "It sure does." I ushered her through the door and into the hallway across from the stairs, resisting the temptation to hint that she could use it to come see me any time. "I usually take the stairs down to the next floor before I get on the elevator, but we'll catch it here since no one else is around." I locked the deadbolt on my door and stepped down the hall.

At this time of night, the building was empty except for the cleaning crew, and I had to use my key-card to call the elevator. After we got on, I used it inside to send the elevator down to the parking level.

Serenity stood beside me all the way down, tense and clutching her small purse. Was she nervous to be with me? I noticed her hands were bare, and my brows dipped. "How come you're not wearing your gloves?"

She twitched before glancing my way. "They're in my purse, but I thought I should leave them off until we get to the club. If something's coming, I'd like to know beforehand."

My brows shot up. It sounded like she'd taken my advice to heart, but was something else going on? "Did you have another vision about me?"

She shook her head. "No. But since someone *is* trying to kill you, we can't be too careful, right?"

"Uh... yeah, right." I wanted to argue that no one was going to try to kill me on the way to the club, but I liked that she wasn't wearing her gloves.

The elevator doors swished open and I stepped out. "We'll take my car. It's right next to the bike."

"Sounds good."

She followed me to my car, and I reached to open the passenger door for her, but she grabbed my arm to stop me.

"Wait. Let me touch it first."

Surprised, I sent her a nod. "Have at it."

She held her fingers to the door handle. After a couple of seconds, she glanced my way. "I guess it's okay."

"You guess?"

"I'm not getting anything dangerous. Like a bomb, or fire, or smoke... you know... that sort of thing?" Before I could comment, she pulled the door open and climbed inside.

Shaking my head, I hurried to the driver's side and got in. She ran her fingers across the dashboard and steering wheel. I wanted to tell her she could do that to me, too, but I didn't. Finished, she glanced my way and nodded. "Okay. We're good to go."

Embarrassingly, it hadn't occurred to me that my car could be a death trap. At least she was sitting here with me, so that had to mean it was safe. With a shake of my head, I started the car and began the drive to the club.

A few minutes later, we pulled around back to my reserved spot and I opened the door to get out.

"Stone. Wait."

"Again?" Sighing, I shut the door and turned toward her. "What?"

"I'd like to try something before we go in. Is it okay if I touch your hand for a minute? I just want to see if I get anything."

A slow smile crept up my lips, but I tried to play it cool. "Sure." Shrugging nonchalantly, I held my hand open. As she placed her hand in mine, sparks danced across my skin. Curling my fingers around hers, I waited for what came next. Would she have a vision? Would she gasp or pull away?

She closed her eyes and hardly twitched, holding my hand in a firm grip. Her fingers were warmer than I expected. Still, I studied her reaction. I expected her to cringe or pull away, even though I didn't want that to happen.

She did neither. Instead, she stiffened and sucked in a breath. Swallowing, she let it out, and her face relaxed. A surge of color spread over her cheeks, and she gently rubbed her thumb across my hand spreading electricity over my whole body.

What was she seeing? Her lips parted, and her tongue darted out to moisten them. A sudden desire to swoop down and kiss those beautiful lips came over me, but I held back, waiting to see what she'd do next.

Finally, her eyes flew open. Her pupils were dilated, holding a dark desire that cut through my defenses. I was ready to lean over and kiss her, but she gasped and pulled her hand from my grip.

Clearing her throat, she whispered. "Uh... I didn't see anything threatening, so we might as well go in."

Her heaving chest told me she'd seen a lot more than she wanted to admit, and it involved me. Had she seen us kissing? Or making love? Heat rushed through me. From her flushed face, it was evident I was on the right track, and I leaned toward her, my voice low and husky. "Was it good?"

An even brighter blush colored her cheeks, and her eyes widened. "I don't know what you're talking about. Um, we should go in." With jerky movements, she opened the door and scrambled out of the car.

Unable to help myself, I chuckled and pushed my door open. So, she saw us kissing, and had obviously enjoyed it. Interesting. I grinned. Did that mean it was inevitable? Or now that she knew, would she make sure it didn't happen? My smile faded a little as I followed her to the door, her back to me.

I wanted to explore her vision more, but now wasn't the time, and I tucked it away for later. Right now, we had work to do. The office was locked since it was after business hours, so I swiped my security access card across the lock pad.

Hearing the lock disengage, I pulled it open and ushered Serenity inside. "I want to check the surveillance room before we head into the club."

"Sure." Flustered, her voice squeaked. It was so adorable.

Wait, did I just use the word *adorable*? What was wrong with me? Women weren't *adorable*, they were sexy. What was I thinking?

Serenity followed me to the security office where we found Patrick watching the feed. "How's the crowd tonight?"

"Just the usual. Not many people yet, but it should pick up in an hour or two."

"Good." I glanced at Serenity. "This is Serenity. She's helping me tonight."

"Hi." She sent him a little wave instead of shaking his hand.

"Why don't you give Patrick the description of our mystery person so he can keep a watch out."

"Oh, right." She gave Patrick the general description of a man with a beard and hat, and his brows rose.

"Really? Without the hat, that could be like... half the people in the club." He glanced my way and I shrugged.

She frowned. "I know, but that's what we have to go on, so if someone looking like that acts suspicious, keep an eye on him and let us know, okay?"

He nodded and she turned to the door, so I pulled it open and glanced at Patrick. "I'll check back before we go home. If you see anything out of the ordinary, send me a text."

"Will do."

I ushered Serenity out, and we made our way to the door beside the bar. Slipping inside the club, no one but the bartender paid any attention to us. I sent the bartender a nod, and led Serenity to my usual corner table where I could watch the crowd. Serenity slid into her seat without touching anything.

"If you're nervous about what you touch, you might as well wear your gloves." Reaching out to take her hand was way too tempting without them, since I wanted to see if I could give her another arousing vision. I held back a grin.

She let out a long sigh before taking a pair of black lace gloves from her bag. After slipping them on, she visibly relaxed. Our waiter, Macy, came over to take our orders. I didn't want anything, but Serenity ordered a Diet Coke with lime.

While waiting for her drink, Serenity glanced around. "This place sure looks different from this afternoon." Her eyes lit up with excitement, and she caught my gaze. "Is it okay if we do some dancing? You never know what I might pick up on the dance floor."

My brow rose. "I wasn't planning on it."

"Oh... well, I think I'll check my bag and jacket, just in case." She looked toward the bar. "Where's the coat-check?"

Macy brought Serenity's drink, setting it down in front of her. "Thanks."

"Why don't I check your things? I need to walk around and see who's here tonight. If you see anything, come find me. I won't be far."

Her brows drew together. "Maybe I should come with you?"

"No, that's not necessary." I'd never be able to focus with her right next to me. "It would be better if we we're both looking from different vantage points, so we don't miss anything."

She shrugged. "Fine. But be careful, okay?"

I raised a brow, secretly loving that she wanted to keep me safe. "You really think I'm going to get killed in the middle of this big crowd?"

She handed over her bag and jacket and gave me a sweet smile. "You never know."

With a slight shake of my head, I strode to the coat check room. After securing Serenity's things. I made a short circuit around the club, keeping an eye out for trouble, and purposefully avoiding looking toward her. Several minutes later, however, I caught a flash of red in my peripheral vision. Turning, I spotted Serenity on the dance floor beside a man who looked like he was trying hard to impress her.

She barely smiled at him, keeping her attention on the people around her, like she was looking for the guy she'd seen in her vision. I couldn't fault her for that, but something twisted in my gut to see her dancing with some loser.

The guy leaned over to whisper in her ear, and wrapped an arm around her waist. She stiffened, but he didn't seem to notice. Growing bold, he put his other arm around her waist and began to sway to the music.

Serenity put her hands on his shoulders, but did her best to keep some space between them. When his hand moved lower toward her ass, fire roared inside of me. That was enough. I strode to his side and grabbed his arm, shoving him away from her.

He took a few steps back, anger darkening his face. "What the hell, man?"

I dismissed him and glanced at Serenity. "You okay?"

Her eyes widened. "I'm fine."

I turned to the man. "She came with me, so she's off limits."

His brows drew together. "Well, she didn't tell *me* that."

"*I'm* telling you, so get lost." I glared at him, unable to hold back the seething anger in my gut.

"Fine. But it's not my fault she wanted to dance with me. Maybe you should pay more attention to your date." He frowned at Serenity before stalking off.

"Now you've done it," Serenity said.

"Done what? Did you really want to dance with him?"

"No, of course not. But you've made a scene. Everyone's looking at us. You'd better dance with me if you don't want to look like a total jerk." She raised her arms to my shoulders and began to sway. A slow second later, my hands came around her waist, and I began to move with her.

"That's better." She arched a brow. "Do you normally treat your dates like this?"

"I don't bring dates here. Ever." My gaze dropped to her lips. "I don't have to, women usually come to me."

"Yeah... I saw enough of that on the surveillance video."

"So why were you dancing with that guy if you didn't want to?"

She blew out a breath. "I couldn't see much from my seat, and he asked. So I thought, why not? I'd have a better chance at keeping an eye on everyone from the dance floor."

"Hmm." I grunted, unsatisfied.

We swayed in silence for a long minute before she raised her gaze to mine. "So... tell me something about yourself, something that no one else knows."

"Why?" I scoffed.

She rolled her eyes. "So I can get to know you better."

My brows rose. "Why would you want to do that?"

"Well..." She sighed. "I'm trying to figure you out. Sorry if that's a crime or something."

"It might be." I grinned, pulling her a little closer. "You might not like who I am."

She searched my face. "And what if I do?"

Heat pulsed through me. "That might be even worse."

"How about I go first, then? So you'll know what I mean." Swallowing, she ran a finger over the collar of my shirt. "I like to snack on peanut butter. Sometimes I leave the lid off the jar, and take little finger-dips all day long."

She met my gaze like she was daring me to complain, so I one-upped her. "I don't mind that. In fact, I'd lick peanut butter off your fingers anytime."

Her eyes widened, cheeks flushing a brilliant crimson, but instead of taking the bait like I'd hoped, she pressed on with her questions. "Your turn. Tell me something you like to do." She paused, a glint of mischief in her eyes. "Aside from licking peanut butter off my fingers. Which... you don't actually know if you like."

"Yet." I grinned. "But... since you're forcing the issue, I guess I'd say that I like to take off on my bike for a few days at a time. Just me, the bike, and the open road." I lifted a hand from her waist and lightly traced one finger over her wrist, gently brushing her skin all the way along her arm, over her bare shoulder, and down her spine, where her silky hair fell over the back of my hand.

She shuddered, taking a deep breath, and I leaned in to whisper in her ear. "I like the back roads, the ones that few people travel. I like to find unexpected places, and I often do." I pulled back a little, a lopsided smile lifting a corner of my mouth. She smelled so good.

"I usually end up in a small town where everyone knows everyone else." I grinned. "You'd be surprised at how many people you get to know when you're on a motorcycle. I once found the best apple pie I've ever tasted on a trip like that." My mouth watered just thinking about it. Or maybe it was because of Serenity. "I'd like to go back there sometime."

She gazed at me, like she was a little dazed. "That sounds amazing."

I tilted my head, leaning in a little closer. "And what about you? Tell me a secret. What's something you've always wanted to do?"

The music thrummed rhythmically, almost hypnotically as I gazed into Serenity's gorgeous blue eyes, now shadowed mysteriously in the dim room.

She bit her lower lip, hesitantly, before finally blurting, "I've wanted to be a PI since I was a kid."

I blinked. "And that's a secret? Why?"

"Well..." She shrugged. "It's not a secret I kept from my family, but I stopped telling people after I turned eleven." She bit her lips again, making me want to bend down and taste them.

"Okay... and what made you want to be a PI?"

"Oh... well... I love to read, and mystery is my favorite genre. Solving cases and putting the bad guys away just seemed so... noble. And, if I'm honest... a little romantic. But I love the challenge of figuring things out, you know?"

Her eyes shone with determination, and, in that moment, I would've agreed with anything she said. "I can see that. So now you're a PI. How long have you been one?" I knew several investigators, but I'd never heard of her.

"It's a recent development." She blushed again. "It took over two years, but that was because I had to work full-time. Then there was the accident... and I got waylaid."

My stomach turned ice cold, and I stopped moving. "You were in an accident? What happened?"

She shrugged like it wasn't a big deal, but from the pain in her eyes, I knew it was all an act. "Car accident. They ran a red light and plowed right into me. I was pinned in the seat and nearly bled out before they got me out of there. It gave me nightmares for a while."

"Holy shit. That's awful. But—you're okay now?" I studied her face, resisting the urge to check her for non-existent injuries.

"Yes." She swayed to the music, pulling me with her. "I'm fully recovered... for the most part."

"For the most part?" What did that mean? Before she could answer, the music changed to a loud, boisterous song, and everyone started going wild on the dance floor.

Her face brightened. "Oh! I love this song!" She began to move to the beat, taking my hand to follow her lead. I moved with her like she'd cast a spell over me. The sheer joy on her face reminded me of that photo of her niece, and warmth filled my chest. Laughing, I let go and enjoyed the moment.

I couldn't remember the last time I'd abandoned my hardened persona. But with her, it was easy. My awareness of everyone around us never faded, but I couldn't help grinning every time she laughed. I caught sight of one of the waiters staring at me with his mouth open, and I chuckled.

As we continued dancing, touching her became easy, almost like it was second-nature. She kept touching me as well and I welcomed it, each tingling caress muffling the alarm bells going off in my head.

A magnetic pulse drew me to her, and my body responded like we were meant to be together. The pull was too strong to resist, so I gave in and rode the wave into the perfect storm. I reveled in her touch and the dark desire in her eyes. Gazing at one another, we swayed in time with the beat, slowing as the song changed to one of love and longing. I couldn't look away to save my life.

A flush stained her cheeks, and her lips parted. They were close enough to taste, but before I could lean in and kiss her, movement caught my eye. As a man reached for her, I pulled her away.

"Serenity?" He scowled, looking her up and down. Serenity's face filled with shock. "What the hell are you doing here?" He shifted his glare to me. "Who the hell do you think you are? Get away from my wife."

"Wife?" My stomach dropped. She was *married?*

"I'm not your wife anymore." Serenity's hands balled into fists, her glare fierce.

"The hell you're not. Last I checked we were still married."

"Yeah, well, last I checked it's because *you* won't sign the damn papers."

"Of course not. You owe me. You ruined my life."

"*I* ruined *your* life? You selfish son of a bitch." Her voice shook. "I nearly got killed, miraculously survived, and *that* ruined your life?"

"Yeah, it did."

She paled.

"Because now you're a freak who can invade anyone's privacy just by touching them." He glanced at me like he'd won the argument. "Did she tell *you* that? Did you know that she can ruin your life just by touching you?"

My jaw tightened. "You know what?" My voice stayed deadly calm. "I think you'd better leave."

"*I'd* better leave? You're the one dancing with a psycho. If you're smart, you'll get as far away from her as you can."

I signaled Macy, who hurried off toward the front entrance. "If *you're* smart, you'll stay away from her. Now. Get out."

His expression turned ugly. "Who do you think you are? You can't kick me out of here."

I raised a brow, a slow satisfaction building in my stomach. I was ready to kick this guy's ass, but sometimes having someone else do it is far more satisfying. "Yes... I can do exactly that."

One of my bouncers arrived, right on cue. "You needed me?"

"Yeah, show this asshole out."

"You got it, boss." He turned to Serenity's ex. "Come with me."

"No way!" His eyes widened. "I have every right to be here."

I narrowed my gaze. "No... you don't."

"Like hell!" He leapt at me, swinging wildly.

I easily stepped aside and grabbed his arm, twisting it behind him. "Looks like I get to do the honors after all."

"Hey! Let me go." His voice squeaked as I held him tight.

I didn't bother to respond. Instead, I forced him out in front of me and pushed him through the crowd, my bouncer clearing the way.

"Brandon?" One guy peeled off and followed. "What did you do?"

Now I had a name. Brandon.

Seeing me, the other bouncer opened the front door. Without pausing, I marched through and shoved Brandon to the sidewalk.

His friend ran by me to catch him. "What the hell, man? We just got here."

"It's not my fault!" Brandon glowered at me. "I have every right to be here. I paid my fee and I'm going back in."

He tried to shove past me, but I pushed him away. "Pathetic."

Brandon bared his teeth and came at me again, but his friend grabbed him. "Dude, stop."

Serenity stepped up beside me, shaking her head at her ex. "For heaven's sake, go home, Brandon. You've had too much to drink."

"How else am I supposed to deal with your mental cruelty?" He sneered. "Meanwhile, you're out here pretending to be normal. You know it won't work. Not when you're a psycho." He shook his head. "You know what? Before I knew what you were, I was happy you survived that accident. But now I wish you would have died. A freak like you doesn't deserve to live."

Serenity gasped, and her hands flew to her mouth like she'd been slapped.

Rage filled my chest, and I shoved Brandon away from her. "Get out of here. Now. Before I do something you'll regret."

"Mind your own damn business. She's my wife. I'll say whatever the hell I want to her."

I got in his face, staring him down. "Not while I'm here, you won't."

Brandon swore and took another swing at me. I sidestepped him, and he threw a punch at my face. I easily sidestepped again and grabbed his wrist, twisting to pull his arm behind him and forcing him to the ground. Cold rage filled every part of me, and I had to strain to keep it in check.

I held his wrist in a firm grip and placed my knee on his back. He screamed and hollered that I was breaking his arm. He wasn't wrong; just a little more pressure, and I could easily dislocate his shoulder. But I shouldn't do that. This guy was an asshole, but he wasn't a criminal I could beat the hell out of without repercussions.

Frowning, I let up slightly so he'd stop screaming, but kept him in a tight hold. "Don't ever talk to Serenity like that again. Is that clear?" I jerked his arm back, just to make my point.

He yelped. "Okay! Okay! Just let me go!"

By now, an even bigger crowd had gathered, but his friend was smart enough to keep his distance. I let Brandon go and grabbed his upper arm to pull him up. He jerked away, stepping back until he was out of my range. Glancing at Serenity, he sneered. "I'm telling my lawyer about this. It won't look good for you in court."

I took a step toward him and he flinched. Realizing he'd shown weakness, he surged toward me again, but his friend grabbed his arm. "Come on Brandon, let's go. Why are you even fighting over her? She's not worth it. Think about the divorce. Think about the money."

Something clicked in Brandon's eyes, and he let his friend pull him away. They continued down the street and got into a car parked on the side of the road.

As they drove away, I turned to Serenity. Seething, she glared after them, but behind her rage, tears were gathering in her eyes, and I could tell it was taking everything she had to hide how much he'd hurt her. Seeing that broke something inside of me, and I wanted to chase down that son-of-a-bitch and beat him until his own mother wouldn't recognize his face.

Letting out a breath, I glanced at the crowd. "Nothing to see here, folks. The party's in there." I jerked my chin at the door, and the bouncers helped direct people inside.

Swallowing my anger, I stepped toward Serenity.

She stiffened. "I'm fine." But her voice shook. In fact, her whole body trembled.

"Well, I'm not." Still enraged at her ex, I tugged her against my chest and rubbed her back.

"Oh." Her breath caught, but she slowly let it out and relaxed into my arms. I held her until she stopped trembling.

"Let's go get your things." Keeping my arm around her, I walked her back into the club, doing my best to shield her from curious gazes. I held her while we got her purse and jacket, and didn't let go until we'd gone through the back door and into the parking lot.

At my car, I moved to open the door, but she pushed my arm away.

"Wait. Let me touch it first."

I waited, watching her peel off her glove and reach for the handle. Brushing the cool surface, she swallowed before nodding. "It's fine."

I pulled the door open and she got in. Heading to the other side, I slid behind the wheel and started the car. After backing out, I pulled onto the road and glanced her way. "Your ex is a piece of shit."

She nodded, but didn't say anything, finally letting her mask fall and the tears come.

"Just so you know. If I ever come across him again, I *will* beat the hell out of him."

She sniffed. "Really? Even if I didn't want you to?"

"You really don't want me to beat him up?" I didn't believe that for a second.

A tiny smile pinched one corner of her gorgeous mouth. "He's not worth the trouble. Besides that, he's suing me, so I need to be careful." Pausing, she sent me a trembling smile. "But once that part is over, I wouldn't stop you."

I nodded. "It's a deal." Glancing at the time, I shook my head. "I'm afraid that taking out the trash means there's not time for you to change."

She sighed. "Oh well. It's okay. I can put my jacket on." Working around her seatbelt, she slipped her arms through the jacket and stuffed her gloves into her purse. Before closing it, she pulled out a tissue and wiped her nose. After checking her reflection in the visor mirror, she dabbed at her eyes and settled back into the seat.

I waited for her to say something about her husband, but when she didn't, I spoke up. "So... on top of getting divorced, he's suing you? What's that about... are you a secret billionaire or something?"

"Hardly." A sardonic laugh burst out of her. "He says it's for mental cruelty, because of the *stress from the accident.*" She made finger quotes. "But all he really wants is the insurance settlement money."

She laughed at the irony. "He thinks I've got it stashed away somewhere, but I don't. It's gone... I had to use it to pay all the hospital and doctor bills. I had insurance, but it barely helped, and the bills piled up. After I paid them and my lawyer's fees, I used the rest to pay off the mortgage.

"Now, he wants half of what the house is worth, along with half of the settlement money. My lawyer says he won't get it, but Brandon's promised to tell everyone I'm a psychopath if I fight him on this. My lawyer says I can't lose, but it's going to cost me a ton of money in fees. Plus—" She waved her hand. "It'll ruin my reputation.

I shook my head. "No it won't. I mean... a lot of men say their exes are psychos."

Her mouth flattened, and she stared at me with a raised brow.

My eyes widened. "What? They do."

"I know." Shaking her head, she pressed a hand to her forehead. "I shouldn't let it get to me, but it does."

"So, is that why you took the job?"

She sent me a furtive glance. "Mostly. Plus, working for Vanetti is a real boost to my business. I should be able to get more clients with his recommendation, you know?"

"True." I shook my head. "The accident must have been bad, but I don't understand why your husband would turn on you. You're a beautiful woman. You're smart, and funny, and you're... sexy as hell. It doesn't make sense."

Her lips twisted. "You're forgetting something." She held up her hands and wiggled her fingers. "I'm psychic. I have psychometry, remember?"

"Well, sure, but didn't he already know that?"

"It's a recent development."

"Oh." My eyes widened, things clicking into place. "How recent?"

"It's a result of the accident I was in. Brandon couldn't handle it, and he... left me."

I nodded. "Okay." Well, damn. But it still didn't make a lot of sense to me. Besides being beautiful, even in the short amount of time I'd known her, I could tell that Serenity was an all-around good person. "So what was it? He didn't want you to touch him?"

"You nailed it. At first, it didn't bother him... probably because I didn't tell him everything I saw." She shrugged. "I mean... when it's no big deal, what's the point, you know? But when I had a vision that didn't make sense, I asked him about it, and he freaked out. After that, he never wanted me to touch him again."

"Why? Was it something bad he'd done?"

"No! That's the thing... it wasn't." Her brows drew together. "I just saw him in a cemetery, and he had a bouquet of flowers in his hands. I wasn't sure if someone had died while I'd been in the hospital for the last two months, so I asked him about it."

She blew out a breath. "He turned white and told me to stay the hell away from him. Later, he told me he remembered visiting his great-aunt's grave, so that was probably who it was." She shrugged. "I never saw the name on the headstone, so I figured that had to be it; but Brandon changed after that."

She shook her head and let out a big sigh. "He said he couldn't live with the way I was now, and he left me the next day."

"That must have been hard."

Her lips thinned, and she nodded. "Yeah... well, someday he'll be out of my life for good. And that day can't come soon enough."

"No kidding." I slowed down and pulled into a parking lot beside a stand of trees. "We're here."

Chapter 9

Serenity

One lone light shone down over a basketball court, leaving the rest of the area in darkness. The remaining light fixtures on the poles surrounding us were broken, and the parking lot was empty.

A chill ran down my spine. "Are you sure we should park here? It looks a little sketchy."

Stone smirked. "It *is* sketchy." But he drove to the other side of the lot anyway, keeping away from the basketball court and the light. He backed the car into the spot for an easy getaway and cut the engine and lights.

"Besides," he said. "They've already seen us."

"The... snake gang?"

"Yeah." He rolled his eyes and didn't correct me. "Over there." He motioned to a small playground on the other side of the basketball court. Because of the darkness, I couldn't see more than a few shadows. "But, uh, don't call them that to their faces."

"As if I would." He started to open his door, but I grabbed his arm. "Wait! For this to work, I need to touch them." This was the part I hated most. "I was planning on a handshake, but is there a cool gang thing I need to do?"

His brows rose, and he stared at me for just a moment. "How about I introduce you, and you just shake their hands?" His lips twitched.

"So... no hissing?"

He closed his eyes, but his lips tilted up. "That would be no."

I smiled back, grateful to relieve some of the tension. "If you say so." Taking a breath, I opened my door and got out. Stone waited for me to join him, and we started toward the playground. I wanted to hold his hand in the worst way, but settled for walking as close as I could get. By the time we reached it, the shadows had blended into the darkness.

He stopped at the edge of the playground, and we waited for them to come to us. I chewed on my bottom lip, every muscle in my body tense, listening for sounds of footsteps approaching us. A second later, a figure emerged from the darkness and stalked toward us. He stopped far enough away that I could barely make out his features.

"I wasn't sure you were gonna make it."

"Joint." Stone sent him a nod. "I hope we're not too late."

"Nah, man."

"Are the new guys all here?"

Joint glanced behind him. "They're here."

My eyes finally adjusted to the darkness, and I could make out the man's features more clearly. I recognized him from Razor's place, but for some reason, he seemed more sinister in the dark. His hair was pulled back with an elastic, and a short beard covered his jaw. He twisted his head over his shoulders and called out. "All right boys, let's make this quick."

Five shadowy figures detached from the darkness and came to stand behind Joint. A few were young, no more than seventeen or eighteen. The others wore the hardened look of street toughs. My stomach squirmed. I did not want to touch any of them.

Joint glanced at the group. "This is Stone. I'm sure you've heard of him." A few of the men straightened, and one even took a step back. "Razor owes him, so just tell him what he wants to know so we can get back to business."

Stone edged closer, so I tagged along, glued to his side. He nodded toward Joint. "I don't think you were introduced earlier. This is..." He paused, like he'd forgotten my name, but then I realized he wanted to protect me.

"Sen." I held my hand out. "We saw each other at the shop."

"Yeah." Shocked that I wanted to shake his hand, it took him a second to reach out. Luckily his touch was brief.

"All right if I meet your men?"

Joint flicked a gaze between me and Stone, but finally nodded.

"Great, thanks." Smiling, I quickly stepped to the next man and introduced myself again. "Hi. I'm Sen."

"Uh, Staples." After a quick shake, I moved to the next, meeting Ajax, Hammer, and Snake. I held out my hand to the last guy, but he didn't make a move to touch me.

"Dude... you afraid of her or what?" Staples, one of the younger guys, laughed.

With a scowl, he finally gave in to the pressure. "Grizzo." The brief touch was enough to let me know that he had a good reason for not getting too close.

My stomach fluttered, but I smiled as pleasantly as I could, and stepped back. Wiping my hand on the side of my dress, I glanced at the street. Were the cops already on their way? Did we have time to question these guys? I hadn't picked up a thing from them about Stone, so they probably didn't have anything to do with the phone call that lured him to the blast. Crap. We needed to get out of there. "Well, it was good to meet you, but, uh... we've gotta get going."

I grabbed Stone's arm and started pulling him toward the car.

He turned around, but didn't budge, sending me a questioning glare.

I leaned in close. "I think the cops are coming. All these guys are going to be arrested."

"Wait! Did you just say the cops are coming?" Joint stood right behind us.

Jumping, I twisted to gape at him. "Uh... yeah. We all need to get out of here."

Hearing that, the group scattered, each of them taking off in a different direction. All but Joint, who stared at me with narrowed eyes. "How do you know the cops are coming? Did you sell us out?" His wild eyes held accusation.

"No! I've got—I know things. Look—we all need to go. I am not getting picked up by the police tonight."

"Fine, but this ain't over."

"We'll talk later," Stone replied.

"Yeah, we will." With a scowl on his face, he lumbered off toward the houses across the street. He didn't seem in any hurry, but I lost sight of him as we continued toward our car. I quickly opened the passenger door and jumped in.

Stone started up the car. Driving out of the parking lot, he glanced my way. "What did you see?"

"I saw most of them in jail cells. I'm not sure when it happens, but from the impression I got, I think it's tonight."

"Most of them? Did a few get away?"

I hesitated, unsure if I should tell Stone about the last guy I'd touched. In my vision, I'd seen him talking to one of the cops, but he wasn't in jail. He was working undercover to bring them down.

"Serenity? What is it?"

"I think the last guy, Grizzo, is an undercover cop. But you can't tell Razor, okay?"

"Dammit." His mouth twisted.

"You won't tell him, right?"

He sighed. "I can't make any promises. This puts us in a tight spot, and it's not helping our case."

"I know, but if they find out Grizzo's a cop... they'd do something bad to him, wouldn't they?"

Stone's lips twisted. "Let me worry about that." He paused. "So, what now? If you didn't see anything else, does that mean the guy we're looking for isn't one of them?"

"Yeah, I don't think it is."

He huffed out a breath. "Dammit. I thought we had a lead."

"I know... it sucks." We drove in silence for a few seconds, then an idea popped into my head and I turned his way. "Hey... why don't we go back to the trailer park and check on Cash? Even if you're convinced it's not him, I think he's connected in some way, and it's late enough that he's probably home. You could convince him to talk."

Stone raised a brow. "I guess it wouldn't hurt." He turned the car in that direction, and I kept my eyes peeled for anyone following us. Traffic was sparse, and nothing stood out to me, so I settled back into my seat and worried about other things, namely, that Stone had found out about Brandon.

As much as I hated to admit it, Brandon had struck a nerve calling me a psycho. But that wasn't near as bad as saying he wished I would have died in the accident. That stung. He'd loved me, once... even cherished what we had. I never thought he could be so cruel.

And... then there was Stone. I hadn't wanted to touch him again after what I'd seen in the car, but then he'd interrupted me on the dance floor. I definitely hadn't liked dancing with the other guy, but it was all part of the job. I hadn't expected the dude to try feeling me up, though, and Stone had appeared out of nowhere, fierce and protective.

After that, I couldn't resist getting him to dance with me. I knew this attraction between us wasn't going anywhere, but it had been so much fun seeing him loosen up. He'd actually smiled and laughed. It had been wonderful.

Not only that, but dancing with him had brought out the old me again. I hadn't realized how much I'd missed that part of myself until then, and it was all because of Sexy Stone. Grouchy, my-way-is-the-only-way, Stone. I'd kept my gloves on, so I didn't see more. But I couldn't believe how much fun I'd had flirting with him.

It was the most fun I'd had in... I couldn't even remember. Touching him had seemed so natural, and to say he was a good dancer was putting it mildly. Even all the women watching him with lust in their eyes made my enjoyment ten times better.

But now I had a problem. How on earth was I going to keep things professional, when all I wanted to do was touch him all the time? Even now, I wanted to lean against him, take his hand in mine, and feel the callouses on his palm. I sighed, my stomach fluttering just at the thought. Ugh. This was *so* bad.

Stone pulled off the road to park beside the entrance to the trailer court and cut the engine, bringing me back to the present. "I don't want him to see us coming and ditch us again."

"Makes sense to me." I sighed, wishing I wasn't wearing my skimpy red dress and heels. Stone began to open the door, but I stopped him. "Hang on. Let me touch you again. Maybe I'll get something this time."

The last time I'd touched him without my gloves, I'd seen him bare-chested and kissing a woman. It had about knocked my socks off. But realizing the woman was me had sent white hot flames dancing through my entire body.

Besides that, I wasn't wearing anything in the vision, either. Of course, seeing us like that didn't mean it was going to happen. Honestly, though? I wished it would, more than I liked to admit, which meant I was in deep, deep trouble.

But I had a job to do. Mainly finding out if Cash, or his friend, Johnny, were in there waiting to kill this man I was crushing on. So really, it was perfectly acceptable to hold his hand. Nothing violating the client-investigator professional relationship I was trying to maintain. I was just doing my job. It also didn't hurt that being with him was something I really wanted to have happen.

Ugh! I was so messed up.

He settled back into his seat and held out his hand. He had nice, big hands with long fingers, and I tried to keep my hand from trembling when I took his. As my hand fit snugly inside of his, tingles zipped over my skin. I tried not to think of all that passionate kissing from my earlier vision, and closed my eyes, concentrating on the vision of when he got hit by the truck.

This time, darkness swirled around him, and I couldn't see through it. I sensed something else, but I wasn't sure what it was. Holding his hand a little longer, I waited to see more, but nothing came.

Letting out a breath, I shook my head. "I think we're okay to go? But let's be careful. Maybe I'll know more once we get closer."

"All right." He reluctantly pulled his hand from mine to open the door, and I already missed the warmth of his touch.

Getting out, I followed behind him. He kept to the shadows until we made it to the last trailer at the end of the row. There weren't any lights on inside, but that didn't mean Cash wasn't there. Maybe that's what the darkness in my vision meant?

Still, what if he was dead and lying in a pool of blood? Just thinking about it gave me the shivers. "This is starting to freak me out."

Stone raised a brow. "You want to go back to the car?"

My eyes widened. "Oh. No. I'm good." I shouldn't have admitted I was scared. "Where you go—I go."

He grinned at my cheesy line, and I did a mental head slap. Ugh, I was such a dork!

"Let's go then." His lips twisted before he continued up the stairs to Cash's front door.

"Wait! Let me touch it first." I managed to step in front of him to touch the knob. If we were lucky, it would be open just like it had been earlier.

Taking a breath, I touched the doorknob. Darkness hit me, the same as when I'd touched Stone, but it seemed like there was more to it. Trying to see more, I grasped the knob. It turned slightly in my hand, and I heard a raspy voice singing *burn, burn, burn, that ring of fire.*

What the hell? Suddenly, a searing heat burned my palm, and I jerked my hand away. "Oh, shit." In a panic, I backed into Stone and nearly fell. "Run!"

He grabbed me around the waist and pulled me down the stairs. Running as fast as we could, we didn't make it far before a fiery explosion blasted through the silence.

The concussive wave sent us flying, and we both landed hard on the pavement. Debris showered around us, and something hard landed on my lower back. Stone crawled to my side and shoved the debris off me. He draped his body over mine, shielding me from the rest of the fallout.

Seconds later, the remnants of the blast had finished landing on the pavement. We both turned to find a blaze of white-hot fire and thick, black smoke billowing into the night sky. Stone spoke, but my ears were ringing so hard that I couldn't make out what he said. "What?"

"Can you get up? We need to move."

Nodding, I swallowed and pushed to my hands and knees, feeling pain in my knees from the fall. Stone staggered to his feet and helped me stand. I didn't realize my shoes were gone until Stone tugged me away and I faltered. Taking in my bare feet, he slung my arm over his shoulder and picked me up.

People came running out of their trailers, most in pajamas and slippers. With their eyes on the blaze, no one paid much attention to us. Luckily, Cash's trailer was the last one on the lane, and not close enough to the others to catch them on fire. Still, with a blaze that big, people were beginning to panic. Not to mention that their neighbor's house had just exploded.

While they called nine-one-one, we made our way toward Stone's car. He set me down and opened the door. After I got in, he hurried to the driver's side and slowly drove away. We made it back to the main road before the sound of sirens cut through the ringing in my ears.

Stone glanced at me, his voice raspy. "Are you okay?"

"I think so. But I lost my shoes! I really liked those shoes."

He raised a brow. "You wanna go back?"

"What? No." I swallowed, my head still a little fuzzy. "What about you? Are you okay?"

He nodded. "Yeah, that was too close."

"I know. I didn't see it coming until I turned the doorknob. I must have triggered it somehow, but I should have known something was off." I shook my head. "Well, that's not entirely true. I did know something was off, but I thought it meant Cash was dead inside, not that there was a freaking bomb."

Now that the excitement was over, pain began to radiate from my knees, along with a few other places. In fact, sitting down wasn't so comfortable, either, and I was starting to shake. I'd nearly died. We'd both nearly been blown up. Holy hell.

We arrived back at Vitality Ventures, and Stone pulled into the parking garage. Still shaking, I got out and limped toward the elevator.

"Hang on, let me help." Stone carefully wrapped an arm high around my waist to help me walk. "I can carry you if you want."

"No... it's fine. I walk barefooted all the time." In the light, I gasped to find charred holes in my dress. Several burned spots dotted the red material, and my leather jacket had taken a beating. At least it had protected my elbows. But a sharp pain low on my back side was growing with each step. I tightened my jaw. It really hurt.

I'd felt something hit me there, but I didn't think it had burned through my clothes. What if it had? I reached back to tug at the bottom of my dress, but Stone stopped me.

"Don't do that. You've got a burn on your... uh... back. I'll take a look at it in the apartment."

"My *back* or my butt?"

He raised an eyebrow at me and I blanched. Could this get any worse? Based on the pain, he'd get a decent look at most of my bare butt if I let him help me. Just the thought of being so vulnerable made it hard to breathe.

Stone used his key-card to call the elevator, and we stepped inside. Closing my eyes, I tried to compose my nerves, but my legs wouldn't quit shaking, and I couldn't seem to catch my breath. My stomach grew queasy, too. I did *not* feel good.

Pulling me a little tighter against him, Stone kept his voice even and calm. "Hey, it's okay. Breathe. Just breathe. I've got you. You're safe. Breathe in... breathe out. Deep, slow breaths."

"I don't feel so good."

"I think you're in shock. Nearly getting blown up will do that to you."

"Uh, yeah. I guess you should know." I licked my lips and took a long, slow breath. The ringing in my ears got softer, and I could focus more clearly again.

The doors opened, and Stone helped me walk to the hallway door of the apartment. Unlocking it, he pushed it open and guided me inside, stopping to lock it behind us. Snaking his arm back around me, he helped me through the hall to my bedroom.

Next to my bed, I let go of him and tried to give him a smile. "Thanks. I think I'll be okay for now. You can go." Turning, I sank onto the side of the bed. As soon as my butt hit the bed, I sprang to my feet. "Ow! That hurt."

"Yeah... it's pretty red."

"You can see my skin?" I reached back to touch my dress and found a big hole right over the top of my bum. "Dammit!"

"Let me help. I promise to be a complete gentleman. I won't even peek."

I studied him with narrowed eyes.

"I swear." He met my gaze, his deep brown eyes warm and sincere. "Besides, I'm an expert at undressing women." A hint of a smile played on his lips.

"Oh, jeez." I couldn't help laughing. "Fine. But go get me a towel or something first."

"You got it." He sent me a lopsided grin. "Don't go anywhere."

I rolled my eyes. As if I could. He was back in no time with a fluffy robe in hand.

"I thought you could get your arms out of the dress and slide this on backwards."

"Oh, good idea."

He laid the robe on the bed in easy reach. "You ready?"

"I guess." I blew out a breath and carefully tugged the jacket off my shoulders. Now came the dress. The side zipper was under my arm, and I tugged it down. I'd worn a strapless bra underneath, so at least I wasn't totally naked under there. I pulled the dress strap off my shoulder and got my arm out, baring both my shoulders and my back to Sexy Stone. At least the long scar down my side and under my breast wasn't visible.

I quickly snagged the robe and put my arms through the sleeves, letting the top of the dress fall. I hissed as the material rubbed against the burn. "Okay, Mr. Expert. Show me what you've got."

"I don't think you could handle what I've got, but I'll make sure this doesn't hurt." He gently took the hem of my dress and pulled the material away from my skin, sending a pleasant tingle over my stomach and legs.

I focused on the burn, fighting the urge to turn around and throw myself at him as he gathered the rest of the material and gently tugged the dress off my hips. It fell to the ground, pooling around my feet. I let out a shaky breath and stepped out of the dress, pushing my hair away from my face.

"Nice thong."

I threw the open ends of the robe around my back. "You do *not* get to comment on my underwear."

"What? I said it was nice."

I turned to face him, my lips twisting. "Thanks. I think I can take it from here."

"You still need help treating your burn." He shook his head. "You can't even see it."

"I'll be fine. Thank you for your help." I swallowed. Being this close to him and practically naked was setting me on fire.

Before I could do something I'd regret, I made a beeline for the bathroom. Before shutting the door, I turned and met his gaze. "Oh, and Stone?"

"Yeah?" He perked up like he thought I'd invite him in.

Yeah right. I smirked. "For the record... I just saved your life."

A grin broke out on his face, and he chuckled. "Thank you, Serenity. I'm only sorry I couldn't save your ass."

Chapter 10

Stone

As soon as the bathroom door shut, my shoulders sagged, and I ran a hand through my hair. I was in trouble. Not only in the *I almost got blown up twice today* kind of trouble, but Serenity was something else. Yes, I wanted her like I needed air, but I also liked being with her... our day together had been *fun*. When was the last time I'd had fun?

Taking a few calming breaths, I stalked to my room and closed the door firmly behind me. I needed a shower. A cold one. I stripped out of my clothes and stepped into my master bathroom, the tile cool against my bare feet. As the water sluiced over me, I leaned against the tiles and caught my breath.

So much had happened today that it was hard to keep everything straight. Besides the attempts on my life, I had a beautiful woman staying here to *protect* me. But she was quickly becoming more than that. What had I gotten into?

Thinking of Serenity naked in the bathroom just down the hall sent my pulse racing. I needed to figure out who was targeting me and why, before I completely fell for her. Of course, that would mean our time together was over. But wasn't that what I wanted?

Too bad everything about her drew me in. I'd never had such an immediate connection to anyone before, and I didn't like the feeling. Usually, I could take 'em or leave 'em, but Serenity just seemed to get under my skin, and her allure ran deep.

The fact that she had a soon-to-be ex didn't even deter me. I usually stayed far away from women like her, but after meeting him, something deep and primitive rose up inside me. What a prick. When he told her he wished she'd died in the accident, I almost came unglued.

She was damn lucky to be rid of him. If he couldn't handle her touch, then he didn't deserve her. Yes, it was a little disconcerting to know she saw things sometimes, but it was also fascinating.

Since Cash had to be the link to my stalker, she'd definitely proved me wrong. I hadn't been sure her visions were actually related until now. It seemed that, even though they didn't always make sense, there was a connection between events. Plus, she seemed to believe that whatever they showed was always for a purpose.

So why was her ex so upset? Did he have something to hide? I'd seen the fear in his eyes when he looked at her. It was almost like he used sarcasm and meanness to cover it. Something didn't gel, and I wanted to know what it was. Next time she saw him, she should try to touch him; then she'd see how fast he ran away.

Breathing easier, I got out of the shower and dried off. I needed to see if Serenity would let me help bandage her cute little ass. Now that we'd both had time to collect ourselves, it wasn't a big deal. Besides, I was a cool and collected hitman with nerves of steel. Nothing got to me.

I had a couple of new scrapes and bruises myself, but nothing as bad as Serenity. Of course, my black blazer was toast, along with Serenity's sexy red dress, which was a huge shame, because she looked amazing in it. At least we were still alive. The image of Serenity standing nearly naked washed over me, and I groaned. Maybe I wasn't so cool and collected after all.

Slipping on a t-shirt and gym shorts, I left my room to check on her. From the sound of the shower running, she was still in the bathroom, so I headed down the hall for a snack in the kitchen.

Pulling out a yogurt, I heard the water turn off and leaned against the counter to eat. A few minutes later, I heard the door open and her bedroom door shut pretty hard. I took another bite of yogurt and decided to give her a minute before offering to help her again.

She'd probably send me on my way, but, since she'd saved my ass by putting hers in the line of fire, I had to ask. I grinned at my pun, but quickly sobered. I genuinely hated that she'd been hurt, so maybe I should leave her alone. But what if she needed my help? Besides, it didn't hurt to ask, and I loved it when she got flustered around me.

After throwing the empty yogurt container away, I stepped down the hall and knocked on her door. "You okay in there?"

"Yeah. I'm fine."

"Need any help?"

"No."

"You sure?"

The door opened, and she stood there in a loose t-shirt that covered her to mid-thigh. "Yes. But I could use some pain reliever. Do you have some handy?"

"Sure. It's in the kitchen." I kept my gaze firmly on her face. Her dress had been revealing, but somehow, seeing her like this excited me even more. Maybe I should have worn my jeans. Turning, I led the way to the kitchen, and she followed slowly behind me. "How's your butt?"

She huffed. "Not too bad. I found the burn gel and slathered it on."

"Good. Would you like me to take a look at it?"

Her brows rose. "Uh... no. It's all bandaged up."

"Oh... okay. Well, let me know if you change your mind. Can you sit down?"

"Yeah. It's not in the worst spot, even if it is uncomfortable."

"That's a bummer." I snickered, unable to resist the stupid joke.

She smacked my arm. "That's not funny."

"Sorry... it's not fun to be the butt of a joke."

Groaning, she held out her hand. "Tylenol. Now."

"Yes, ma'am." I opened the cabinet doors over the sink. Rummaging around, I found the bottle and handed it to her.

"Ma'am? Really" She took a couple out, filled a glass with water, and swallowed them down.

"Would you rather I addressed you as sir?"

She rolled her eyes. "No. Thanks for the pills." She set the glass in the sink and leaned her elbows against the counter. "What's the plan for tomorrow?"

"It's nearly two in the morning. Why don't we start at nine? That would give us a few hours of sleep."

"Sure."

She straightened, but I wasn't ready to let her go. "Hey... do you think Cash was in the trailer when it blew?"

"Yeah... from my vision, I'm pretty sure of it. Plus... there's something else—"

She lowered her head and wouldn't look at me.

"What?"

Taking a breath, she glanced up at me, and her mouth twisted. "You'll never believe this, but I heard a Johnny Cash song when I touched the doorknob."

"What? No way! Which one?"

She shook her head. "The *burn, burn, burn... that ring of fire* one."

I nearly choked. "Holy hell!"

"Yeah... pretty crazy, huh?"

"Damn. So, I guess they're connected then."

"That's what I'd say."

"Shit... then I guess talking to Cash about Johnny is a dead end."

She squeezed her eyes shut, but her lips quirked up. "You're just full of puns tonight, aren't you?"

I shrugged, not admitting that last one had been unintentional. "I guess so." A chuckle burst out of me, and I couldn't stop laughing. "I'm gonna be singing that song all night, now."

She chuckled and shook her head as well. "I know... me too!"

We mused together in comfortable silence for a minute before Serenity sighed and met my gaze. "Okay... well, I'm going to bed. I sure hope we can figure this out by tomorrow."

Really? Was she that ready to get away from me? I raised a brow to hide my disappointment. "Me too. I'm kind of tired of dodging bombs."

"No kidding." She rolled her neck to work out the kinks. "It's got to be someone who wants revenge pretty bad, because they're going to a lot of trouble to kill you."

Sighing, she moved her hand toward my chest, like she was going to pat me, but caught herself and pulled back. "Uh... goodnight. I'll see you in the morning."

My heart twisted, and I shook my head as she limped away as fast as she could. I opened my mouth to ask her if she wanted some company, but her door shut before I could. It was probably for the best.

A woman like her wanted different things than I did. And, since I was a cold-hearted bastard, I didn't want to hurt her. Besides that, nearly getting blown up twice in one day was tiring. Plus... I wanted her to enjoy my company, and she couldn't do that with a burn on her butt. I grinned before downing a couple of pills, and turned out the lights.

Lying down on my bed felt amazing. Still, as tired as I was, my mind wouldn't rest. Serenity was right. Someone was going to a lot of trouble to end my life, and I needed to figure out who it was before they succeeded.

Like she said, it had to be someone with revenge in mind. In my line of work, that added up to a lot of people. I'd kept most of that information tucked away, but now it was time to look a little closer.

Sure, I'd killed a few people, but they were all criminals who'd gotten out of control. Vanetti lived by a code, and I helped him maintain it. It's how he'd become so successful. Hell, even the police appreciated that we could clean up things they couldn't.

It was time to dig deep into the past. Something I should have done before now. Three people came to mind, and all of them had the guts to use explosives.

First was Needles. I'd killed his brother in a shootout, leaving Needles wounded and several members of his gang in the hospital. I'd tipped off the cops, and they'd conveniently found all the drugs and money he and his gang had been dealing. He'd gone off to prison, along with several members of his gang. I hadn't thought of him for a while, but what if he'd gotten out?

There were a couple of others who came to mind as well. That gang fight last month was one. I'd stepped in to settle things between the members who didn't want to play by Vanetti's rules. They didn't like that much, and I'd had to make an example of the biggest asshole of the bunch. I'd left Jangles alive, but in hindsight, maybe that had been a bad idea.

The last person I worried about was Anna. She'd tried to cheat Vanetti out of a boatload of money, and it had backfired. Her boyfriend had ended up in jail, and she'd lost her job along with her reputation. She definitely had a bone to pick with me.

Sighing, I closed my eyes, too tired to think anymore, and finally drifted off.

A noise brought me awake, and it took a minute to remember where I was. I sat up and tried not to groan. Every muscle in my body had stiffened during the night, and I spent the next few minutes stretching the kinks out.

The noise sounded again, and I realized it was coming from the kitchen. I almost ran out in my boxers, but remembered my shorts just in time. I hurried out, hoping Serenity hadn't destroyed my expensive coffee brewer.

I found her wearing the same t-shirt as last night and standing beside my coffee grinder. She glanced up, and her eyes widened. Her gaze landed on my bare chest, and her mouth dropped open. "Uh..." She swallowed. "I'm sorry if I woke you. I thought I'd make some coffee."

"It's fine." I shook my head and crossed to her. "Do you know how to use that?" I motioned to the coffee grinder.

Her lips turned down. "Of course I do." She pulled the ground coffee beans out and stepped to my precious coffee brewer. She hesitated, and it was all I needed to hurry to her side.

"Here. I've got it, why don't you sit down?"

She pushed my reaching hands away. "You don't think I know how to make coffee?" She settled the beans into the top of the machine and moved to push the button.

"Wait. Do pre-infusion. It's this button." I pushed the button and waited for the beeps. "There. Now you can start it up."

Twisting her lips, she pushed the start button and glanced my way, freezing when she realized how close we were standing to each other. "I'm, uh... it's a little chilly in here. I'm going to get dressed while it's brewing." Her throat bobbed as she stared at my lips.

"You sure?" My voice went husky. She wore a too-big t-shirt, and all I had on was my shorts. I could remedy that. "I could give you my shorts if you'd like."

Her eyes widened. "No— I mean, *yes.*"

I grinned, wanting to step forward and run my hands under the shirt and over her bare stomach and waist. "So... no, you're not sure about getting dressed, or yes, you're sure you want my shorts?"

A bright red blush covered her cheeks. "I'm only sure that you're bad news."

She quickly turned and practically ran to her room. The sound of her door slamming brought a smile to my lips. Shaking my head, I hurried back into my room to get dressed for the day.

Chapter 11

Serenity

I closed the door and leaned against it to catch my breath. I was in so much trouble. Part of me had wanted to run my hands all over his perfect chest. The sane, rational part was yelling to run as far away as I could.

Letting out a sigh, I quickly made the bed and tried to figure out what to wear today. I wasn't so sure I could handle wearing pants over my burn, but I didn't have a skirt or dress that would work.

Needing to take a look at it, I slipped off my shirt and tugged my undies down. The burn was on my right side, high enough that I wouldn't sit on it if I sat on the edge of my seat.

I twisted and turned, but couldn't see it at all. If not for the mirror in the bathroom, I never would have been able to bandage it last night. I gingerly pulled the tape away on one side, but the gauze wasn't coming off.

I tugged at it, and gasped at the sharp pain. Was it stuck to the wound? "Dammit!" I should have waited until I was in the bathroom across the hall to look at it. Now what was I going to do?

Maybe if I got it wet it would come off? But I couldn't go across the hall half naked. I heaved a sigh and got dressed, pulling my pants to just below the wound and leaving them undone. I slipped on my bra and a t-shirt, pulling it down to cover me up. The shirt wasn't big enough to do the job, so I put my sleep shirt back on.

I really didn't want Stone to see me with my pants undone. Hopefully I could make it to the bathroom before he noticed. I hurried to the door, just as he knocked.

"Is everything okay in there?"

Damn! What lousy timing. I pulled the door open a crack. Stone stood in the hall holding a cup of coffee. "Coffee's ready."

It smelled amazing, and I realized there was nothing for it. I needed his help. "I'm having trouble with my burn. I think the gauze is stuck, and I can't see what's going on."

"Oh... that's too bad." He glanced down at my unbuttoned pants and nodded. "That's gotta hurt. Let's go in the bathroom, and I'll take a look at it." Instead of waiting, he stepped to the bathroom.

Heaving out a breath, I followed, holding my pants up with one hand, and letting my t-shirt hang down. I waited while he got the crate with the supplies out of the cupboard and set everything on the counter. After washing his hands, he turned my way. "Okay. I'm ready. Let me take a look at that *ring of fire* burn."

My brows rose. "You're really calling it that?"

He shrugged. "Why not?"

Shaking my head, I turned to face the sink and pulled my shirt up with one hand, holding my pants up with the other. He had to squat down to see it, and I squeezed my eyes shut, my face impossibly hot.

"Yeah... it looks like a blister broke. That's why the gauze is stuck. Let me get it wet and see if it'll come off." He wet down a washcloth and gently placed it over the gauze. While he held it there, I dropped my head, letting my hair cover my face.

Sexy Stone was holding a wet washcloth to my butt. He was probably examining every inch of bare skin while he did it, and all I wanted to do was hide. "I think it's probably wet enough now."

"Okay. I'll try pulling it off."

The bandage came off, and I let out a sigh. He took out the ointment and began to slather it on before setting the tube back down. He looked through the crate for a bandage, and my patience was getting the best of me. "It's right there." I pointed. I knew, because I'd gotten it out last night. "Or are you just being slow to see if I'll die of embarrassment?"

He huffed a laugh. "No, I'm almost done. I was looking for a different pad. And, just so you know, the worst of the burn is only a little bigger than a nickel."

"Oh, that's good." It felt a lot bigger than that, so it was nice to know it probably wouldn't take too long to heal. "How blistered is it?"

"It's mostly just red, though there are a few small blisters. And here is the non-stick pad I was looking for. It's a lot better than the gauze you put on it last night."

"Get blown up often?" I asked. He really knew his medical supplies.

He stiffened, but instead of answering, he tore a couple of strips of medical tape and set it on the counter before laying the pad over my wound. Grabbing the tape, he gently placed them over the pad onto my skin. I couldn't get a look at his face.

"Stone?" Had I said something wrong?

"There. All done. That wasn't so bad, right?" He gave me a tight smile.

I straightened and yanked my shirt down. "I guess not."

He concentrated on putting the supplies back in the crate.

"Are you... okay?"

"I'm fine." He tried to smile again, but his face held a gravity that hadn't been there before.

My stomach twisted, and I almost pushed him to tell me what I'd done wrong. Instead, I hurried back to my bedroom to finish dressing, and shut my door. I'd only been joking about getting blown up... why had that struck a nerve?

He'd talked about it yesterday like it was nothing. So what was it? I *couldn't* have made him feel bad. Maybe it was having him so close that was unsettling. Maybe our fun last night was a fluke? I'd just have to keep my distance, concentrate on doing my job, and forget about how much I wanted to touch him.

Sighing, I managed to pull up my pants and fasten them with hardly any pain. Taking off my night shirt, I rummaged through my suitcase for a cute top, and found a white tee with a colorful sunflower on the front. I loved this shirt, since sunflowers were my favorite, and I hoped wearing it would put me in a sunny mood.

Needing to put on my shoes and socks, I sat on the edge of the chair. Leaning over, I felt only a twinge of pain, and relief washed over me. I could do this. I quickly slipped on my shoes and opened the door to head into the bathroom.

After combing my hair and applying a touch of makeup, I grabbed my purse, leather jacket, and gloves, and hurried into the kitchen for some of that coffee.

Stone stood beside the dishwasher, putting his empty plate inside. "Help yourself to whatever you want for breakfast. I'm leaving to check in with Vanetti. Why don't you join us in his office after you've had something to eat?"

"Sure. Thanks."

He nodded and hurried out the door. Was he happy to get away from me? My shoulders sagged, and I set my things on the table, put a piece of bread in the toaster, and poured a cup of coffee. Maybe it was for the best. Straightening, I decided to be totally professional today. Minus the sunflower t-shirt.

Sleep had eluded me last night, mostly because my mind kept taking me back to the moment I turned the doorknob on the trailer and knew there was a bomb ready to go off.

I glanced at my palm, still surprised that the heat I'd felt was just part of the vision and not real. I'd never felt actual pain from a vision before, and it worried me. If I got shot in a vision, would I physically feel it? There was so much I needed to learn about my ability. Too bad there wasn't someone to teach me.

Finished with my toast, I cleaned up and hurried out the door. Stepping out of the apartment and into the middle of a large corporate office seemed strange, but I shook it off and headed down the hall.

I got to Julia's desk, before anyone noticed me, and paused. "Hey, Julia. Stone told me to meet him in Mr. Vanetti's office. Is that okay?"

She glanced my way before nodding. "Yes. They're in there. Since you're headed that way, would you give Mr. Vanetti this envelope? He wanted it as soon as it came in."

"Sure. I'd be happy to."

"Thanks." She held it out for me and I took it, totally forgetting that I'd left my gloves on the kitchen table. Unfortunately, it triggered a vision, and I blinked a few times to see Julia and Mr. Vanetti in a heated embrace, kissing each other passionately.

It only lasted a couple of seconds, and luckily, Julia hadn't been watching me. Sighing, I ignored the flutter in my stomach and stepped down the hallway.

So... Julia and Vanetti were lovers? Who would have thought? At least she wasn't twenty years younger than him, so that was good. I'd bet anything their relationship wasn't common knowledge. I shook my head and pushed it to the back of my mind. It was better to act like I didn't know. Still... what the freak?

Not wanting another vision, I rapped on Vanetti's door with my knuckles and used the bottom of my shirt around the knob to open it.

"Serenity," Vanetti said. "Come in. Stone was just filling me in on what happened last night. Sounds like you barely made it out of there alive."

"Yeah, it was close. Uh... Julia asked me to give this to you." I held out the envelope to him. Taking it, he looked it over while I sat in the empty chair beside Stone, easing diagonally onto the edge of the seat. It probably looked a little weird, but it was better than sitting on my burn. "I guess Stone filled you in on *everything*?"

Vanetti glanced up from the envelope, and his brows drew together. He stretched his neck to look at my chair, but was too polite to ask why I was sitting on it sideways. "Yeah, he did. I'd like to know your take on things, especially if you picked up anything at the club that would be important for me to know."

I raised my brows, totally surprised.

His lips twisted. "Just start with what happened when you got there."

"Oh. Sure." That surprised me, but I quickly went over what happened from my perspective, glossing over how much fun I'd had on the dance floor. I only hesitated when it came to Brandon. He didn't need to know about him, right? Unless Stone had already told him. Now I *had* to bring it up. "Uh... did Stone tell you about meeting my ex?"

"Yes." His lips flattened. "That was unfortunate, but it didn't seem to stop you from doing your job."

"No, it didn't." I hadn't thought of that. He was right, I hadn't let Brandon derail me at all. In fact, I'd *saved* Stone's life last night. Go me!

"Good." He met my gaze and raised his brows. "And there was nothing you picked up about the club that I should know?"

I squirmed. "Um... not really. I was concentrating on Stone, and I kept my gloves on most of the time." He narrowed his gaze, so I continued. "I may have accidentally picked up a few personal things about people, but it's nothing that concerns your business."

He rubbed his chin and twisted his lips. "What about here at the office?"

My eyes widened. "Nope." I said that pretty quick, but I wasn't about to tell him that I knew about his affair with Julia. I didn't know if he had a wife, and I wasn't about to ask. Besides, if he wanted me to snoop around his club and office, he was going to have to pay me for it.

"Hmm. Okay. Good to know." He wrote on a notepad before glancing back at me. "At the beginning, you mentioned that you sometimes see visions of future events. So I'm wondering if you've ever been able to prevent one of your visions from happening."

I relaxed and nodded. "Good question. I've tried to intervene at times, but I honestly don't know if it helps. I mean... sometimes it does, but not always."

"Can you give me an example?"

"Uh... sure." I paused to think. Why was he questioning me? It felt like I was being interviewed all over again. "Last week, there was this guy at my lawyer's office. On my way in, I dropped my notebook, and he picked it up. When he handed it to me, his fingers brushed my hand, and I saw him trip and fall over a step on the sidewalk outside. After thanking him, I told him to be careful outside on the steps. He gave me a weird look and walked away."

My lips twisted. "So, I sort of followed him, to see if it would happen, and... it didn't turn out the way I thought."

"Why not?"

"Because he started down the steps and glanced back to see me watching him and..." I heaved out a breath. "That's when he fell."

Stone snorted and shook his head. "So, *you* made him fall."

My eyes widened. "No, I didn't! He might have glanced back and fallen anyway. Even if I hadn't been watching. If he would have just paid attention to the steps like I told him to, he would have been fine."

Vanetti nodded. "I see what you mean, but would he have fallen if he hadn't interacted with you in the first place?"

"Maybe? I don't know." Ugh.

Stone's eyes sparkled. "So maybe things happen to people *because* Serenity's involved."

Was he teasing me? I glared at him. "Come on, you're making it too black and white. Sure, there's cause and effect, but don't forget that most of these things are based on our choices. That guy chose to look back instead of paying attention to the steps. I didn't make him look at me."

"True." Stone's lips twisted. "But what about this? Would he have fallen if he hadn't picked up your notes in the first place?"

I glanced at the ceiling before meeting his gaze. "Who knows? It could have happened anyway. And since I saw a vision of him falling, I was able to warn him." I shook my head. "Of course, it didn't change anything. But it could have."

Vanetti shook his head, and his lips quirked up. "That's true, but don't underestimate yourself. I think if someone told me I was going to be stabbed in the back, I'd take it seriously. Even if I didn't believe them, I'd still be extra cautious." He glanced at Stone and narrowed his eyes.

"I'm taking this seriously." Stone raised his eyebrows. "But—" He turned to me. "This is still pretty new to me... and to you."

My stomach plunged. Was he throwing me under the bus? Before Vanetti could fire me, I turned to him. "You know how good I am. I figured out where your document disappeared to, right? And everyone has to start somewhere." I glared at Stone. Why was he doing this?

Vanetti met my gaze, eyebrows quirking. "Yes, you did." He glanced between me and Stone. "When you say 'new to this,' do you mean to being a PI or a psychic?"

Oh, hell. "You know I'm a fairly new PI."

He nodded. "And how new are you at being a psychic?"

I blew out a breath. "About a year."

"I see." Vanetti narrowed his eyes at me. "And would you mind telling me how your powers came to be?"

I didn't have to explain, but I wanted both Vanetti and Stone to trust me, so I went ahead with the story. "Sure. I was in a car accident. It happened after that. I don't know exactly what triggered this psychic ability, but I think it's because I died while they were trying to stabilize me. Obviously, they brought me back, and now I have psychometry."

I glanced at Stone. Had he told Vanetti about Brandon leaving me over that, too? I shrugged. "It was weird at first, but now I'm trying to use it to help people."

"Remarkable." Vanetti nodded. "So, you never had a sixth sense about things like that before the accident?"

"You mean like... premonitions?" He nodded, and I shook my head. "No. I mean... I guess I've always been intuitive, but since I married a guy who turned out to be a total jerk, maybe I'm just kidding myself."

"So the reason you became a PI was because of your new psychic abilities?"

I cleared my throat, glancing at Stone. "Well... not really. I mean... it was something I was already working on, and gaining this ability kind of sealed the deal... if you know what I mean." I'd told Stone about my childhood dream and my passion for detective books, but that was meant only for him. I wasn't about to tell Vanetti.

Vanetti's lips tilted up. "Excellent. I like your attitude. It takes initiative and courage to start your own business, and I applaud you for it, especially since you've helped me out already."

"Uh... thanks." I perked up a little. That was more like it.

He nodded. "And... if you need a good lawyer, I'm happy to lend you mine. He's not a divorce lawyer, but his firm handles them." He opened his top drawer and pulled out a card. "His name is Christopher Nichols."

"Oh... thanks, but I've got someone."

Vanetti's brows dipped. "Sure... sure. But with your connection to me, I guarantee that he'll give you a nice discount. Think about it."

"Of course." I slipped the card into my bag. "Thanks."

He smiled, pleased with himself, like he'd done me a big favor. "Now let's get back to business, shall we?" He raised his brows at Stone. "Do you have any other leads?"

"Yes." Stone glanced my way. "Since talking to Cash is no longer an option, I've thought of a couple more people we can check out."

Vanetti nodded. "Good. Let's hope one of them is who we're looking for." Vanetti turned to me. "I'm confident you'll be able to figure it out."

"Thanks. I won't let you down." Warmth blossomed in my chest. It was nice that Vanetti believed in me, even if Stone didn't. Giving him a quick smile, I stood, only wincing a little at the pain in my butt. Stone, the other pain in my butt, stood as well and followed me to the door.

Chapter 12

Serenity

Stone held the door open for me, and we walked to his office in silence. Was he ever going to tell me what I'd said to make him mad? He ushered me inside before taking his chair behind the desk. While he turned on his computer, still more stoic than he'd been this morning. I folded my arms and leaned against his desk.

He glanced up at me and raised a brow. "If you want to sit down, I could get you a pillow."

"No, I'm fine." I tried for a haughty expression.

The corner of his mouth twitched. "I think I've got one in here, somewhere." He pushed his chair back to stand, but I held up a hand.

"Don't bother. It's not that big of a deal, I just want to stand for a minute. So what have you got on these new guys?"

I wanted to tell him that it might have been helpful if he'd done this research earlier, but now wasn't the time to complain. Too bad Cash was dead, but wasn't there another angle we could check out? Something to do with Razor and his gang?

Stone scooted his chair back to his desk and logged into his account. "I remembered someone who might be behind this. I helped put him in jail, so I need to find out if he's still there."

My eyebrows shot up. "You did? Really? I'm impressed." For some reason, I didn't think of Stone as a guy who got the good guys involved. It was reassuring to hear.

"Yeah, I told you I'm good at this stuff."

I rolled my eyes. "Yeah, okay. So what happened? I mean... you put him in jail, so now that he's out, he wants you dead? That doesn't seem bomb-worthy."

Stone sat back in his chair and folded his arms. "It's a little more complicated than that. Needles ran a gang that went rogue. It was my job to bring them back into the fold, but things got out of hand and—" He shrugged. "I had to protect myself. His brother was killed, and most of the gang went to jail with him."

My brows rose. "Oh... so... you're the reason his brother is dead?"

"It was self-defense."

"Oh... okay. Yeah... I can see why he'd come after you."

He logged onto a paid search engine and typed in the guy's name. "Yeah... in fact, after they dispersed, Razor and the Shadow Serpents took over his territory."

"Would his real name happen to be Johnny?"

Stone's mouth quirked up. "No. His name's Nico Navarro." He tapped on his keyboard, and sighed. "It looks like he's still in jail, so it can't be him." He glanced my way. "That leaves Anna and the South Side Gang."

"Anna?" My stomach twinged. "It couldn't be a woman. The person I saw had a beard."

He rubbed his face. "She could be working with someone."

"I guess." Was she a jealous ex? Why would she want to kill Stone?

"We'll have to find her to make sure, but I have a good idea where she is. She used to work at the Tiki Tabu Bar and still has friends there. Do you know the place?"

"No. But why do you think it could be her?"

"I had a run-in with her boyfriend, and he ended up in prison."

"Oh." Relief rushed over me. "Wow... you sure send a lot of people to prison. Are you sure you're not working for the cops?"

His lips twisted. "I don't mind helping them when it helps Vanetti."

"Right. So why do you think she's bomb-worthy?"

"I guess she thinks I ruined her life, and she swore she'd get back at me." He shrugged. "It's worth checking out. But the bar won't be open for a few hours. In the meantime, we could head to the game store and talk to the leader of the South Side Gang." He motioned in the direction of my butt. "Do you think you could ride the bike?"

"Yes." I nodded before really thinking about it. Even if it wasn't the most comfortable place to sit, I couldn't pass up a ride. It made me realize that riding with him could become an addiction. But there were worse things to be addicted to, right?

With a slow smile, he nodded. "Great. Let's go."

"Sure... but I left my gloves in the kitchen."

"That's fine. I need to get a couple of things from the apartment myself."

I followed him down the hall and waited while he unlocked the door. Inside, I went straight to the table and grabbed my purse and gloves.

Stone hurried to his room and came out wearing his shoulder holster and gun. He slipped his leather jacket over it and grabbed his keys. "Let's go out the back way."

"Hey... I have a gun. Should I bring it?"

"You do?"

"Yeah. It's in my luggage, but it fits in my shoulder bag."

His brow crinkled. "You have a concealed carry permit?"

"Of course."

"And you know how to use it? I mean... I don't mind having backup, but I don't want to get shot by accident."

I huffed out a breath. "Jeez. I would never... I know what I'm doing."

"Have you ever shot at anything that's alive?"

My lips drew in. "No. But I've still gone through all the training."

He shrugged. "Okay. Then go get it."

Scowling, I hurried to my room and pulled the gun case from my luggage. After taking it out, I slid the loaded clip into the grip, flipped the safety on, put it in a holster that I could wear if I needed to, and stashed it in my shoulder-bag.

I hurried back into the kitchen, finding Stone drinking another cup of coffee. He raised his mug. "You want some?"

"No, I'm good."

My phone began to ring, and I pulled it out of my purse. Glancing at Stone, I raised my brows. "It's my sister. Do you mind if I take it?"

"No, go ahead."

I swiped to answer. "Hi, Felicity. Sorry I didn't call you yesterday."

"That's okay. I figured you got the job."

"Yeah. I did."

"So how's it going?"

"It's good." I swallowed, not about to tell her I barely escaped death last night. "Not quite what I expected, but the pay's a lot better than I thought... which is a good thing since I found out that Brandon's suing me."

"What? I thought it was all settled. What does he want now?"

"I guess he wants more money, because he's suing me for mental cruelty that occurred after the accident. He's claiming the divorce is my fault because I changed. It just makes me so angry I could scream."

"That asshole."

"Yeah." I contemplated telling her about bumping into Brandon last night, but decided I didn't have time to go into it. I glanced at Stone, and found him eating a bagel, so I hoped he didn't mind if I kept talking.

"Well... hang in there. I know you're busy, but I just wanted to make sure you're bringing the chips and dip to Gracie's birthday party tomorrow."

My heart dropped. I'd totally spaced it. "Oh... yeah... uh... I'm not sure I can make it. This is one of those jobs where I can't leave my client... alone. But... maybe I'll have the case solved by then." I winced, knowing that was a lame excuse.

"What are you talking about? You can't miss Gracie's seventh birthday party. She's expecting you. I get that you're busy, but... can't you take a couple of hours off?"

I squirmed. "Well... I'm a little stuck since I agreed to being on the case twenty-four seven. With the way things are going, I don't think I'll have a choice."

Felicity blew out a breath. "I can't believe what I'm hearing. Sen... you have to come. Think about Gracie. You'll break her heart."

I closed my eyes. "I know... you're right, but this job is not like the others. It's a lot more intense. But listen... I'll try and get away for a half hour or so. I know that's not much, but it's better than nothing, right? When this case is over, I'll do something fun with Gracie. I promise."

I glanced at Stone and found him leaning against the counter, his brows dipped. Was he mad that I was still on the phone?

"Uh... I've got to go. Why don't I call you tonight when we can talk. I'll explain everything then."

"Fine. But you *have* to come tomorrow. No excuses, so figure it out, okay?"

"Sure. I'll do my best."

She sighed. "Okay. Bye."

"Bye." I disconnected and let out a breath. Damn. Why did everything always have to happen at the same time? I finally get a good-paying job, and now I have to let down my niece because of it. Life just wasn't fair.

"Sounded like your sister wasn't happy with you." Stone's low voice sent a shiver down my spine. "What's going on?"

I rubbed my forehead. "It's my niece's seventh birthday tomorrow, and they're having a party for her. But don't worry about it. I'll just make it up to her on another day."

"I'm sure I'll be fine without you for a couple of hours. You should go."

I shook my head. "No. We have to stick together. It's in my contract. I'll just have to figure something else out."

Stone shook his head. Then his eyes lit up. "Hey... I could come with you."

"What? No."

He flinched, and his brows dipped. "Why not?"

Oops. Had I hurt his feelings... again? Backtracking, I shrugged. "Oh... well, sure you can come if you really want to. Let's just hope we solve the case by tonight. Then it won't matter, right?"

His right brow rose, and his lips turned down like I was full of crap. "With the way things are going, I wouldn't count on it."

I huffed. "Yeah. Maybe not."

He gave me a half-smile full of sarcasm. "If you're worried about me, I usually get along fine with most people."

I blinked. "So, you really want to come? Why?"

He shrugged, rubbing the back of his neck. "Well... I don't think you should let your niece down because of me. Family is important. And it's only an hour or two."

"Oh... well... yeah. Of course." I bit my lips. "Hey, I'm sorry if I made you mad, earlier."

"You didn't." He smiled tightly. "Don't worry about it."

"Okay." I hesitated, but decided that it was best to move on. "So, I guess it's settled?"

"Yup. Tomorrow at five, right?" At my nod, he set his coffee mug in the sink. "Then let's plan on it."

I heaved out a breath and shook my head. "Okay." Sexy Stone was officially coming with me to a family gathering. What had I gotten myself into?

"You ready to go?"

"Uh... yeah."

"Good." He stepped down the hall to the laundry room, and I quickly followed. We slipped out the door into the hall, and I waited while he locked up. After that, we trailed down the staircase to the lower floor before getting on the elevator and taking it down to the parking level.

It was on the tip of my tongue to question his sanity about going to the party with me. He said he didn't want me to disappoint my niece, but it seemed like there was more to it than that. But what? He certainly couldn't be interested in meeting my family, right? Damn! This was going to be the worst. Awkward didn't even come close.

Now I really needed to figure this out before then. How would I even explain who he was?

We made it to the bike, and I slipped my gloves on before taking the helmet. It wasn't any easier to get the strap snapped together this time, and it took me a couple of tries before I got it done.

As I climbed on the bike behind Stone, butterflies rose in my stomach. I wrapped my arms around him and closed my eyes to savor the moment, grateful he couldn't see my face. Why did I like this so much? It wasn't just the bike. I liked wrapping my arms around him because it felt amazing. It was the one time I could touch him without needing an excuse.

Of course, it also distracted me from the discomfort of the burn on my butt, so why not enjoy it? Oh, crap. A physical pain gnawed in my chest to realize that once we figured out who was after him, my riding days would be over. Pushing that depressing thought away, I squeezed Stone a little tighter.

We exited the parking garage, and the butterflies began to dance through my chest. Yup... I was totally addicted, so no matter what the future held, I'd take this moment and enjoy it.

Several minutes later, we pulled off the street into a strip mall on the south end of town. We parked in front of a game store with all kinds of video game posters in the windows.

Before heading into the store, Stone caught my gaze. "Just a heads up... they won't be happy to see me, so watch my back, okay?"

My eyes widened. "Really? What do you think they'll do?"

"Depends on who's there. Just don't shoot me."

I narrowed my eyes. "Are you teasing me?"

His lips twisted. "Maybe a little." With a lopsided grin that did funny things to my stomach, he pulled the door open and motioned me to go in first.

I rolled my eyes and hurried inside the store. A chime sounded, and the man at the counter glanced up. His smile faltered as he caught Stone coming in behind me.

"Uh... hey, Stone. Didn't think I'd see you for a while. What can I do for you?"

Stone stalked to the counter, a friendly smile on his face. It seemed to scare the guy even more. "We came to find a game for Sen."

He motioned toward me and winked. My mouth dropped open. Not only had he remembered my nickname, but I loved how it sounded when he said it. Oh jeez, could it get any worse?

"She's real interested in the..." He glanced my way. "What game was it again?"

Since I had no idea, I glanced at the games on display. "It was this one." I picked one of them up and smiled at him, surprised by how expensive it was. I turned to the manager. "Stone's buying it for me. Isn't that sweet?" Before he could answer, I held out my hand to shake his. "I didn't catch your name."

"Oh..." He quickly shook my hand. "I'm Grady."

"Nice to meet you, Grady." Touching him had given me a quick flash of a video game cover. I had no idea what that meant, so I glanced around the store, hoping to find it.

With shaky fingers, he grabbed the video game I'd pointed to and began to ring it up. "Is there anything else you need?"

I swallowed. "Well, I'm not sure that's the only one I want, but I can't remember what the other one is called." I chewed on my bottom lip and continued to glance at the games. "Is there one that has a man fighting on the front?"

Grady looked at me like I was nuts. "Can you be more specific? I mean... look around... most of them have someone fighting on the cover."

"Oh! Right." I chuckled. "This one is for my... nephew, um..." I closed my eyes, trying to picture the game I saw in my vision. "I think it's actually got a tank on it."

Grady's eyes widened. "Uh... sure. We might have a few like that." He motioned toward the back wall. "They're back there."

Stone glanced my way, narrowing his gaze before turning to Grady. "That reminds me. Is Tank around? Someone's messing with me, and I'd like to talk to him."

Grady blew out a breath. "Look... we don't want any trouble with Vanetti. My guys are sticking to the agreement."

Stone shook his head. "Even Tank?"

"Especially Tank."

A shuffling noise came from the back room, followed by the banging of a door. Stone rushed around the counter and into the back. Grady ran after him, and I chased after them both.

I followed Grady out the back door and to the left, where we found Stone holding a man by the throat against the wall. The guy was shorter than Stone, but larger around the middle, so it made sense that he was Tank. In the tussle, Tank's phone fell out of his pocket, and I cringed to hear it crack.

"Let him go!" Grady ran toward Stone and tried to pull him off Tank.

Grady's puny efforts didn't make a difference, but Stone let Tank go anyway. Tank slumped and leaned over, heaving in big gulps of air. Grady patted him on the back. "Why did you run, man? I had it handled."

Tank couldn't answer, so while we waited for him to catch his breath, I picked up his phone to see if I could get anything from it. I closed my eyes and concentrated, but nothing happened, and I knew he wasn't our guy.

Finally, he straightened. "I didn't do nothing... I just panicked... okay? I didn't plan anything. It's not me. Okay?"

Stone raised a brow. "Then who? Who's behind it?"

"Who's behind what? I don't know what you're talking about."

"You said it wasn't you. What did you mean by that?"

He threw his arms up. "How the hell do I know? You're the one who came after me. I figured something must have happened, and that's why you're here. I'm just telling you that whatever it is, I didn't do it."

Stone closed his eyes before glancing at me with a raised brow. "You have anything to add?"

They all glanced my way, so I sent them a small smile to put them at ease. "Do either of you know how to make a bomb?"

Grady jerked. "What the hell? No way."

"Hell, no." Tank's brows drew together.

I glanced at Stone. "I don't think it's them." I held up the phone and handed it back to Tank. "You dropped this."

"Thanks." He took it, glancing between Stone and me.

Stone heaved a sigh. "Fine." He shook his head and stared daggers at both of the men. "But if either of you get in my way, it'll be the last thing you ever do."

"You got it," Grady agreed. "Like I said before, we know better. What the hell's going on, anyway? Why come after us?" Stone turned the full force of his intensity on Grady. He flinched, but held his ground.

"Someone's targeting me, and I don't like it. They're going to pay, so if you know anything about it, now's the time to speak up, because if you don't, you'll pay, too."

"Shit, man, I don't know a thing." He turned to Tank. "You hear anything about this?"

"No. This is the first I've heard of it."

Stone stared them down before giving in. "I believe you. But be sure to let me know if you do hear anything."

They both nodded, and Stone motioned me back inside. As we all marched in, Grady stopped us at the register. "Wait. Don't forget your game."

Stone gave him a menacing stare, but Grady didn't back down. "You wouldn't want to let your girl down, right?"

I couldn't stop the grin that spread across my face. While Stone paid for the game, I ran my fingers over the counter and a few of the other games, but nothing came to me. As far as I could tell, these guys had nothing to do with Stone's problem.

"Here you go." Grady handed me the game, and I slipped it into my purse. "Enjoy."

"Thanks so much."

We hurried out of the shop to the motorcycle. I slipped my leather gloves on before grabbing my helmet, and met Stone's gaze. "If you didn't guess it already, I'm sure they have nothing to do with your stalker."

"Yeah. I got that." His brows dipped. "What did you see when you shook hands with Grady, anyway?"

"A video game with a tank on it. I wasn't sure what it meant, but when you asked about Tank, it made sense."

"Does that happen often? Where you see something but you don't know what it means?"

Shrugging, I nodded. "Yeah. Sometimes it's like a puzzle that I have to put together."

"So you don't always know what your visions mean?"

"Not exactly. Most of the time, what I see is fairly obvious. But with this case, I feel like I'm missing something. It would help if we had more to go on."

Stone rubbed his face. "Yeah. It's frustrating." He checked his watch. "It's still too early to head to the bar, but I don't know what else to do. Do you have any ideas?"

I met his gaze. "Actually, yes. There's one place I haven't been yet, and that's your house. Since this is about you, I might pick up something there. The apartment really doesn't give off your personal vibe so much, but your house should be full of it."

His brows rose. "Really?" He shrugged. "Well, if it helps find our guy, I'm willing to give it a shot. Let's go."

It surprised me that he was so nonchalant about me invading his personal space. Didn't he realize I might pick up something he'd be embarrassed that I knew?

On the other hand, maybe he didn't care because he didn't get that same thrill I did when I touched him. So why care if I saw something personal about him? As long as it didn't include a vision of him sleeping with a woman. Yikes. I sure didn't want to see that.

We rode the bike back into the city and continued up toward the better, pricier side of town. Here, the houses were older and packed more tightly together, with stately trees and long driveways.

He took us through the neighborhood and along a street filled with older, craftsman-style homes. They were mid-size and cozy, with low-pitched roofs, protruding gables, and overhanging eaves.

I didn't picture him living in an area like this. I thought he'd be more of a condo person. A minute later, he pulled into the driveway of a beautiful, stately house, with a wide, open front porch held up by two thick, tapered columns, covered in beautiful stonework. This was his place? It was gorgeous.

A heavy, wooden front door, framed by two large windows on either side, looked inviting, and the wood siding, painted in earthy green tones with cream colored accents, complimented the design.

Softly rounded shrubs with colorful perennials and a stone paver walkway to the front door tied it all together, totally impressing me and making me a little jealous.

Stone drove down the driveway to the garage and parked in front. We got off, and I followed him through the gate into his backyard. A tall fence surrounding the space gave him privacy, and the garden landscape held trees and a water feature that made it cozy and secluded.

My mouth dropped open. What a great place to unwind. It was almost magical. There were even plenty of things I could photograph. I closed my mouth, totally enamored and wishing I could stay for a while.

He stepped to the back door and hesitated. "You want to touch the knob before I open the door?"

"Oh! Yes. Of course."

Pulling off my glove, I placed my hand on the knob. Nothing came through, and I nodded. "It seems fine."

Stone unlocked the door, and I followed him inside. After closing the door, he entered a security code into a panel beside the door and reset the alarm.

I stepped into his kitchen and dining room area, finding that it continued to the front of the house, leaving it open and airy. The kitchen sported a farmhouse sink, light wood cabinets, a stone tile backsplash, stainless steel appliances, and white countertops.

Standing still, I soaked it all in. It was amazing, and somehow it fit Stone perfectly.

He came to my side and raised his brows. "You want to start in here... or my bedroom?"

The way he said it sounded like an invitation, immediately sending tingles down my spine. I quickly stepped away, hoping he didn't see how his closeness rattled me.

Not only that, but this house and his yard made me view him in a totally different light. I needed to get the stars out of my eyes before I made a fool out of myself.

Our gazes met, and I saw a hint of mischief in his eyes. Narrowing my own, I played along. "That sounds like a good idea. Where is it?"

"At the end of the hall. I'll show you."

He took a step in that direction, but I put my hand on his chest to stop him. "That's okay. I can find it. You should stay out here. It's better if I do this alone." Smiling, I patted his chest and hurried to the hallway, hoping he'd stay where he was.

"Chicken."

I ignored him and stepped to the last door in the hallway. The door was partially closed, and I slipped my glove back on, wanting to make sure I only touched what was necessary, and hoping to avoid seeing him with some woman.

Inside, his bedroom held a king-sized bed covered in a plush, black comforter. The wooden headboard and dresser had a rustic, outdoorsy finish, and the walls were painted a dark forest green. It was earthy and masculine, completely different from the contemporary look of his apartment.

Finding his closet door ajar, I hurried over and pulled it open. The large walk-in closet had clothes and shoes neatly organized on one side. The other side was empty, except for a sexy, ice blue lingerie set with a matching bathrobe. Hmm... I was not touching that, I didn't want or need to know who *those* belonged to.

Closing the door, I wandered over to his dresser. Loose change and a tube of lip-balm sat on top, along with a framed photo of a much younger Stone standing beside a beautiful woman. From their similarities, it was easy to tell the woman was Stone's mother.

A round, polished stone sat next to the photo. It was black, with white veins running through it, and would easily fit in the palm of your hand. From the shine, it looked like Stone had handled it a lot, maybe even running a thumb or finger over the smooth surface.

Should I touch it? It had to be something personal, and definitely important to Stone. Maybe it had something to do with his name? It might be just what I was looking for. Pulling off my glove, I held my breath and reached out to pick it up.

The moment it touched my palm, my vision went dark. The room disappeared, replaced by hot desert sand and blinding sun. Shouting sent my pulse racing, right before a huge explosion rocked the ground.

Screaming filled the air, and gunfire erupted. Stone emerged from the smoke, wearing military gear and dragging a wounded soldier to safety. More shots sounded and he hit the ground, instinctively covering the fallen soldier with his body.

The gunfire stopped and he jumped to his feet, rushing to pull the soldier toward a gate and the compound on the other side. Another explosion rocked the ground, and shots sounded again, but he didn't stop. Ducking into a crouch, he moved faster, continuing to pull the soldier behind him. The gate swung open and he—

"Hey! Give me that!" Stone grabbed the rock from my hand.

The vision disappeared, jerking me back to his room. Gasping, I staggered back and collided with the edge of the bed. Off balance, I fell backwards, landing right on my wound. With a yelp, I tried to get up, only to have my feet slide out from under me. Right before my butt met the hardwood floor, Stone grabbed me under the arms and pulled me to my feet.

I shoved away from him, fury tightening my chest. "What did you do that for?"

"I... I didn't want you to see—" He shook his head. "This doesn't have anything to do with the current situation."

My brows shot up. "How do you know? There were explosions. It could have everything to do with it."

His jaw tightened, and his gaze hardened. "It doesn't. It's in the past. It's over."

I studied him, seeing the way his whole body had tensed up. That had been a bad time in his life. I let out a breath and softened my voice. "You knew I was here to touch things. If you didn't want me to touch it, you should have said something."

Swallowing, he shook his head. "I came in as soon as I remembered it, but you already had it in your hand. I just reacted." He absently rubbed the rock with his thumb, like it was something he'd done many times before. Realizing what he was doing, he hastily set it back on his dresser. "Look, let's just forget it, okay?"

"It could be important." I wasn't trying to be a jerk, but I got my visions for a reason.

His mouth pulled into a frown, and he shook his head again as if fighting back strong emotions.

I softened my voice. "I saw a battle. It looked like you were in the middle of a war zone. There was an explosion, and guns were shooting, with bullets flying everywhere. You were helping someone—dragging them to safety—"

"Stop." Stone tensed, the muscles in his arms tightening. "You don't need to tell me the rest."

I paused. "You were a soldier?"

"Yeah." He glanced away. "The... rock was kind of a... good luck charm."

"Oh."

He shook his head. "But I'm sure it has nothing to do with what's happening now."

I raised a brow. "But what if it does? Where were you when this happened? It looked like the Middle East. I'm guessing you were in the army?"

He took a deep breath. "It happened a long time ago."

"Sure. But at least tell me what happened to the other soldier. It looked like you were trying to help him."

He closed his eyes and rubbed the bridge of his nose.

Unsure if he would tell me, I pushed a little harder. "You were dragging him toward a gated compound. The soldier looked pretty bad. I lost what happened after that because you pulled me out of the vision. I know you made it out, but... what about the other guy? Did he make it?"

Shaking his head, Stone let out a sigh. "I was in the service for six years. My specialty was security—kind of what I do now." He swallowed and rubbed the back of his neck. "I was good at what I did, but that doesn't matter when all your intel is wrong." He swallowed, a haunted look in his eyes. "Everything went tits-up— it went all wrong, and a lot of good guys died."

Stone dropped his arm and met my gaze. "So, to answer your question—no, he didn't make it." Glancing away, he let out a long breath. "I got out as soon as my time was up."

I raised my brows. "I see." It didn't take a psychic to know it bothered him. A lot. He could probably use some counseling. Still, even knowing that, I couldn't shake the feeling that this was linked to his current predicament. "So, you're *sure* your service there isn't related to what's going on now?"

His steely-eyed gaze met mine. "Positive."

Rubbing my forehead, I licked my lips. "Okay. But I think you might be making a mistake."

"I'm not. Unless you saw something else?"

"No." I closed my eyes. "It's just a feeling I have that it's related. That's all."

"Well, I have a feeling that it's not." He huffed and took a calming breath. "You've been wrong before, but I'll try to keep an open mind." He glanced around the room. "Is that your 'vision-quota' for the day, or was there something else you wanted to touch?"

I followed his gaze to the bed.

A smile twisted his lips. "How about my pillow or the comforter? You might get something from that."

Naturally, he was goading me. Probably payback for pushing him so hard on the rock. I opened my mouth to tell him no, but the smirk on his face sent me over the edge. With a show of bravado, I reached down and grabbed his pillow.

"Sure. Let's see what other secrets you're hiding." I closed my eyes, ready to make up an embarrassing story, but my vision went dark.

Chapter 13

Stone

Serenity froze and her eyes glazed over.

Oh, shit. I hadn't expected her to actually see something. Was she seeing me with one of my exes? I cringed. That would be the worst. I opened my mouth to interrupt her, but that hadn't gone so well last time, so I bit my lip instead. Closing my eyes, I prayed to God that whatever she saw was the clue we needed, and not me with another woman. I shook my head. What was I thinking?

She hugged the pillow against her chest, and finally, her eyes flew open. "Stone!"

The alarm in her voice sent adrenaline rushing down my spine. "What?" I grabbed her arms. Did we need to run?

Her frantic gaze met mine for a fraction before flying to my chest. She reached out to press her hands to the skin right over my sternum. Swallowing, she rubbed her hands over my heart before raising her eyes to mine. "Thank God. There's no blood. You're okay."

My stomach tightened, but a sliver of relief washed over me. "What did you see?"

"You got shot. Right there." She patted my chest again. "There was so much blood." Her vivid blue gaze met mine. "You—" Her voice trembled. "You died."

Her certainty hit me like a punch in the chest. "I died?"

She nodded, her lips trembling.

"Hey, it's okay." I pulled her against me, trying to reassure her, though my heart pounded like a jackhammer. "I'm sure we can stop it from happening."

She shook her head. "I've never had a vision like that before. It was like I was there. You got shot, and you died right in front of me. All that blood. And the pain in your eyes. It was awful."

"Did you see who did it?"

"No." She pressed her head into my chest. "The light was blinding, and everything else was faded and washed out."

"Okay... where did it happen?"

"I don't know." Her voice hitched. "I don't know, and I don't know how to stop it." She held me tight.

"It's okay," I soothed. "Did you see anything else? From before I got shot?"

"I... I did see something. You were..." She trailed off, holding perfectly still.

I kept my mouth shut, not wanting to interrupt her concentration.

"You must have been outside, because the sun was shining so brightly. You also held something in your hand, but you dropped it when the bullet hit you."

She pulled back and met my gaze, determination sparking in her eyes. "I think if you don't spend a lot of time standing around in the sun, you should be okay."

I couldn't keep a smile from tugging the corners of my mouth. "You want to hide in a cave with me somewhere?" If someone was after me, I didn't think it would matter where I was. If they were determined, even changing something she saw might not be enough. I needed a lot more to go on than being outside, but her determination to save me warmed my heart. If I wasn't a complete fool, I'd say that she really cared about me.

"That's not what I meant." She scowled and started to pull away, but I stopped her, and she relaxed against me again.

"Hey, I know." I liked having her in my arms. "I just liked the mental image of being hidden away with you." I glanced at the bed. "Preferably somewhere warm and comfortable."

She met my gaze, hers searching. "You want to hide away with me?"

I smiled again. Her lips were just inches from mine. "Yes," I whispered. Unable to resist, I closed the gap, pressing my lips against hers.

She responded with an eagerness that took my breath away.

Like a dam breaking open, the desire I'd been denying came flooding out, scorching me with heat. Her scent filled my senses, and I deepened the kiss. She held me tighter and ran one hand through my hair. I groaned; my need stronger than my reason. Twisting, I sank onto the bed, pulling her down on top of me. She didn't hesitate to follow, maneuvering to straddle my hips, her knees on either side of me.

Our lips met in a wild frenzy, our tongues dancing and pulling, sucking and caressing. Lost in a haze of sexual desire, I barely heard my phone ringing.

Like coming out of a long, dark tunnel, the tone pulled me back to my senses. Serenity broke the kiss. Sucking in a deep breath, she rolled off of me, her lips red and swollen, her pupils still dark with desire.

Breathing heavily, I reached into my pocket and pulled out my phone, barely able to contain my low growl of anger when I answered. "What?"

"Hey Stone, it's Scardino. You sound more surly than normal. Did I interrupt something?"

"Yes... what do you want?"

He sucked in a breath. "Look, bigshot... I'm doing you a favor. You should be more respectful."

My nostrils flared. "Just spit it out. Am I in trouble or something?" It wasn't every day that the police detective on Vanetti's payroll called me, so it had to be something I didn't want to hear.

"Were you involved in an explosion yesterday?"

"Was it in the morning, or last night?"

"Are you shitting me? You were at both?"

I rubbed my forehead. "Unfortunately, yes. I think someone's trying to kill me."

Serenity met my gaze, her blue eyes wide and worried. "Seriously?"

I tried not to growl as she slipped off the bed, straightened her clothes, and pulled on her gloves. Why did she put her gloves back on? She didn't have to.

"Stone? Mr. Bigshot?"

I stood and began to pace. "Look, the explosion wasn't my fault. Someone set me up."

"Well, that's good to know, but I've got more bad news for ya. They found a body in the trailer. There's also a couple of eyewitnesses that gave a pretty good description of you and a woman leaving the scene. No surveillance cameras, and it was dark, so you're in the clear, but that's how I figured it was you."

"Damn. I was afraid of that. Thanks for covering for me."

"Don't thank me yet." He hesitated. "There's more."

"What?"

"A drug raid was supposed to go down last night, but the perps were warned. Our inside man told them it was you and a woman in a red dress. I'm guessing it was the same person?"

"Shit."

"Yeah. What happened man? I told you to keep your distance for a while. Did you forget?"

I rubbed the back of my neck. "Look, someone's trying to kill me. I have to chase down every lead. And I found out that he's linked to the gang... or at least to the dead guy in the trailer who's part of the gang. I was at the park for more information. I need to know who's behind this. When everyone scattered, we went to Cash's trailer to talk to him and got our asses handed to us."

Dino huffed out a breath. "You're talking about you and Sen, right? Grizzo said that was her name. What does she have to do with all this? Besides which... I'm surprised you'd take a woman to a drug meet. What the hell were you thinking?"

I closed my eyes and wandered into the kitchen for a glass of water. "It's not what you think. Vanetti hired her to help me find the guy who's trying to kill me. She's a—" I sighed and bit the bullet. "She's a psychic. She warned the gang members, but not on purpose."

Scardino actually laughed. "You're shitting me. Who is she really?"

I ground my teeth. "I'm not shitting you. It's true. When she met them, she had a vision that they were all in jail... except for your guy, Grizzo. She knew he was an undercover cop, but she didn't give it away. Someone overheard her telling me about the raid, and they all took off."

"So, this Sen person is a psychic? An actual, honest to God, psychic?"

I glanced at Serenity and found her studying me. Worry tightened her mouth, but she looked more angry than frightened. "Yeah, that's right."

"What's her real name?"

I hesitated. "I'm not going to tell you."

"Come on, man." Dino huffed out a breath. "If she's for real, then maybe I should hire her to work for us. The fact that she didn't rat out the Grizz is a real good sign."

Serenity mouthed *who is it?* I muted the phone. "Dino wants to know if you want to work for the cops."

Her brows rose. "Dino? Wait, do you mean *Detective* Scardino?"

My stomach clenched. "You know him?"

Her lips twisted and she nodded.

"How the hell do you know him?"

"He's the one who worked on my case. I needed his testimony about the accident so I could get my settlement money."

The phone squawked. "Stone! Stone? You there? You talking to her? What's she saying?"

Shaking my head, I un-muted the phone. "I'm still here." I paused and raised my eyebrows at Serenity. She nodded reluctantly. "And I guess you already know her. Serenity Jones? Ring a bell?"

"Oh... yeah... sure. I worked on her case. So wait. She's a psychic? For real? She never mentioned it. Do you believe her?"

"Yes I do... she's the real deal. But you can't have her. She's mine." For some reason, saying that settled something in my gut.

"Hmm... I guess we'll see about that."

"So, are we done?"

"Sure... for now. You're on the narcotic squad's radar, but that's nothing new. Just be careful who you talk to for a while. And Stone..." He paused to let out a breath. "Be sure to fill me in on what you find out about these bombings. I'll try to keep you out of it, but if you figure out anything, let me know. Okay?"

I rubbed my face. "Sure. As long as you keep me updated on your end."

"Well... now that I know they're after you, it will help me narrow down my search."

I snorted. "I thought the same thing... but I have no idea who it could be. I'm just hoping to stay alive long enough to figure it out and end it."

"I'm gonna pretend I didn't hear that last part."

"You do that."

"Shit, Stone. I can only do so much, you know?"

"I'm discreet. You have nothing to worry about."

"Be sure and keep it that way."

I growled. "Don't tell me how to do my job."

"Fine. At least you've got Serenity to help you. Hey... be sure and say 'Hi' to her for me. Too bad she's married... she's a real babe."

"Yeah... too bad." I ended the call, not about to tell him she was getting a divorce.

"What was that all about?" Serenity met my gaze, her arms crossed and her brows furrowed.

"I guess their guy Grizzo made us last night. Told his squad all about it, so Dino called to warn me."

"Why would Detective Scardino do that? How does he know you, anyway?"

"Well... you know Vanetti's a..." I hesitated. "A *business* man. He's got connections."

Her mouth tightened. "You mean... he's a mob boss?"

We both froze for a few seconds. "Yeah," I finally admitted.

She let out a breath. "I, uh... figured that out on my first job, but I didn't want to believe he was a bad guy. He's so nice and normal. He doesn't seem like a criminal, you know?"

"Oh... he's not a criminal." I smirked. "He's never been convicted of a crime in his life."

"Well... that's a relief." Sarcasm dripped off her words.

"Sure is." I sent her my trademark smile. Before she could comment, I brushed my fingers across her forehead, moving a strand of hair out of her eyes. "Now... I believe we were starting our lives of hiding out together."

Her eyes widened, but instead of leaning into me, she took a step back. "Um." She licked her lips. "I think... that maybe we made a mistake."

My heart twisted. "A mistake?" The space she'd opened up between us left me cold and aching.

"Um." She still looked at me like she wanted me. "I mean, you can't hide away forever. We've got to find the guy who's after you. We can't do that in... hiding."

A corner of my mouth quirked, though my chest tightened. "Right. We need to find him and... end this?"

She nodded. "Right. I... I really don't want you to die."

"Well, that's something at least." I stepped forward, and she swayed toward me but didn't take the bait.

She held up a hand. "And this, uh, that... kissing... can't happen again. I need to be professional. You're like... my boss; and that's gross, so no more... uh... shenanigans."

"Gross?" I was a little offended. No woman had ever called me gross.

"Not *you*." She widened her eyes at me. "But I'm not sleeping with a client. I'm a PI, for heaven's sake, not a—" She cleared her throat. "So, professional. Got it?"

"Fine." My brows rose. "No more *shenanigans.*"

"Good." Frowning, she stepped toward the door. "We need to go. Aren't we supposed to look for someone at a bar?"

I leaned my back against the table and crossed my arms. "Yeah. But first, I think we should talk about this vision of my death. I'd like to keep it from happening. Are you sure you didn't see more... like when it's supposed to happen?"

She pursed her lips and shook her head. "No. But I don't think it'll happen today."

My brows rose. "Why not?"

"You were wearing a different shirt."

"Oh... well, I guess that changes things."

"So, can we go now?"

It pained me that she was so eager to leave. That kiss had rocked me to the core, and she acted like it was nothing. Of course, her eagerness to leave also implied that she knew if she kissed me again, she'd never be able to stop. She'd also said that wasn't the kind of... *professional* she wanted to be. I could respect that... even if I teased her a little.

I checked the time. "Sure. The bar should be open by now." I shook my head. "But, from what's happened so far, it doesn't seem like Anna has anything to do with this."

"I tend to agree. But it won't hurt to eliminate her as a suspect. I mean... what have we got to lose?"

Chapter 14

Serenity

I sent Stone a *professional* smile, hoping to convince him that the kiss we'd shared was no big deal. Of course, since it had shattered every last shred of defense I had against him, he'd see through my facade pretty quick. Still, if it got me out of his house without me throwing myself at him, I'd have a chance to control my impulses and make sure it never happened again.

Something inside me wilted at the thought. All those imagined kisses had never amounted to a sliver of how amazing the actual kiss had been. Stepping away from him had taken more will-power than I knew I had.

I wasn't sure I could do it a second time, let alone a third or fourth. I was doomed. Thank goodness for that phone call, or I would've gone all the way with him. It didn't help that seeing him get shot and die in that stupid vision made me want to throw myself at him right this very minute.

If he died, I'd never have the chance to make love to him and know how it felt. Just the thought was nearly enough to make me throw caution to the wind and shove him back into his bedroom.

I glanced out the window. It was a beautiful, sunny day, but as long as we didn't stay outside, he wouldn't die today. That gave me plenty of time to figure this out, right? "You coming?"

Stone raised a brow, but didn't budge. It was almost like he was testing me to see how long it would take before I gave in and rushed into his arms.

His intense gaze left me even more shaken than normal, and I swallowed, unable to look away. If something didn't happen soon, my heart would probably burst right out of my chest.

His lips twisted into that sexy smile of his, only this time a small smirk crinkled his eyes. He'd gotten to me, and he knew it. That smirk unfroze me, and I managed to breathe again. I even sent him a small eye-roll. Go me.

He let out a huff and shoved away from the table, following me to the door. He tapped in the code and opened the door. I hurried to the bike while he re-set his alarm.

I pushed my helmet on, but had trouble fastening the strap. It might have had something to do with my shaking fingers. As much as I tried to look cool and collected, I was far from it.

This time, Stone pushed my fingers away and snapped it himself. He met my gaze with a knowing smile and mounted his bike. I huffed out a breath and got on behind him, though wrapping myself around him only heightened the sexual tension. But it was fine. I closed my eyes, savoring the moment. Holding him like this would be enough to sustain me for now, but I knew it would be hard not to touch him as often as I could from now on.

I was doomed.

Stone maneuvered through traffic like an expert and took us all the way over to the west side of town. We came to an area with a corner drugstore and a few shops.

Across the street, a square building with a blinking neon sign over the double-doors read "Tiki-Tabu Bar." It fit right in with this part of town, and I couldn't wait to see what the inside looked like. Stone pulled in front of the bar and cut the engine.

"This is it." He pulled off his helmet and held out a hand to help me get off the bike.

I got my leg over the bike and stood beside it. While Stone dismounted, I pulled off my helmet and set it on the seat, then took off my right glove so I could fix my hair. Satisfied that it wasn't a huge mess, I slipped the glove back on.

"You ready?" Stone glanced my way. At my nod, he started toward the door. Pulling it open, he held it for me and we stepped inside. The lights were dim, and I had to blink a few times before I could see much.

The walls had wood paneling and an open ceiling, with spotlights that shown down on the walls and the side tables. The clean floor and shiny counter showed a great deal of care. Whoever owned it kept it up.

Only a few people sat at the bar, but there were several others in the back shooting pool at a couple of tables. One of them noticed our entrance and headed straight for us. He was a Pacific Islander with a straight nose and a huge build. I could picture him playing professional football somewhere. As he approached, I stepped back, bumping into Stone's chest.

Amused, Stone raised a brow at me, and I glanced between them, realizing they were about the same size. Stone stepped forward and gave the man a complicated hand shake. "Keola... how's business these days?"

"Not so bad, bro. It's been a while since you've been in. Who's this pretty lady?" Keola glanced at me and his brows rose. "Never seen my bro bring a woman in. You must be special."

Delighted by his warm nature and open face, I sent him a smile while pulling off my glove, and held out my hand. "I'm Serenity."

Smiling, he took my hand and held it. His warm touch sent a wave of dizziness over me, but it wasn't because of a vision, it was more a feeling of power. Whoa. This guy was going places. Taking a breath, I pulled my hand away and blinked a few times.

"So, what can I do for you?" Tilting his head, Keola glanced at Stone. "Does Vanetti need something?"

"No. I'm here on my own, looking for Anna. Does she still work for you?"

He shook his head. "Not anymore. She got into some trouble and took off. If you catch up with her, tell her I want the five grand she stole from me."

"Damn. Then I guess she's not coming back."

"Not if she knows what's good for her. Last I heard, she was headed to Texas."

Stone shifted his stance. "Okay. Well, I knew it was a long-shot, but I had to try."

"She owe you money, too?"

"No." Stone glanced at me before meeting Keola's gaze. "Someone's trying to kill me. I thought she might have something to do with it."

"Bro, that's mental. Don't they know who you are?"

"Doesn't seem to matter."

Keola shook his head. "I'll ask around. If I hear anything, I'll let you know."

"Thanks man, I appreciate it."

"No prob. You have time for a game? You could show Serenity your mad skills at the pool table." He glanced my way. "He's got his own stick here, but he hardly ever uses it."

Stone shook his head. "Thanks, but we should go."

Keola nodded. "Sure. I hope you find your guy." He glanced at me. "Come back sometime, Serenity. You don't even need to bring this jughead with you."

I grinned. "Thanks. Maybe I will."

"Later." Stone's lips twisted, and he turned toward the door without waiting for me. I gave Keola a quick wave and followed him back outside.

Meeting Keola had given me a lift, totally different from the last people Stone had introduced me to. I wanted to ask Stone how they knew each other, but held back, since it was clear he wasn't in a talking mood.

At his bike, Stone glanced at me. "You got a dazed look when you shook Keola's hand. Did you see something?"

I slipped my glove back on and shook my head. "No, but I got an impression that Keola is important. You should keep in touch with him."

Stone's brows rose. "So you get impressions, too?"

I shrugged. "I guess. That's never happened before. Well... I take that back. When I shook Vanetti's hand, it was kind of the same thing... only more powerful."

"And what about me? What did you get when you shook my hand?"

My eyes widened. I didn't want to tell him that his touch took my breath away and just about knocked me over. "Um... you know... I can't remember, so I guess it wasn't a big deal."

"Liar."

I grabbed my helmet and ignored him. "So what should we do now? Go back to the office? Maybe you should check your messages and emails in case the killer's trying to set you up again."

Stone's lips twisted. "I'm beginning to think that baiting him might be the only way to flush him out. Since you saw me get shot, I guess that means he's not giving up any time soon."

A chill passed over me. "Yeah... in fact, we should get going. Don't want to stand around in the sun for too long, you know?" I glanced at the street with different eyes, looking for anyone suspicious. Could the killer be watching us right now?

I glanced at Stone's chest, remembering the blood that spread over his gray t-shirt. The shirt he wore today was black, so he was fine, right? "Is there somewhere else we could visit? Maybe the other places where he tried to kill you?"

"I go to the gym a lot. You want to try that?"

"Sure. Maybe you could take me up to the roof of the building where the AC unit fell. I might pick up something there."

Stone shrugged. "I guess it's worth a try."

With that decided, I slipped on my helmet and even managed to snap the chin strap all by myself. We motored off, heading closer to the downtown area and the office.

On the way, a shiver ran down my spine. It didn't help that the sun had gone behind a cloud, but that was a good thing, right? Still, it felt like we were just running around in circles, while the killer just got closer and closer to cornering us.

I was missing something, but what?

We arrived at the gym and I got off the bike. After pulling off my helmet, I waited for Stone to do the same, and couldn't help admiring how handsome and commanding he looked.

His chiseled jaw and tousled hair sent butterflies through my chest. Then he glanced at me and grinned, like he knew I couldn't take my eyes off him. I sighed. Why couldn't he be ugly? He stepped to my side with a raised brow. "What?"

Flustered, I improvised. "We should get out of the sun."

He rolled his eyes and followed me inside. The smell hit me first, and I tried not to wince, but I hated that locker room scent. Glancing at all the equipment, and people on the machines, my heart sank. "I just realized something. With so many people in and out of the gym, I'm not sure I'll find anything specific enough to give us a clue."

His brows rose. "So you don't want to try?"

My lips drew down. "No... I mean... sure I'll try, I'm just warning you that it might not work the best. You know?"

"I guess."

"There's also the fact that I'll probably see stuff I'd rather not, so I hope you appreciate what I'm putting myself through for you."

That startled a chuckle out of him. "Hey... you're getting paid very well, so don't expect any sympathy from me."

I shook my head. "Fine. Let's get this over with." Keeping my gloves on, I followed Stone to the counter, where he explained that I wanted a tour of the facilities, and he'd show me around. The attendant nodded, and I followed Stone to the weights.

He picked one of the hand weights up. "I always use these when I work out. Want to try it?"

He held it out, and I took hold of it. He let go, but did it gradually. Still, I staggered and nearly dropped it on my foot. "Holy hell. This is heavy. Here. Take it back."

He took it from me like it weighed nothing, and a big grin split his face. "You know it won't do any good with that glove on."

"Oh... right." I pulled the glove off my hand and glanced around at the equipment. Touching the handle of the multi-functional work-out machine, I braced for a vision, but nothing happened. Maybe there were just too many hands on these to get anything. Since that seemed to be the case, I felt along the rest of the machine, but came up empty.

"Nothing."

"Try this."

I followed behind Stone, touching all the other surfaces he pointed out, and still got nothing. "Sorry. I'm not getting anything."

He led me around the rest of the gym, and I got one or two images, but they had nothing to do with Stone or my previous vision of the guy, so I shook my head. "Nothing. Is that it?"

"Yeah. We might as well head to the building with the AC unit."

"Sure."

Only a short distance down the street, Stone pointed out where the AC unit had landed on the sidewalk. "It was right here."

"Okay. But you go stand next to the building in the shadows."

His brows rose. "Really?"

"Yes... really. Sunshine, remember?" Stone let me push him into the shadows, and I knelt down to touch the cement, hoping for something, but came up empty as well.

I met Stone's gaze. "Nope."

He scowled. "Too bad. Let's head up to the roof."

I followed him into the building and exited on the roof. "Stay here in the doorway. Just point out where I need to go."

Stone sighed before pointing straight ahead. "Look for scuff marks."

I followed his directions and found them. Kneeling down, I touched the marks, but only got a vague impression of anger. I tried again in several different places, but not one vision opened up to me.

Standing, I wiped my hands on my pants, and returned to Stone at the door. "The person who did this has a lot of anger issues, but that's all I'm getting."

Stone let out a breath. "All right. I guess it's a bust." He checked his watch. "We missed lunch. Why don't we grab a sandwich and head back to the apartment?"

"Sounds good."

Half an hour later, we pulled into the parking garage at Vitality Ventures with a couple of sandwiches, and took our food up to the apartment to eat.

At the door in the hallway, I stopped Stone and laid my hand on the doorknob. "It's clear."

Stone unlocked the door and we stepped inside, putting our food on the table. I cleaned up in the bathroom, while Stone got a couple of sodas from the fridge.

Grateful I didn't have to worry about Stone getting shot, I sat down to eat. Just as Stone finished up, his phone rang. He pulled it out and scowled. "I've got to take this." Throwing his napkin on the table, he pushed his chair back and went around the corner to talk in the living room.

From where I sat, I couldn't hear him well enough to know what he said, but, from his tone, I knew he wasn't happy.

I began to clean up, grabbing his sandwich wrapper to throw away. He still had some chips left, so I stepped toward him to see if he still wanted them. I came around the corner and caught sight of Stone as he stood in front of the large, plate-glass window. A sudden vision of him standing closer to the glass window filled my mind. A crack sounded, and Stone fell backwards, shock on his face and blood pouring from his chest.

I blinked out of the vision and found Stone standing in the same spot. With the sunlight streaming into the room, his black t-shirt had turned gray, and the light washed the color out of the room, just like in my vision. Shit! Shit! Shit!

"Stone!" I began to move, hoping I could make it in time. "Drop! Now!"

Before he could respond, I barreled into him. A loud crack sounded, and we both fell to the floor. The glass on the painting behind us shattered, and the painting flew right off the wall.

"What the hell?" Stone's harsh breath came fast.

I raised my head to glance out the window, but Stone pulled me back down and away from the window. "Stay back. They might take another shot."

My chest heaved. "But where did it come from? We're up on the twenty-sixth floor. It was supposed to happen outside!"

"It has to be the building across the street. The upper floors are at the same level as this one." He felt at his pocket and swore. "Dammit, my phone."

The device lay in a bright patch of sunshine in easy view of anyone waiting to take another shot. A whistle of wind came through *several* bullet holes in the window, sending a shiver down my spine. Holy hell.

"We need to move." Stone tugged on my arm. "Stay low and crawl to the kitchen. We should be safe there."

I followed his lead and breathed easier after making it to safety. Stone jumped to his feet, ready to rush out the door.

"Wait." I got to my feet. "Where are you going?"

"I need to—" He glanced at me and froze. Raising his hand to my head, his fingers came away bloody. "You're hurt."

I blinked, suddenly feeling the sting on my head and something wet running down the side of my face and neck. Touching the area next to my forehead, blood coated my fingers, and I gasped.

"Here... sit down." Stone pulled me into a chair and moved my hair out of the way to uncover the wound. "It looks like a piece of flying glass hit you. Maybe from the painting. I think you just need a few stitches and you'll be fine."

"Oh... good. For a minute there, I thought maybe I got shot in the head." Dizzy, I slumped back in the chair and closed my eyes.

"No. It's nothing like that. Do you feel pain anywhere else?"

"No. I'm fine." I shook my head.

Nodding, Stone left my side, coming back a few seconds later with a washcloth. "Here. Hold that against the wound. It should help stop the bleeding. I have to go. Will you be okay?"

"I'll be fine."

He nodded. "Hang tight, and I'll be right back."

Stone rushed out the door, leaving me holding the cloth to my head. My vision began to fade, so I slipped off the chair and laid down on the floor, hoping I wouldn't faint.

The sight of blood always did this to me, but hopefully I'd feel well enough to get back on the chair before Stone came back. If he was headed to the building across the street to catch the shooter, there was nothing I could do to save him now.

I just hoped he didn't run into another trap while I was stuck here, lying on the cold floor.

Chapter 15

Stone

I rushed out of the apartment and straight to Julia's desk. "I need the doctor here, *now*. Is Vanetti in his office?"

Her eyes widened, but she kept her cool demeanor. "Yes."

While she picked up the phone, I hurried into his office, finding Vanetti sitting behind his desk. "We have a problem. Someone just tried to kill me. They shot through the window in my apartment. It must have come from the building across the street. I need to get over there now and check it out, but Serenity's hurt."

"How bad?"

"Not bad. It's a head wound. I think from flying glass. She just needs a few stitches. I already told Julia to call the doctor. I had to leave my phone."

"Is the apartment safe?"

"The kitchen is."

He nodded. "Good. Go back to Serenity. I'll send Ricky over there with a team."

"But I need to go."

"No. It's too risky. He's downstairs. He can get there faster than you anyway."

I huffed out a breath. He was probably right, and I'd left Serenity alone and bleeding. "Fine. But he needs to catch that son-of-a-bitch."

Vanetti picked up his phone. "Go. I'll come to the apartment as soon as I'm done talking to Ricky."

I hurried out the door, slowing at Julia's desk. "Did you get the doc?"

"Yes. He'll be here as soon as he can."

"Thanks." I rushed back down the hall and through the door to the apartment. I stopped short to find Serenity lying on the floor with her eyes closed." My heart stuttered as a memory of a dead soldier crossed my mind. Dammit.

I rushed to her side, worry tightening my chest. "Serenity?" Was she hurt worse than I thought? No, she couldn't be; she was still holding the cloth to her head.

She blinked her eyes open. "You're back already? Did you catch him?"

"No... I didn't go over there. Why are you on the floor? Are you hurt somewhere else?" She'd said she wasn't, or I wouldn't have left.

She shook her head and winced. "No. The sight of blood... especially mine... always makes me feel faint, so I had to lie down. I'm feeling a little better now. Can you help me up?"

"Maybe you should stay there."

"No... I'm okay now. Besides, the floor's hard, and the whistling is starting to get on my nerves."

"Right." I resisted the temptation to glance around the corner into the living room. I didn't want to risk getting shot if the bastard was still waiting for me. That was too close. How had the shooter known I would be standing right there at precisely that moment? It made my skin crawl.

What about Serenity? The glass in the painting had shattered, sure...but what if the bullet had actually hit her? I swallowed. If so, she'd nearly died saving me.

"Stone? What's wrong? You look a little pale."

I shook my head. "Nothing. I just realized how close that was." I met her gaze. "How did you know?"

She held out a hand, and I helped her back into her chair. "Oh that. You still have some chips left."

"What?" I raised my eyebrows.

"I was clearing the table, and you hadn't eaten all your chips, so I was bringing them to you." She swallowed. "When I came around the corner, I saw a vision of you getting shot, just like before, only this time there was more to it. When the vision cleared... you were standing in the same spot." Her eyes widened. "I wasn't sure I'd make it in time."

My breath came out in a whoosh. "Shit. I'm sure glad you did. But... you got hurt instead."

"I'm fine... barely a scratch, right?" Her brows dipped. "I heard the glass shatter, so a piece of it must have hit me."

"Yeah... looks that way." I wasn't about to tell her otherwise. From what I'd seen of the wound, it wasn't that deep, but I was grateful that Dix, our doc on call, was on his way and could patch her up.

From my position in the kitchen, I could barely make out the hole in the wall where the bullet— *bullets*— had ended up, so at least they weren't in her... thank God. Serenity let out a breath, and I noticed she'd slumped a little in her chair. "Do you need to lie down? I don't want you to faint."

"I'm fine. My arm's just getting tired from holding this cloth."

"Here. I've got it." I gently placed my hand over the cloth, and she let go. The cloth was pretty bloody, so I applied more pressure.

"Ow." She tried to pull away.

"You need pressure to stop the bleeding. Were you just holding it there?"

"No. I put pressure on it." She scowled. "Just not that much because it hurts."

"Sorry." I grimaced. "There's just a lot of blood."

"It's fine." She sighed. "I guess this means I have to go to the ER. I really hate hospitals, you know?"

"Actually... we have a doctor on call. He should be here any minute."

"Wow... that's... uh... really great. I guess it pays to be a..." She closed her eyes. "A... *businessman.*"

I chuckled. "That's for sure."

A knock sounded at the door, and Vanetti pushed it open. He gave me a nod before focusing on Serenity. "How are you doing?"

"I'm okay."

"Good." He motioned to the man who had followed him inside. "I brought Dr. Pettey with me. Dr. Pettey, this is Serenity."

"Nice to meet you, Serenity. Call me Dix. Let's take a look at this cut on your head." He got right down to business, moving my hand away from the cloth. That was one of the things I liked about Dix, he was no nonsense.

"Okay. It doesn't hurt too bad right now, but it's still bleeding."

"Head wounds bleed a lot." He peeled the cloth back to get a look.

Vanetti came to my side and motioned me toward the hall where we could get a look at the living room wall without being in the line of fire. The guy was probably long gone by now, but assuming things were safe got a lot people killed.

Vanetti motioned toward the building across the way. "Ricky's over there. He should be calling any minute, but I'm sure the shooter's long gone."

"Probably." I gazed at the holes in the wall.

My phone still lay on the floor, but I could probably reach it with a broom. Grabbing one from the kitchen closet, I managed to retrieve it and found that I'd missed several calls, all from Aubree. She was probably wondering what had happened since I was talking to her at the time of the shooting. I'd have to call her back once things settled down.

The whistling sound coming from the bullet holes in the window was definitely annoying. I could patch the window with duct tape, but not if it was evidence for the police. Slipping my phone in my pocket, I turned to Vanetti. "You thinking of calling the police?"

"Not sure. I mean... if we want some answers, they could run prints on the bullets."

My lips turned down. "Yeah... but I doubt there'd be any. Besides, Dino called me earlier and warned me off. He knows I was there when the trailer exploded, and I had to tell him about Serenity warning the gang about the raid. Their inside man identified me, so I'm on their radar now."

Vanetti sighed. "Okay. We'll keep it quiet, but I'd feel better if you let Dino know what happened here. It might help us catch the guy."

"Yeah. I'll tell him about it."

"Good." Vanetti shook his head at the painting on the floor. "Damn. I really liked that one." His phone rang, and he quickly answered. "Yeah?" He listened for a few seconds. "That's what we thought. Stay there. I'm sure Stone will want to take a look, and I don't want anyone messing with the scene."

Slipping his phone into his pocket, he nodded at me. "Looks like our guy left in a hurry and forgot to clean up. Ricky found the shells and the broken window. This might be what we need, especially if Serenity can get a reading on who the bastard is."

Nodding, I glanced into the kitchen. Dix and Serenity had moved closer to the sink. With his medical bag on the counter, it looked like he was just about finished stitching up her wound, and I sighed with relief.

Stepping closer, I caught the last of Dix's instructions to Serenity. "You need to take it easy for the rest of the day. Getting shot in the head can be traumatic, even if it didn't do any major damage. You can shower in the morning, but try not to get it wet before then. Why don't you come into my office in a week, and I'll take the stitches out. And don't hesitate to call me if you have any questions. Here's my card."

Serenity took his card, but could barely nod. Her eyes had glazed over right after he told her she'd been shot in the head. It kind of shocked me, too.

Vanetti stepped beside him. "Thanks, Dix. I'll see you out." He ushered Dix out the door, leaving me and Serenity alone.

Serenity glanced my way, her eyes still wide with shock. "Did he just say that I got shot in the head? With a bullet?"

Her face had drained of color, and I hurried to her side, grabbing her arms to steady her. "Are you going to faint now?"

She stiffened, and fire lit her eyes. "Of course not."

"Good, because we need to take a look at the building across the street. Ricky's waiting for us at the window the shooter used to take his shot. You might pick up something. Do you think you can manage a trip over there?"

"Oh... sure. That's a good idea."

I knew that made me look like a big asshole, so I quickly continued. "Once we do that, we can take the rest of the day off. Okay? I know you need to rest... but this might be the clue we're looking for."

She closed her eyes. "You're right. Of course we need to check it out."

"Good. We can go whenever you're ready."

She shrugged. "We might as well go now. My head's numb, so I can't even feel the wound, although I do have a slight headache."

"I've got something for that." I opened the cupboard above the sink and got out the pain reliever. I gave her a couple of pills, and grabbed a glass of water for her.

"Thanks." She swallowed the pills and finished off the water before examining her hands. Bloodstains covered them. "I think I need to clean up first."

"Oh yeah." I glanced at my own hands, finding blood on them, too. "I guess Ricky can wait a few more minutes."

She glanced at me with raised brows.

"Come on... I'll help you walk to the bathroom."

"What?" She waved me off. "I'm fine... really." To prove her point, she stood and carefully picked her way across the kitchen. I followed behind, making sure she didn't faint. Making it to the bathroom, she stepped inside and closed the door in my face.

Letting out a breath, I hurried into my bathroom, and washed her blood off my hands. As the red-tinged water ran down the drain, I tried not to think too hard about the close call, but the fact that she'd almost died saving me made something in my chest ache.

How had I been so blind to the fact that being stuck with me could get her killed? I wasn't sure I was worth her life. In fact, I knew I wasn't. She was kind-hearted and wholesome, with a bright future ahead of her... nothing like me. She deserved better than a hitman for the mob.

So why did she risk her life to push me out of the way? According to the contract, she still would have been paid if I'd died. Did that mean she cared about me? The ice around my heart cracked a little, sending a small drop of hope into my blood.

Did I want her to care? I wasn't worthy of her, and I was pretty sure she knew that, but she'd saved me anyway. I sighed. I only knew one thing for certain... I'd have to make sure nothing ever hurt her again, because, if it did, I'd never forgive myself.

Chapter 16

Serenity

After one look in the mirror, I sank onto the toilet seat and closed my eyes. I breathed in through my nose and out through my mouth to calm down. Still, I'd just been shot in the head. Well... maybe not shot, but grazed by a bullet. What the freak?

After seeing Stone get shot in my vision, I hadn't even hesitated. I'd just run right at him like a freaking kamikaze. Of course, how could I stand by and watch it happen when I could stop it? I couldn't. Plain and simple... I did what I did because I had no choice.

A tiny little voice whispered that wasn't the only reason. Besides the physical attraction, I cared about him. He might be a pain sometimes, but he wasn't a bad person. I knew he'd spent his time in the army trying to save people. He could have left that soldier behind, but he was fiercely loyal, and that was something I admired. Besides that, my psychic ability didn't seem to faze him, which was even more unusual.

I sighed. Whatever the reason, I'd do it all again in a heartbeat. My vision of seeing him die had hurt my heart a lot more than I'd let on. I craved his touch, his nearness, and that sexy smile. I didn't want to lose him, even if he was a pain in the ass.

Feeling more settled, I let out a breath. No one had died. My head hurt a little, but other than that, I was good. It was also kind of nice to realize I'd made a difference with my psychic ability. I'd changed Stone's fate. He was alive because of me, *twice* now, and that meant I could finally trust my visions.

Feeling stronger, I went to work washing my hands. Then I pulled my shirt off and tackled my neck and face. While I was at it, I took a look at my wound. Stitched up tight, it was only about an inch and a half long, and there was plenty of hair around it to cover it up.

I might end up with a scar, but it wouldn't be visible. Considering all my other scars from the accident, this was nothing. In fact, after going through that awful experience, this was hardly worth mentioning.

It took a little longer to get the blood out of my hair, but I did the best I could and hurried into my room. I found a turquoise scoop-neck t-shirt and slipped it over my head. Feeling a slight chill, I slipped on my black leather jacket and opened the door. I found Stone sitting at the kitchen table.

"I'm ready."

Glancing my way, the worry in his eyes changed to relief, and he jumped to his feet. "Great. Let's go out the back."

"Okay."

I led the way down the hall to the laundry room and unlocked the deadbolt on the door. Out of habit, I touched the knob. Sensing nothing bad, I pulled the door open.

Stone followed me out and locked the door behind him. "Are you okay to take the stairs down a couple of floors?"

"Yeah... sure." I held onto the railing and started down. Surprising me, Stone wrapped his arm around my waist. I hesitated and met his gaze.

"I know you're fine, but I'd feel better if you let me keep my arm around you. Okay?"

I didn't need it, but having him to lean on was too much of a temptation to resist. "Okay... but only to help *you* feel better."

He huffed, but a grin tilted his lips, and I enjoyed having him so close. For the first time, it felt like we were finally a team.

We came out of the stairwell a couple of floors down, and waited for the elevator. After it came, we took it to the lobby so we could cross the street to the building.

Outside, the sun had gone behind a cloud, which relieved my worry that he'd get shot again. Still, we walked quickly across the street to the building.

In the lobby, we found a directory of businesses listed beside the elevators. The twenty-sixth floor didn't have a business name attached, and I narrowed my gaze. "Is it safe to go up there?"

"Yeah. Ricky's waiting for us. He said they're doing renovations on that floor, so no one's there."

"Oh... that makes sense."

We stepped into the elevator, and it soon opened on the twenty-sixth floor. A tall man with wavy dark hair and a short beard stood in the hall waiting for us. He gave me a nod. "Hey Serenity. I'm Ricky. Mr. Vanetti filled me in. If you'll follow me, it's this way."

Stone waited for me to go first, and we followed Ricky down the hall to where another man stood in front of the doorway guarding an office. After a quick nod to us, he stood aside, and I stepped into an empty office space. The broken window let in a cool breeze, and a shell casing lay on the floor.

"I didn't touch anything." Ricky glanced my way, giving me a nod before turning to Stone.

"Thanks." Stone knelt on one knee by the casing, looking it over, before catching my gaze. "You ready to touch it?"

"Yes. Should I be careful about ruining the prints?"

"We're not involving the cops, so you're good to go."

"Oh." I licked my lips and crouched down. I hadn't worn my gloves, so I didn't have an excuse to hesitate before picking it up. Still, it took me a moment to center myself and open my mind before I touched it.

As my hand closed around the casing, I saw a vision of a man holding a rifle to his shoulder. His face was obscured behind the rifle, but I caught signs of a beard. His finger moved on the trigger, and his body jerked from the shot. The casing fell out of the gun and into my hand as the vision cleared.

I met Stone's gaze. "It's the same guy. His facial features aren't as clear, but I'm sure it's him. I saw his hand pretty clearly though, and each of his fingers had tattoos on them. I couldn't tell if they were numbers or symbols. But they were on his fingers right here." I pointed to the skin between my knuckles and the first joint of my finger.

"Sounds like he's part of a gang," Ricky said.

"That's what I thought," Stone answered. "But it doesn't add up." He met my gaze. "You want to try the window?"

A perfect circle of glass had been cut out of the window, like I'd seen in spy movies. "Wow... this guy must be a professional to do that."

"Yeah... that's why the tattoos don't make a lot of sense. A professional hitman wouldn't have any kind of identifying marks on him because it would make it easier to track him down."

I shook my head. "I'm not sure I'll get anything if he used tools to cut the glass, but I'll give it a try."

"Just don't cut yourself."

I met his gaze and nodded. Warmth flooded my chest that he was looking out for me, even though I was smart enough to know better. Taking a breath, I placed my hands on both sides of the circle and closed my eyes.

At my touch, sudden darkness engulfed me, along with a sharp stab of hatred and loathing. The darkness seeped into my soul like black oil, pulling me into a deep void that I couldn't escape.

I fought against the dark, but it just sucked me in deeper. Then a rasping voice filled my head, repeating the same words over and over. I opened my mouth to scream, but nothing came out. Fighting to pull away only seemed to drag me further in, and, like quicksand, I couldn't get out.

In the distance, someone called my name. I turned toward that voice and felt strong arms wrap around me, pulling me to safety. The darkness began to retreat, and relief sapped my strength.

"Serenity! Sen!" Stone held me against him, and the remaining darkness fell away. His frantic gaze met mine. "You didn't come out of it. What happened?"

"I... I don't know." As I caught my breath, he pulled me tight against his chest, and I closed my eyes. "It was awful... like a black void full of anger and blame. I kept hearing the words, *die, die, die,* over and over. It wouldn't stop." I took a halting breath and began to shiver.

"It's okay. I've got you."

I leaned into him, needing his solid presence and comfort. I'd never been so scared of the dark in my life. I squeezed my eyes tightly together, hoping to stop the tears. Stone rubbed my back, whispering words of comfort. His soothing voice began to penetrate the darkness that wouldn't let go.

At last, I relaxed into his arms, and my shivering stopped. My breathing slowed, and I could finally open my eyes.

Stone pulled away from me, holding my arms, and met my gaze. "Feeling better?"

I managed a short nod. "Yeah... thanks for...bringing me back." My voice shook, and I had to swallow the tears before I cried again.

Stone held me against him. "Anytime, Babe. Anytime. We should get you back to the apartment. Even *I'm* getting a bad vibe from this room. Can you walk?"

"Yes." Thoughts of leaving this place sent a burst of energy through me. I turned toward the door, grateful that Stone kept me tucked under his arm, and we stepped out together.

The further away from that room we got, the more my strength returned. It was like a gentle, calming breeze after a category five hurricane.

What the hell was that? Why had it affected me so strongly? A shiver ran down my spine, and I took a deep breath to push the fear away. Needing tranquility, I retreated into a state of meditation and hardly noticed when Ricky left us at the door to the apartment.

Inside, Stone took me straight to my room. Without hesitation, I kicked off my shoes and crawled onto the bed. As soon as my head hit the pillow, I let sleep overtake me, barely registering the soft blanket that Stone used to tuck me in.

Chapter 17

Stone

I closed the door, leaving Serenity asleep on her bed. Running a hand through my hair, I stepped into the kitchen and grabbed a beer. Sitting at the table, I drank half of it down and closed my eyes.

What kind of shit was that? Serenity had scared me half to death. Her contorted face held such anguish that I had to physically grab her in order to pull her out of the vision.

I shook my head. She'd barely missed death once already today, and then this? It was still hard to believe that the bullet had grazed her head.

This day was turning into a real shit-show. It didn't help that we were no closer to figuring out who the guy was, either. This had to end before Serenity got killed.

It was time to set up a sting. Let him walk into my trap, for a change. That meant I had to bait him. Even if there were some downsides to that idea, it was better than running around like a chicken with its head chopped off.

A knock sounded at the door, and Vanetti stepped in. He took in my beer and raised a brow. "Ricky told me what happened. Where's Serenity?"

"She's asleep. She passed out as soon as she laid down."

"Good." Vanetti stepped to the fridge and grabbed a bottle for himself. He popped the cap and sat down at the table, taking a long swig. "It sounded like she got something from her vision."

"Yeah... the tattoos on his fingers. That's pretty vague, but I guess it's better than nothing."

"Did she tell you about the vision she saw at the window?"

I rubbed a hand through my hair. "Not really... I mean... this vision seemed like it was full of dark emotions. I think she tried to pull herself out of it, but was stuck there until I pulled her into my arms. It scared her. Hell, it scared me. I thought she was a goner there for a sec." I shook my head. "I'm not sure how much longer we can do this. I think we'd better change tactics."

"I tend to agree." Vanetti splayed his fingers on the table. "Let's see what we can come up with. We need to set up a sting. Where would be a good place for that?"

"The first thing that comes to my mind is Razor's shop. But I doubt he'd go for that."

Vanetti huffed. "Probably not, but I'm sure we could convince him to cooperate."

—◦► ⟨⟨⟨⟩⟩⟩ ◄◦—

An hour later, Serenity came into the kitchen, her hair tousled, and her eyes still a little droopy. She stopped short to see Vanetti and me. "Oh... hey."

I gave her a small smile. "Feeling any better?"

"Yeah. My headache finally went away, and my butt doesn't even hurt anymore. Small miracles, right?"

Vanetti's brows rose, and he sent me a pointed stare.

"She got hit by a piece of burning furniture in the explosion last night. It burned right through her dress before I got it off of her."

Vanetti raised a brow. "The dress?"

"No! The furniture."

He snickered. "Right."

Serenity shook her head at me before opening the fridge and taking out a can of Diet Coke. She brought it to the table and sat down. "I just realized I should have added hazard pay to my contract." She raised her brow at Vanetti. "You got off easy, considering all the times I've nearly died, and we're not even close to being done yet."

His lips turned down, but he nodded. "You have a point, but I think you're being more than compensated."

Unable to argue with that, she shrugged. "So, any ideas on what to do next?"

"We're working on it," Vanetti replied. He sent me a pointed stare. "But first, we need to find somewhere else for you to stay." He glanced toward the living room. "It's not safe here."

"I've got a great security system at my house. We can stay there."

Vanetti shook his head. "I don't like it. Besides, you don't want your place to get blown up, right?"

"You have a point. So what did you have in mind?"

"I could put you up in a hotel for tonight, then you could go to a different one the next night, and so on, until we flush the guy out."

"I have a better idea," Serenity said. "Why don't we just stay at my place? Stone's enemy doesn't know anything about me. We should be fine there while we figure out our next move."

Vanetti nodded. "I like it. What about you, Stone? Think it will work?"

"Yeah. It's a good idea, as long as no one knows."

"Then it's settled." Vanetti stood. "Leave your bike and car here, and go home with her. That should throw him off your trail for now. In the meantime, I'll look into those ideas we discussed. We'll talk some more tomorrow."

"Sure."

As Vanetti walked out, Serenity's brows drew together. "How long was I out?"

"It's after five, so almost two hours. Let's grab our things and we'll head out."

"Okay."

It didn't take long before Serenity was leading me to her car in the parking garage. She stopped in front of a gray Corolla and popped the trunk. "I know this isn't what you're used to," she began. "But it's all I've got."

Her cheeks warmed with embarrassment and she shook her head. "I had to sell my Tesla to help pay my lawyer's fees. I loved that car. Luckily, my dad kept this from my college days and let me take it."

"It's fine. Do you need me to drive? I can if you're not feeling up to it."

"No. I'm feeling a lot better after that nap." She unlocked the car, and I opened the passenger door. I had to push the seat all the way back in order to fit inside. There were signs of wear and tear, but it was in pretty good shape considering how old it was.

She pulled out of the garage, and I slipped my ball-cap down over my head in case my stalker was watching. Twenty minutes later, we turned into her driveway. She pulled the car into the garage, shutting the door behind us.

"I have a guest bedroom for you."

It was on the tip of my tongue to tease her about sharing her bedroom, but I held back. Now wasn't a good time for that. I followed her inside the house and down the hall to a small room with a double-bed, noticing that it was directly across from the master bedroom.

"The bathroom is right there." She pointed to a small bathroom with a tub and shower combo.

"Got it." I took my bag into the bedroom and left it on the bed. It seemed like hours since we'd eaten our sandwiches, and I was starving. I stepped to her bedroom door and leaned against the frame as she put her things away. "Any chance we can get some dinner? I could take your car and pick up something if you want to stay here."

"That would work, but I could probably whip up something faster if you don't mind an omelet."

I shrugged. "Sounds good to me, but you should let me help."

Her eyes widened. "Okay. I won't say no to that."

I followed her into the kitchen, and she put me to work slicing up an onion and some peppers while she cooked up some bacon and potatoes. It surprised me how well we worked together, but then, she was easy to be around.

"How's your head feeling?"

She smiled at me. "Not too bad, but I'm afraid the numbness is wearing off. Want to see the stitches?"

"Sure."

She stepped close and turned her head, lifting her hair from the area. I helped move her hair away, enjoying the feel of her soft tresses between my fingers. I examined the neat, even stitches, grateful the wound was smaller than I thought. "Wow. He did a great job. No one would believe you got grazed in the head."

She winced. "I know, right? I have a hard time believing it myself. I thought for sure it was from the glass."

Unable to resist, I wrapped my arms around her. "Yeah. I could hardly believe it either." She snuggled against me, and I closed my eyes, grateful she didn't pull away. "I never thanked you, so... thanks, but don't ever do that again. I'm not sure I'm worth the risk."

She pulled back to meet my gaze. "What? Of course you are. Besides... it's my job." She made a flipping motion with her hand. "And I don't think I'd like it if you... if you got shot. Besides, I signed a contract."

"Wait. Are you saying you like me? So I'm not *just* a job?"

She blinked a few times and shook her head. "I never said that."

I tugged her back into my arms. "But you'd be upset if I got shot?"

She tilted her head to meet my gaze, and her right brow rose. "Of course. You know how I am with blood. I might have fainted."

I nodded, grinning. "That's right. How could I forget that?" Her lips were inches from mine. All I had to do was lower my head just a little more—

Her gaze darkened, but instead of giving in, she pulled out of my arms. "What happened to being professional?"

"I didn't say *I* was going to act professional," I teased.

She rolled her eyes. "How are you coming with the peppers. About done?" She turned back to her bowl with the eggs and started beating them to death.

I smiled and picked up the cutting board. "All done. Want them in the pan?"

"Yes."

Using the knife, I slid the onion and peppers into the hot, buttered pan. She took over and began to stir them around. I leaned back against the counter and watched her work. A few minutes later, she added the eggs and spices, and the smell was heavenly. It was fun to watch her get lost in her cooking, and I could tell that she enjoyed it.

She glanced my way. "Want to set the table?"

"You bet."

She directed me to the place-mats, plates, utensils and glasses. We finished up at about the same time, and my mouth watered with anticipation. "This looks amazing. I cook for myself now and then, but I usually order out, so this is a treat."

"Then I hope you like it."

"I'm sure I will."

While she dished up the food, the doorbell rang. It startled her so badly that she nearly dropped the plate of eggs.

"Whoa." I grabbed the plate. "You okay?"

"Yeah. Sorry." She swallowed, wiping her hands on her apron. "Guess I'm a little jumpy." She hesitated.

"Were you expecting someone?"

"No." She shook her head.

The doorbell rang again, followed by a couple of hard knocks.

"Want me to answer it?"

She shook her head. "No. It's fine. I don't know why I'm so rattled. I'm sure it's just a neighbor. I'll be right back."

She left the plate in my hands and hurried toward the door. Not about to stay behind, I set the plate down and followed her into the living room.

I moved the curtain aside for a quick peek before she pulled the door open. Getting a glimpse of a man with dark hair on her porch, I stepped behind her to see his face.

"Brandon? What are you doing here?"

"I saw the light on and—" He caught sight of me, and his face darkened. "What's he doing here?"

Surprised, Serenity glanced over her shoulder to find me standing right behind her. "I invited him. We're having dinner. But that's none of your business. What do you want?"

He glanced at me and clenched his jaw. "I wanted to talk to you. In private."

"Anything you have to say, you can say in front of him." Serenity straightened and crossed her arms. "So hurry up. Our food's getting cold."

Brandon let out a huff and his nostrils flared. "Fine. I came to apologize for what I said last night. I'd been drinking. I know that's not an excuse, but I shouldn't have said those things. I didn't mean it. I... I was hoping we could—"

He shook his head and let out a breath. "I don't want to go through with it. I don't want a divorce. Will you at least consider giving me another chance to work this out? I'm still in love with you, Serenity. I was stupid and mixed up, but I've come to realize you mean more to me than anything, and I'm an idiot."

Serenity shook her head. "Brandon. I—"

Brandon held up a hand. "Don't answer me right now. Just think about it. Okay? At least give me that much. You can tell me tomorrow. Or the next day. We had something special once, and I want that again. I want you back in my life. I want what we had, and I'm not ready to throw it all away."

Serenity huffed out a breath and dropped her arms. "Then why are you suing me? Why go to all that trouble? Don't you realize how much that hurts? Why would I ever want you in my life again after everything you've put me through?"

"I get it. I'm an ass. It was a stupid, mean thing to do, and I lashed out because I was hurting. You changed, and I didn't know how to handle it. But I'd like to try again. I never really gave it a chance, and I don't want to regret it. I just need one more chance. If it doesn't work, then I'll sign the papers, no questions asked."

His eyes held remorse and pain, and I hoped Serenity didn't fall for it. This guy was as shady as they came. With a slight shake of her head, she opened her mouth to respond, but he raised a hand. "You don't have to answer me now. Just think about it. Please. At least give me that much."

She threw her hands up. "Fine. I'll think about it, but don't expect me to change my mind."

His shoulders drooped and he closed his eyes. "Thanks sweetie. That's all I ask. We'll talk soon, all right?"

"Sure." Serenity stepped back and began to close the door, missing the sudden hardness in his eyes. His gaze met mine and his nostrils flared as the door clicked shut.

Serenity turned to me. "That was awkward."

I quickly stepped to the curtain and tugged it open to watch him leave. He stuffed his hands into his pockets and hurried to the street where his car was parked. After he got in, he started the car, and I watched until his tail lights vanished down the road.

One thing was for sure... this little display was all an act, and I hoped Serenity hadn't been fooled. The man I'd met last night wasn't drunk. He'd meant every word he'd said to her, so what was he up to?

Chapter 18

Serenity

Embarrassment flooded over me. How could Brandon just show up like that? What was wrong with him? How could he possibly believe that I'd ever want to get back with him after everything he'd done?

I'd seen his true colors, so nothing would ever change my mind, but now I was back to playing this little game of his, and it made me so angry.

Stone stood at the window, watching Brandon leave. I hurried into the kitchen, hoping to salvage our meal. I'd enjoyed working on it, and now it was probably ruined.

I slipped the omelet back into the pan and turned on the cook-top, hoping I could heat it up again without too much trouble. It was a simple meal, so it should still taste good.

Stone came into the kitchen, and I finished warming everything up before setting it on the table. With the omelet, bacon, hash browns, tomatoes and cheese, it looked pretty good. The toast popped up, and I quickly brought it over to butter.

"This looks amazing," Stone said. "Thank you."

"Of course. Help yourself."

We began to eat, and I savored each bite, grateful it had turned out so well. Nearly finished, Stone cocked a brow. "So. What do you think Brandon really wanted?"

I shook my head, sorry we had to talk about him. "I don't know. To be honest, I think he takes delight in messing with me. But he should know by now that I'd never consider getting back together. It blows my mind that he'd even suggest it. After what happened, I could never trust him again."

Stone nodded. "I agree. There's got to be something else he's after."

I shook my head. "You don't think making my life miserable is enough?"

He shrugged. "Could be, but I think there's more to it. It's too bad you didn't try to touch him. Now that would have been telling."

My eyes widened. "Dang. I didn't even think about it."

His lips twisted. "It's okay. You'll have to remember it for next time though, since it's obvious he's planning on seeing you again." His brows drew together. "So tell me. It sounded like you already had a divorce agreement drawn up, but he wouldn't sign it, right?"

"Yeah... pretty much."

"Why wouldn't he sign it?"

I set my fork down. "He wants half of the settlement money from the accident. I guess he forgot that I used most of it to pay all the hospital bills along with my lawyer's fees. Technically, he should only get what's left over after all the bills were paid, but now he's suing me to try and get more.

He must think suing me for mental cruelty would entitle him to that."

I shook my head. "I also paid off this house and bought a new car... that I had to sell. I lost my job after the accident, so I decided to start my own business. That took every last penny I had, but I thought it was a good investment, you know?"

Stone raised a brow. "So basically, if he signed it now, what would he get?"

"We'd split the market value of this house... that's it. I don't mind doing that. He took everything he wanted and left the furniture... that sort of thing. He also cleared out our shared checking account, but there wasn't much in it, so I didn't bring it up."

I picked up my fork, but I'd lost my appetite, and I pushed my remaining food around on my plate for something to do. "But what I really want is to have him out of my life. I'm sure once I get my business up and running I could qualify for a loan to pay him off, especially with the money I'm getting from Vanetti. But if it goes to trial, most of that will be gone, too."

"You need to withdraw your proposal and write up something new."

I set my fork down. "Like what?"

"I don't know. Half the equity in the house would be better than the market value. Then you should threaten to counter-sue him for mental cruelty. See how he likes that."

"Yeah. Maybe. But that just takes more money away to pay my lawyer." I rubbed my forehead, feeling another headache building. "I just want this to be over. I'm so tired of it dragging on and on."

He sighed. "I'm sure you are, but he's dragging this out no matter what you want."

"Okay. I'll call my lawyer tomorrow and see what he says."

"Just out of curiosity, did you get the locks changed on your doors?"

I sucked in a breath. "Uh... no. He gave me back his keys, so I didn't think I needed to."

Stone raised a brow. "I didn't think you trusted him."

"I don't... but..." I glanced away, worry tightening my chest. What if Brandon had a spare key I didn't know about? He could come into the house anytime he wanted. Take whatever he wanted. "You're right. I should have changed them."

Stone checked his watch. "The hardware store should still be open. Want to make a run and get new locks? And a security camera for the porch would be nice. It wouldn't hurt to set you up with a security system, either."

"I can spring for the locks. But I don't have the money for a security system. Don't you have to pay a monthly fee for that?"

His brows dipped and he looked me in the eyes. "Don't worry about it. I know a guy."

My eyes widened. "Are you joking with me right now?"

He grinned, his sexy smile doing funny things to my stomach. "Babe, I'm talking about myself. Besides, you should have done this right after he left. Now I can do it for you, and it'll help make us even."

My brows rose. "You mean for saving your life today... *and* yesterday?" I twisted my lips. "I'm not sure that's enough to make us even."

"Maybe not, but if you think of something else, we can add it to the tab."

His smoldering gaze sent a different kind of message, and heat filled my veins. Was he propositioning me? Just the thought made it hard to think straight. I swallowed and shrugged, hoping he didn't notice. "I guess I'll have to see how good of a job you do on the locks before I decide."

He raised a brow. "Well... I am good with my hands, so you're on." He grabbed his jacket and headed to the back door. I snatched mine, and quickly followed.

The hardware store wasn't far, and I ended up following Stone around the aisles, since he knew where to go and I didn't. He helped me pick out everything I needed. Then he paid for it before I could stop him, and we ended up back at the house in no time.

While he got to work on the locks, I cleaned up the kitchen from our dinner. I had to admit that it was nice having him here to take care of this for me. I probably could have done it myself, but why not take advantage of him while I could, right?

Too bad I couldn't take advantage of him in other ways. Just knowing he was spending the night sent shivers down my spine, and I shook my head. I couldn't go there. Nope. I definitely wasn't ready for that, no matter how much my body ached for his touch.

Feeling drained, I stepped into the living room, leaning against the doorway to watch him set up the security camera on my front porch. Wanting to sit down, I started toward the couch, and the vision of us kissing and naked hit my chest.

That was where it happened. On my couch. Shit. I swallowed and tried to put it from my mind. Seeing a vision didn't mean it was going to happen. Besides, I wasn't ready for that. At least, I didn't think so.

"Serenity?"

I jerked. "Huh?"

"Your phone. I need it to connect everything."

"Oh, right. Here." I unlocked it and handed it over. Instead of sitting on the couch, I stepped to the chair beside my bookcase. Sinking down into it, I let out a breath and relaxed. So much had happened today that it boggled my mind.

The vision of Stone getting shot popped into my head. If I'd reached him just a second later, he'd be dead. It still unnerved me that the bullet had hit me instead. I could be dead right now too. Just thinking about it made my head hurt.

And what about getting sucked into the darkness of that vision and not being able to pull myself out? But it was a lot more than just that. Stone and I had barely escaped the blast from the trailer. On top of that, Brandon had shown up and ruined a perfectly good meal.

The last few days were catching up to me, and a sudden pain arched behind my eyes. It stretched across the front of my skull to the back of my neck. Oh no. Not now. The pain intensified, and I winced.

Stone handed me my phone and his brows rose. "Are you okay? You look a little pale."

"My head's hurting. It usually means a migraine is coming on. I think I can stave it off if I get some sleep. Are you okay if I go to bed?"

"Of course."

"Thanks. I never got migraines before the accident. But with all the trauma I've experienced lately... along with a head wound, I should have expected it."

"I'm sorry. I'm pretty good at neck massages. Would that help?"

My eyes widened. "I don't know. I've never tried it before."

"It might make a difference."

I shrugged. "Okay. Should I lie down?"

He grabbed a pillow from the couch, and had me sit cross-legged on it while he took my place in the chair. I closed my eyes and tried to relax. His touch was gentle but firm. As he expertly rubbed his thumbs over my shoulders and neck, the tension drained out of me, and my headache lessened. I may have groaned a few times, and, after several of minutes of this, I was a spineless blob.

"Let's get you to bed." Stone got to his feet and helped me up, his arm coming around my waist. He walked me into my room and sat me on the bed, where I laid back on my pillow. "I'd offer to help you undress, but I don't think I'd be able to leave." His intense gaze left me breathless. "Goodnight, Serenity."

He walked out of my room and closed the door. Part of me didn't want him to leave, but another part breathed a sigh of relief. Totally confused, I quickly undressed and climbed under my covers. After a few cleansing breaths, I dropped into sleep.

———•+ ◆≪◆≫◆ +•———

I woke to the gray light of dawn filtering through my window. The events of the last few days came flooding back, but none of it brought the anxiety I expected. Even my headache was gone.

I stretched, realizing that I probably felt so good because of the great massage Stone had given me. Not only that, but he was here in my house and I wasn't alone. For the first time in a long time, I felt safe and protected, which seemed a little strange since I'd nearly died yesterday.

I took a quick shower, careful with my stitches, and put on a little makeup before blow-drying my hair. It had a natural wave to it, so instead of straightening it, I put some hair product in and scrunched it using my diffuser. With a side part, it turned out great, giving me a sassy look.

To show off my blue eyes, I wore my favorite deep blue crew-neck tee that had a black dragonfly pattern on the front. Next, I found my form-fitting black jeans and slipped on my ankle boots.

By the time I finished getting ready, sunshine splashed through my windows, mirroring my good mood, and I could hardly wait to see Stone. I opened my door to the smell of coffee and found him in my kitchen using my coffee brewer.

He wore a t-shirt and gym shorts, and I wondered if he'd slept in them or just thrown them on to make his coffee. Thinking of him naked in my guest bedroom quickened my heart.

After taking a cleansing breath, I stepped toward him, noticing his hair curling over his forehead. This morning, it seemed darker than normal, making it look like deep, silk chocolate, and my fingers itched to see if it was as soft as it looked.

His dark eyes, strong jaw, and unshaven face seemed to lure me to him, and I wondered what it would be like to wake up with him in my kitchen every morning. Preferably after a night of amazing sex. Yikes! Just the thought turned my insides to mush.

He glanced my way and smiled. My heart did little flip-flops in my chest and I swallowed. I was in so much trouble. "Hey. How's it going?"

As I stepped to his side, he studied my face. "I'm good. You look better today. Did you have a good sleep?"

"Yes. It's probably due to that great massage. It really helped."

He raised a brow and gave me a sexy, lop-sided grin. "Yeah... like I said last night, I'm good with my hands."

I snorted and shook my head, not quite ready to go there. "Uh... yeah. That's..." I heaved out a breath. "Uh...

besides the massage... I think it helped to sleep in my own bed."

His lips twisted, but he let me off the hook. "Makes sense. I don't have that problem. I can sleep just about anywhere. I'm sure it's from my days in the service."

"That's right. What made you join up, anyway?"

He snorted. "Well, it was either that or be homeless."

"Why? What happened?"

His lips twisted. "I guess I can tell you since we're... friends?" He met my gaze with a raised brow.

"Uh... yeah... of course."

With a nod, he poured steaming coffee into our mugs. "Right after high school, I got into some trouble, and my old man told me that I could join up or he'd kick me out of the house. I was ready for an adventure, so I joined up the next day."

He took a few swallows and glanced out the window, his eyes unfocused. "I thrived on the challenges and did all I could to be the best in my unit. I moved up through the ranks, got my education, and then was sent overseas. It wasn't until I arrived in the Middle East that the whole experience began to sour. They don't tell you how it feels to watch people die."

He shook his head. "But when the killing started to be easy... that's when I was done. I lost some good friends... and made a few bad ones. So, when my time was up, I resigned with an honorable discharge and ended up here. Vanetti needed a security specialist, and I met all of his qualifications." His lips twisted. "Plus... the pay is excellent."

I grinned. "Yes... I believe that."

His phone began to ring. He pulled it out, and his brows dipped. "Excuse me." He strolled down the hall to his room to answer, closing the door so I couldn't hear his side of the conversation. I knew it wasn't any of my business, but I couldn't help wondering who it was.

Still, I was happy that Stone had confided in me. After my vision of him in a war zone, I knew it wasn't easy for him to talk about his time in the army; but he'd answered my questions without batting an eye.

But now it was back to reality. As good as it felt to have him here, it wasn't going to last. Being with him the last couple of days had given me a glimpse into his life. Sure, it was more than a little messy, but also a lot more interesting than anything I'd ever known.

Still, once the job was done, he'd be back to working for a mob-boss full time. That alone should be enough to warn me away from him. Of course, didn't I work for a mob-boss too? Part of me had come alive the last couple of days. If Vanetti asked me to do more work for him in the future, would I?

Yes. Even with all the danger involved, if it meant being with Stone, I'd do it in a heartbeat.

Chapter 19

Stone

I slipped into my room and shut the door, needing some privacy to hear what Patrick, my security man at the Comet Club, had to say. "Hey Patrick, you got something for me?"

"Sure do. Remember that guy you threw out of the club the other night? The one bothering your girl?"

"Yes." I didn't correct him about Serenity being my girl. I liked it too much.

"Well, he was back last night, only he was with a woman, and they seemed pretty into each other."

"Oh yeah? Did you happen to catch them on security?"

"You know it. I'll send you a photo."

"Thanks. How long did they stay?"

"They got here about nine and stayed until eleven-thirty or so."

I shook my head. Serenity was not going to like this, but, since it was recorded, it would help her feel better about her decision. Plus, it could work out for her with her court case. "Do me a favor and take some time-stamped screen shots of them. Text them to me when you're done."

"Sure thing."

We disconnected, and the screen shots came through a minute later. There was no mistaking Brandon, but I'd never seen the woman before. Maybe Serenity knew her?

I stepped out of my room to find Serenity finishing up a piece of toast. "That was Patrick. He runs security at The Comet Club."

"Oh, right." Her eyes brightened. "Did he see something?"

"Yeah, but it wasn't about me. Brandon showed up there last night."

"At the Comet Club? Was he with his friend again?"

I shook my head. "No. I'm afraid he was with a woman. Patrick sent me some pictures. Want to take a look? Maybe you know her?"

She blinked a couple of times. "What? Are you freaking kidding me? Let me see." She held out her hand for my phone. I handed it over, and she quickly scanned through the photos, her brows growing tighter with each passing second.

"You know her?"

She shook her head and handed the phone back. "I can't believe it. This was after he asked me for a second chance? What a conniving bastard."

"Yeah. I guess he didn't mean a word he said to you." I shook my head. "But why the ruse to get back together? And why drag out the divorce, especially if he's hooked up with someone else?"

She pursed her lips. "I don't know. It doesn't make sense. They looked pretty chummy, too. I wonder how long he's been seeing her?"

"You want me to text you the photos?"

She nodded, her shoulders slumping and her eyes closed. A sudden desire to beat the shit out of Brandon came over me, but I tamped it down. "They're date and time-stamped, if that helps."

She took a deep, shuddering breath to get back under control. "Yes. It does. I might need to stop by my lawyer's office today. I could show these to him. Is that all right?" I nodded, and she continued. "Good. If nothing else, it will help me feel better."

I hated that he'd hurt her. Brandon was a piece of shit. What was he trying to prove? Was he just a sadistic bastard who got off on hurting Serenity? There had to be more to it. Serenity might not like it, but if I could confront him, I was sure I could beat it out of him. If he showed up at The Comet Club again, I could tell Patrick to let me know, and I'd gladly let him have it.

While she put the call through to her lawyer's office, I made a quick call to Patrick and told him what I wanted. That done, I finished my coffee and put my mug on the counter next to Serenity's. It looked good beside hers, like I belonged here, and a surge of satisfaction rolled over me.

"Okay." Serenity put her phone away. "He's got ten minutes at eleven. You can stay here. I think you'll be safe enough while I'm gone."

I raised a brow. "But what about sticking together twenty-four-seven? Isn't that in your contract?"

"Well... yeah, but it's different now."

"How so?"

"Your stalker doesn't know you're here."

Being stuck here was not my idea of a good time. "Maybe... maybe not. You want to take that chance?"

"No. That's not what I meant—" She blew out a breath. "You're right. I guess you'd better come with me."

"Good." I nodded, holding back a pleased grin. She couldn't get rid of me that easily.

"What's the plan for today?"

My morning routine usually included a workout, and I was itching to go to the gym, but that was out of the question, unless... "Do you have a home gym set-up or any exercise equipment?"

She raised a brow. "I have a small workout station downstairs. You want to see it?"

"That's perfect. Yes."

Her lips twisted, like she didn't want to show me.

"Is there something wrong with it?"

"The basement's kind of a mess, that's all."

"Oh. I don't mind."

She shrugged and led me to the basement staircase. Boxes were stacked in the main room, and she turned the corner to the room with the workout system. It wasn't much, but it included an arm press, a high-and-low pulley system, and a four-roll leg developer. It was just enough to give me the workout I craved. "You use it much?"

"Yeah. I got it to help with my rehab after the accident. You're welcome to use it if you want. I guess we have time."

"I just need half an hour, and I can start right now." I pulled off my t-shirt. "You can watch if you want."

Her eyes widened, and her gaze flew to my bare chest. A flush spread up her neck, and her mouth dropped open. I held back a smile and began to change the settings on the pulley.

Her jaw snapped shut and she shook her head. "I'll be upstairs."

She turned to leave, but I caught her looking over her shoulder, and smiled. I settled into a quick routine of weight lifting and used the time to think about my plan to draw my stalker out. By the time I got done, I had a rough idea, but I didn't think Serenity would like it.

An hour later, I had showered and dressed for the day. I found Serenity in her office and sat down in the chair opposite her desk. She hardly glanced at me. "Have a nice workout?"

"Yeah. It was great. What are you working on?"

She sighed. "Just paying the bills. What's the plan for today, anyway?"

"Well, besides going with you to visit your lawyer, we have your niece's birthday party. When is that?"

She raised her brow. "Uh... it's at five. But what about finding your stalker? That comes first, especially after yesterday."

"I think we'll be okay for an hour."

"But why would you want to go to my niece's party?"

I crossed my arms. "Isn't she counting on you? You really want to let her down?"

"Well, no, of course not. But why would you care?"

I glanced at a picture of her family on the wall above her desk. It had to be recent, since there was no sign of Brandon, and a small twist of pleasure rolled over me. "Family's important. If you let work get in the way of that, you'll regret it."

Her gaze settled on mine. "You must be talking from experience."

I shrugged. "My dad and I haven't spoken in years. I don't think I quite lived up to his expectations."

"What about your mom?"

"She died when I was in high school." I swallowed. It had been a long time since I'd spoken about her. "I think that's why I got into so much trouble back then. My dad was lost in his grief, and he didn't want to deal with me."

"I'm so sorry."

Why had I opened up? I didn't tell anyone my personal history, but I felt a connection with her that was undeniable. It dawned on me that being with her had opened a part of my heart that I'd always kept closed.

Her lips twisted. "Life has a way of grinding us up and spitting us out. We're never put back together the same, and sometimes it feels like parts of us are missing."

She gave me a wry smile. "I used to think that everything happened for a reason, but now I'm not so sure. Sometimes things just happen, and we're left to pick up the pieces. We can always make up a reason, or find someone to blame if we want, but it never changes what happened. Like... why a bullet kills one person, and the person right next to them is fine. Most of the time it's just dumb luck."

At my raised brow, she took a deep breath and shook her head. "Sorry. I went off on a tangent. I didn't mean to say all that."

"No. It makes perfect sense. When I was deployed, you'll never believe it, but my nickname was Lucky Stone."

Her eyes widened. "Does it have anything to do with the stone I touched in your room?"

I snorted. "Yeah. That was the only thing I took with me from home. A stupid rock, but it reminded me of my mom, so I carried it in my pocket. Most people have pictures of their girlfriends, or their family, but not me. I carried a rock."

I shook my head. "It wasn't long before my team noticed and figured it was because of my name. So I went with it, and called it my lucky stone." I closed my eyes, seeing the army base in the desert sand. "But that was just at the beginning. After about six months in, the meaning got a little twisted. My platoon called me Lucky Stone because I always made it out alive. It got so that people didn't want to go on missions with me because it meant they might die."

Her brows dipped. "That seems counterintuitive. Wouldn't they want to go with you because the odds of coming back were better for them as well?"

My lips thinned. "You'd think that. But there were plenty of times when I was the only survivor. My last mission... the one you saw in your vision?" She nodded. "I barely made it. I don't pretend to understand it, but that's what happened. I got out of the service right after that."

I met her gaze. "And now it's happening again. I should have died yesterday. Or in the bombing the day before, but you saved me. I'm starting to get a complex."

"Well, at least cheating death isn't making you reckless. If you really believed you couldn't die, you'd put yourself in more dangerous positions."

"And you don't think I do?"

That made her pause. "Well. I guess that's debatable. I mean... your job is kind of dangerous. And now Johnny is after you."

"So, you think it's Cash's friend?"

She nodded. "Yes, I do, especially after hearing that Johnny Cash song, it's the only thing that makes sense. He has to be tied to Razor and the snakes... even if it's only a remote connection."

"I think you're right. We can use that tie to draw him out." I shook my head. "You know, it's crazy, but I've already come up with a plan that involves Razor."

"Oh yeah? What is it?"

"We set a trap. With me as bait."

Her eyes widened. "You can't be serious. That's just asking for trouble."

"Maybe. But nothing else has worked."

She closed her eyes. "There has to be another way."

"I can't think of anything. Can you?"

"Well... not right off the top of my head."

"That's what I thought."

"Fine. Then tell me what you have in mind."

"I'm still working on it, but I think setting up a meeting at Razor's place might do the trick. I could install a bunch of security cameras around his place before the meeting. I'd tell him to make sure all of his guys knew about it, and hopefully one of them would tell Johnny. Then he'd make plans to take me out at the meeting, and we'd catch him."

Her eyes narrowed. "If you think someone else in the gang has connections to Johnny, then why not just talk to them?"

"Look what happened to Cash. He'd probably kill them, and we'd be right back where we started."

"Okay... I get it. So, then what?"

"We'd watch for him on the security footage. When he showed up, we'd move in and catch him, long before he could plant a bomb or set a trap for me."

"I guess that could work."

I nodded. "As long as I get Razor to agree."

She sniffed. "Good luck with that. After all the bombs, I doubt he'll go for it."

"I know. But it's worth a try." I twisted my lips. "If that doesn't work, I'm hoping we can come up with another plan to draw Johnny out, and then you use your psychic powers to foresee if that plan will work."

Her brows dipped. "What if my powers don't tell us anything?"

I shrugged. "Doesn't matter. It's worth a try."

"I don't know... I've barely kept you alive as it is."

"I know. But we have to do something." I started to pace back and forth in front of her desk. "Let's start with this. What do we know about Johnny?"

"That he's angry and wants you dead?"

I shook my head. "Besides that." I held up my fingers to count them off. "He knows where I live. That I drive a Triumph. That I work for Vanetti. And that I go to the gym by the office. He also used my connection to the gang."

"Yeah... and he knew Cash. Maybe we need to find out more about Cash, and that will lead us to him. He must be a friend or a relative, right?"

"Looks that way."

"Okay. Let's dig into this. When I took my private investigator course, I signed up for a few websites that have information like that." She turned to her computer and opened the sites.

Grabbing my chair, I pulled it around her desk and settled next to her. I didn't have the heart to tell her that I had better resources at my office, mostly because I enjoyed being with her in the privacy of her house. Besides, the more I went back and forth to the office with her, the more likely it was for Johnny to find out where she lived. The thought sent shivers down my spine. I had to protect Serenity from him at all costs.

Watching her work, I liked how she chewed on her bottom lip, and how the angle of the sun hit her face just right, giving her an ethereal glow. She had one of the most expressive faces I'd ever seen.

Probably because she didn't know how to be guarded. I knew instinctively that there wasn't a devious bone in her body, and she was someone I could trust. That was rare. Most people I dealt with always had a hidden agenda.

"Okay. Here are my websites. Let's put in Cash's real name and see what the results are. What is it, anyway?"

I shrugged. "I have no idea. I'll call Razor and see if he knows." I pulled out my phone and put the call through. A few minutes later, I had a name. "It's Steve Cashell."

"Really? Okay." She typed in the name, and several hits came up. We scrolled through the list before finally finding the right one. After perusing all the websites and records we could find, there wasn't much to link him to Razor's gang.

We cross-referenced him with the name Johnny, but didn't find a lot there, either. Soon, it was time for her appointment, and Serenity shut off her computer.

"We can pick it up when we get back." I assured her.

"I guess, but it feels like a dead-end. It's so frustrating." She pushed away from her desk. "I'll get my things and we can go."

It was a beautiful spring day, with the temperatures climbing into the lower seventies, and I hated being in a car. At least her lawyer's office was closer to the south end of town, and nowhere near Vitality Ventures and my office.

We had to wait a few minutes before her lawyer was free. He came out to get Serenity, and I got up to go with her. She wasn't expecting that, but I just shrugged. "Twenty-four-seven, remember?"

She shook her head before introducing me. "This is Nathan Stone. I'm working a sensitive PI case with him. He's been there to witness Brandon's behavior, so that's why I want him here now."

Ethan held out his hand. "Nice to meet you. Come on back."

The guy seemed nice enough, especially when Serenity showed him the photos of Brandon. "These are great. We can definitely use them if it goes to trial. Heck, we could even use them in mediation to avoid the trial completely. Even then, most judges can see through Brandon's BS."

Serenity glanced my way and took a breath. "Okay... but if it ends up going to trial, I want to counter-sue for mental cruelty against him. Let's see how he likes that."

Ethan pursed his lips and nodded, but he didn't seem convinced. "It might look better for you if you don't. These photos might be enough to get him to back off and sign the papers without a trial."

Her lips drew down, and she sighed. "I hope so. Is this ever going to end?"

"Yes." Ethan leaned forward in his chair. "It will. I'll reach out to his lawyer. If he's still set on going to trial, it will take a few months to get a date, but if he's with this other woman, he might not want to wait that long, and we can settle out of court. We'll just have to see how it plays out."

Serenity shook her head. "That much longer? What a joke."

"I know it's not what you wanted to hear, but like I said. He might want to end it sooner."

"Wait. I forgot to tell you that he stopped by my house last night. He said he didn't want to go through with the divorce. Why would he say that and then go out with that woman later?"

Ethan's brows rose. "I don't know. Did he threaten you at all? We might be able to get a restraining order."

"No. He might have, but Stone was there." She motioned toward me.

Ethan's brows rose and he nodded. "Makes sense."

"Stone also suggested making a couple of changes to the decree." She pulled out the first one and showed him the changes.

Ethan beamed. "This is so much better for you! I'm so glad your partner talked you into this. I'll make the changes and send a copy to his lawyer today."

Her eyes widened. "Okay. Thanks."

He checked his watch and stood. "I don't have more time right now, but I'll let you know what I find out."

"Sounds good."

Ethan ushered us to the door. "We'll get this figured out." He shook Serenity's hand. She wasn't wearing her gloves, and she froze for a split second before pulling away. He shook my hand next, and I followed her down the hall and outside to the parking lot.

Not looking at me, she unlocked the car doors and got in. After I settled into my seat, she turned toward me. "Where to, now?"

I raised a brow and gave her a smirk. "You know... I kind of liked how he called me your partner." She rolled her eyes, and I grinned. "So, what happened when you touched him? Did you see something important?"

Closing her eyes, she shook her head. "I don't think so. He was in a courtroom, standing in front of a jury and talking about a hit and run. He said he could prove that it wasn't an accident." She sighed. "That's all I got. I didn't see anyone there that I knew, so it must be about a case he's working on." She met my gaze. "Since it wasn't life-threatening, I didn't say anything. That's my new motto. If it's not life-threatening, keep my mouth shut."

"That's probably a good idea."

"Yeah... well, I'm learning as I go. Should we head back to my house?"

My phone began to ring. I checked who was calling and frowned. "It's Razor. I wonder what he wants?" I swiped to answer. "Razor. What's up?"

"We need to talk. Can you stop by my place sometime today?"

"I don't know. What's this about?"

"Cash is dead, and you were looking for him, so I need to know what happened."

"Why? You think I did it?"

He hesitated. "That's what I need to talk to you about. Some of the guys are upset. We just need to clear this up." I didn't answer right away, so he continued. "Don't worry. It's not an ambush. I've got your back."

"Fine. I'll be there soon." I disconnected and put my phone away. "It looks like we need to talk to Razor about what happened to Cash. You okay to head over there?"

"I guess so. I mean... last time I shook his hand, I didn't get anything, but I can't say the same about everyone else."

"I think we'll be fine. I trust Razor, and I'm carrying."

"Oh... well... that's good. Give me your hand, just in case."

She held her hand out to me, so I took it. I waited for her to gasp, and watched to see if her eyes went out-of-focus, but nothing happened.

She shrugged. "Um... I've got nothing, so it must be okay."

I raised a brow. "Maybe a kiss would work better. Want to try it?" I knew she wouldn't go for it, but I couldn't resist teasing her.

"And if I said yes?"

I did not expect that, and she knew it, before she could say another word, I cupped her cheek and leaned in for a kiss. As our lips touched, a soft moan escaped her throat, and she began kissing me back, pulling and sucking on my lips like she was starving. All at once, she broke the kiss and sat back in her seat, her chest heaving. "I shouldn't have done that."

I shrugged, not about to agree. "Did it work?"

She pursed her lips. "No."

"Maybe we should try it again?"

"You wish." She shook her head. "So where's Razor's shop from here?"

Knowing she was done, I let it go. "I can drive if you want."

"No. I got this. Just remind me how to get there."

I gave her the directions, and we arrived in short order. She pulled up in front and stopped. "I thought it would be safer to park out here instead of in the back like we did before."

"Good idea. We might need to make a hasty exit, so keep your keys handy."

I got out of the car and headed into the front office of the car shop, Serenity stuck close to my side, almost like she was protecting me. It would have been funny if she hadn't actually saved my life already.

I wasn't too worried about this visit, since I trusted Razor wouldn't double-cross me, but there was always a first time. Inside, the guy at the front desk raised his brows, like we'd surprised him.

"Razor's expecting us."

"Uh... sure. Go on back."

I stepped toward the doorway, and Serenity grabbed my hand. I glanced back at her, but she just shrugged, so I continued through the shop to Razor's office. It felt nice to hold her hand, and, who knew? Maybe she'd get something for a change? A few of the guys stopped what they were doing to watch us pass, and it put me on edge.

Razor's office door was open and I stepped inside, still holding Serenity's hand. Joint stood beside Razor's desk and straightened to see us. He chewed on a toothpick and crossed his arms, his face tight.

"Stone," Razor said. "Thanks for coming. Have a seat. This shouldn't take long." As we sat down, he glanced at Serenity. "I don't think we were introduced before."

"Her name's Sen," Joint said. "She's the one who told us we had to run." He met her gaze, and his eyes narrowed. "So... do you know who the informant is?"

Her eyes widened, but she shrugged. "No."

Joint moved to loom over her, and I rose to my feet, stepping in front of him and getting in his face. "Back off, Joint. She doesn't know. So deal with it."

He flinched but stood his ground.

"Joint." Razor's low voice held a hint of menace. With flaring nostrils, Joint stepped away from me. Razor shook his head and motioned to the door with his hand. "Get out."

Joint's brows rose. "What?"

"You heard me. Get. Out."

Muttering under his breath, Joint left the room, slamming the door behind him. As Razor's second in command, he'd just been humiliated, and I wasn't sure Razor had done me any favors. Joint had a reputation for his brutality in the boxing ring, and could cause a lot of damage without breaking a sweat.

"Sorry about that." Razor rubbed the back of his neck. "He's upset that Cash is dead. Not because he cares, but because Cash had some guns stored in his trailer, and now the police have them. He's worried one of them might be traced back to a shooting he was involved in."

"That's too bad, but Cash's death had nothing to do with us. The bomb was already set, probably for me."

"So you think Cash's friend double-crossed him?"

"Yes."

"Makes sense. So have you got any clues about who this friend is?"

"The only thing we have right now is the name Johnny. Do you know someone by that name?"

Razor's brows rose. "Johnny? That's interesting, because Joint mentioned that Cash met with someone named Johnny. But that's all he said. Does this Johnny person go by a gang name?"

"If he does, I don't know what it is, but maybe I'd better have a chat with Joint."

Razor shrugged. "Maybe... but I'm sure he has nothing to do with your business... he's loyal to me. In the meantime, is there anything you can tell us about the informant that's got Joint so upset?"

I knew that was the real reason he wanted to talk to me. "My source in the police department doesn't want me involved. But if I were you, I'd tell Joint and his drug dealers to take some time off and see what shakes out."

Razor nodded. "I appreciate the info. But I'm afraid Joint won't be too happy for you to leave without giving him a name. Maybe you could make a deal. The name of the informant for what Joint can tell you about Johnny. What do you say?"

I glanced at Serenity, and she pursed her lips. "We can't give you a name, because we don't have one."

"That's too bad."

I shook my head. This was not going the way I wanted. "I might be able to find out, but I need a favor from you first." Serenity jerked her head in my direction. I patted her knee and she relaxed.

Razor's brows rose. "I can get behind that."

"Good." I sat forward in my chair. "I need to draw out Cash's killer. If this Johnny person somehow found out that I would be here at a certain time, it's possible he'd show up."

Razor's brows rose. "You want me to spread the word, and then use my shop for a meeting? I don't know. The last two places he knew about got blown up."

"I'd make sure I caught him long before it went that far. We can figure out all the details later."

Razor's eyes narrowed. "And you'd give me the name in return?"

"If I can get it. But if not, I have something else you might like better."

"Like what?"

"Mr. Vanetti has a deal he'd be willing to offer you. I can't go into the details right now, but if I tell him what you're doing for me, I'm sure he'd be happy to generously compensate you."

Razor stared at me before dipping his head. "Fine. I agree."

"Good. I'll let you know later today."

Razor rose to his feet, and I stood as well. I motioned for Serenity to go ahead of both of us. She stepped into the hall and hurried through the garage like her life depended on it. I had to hurry to keep up, and didn't realize that the men were missing until we got outside.

Joint and three of his crew stood in front of her car, blocking our way. It surprised me that one of them was Grizzo. Serenity stopped short and backed into me. I stepped in front of her, moving her behind me.

Joint stepped closer. "I just need a name. Then you're free to go."

I glanced behind him at Grizzo, who had paled a bit and looked ready to bolt. I opened my mouth to respond, but Serenity stepped to my side.

"I never got a name. I just had a premonition that you were all in jail. That's it. I don't even know if there is an informant. All I know is what my vision told me."

Joint's brows scrunched together. "A premonition? What the hell does that mean?"

"She's a psychic," I said. "Sometimes she gets visions. Now back off."

Joint stepped back, but his eyes held suspicion. "If that's the case, then you can tell me which of these guys—" He pointed to the men behind him. "—is loyal to me."

My jaw clenched. Why had Serenity told him about her visions? "It doesn't work that way."

Serenity opened her mouth to explain, but I held my hand up. "Look, Joint, she doesn't owe you a thing. You know why? Because, right now, she's working for me and Vanetti, so like I said before. Back off."

Joint glanced between the two of us and shook his head. "I think you're both full of shit." His gaze landed on Serenity. "So tell me this. If you're the real deal, then you know the future, right? So you can stop something from happening, right? Well stop this." He sent a powerful left jab to my chin.

I'd been expecting a move like that, and managed to pull my head back before he hit me. Gasping, Serenity jumped out of the way, and I locked gazes with Joint, my eyes narrowing and my lips twisting with a challenge. "She doesn't need to see the future to know I'm gonna kick your ass."

Anger sparked in Joint's eyes, and he came at me. My training kicked in, and I relished the opportunity to use all my pent-up frustration on him. I'd sparred with him before, but I'd always held back. Not this time.

His specialty was boxing, but I had several years of martial arts and combat training that he couldn't even dream of, and I let him have it.

He managed to get in a couple of solid punches, but I quickly got the best of him, and knocked him down. I pinned him with my knee in his back, twisting his arm in a painful grip. He refused to tap out, so I pulled just enough to hear his shoulder pop, along with his cry of pain.

I might have gone too far, but he needed to be put in his place. Standing over him, I released his arm, noticing that most of the gang had come out to watch, including Razor, who stood beside Serenity.

Joint moaned and rolled over, holding his dislocated shoulder to his side. Someone would have to put his shoulder back in the socket, but Joint had to know I could have done worse. I met Razor's gaze, and he shrugged before telling everyone to get back to work. The men began to leave, and Razor hurried to Joint's side.

I brushed the dirt off my clothes and followed Serenity to her car. She stepped to the driver's side and got in. Starting the car, she wasted no time in pulling onto the street.

She spared me a glance, and I cocked my brow. "What?"

Shaking her head, she let out a breath. "You. I... I don't know what to say. You're like... those actors in the movies. Only you're real. Those guys are just faking it."

I snickered. "What do you mean?"

She shrugged. "It's just... I've never met someone like you. I mean... you're tough and all, but Joint is huge. I was a little worried, but you took him down so fast, it took me by surprise."

"So... does that mean you're even more impressed with me now?"

She sniffed and glanced my way, shaking her head. "I'm just glad you didn't mean it about giving Joint Grizzo's name."

"To be honest, I thought about it, but since I knew you'd be upset, I came up with a backup plan."

Her brows rose. "What? Does Vanetti know?"

"Of course. We came up with a deal yesterday while you were asleep."

"Oh... good." She glanced my way, her gaze focusing on my forehead. "We should head back to my place so you can clean up. You've got a cut above your eyebrow." She pointed to the dashboard. "There's a tissue in the glove box."

I opened the box and grabbed a few tissues to dab at my forehead. My knuckles were scraped as well, but it was totally worth it to put Joint in his place. Of course, I hadn't scored any points with him, since I'd taken him down in front of his gang. But at least the others would think twice about taking me on. Besides, he started it, and I had a reputation to keep up.

We arrived at Serenity's house, and I took a quick shower to get all the grime off. At least the cut above my brow didn't need stitches, and Serenity made me sit down on the edge of the tub while she used a butterfly bandage to pull it together.

She stood close, her chest even with my nose, and I wanted to bury my face against those perfect breasts. Her intoxicating scent made it hard to sit there without wrapping my arms around her and pulling her against me.

"There, that should do it." She let out a breath. "I guess you can add that to the list."

It would be easy to circle her waist with my hands and hold her captive. It might be worth it just to smell her amazing scent a little longer. "What list?"

"Of the things you owe me for. I think you're still in my debt, even with the locks and the security camera."

"Hmm... I didn't know we were keeping track."

She stepped away, and I gave in, circling her waist with my hands and tugging her back. Surprised, her palms came down on my shoulders. I glanced up to find her mouth open and her face suffused with a pink flush. "I can think of a way to pay you back. You'd enjoy it so much that you'd beg for more."

Her breath caught and her eyes darkened. Then her brows drew down and she pulled away. "Is that all you think about?"

I let her go and sighed. "Not usually, but you—" I swallowed what I wanted to say and shook my head. "Never mind."

She pivoted and hurried out the door like an escaping convict. I followed more slowly, glad to know she was just as attracted to me as I was to her. On the way to her office, she threw an irritated glance over her shoulder. "We need to figure out who this Johnny person is, remember?"

"Yeah... got it." I waited while she sat down. As much as I wanted this to be over, I liked spending all my time with Serenity. Once we figured it out, she'd move on, and I wasn't ready for that.

"Okay. So let's think about it. Johnny's been a step ahead of you. So that means he's got to have a way to get information on your whereabouts. That means someone's feeding him information, or he's bugged you with a camera or tracking device. Did you check your car, or motorcycle for a tracker?"

My brows drew together. Could it be that simple? "I didn't."

Her eyes widened. "Well. We'll have to do that when we get back to the office."

I shook my head. "I think I would have noticed something like that on my bike... but not the car." I closed my eyes. "I should have checked."

"You know what? It could be a good thing. If there is a tracker, we can use it to set him up and draw him into that trap of yours."

Sitting in my chair, I leaned forward, resting my hands on my knees. "You're right. I knew I was missing something. That must have been it. Let's go back to the office and see."

Her brow puckered. "You sure you want to do that? Why don't we call Vanetti and have him take a look. Or Ricky... you trust him, right?"

"Yeah, but I'll call Forrest Slater since he's on my security team. He'll know what to look for. He usually does sweeps for bugs once a week, but I'll have him start doing them every day."

"Sounds good. Make sure he looks for hidden cameras, too. Maybe in the parking garage, or by the elevators."

I rolled my eyes. "You don't need to tell me; I know what I'm doing." I put the call through, and Slater agreed to take a look. I stayed on the phone with him while he checked things out. After directing him to every place I could think of, we disconnected. I gave Serenity the news. "No trackers or hidden cameras anywhere."

"Dang! That would have been so helpful." She shook her head and met my gaze. "Could someone in *your* office be feeding Johnny information?"

"Not a chance." At her raised brows, I rolled my eyes. "A move against me is a move against Vanetti. No one who works there would be that stupid."

"You're probably right. But what about the club? Does anyone there hold a grudge against you?"

"We've been over this before. It's not an inside job. I think we need to go ahead and set something up at the car shop. I'll call Vanetti and get Razor on board. I'll see if tomorrow night will work."

She sighed. "I don't like it, but okay."

I spent the next couple of hours working on the deal. It took a call from Vanetti to get Razor to commit to the plan, but Razor finally agreed to tell everyone that I would be there tomorrow night for a special meeting. "But don't tell them until tomorrow."

He agreed, and I told Serenity we had a deal. "That means I'll have to stop by the shop sometime during the night tonight and set up a couple of cameras."

"Does Razor know that?"

"Yes. He'll meet me there. But don't worry, he knows to keep quiet about it."

"I sure hope so. What about the cameras? Do you need to buy them?"

"I have the equipment at the office. We can stop there on our way to the shop and pick them up." At her raised brows, I continued. "It will be in the middle of the night. We'll be fine." She still didn't look convinced, so I pulled the psychic card. "Besides, I'll let you touch me. Maybe you'll get a vision?"

"Fine." She checked her watch. "Oh, jeez, I've got to make my chip dip for the party."

Leaving me behind, she scurried into the kitchen, so I called Vanetti to verify that Razor was good with the plan. I also told him I'd set up the cameras at Razor's place tonight.

I had one last thing to ask, but I hesitated, knowing he wouldn't like it. "One more thing. Just on the off chance, I'm wondering if someone at the office could be feeding Johnny information. I'm not saying someone is, but it could be a possibility."

Vanetti narrowed his eyes. "I hate to believe it, but if anyone knows, it would be Julia. I'll get her to check it out."

I hoped Julia was trustworthy, but since they were into each other I kept my mouth shut. "Sounds good. I'm going to a family thing with Serenity tonight, so let me know if Julia finds anything. Otherwise, I'll get the cameras set up, and we'll take it from there." He agreed, and we disconnected.

With nothing left to do, I got ready for the party. Wanting to make a good impression, I ran my electric shaver over my face and changed into the one dress shirt I'd brought, just for the occasion. I didn't usually give a damn about looking the part, but this was important to Serenity, so I made an exception.

Part of me looked forward to meeting her family. Not that I cared, but the last time I'd been to a family gathering had been a disaster. My dad had remarried while I'd been in the service. His wife had wanted to meet me, but since she was closer to my age than his, it hadn't gone well. Last I'd heard, they even had a couple of kids, but I'd never been invited back.

I was curious to see what a family who actually cared about each other was like. A small part of me questioned why I bothered, but I shoved that thought away and tucked in my shirt. Grabbing my leather jacket, I headed into the living room to wait.

Chapter 20

Serenity

I finished making the cream-cheese-pineapple chip dip my niece loved, and grabbed a bag of chips. After Vanetti offered me this job, I'd packed my bags and delivered Gracie's gift to Felicity's house, on the off chance I couldn't make it. That was before I'd met Stone, or I might not have been so proactive.

I found Stone in the living room, looking at his phone while he waited for me. As I entered the room, he glanced up, and his handsome face sent a thrill through my stomach. Not only that, but warmth rushed through my heart, expanding my chest and pushing outward toward him. Damn. I cared about him, and I couldn't deny it.

He'd changed into a navy dress shirt, which stretched across his chest, revealing the muscles underneath. His sleeves were rolled up, showing corded muscles and dark hair on his forearms and hands. I'd never realized how sexy arms could be.

He'd shaved the stubble off his chiseled jaw and cheekbones. Usually I liked the rugged look, but without the stubble, it took the edge off the deadly vibe he usually gave off, making him more approachable, but still too hot to believe he was real.

His dark, wavy hair flopped across his forehead, making me yearn to run my fingers through it. Then there were his eyes. Dark pools that held a touch of amusement. He raised a brow, knowing I was staring at him, and enjoying every second of it.

I had to tamp down my urge to throw caution to the wind and kiss that mocking smile right off his face. Sheesh! This was terrible. I needed to pull myself together. I needed to be serene. Ha! I couldn't even live up to my own name with him anywhere near me.

"Uh... I'll be right back." Since he looked so amazing, I knew the shirt I wore needed an upgrade. Rushing into my room, I skimmed through my tops and found the black one I wanted. The long sleeves were a sheer mesh that connected at the crew neck to hug the black camisole underneath. I'd never worn it, but it fit the bill for this moment, looking both sexy and alluring.

I'd bought it as a reward for getting out of the hospital, but after Brandon's meltdown, I'd never felt like wearing it... until now. I touched up my makeup and hair before stepping into the living room.

Stone glanced over me with darkening eyes and an appreciative nod. My heart did a little happy skip before it hit me that I was introducing him to my family... as what? My new boyfriend?

Holy hell. Maybe this wasn't the best idea. "Are you sure you want to come?" His brows rose and I hurried to explain. "Not that I don't want you there... it's just that... my family will probably want to know all about you, and you'll never hear the end of it."

He snorted. "Oh, I doubt it will be as painful for me as it is for you."

"Exactly. I didn't even tell Felicity that you were coming... she's not expecting you. They're going to think you're my boyfriend or something." Eyes widening, I shook my head. "Maybe you should just... lay low here." Having my family think that Stone and I were together would be awful.

"Sounds boring. I'd rather come with you. Besides, would it really be so bad if they thought we were together?" He stepped close enough that I could smell his amazing cologne.

"What?" I tried not to let it overcome my reasoning, but it was hard to think with all that masculine perfection staring me in the face. "Yes!" I shook my head, stepping back. "I'll... I'll just have to tell them that I'm your bodyguard."

"My bodyguard?" His brows lifted.

"Yeah. I mean, it's true. And... I'm working on your case and I *have* saved your life. That would work. Why else would we have to stay together twenty-four, seven?"

"I like the boyfriend angle better." He grinned, sending my heart fluttering.

"No, I'm still technically married." I shook my head. "I'm a PI, you're my client, we're working on a sensitive case together. Done."

He raised a brow. "Did they even like your ex?"

"Oh. Sure. At first, but not since the accident when my psychic ability started happening. Brandon didn't keep it a secret that it freaked him out. He may have tried to get them to agree with him, but it backfired. They're on my side."

His lips curved up. "So... I'm curious. What do *they* think about that? Do they mind it if you touch them?"

I twisted my lips. "They don't mind, but that's because if I saw something about them that could keep them safe, they'd want to know. I mean... it's not like they run around killing people and hiding the bodies, so there's nothing like that to hide. Sure, it can get uncomfortable if I see an argument they had, or something stupid they did, but I've gotten pretty good at being someone they can trust."

"That makes sense. Trust is important in any relationship."

"Exactly." Was he saying that so I wouldn't blab about his past? "I'm not going to tell them your secrets."

He nodded. "I know."

"Good." I let out a breath. "It might be a little awkward, since you're my client, but they'll warm up. Just... don't let them get to you, okay?"

He snorted. "Babe, I can take care of myself. You're the one who's worried about it."

From the mischief in his eyes, I could tell he was looking forward to the show, and a knot of worry tightened my stomach. Would he do something to embarrass me? He might, but knowing my family, he would have to get in line.

I slipped on my black leather jacket and grabbed my purse, praying this whole family meeting wouldn't be too bad. "I'd better text Felicity."

Stone's eyes lit up. "Do you have to?"

I smacked him. "Yes." I pulled out my phone and texted that I was coming after all, and I was bringing my client. I pushed send and hoped she looked at her phone before we got there, or I was going to have a lot of explaining to do.

"Okay. Let's go."

We arrived a little late, so I had to park my car across the street from the house. Stone hopped out, and I followed more slowly, mentally preparing to be bombarded with questions.

I automatically reached out to take Stone's hand, but stopped. He didn't need protecting at my house, so if I took his hand now, he might get the wrong idea, and that would be a disaster.

Before I could put my hands in my pockets, Stone grabbed my hand.

"What are you doing?" I hissed, trying to discretely tug out of his grip, but he didn't let go.

"There's no way I'm letting you say you're my *bodyguard*." He gave me a cocky grin that turned my insides to mush, even while my face went crimson.

"No way," I argued.

But he just winked and rang the doorbell. Dammit! It would be even weirder if we waited for them to answer. So, I pushed the door open and stepped inside, pulling Stone with me.

My parents, along with Felicity's husband, Ryan, and their four-year-old son, Hank, my older brother Will, his wife, Emma, and his three kids were crowded into the living room. They all turned to me, mouths open with greetings, but froze when Stone entered behind me. Oh, hell. The doorbell brought Felicity in from the kitchen with Gracie at her side, and Gracie let out a squeal, breaking the tension.

"Aunt Senny!! You came!!"

"Hey sweetie! Happy Birthday!"

Stone finally let go of my hand as she ran into my arms, nearly knocking me over with her enthusiasm. After a big hug, her gaze landed on Stone. "Who are you?"

"Gracie... this is Stone."

"You can call me Nate." He smiled and knelt down to Gracie's level. "I came with Serenity so I could wish you a happy birthday. I also brought you something."

By this time, my parents had stepped over to see what was going on, confusion written all over their faces, and we all watched Stone pull an object from his pocket. He held it out, showing us a black, polished, oval-shaped rock with several gold and white veins running through it.

"What is it?" Gracie asked, her voice hushed.

"It's a dragon egg. It's old, so there's not a real dragon inside, but see all those gold and white streaks?"

"Yeah."

"Dragons love gold, and it gives the stone special powers." He handed it to Gracie, and she took it, her eyes sparkling with awe.

"Wow."

"What do you say, Gracie?" Felicity prompted, glancing back and forth between me and Stone.

"Thanks Nate! I've never seen anything like this. Look everybody! A dragon egg!"

My heart swelled in my chest, warmth washing through me. How could I not help falling for him even more? Sheesh! Who knew he'd be so good around kids? Did he have nieces and nephews? He'd never mentioned any siblings, so probably not. And who knew he was into dragons?

While Gracie showed off her stone to everyone in the room, Felicity stepped beside us. "Wow, thank you so much!" Her cheerfulness came out a little forced. "Gracie loves make-believe with princesses, and knights, and dragons, and all that. Did Sen tell you? Oh, I'm Felicity, by the way." She glanced at me. "Sen forgot to mention she was bringing someone with her."

"I sent you a text."

"Really? Oh, well, I didn't see it."

Stone put his arm around me. "When she told me about the party, she wasn't sure she could take the time. But I managed to convince her we should come. I hope that's all right?"

What was he doing?

"Of course it's all right. I'm so glad you're here." She sent me another *we need to talk* look.

"Thanks." He sent her his sexy smile, and she nearly swooned.

My mom chose that moment to step closer, putting her arm around Felicity to get her attention. "Oh... these are our parents, Kristin and Jack. Nate Stone, right?"

"That's right. A pleasure to meet you." He held out a hand, his low voice sending shivers down my spine.

"Nice to meet you, too, Nate," Mom said, taking his hand.

He smiled. After shaking her hand, he shook my dad's hand, and Felicity introduced her husband, Ryan, then continued to pull him around the room, introducing him to the rest of our family. I watched him closely to see what else he was going to do, or if he'd start to crack under the pressure of meeting so many people, but it didn't seem to faze him.

My mom came to my side, glancing between me and Stone. She spoke softly, but it was still loud enough that Stone could hear her. "So how long have you two known each other? You didn't tell me you were dating."

I opened my mouth to tell her we weren't dating, when she knocked her shoulder against mine. "Does he know you're still married?" She raised a brow at me.

My stomach twisted. "Mom! Of course he knows. And we're *not* dating. I'm—Stone's bodyguard." There, I'd done it. No more misconceptions.

Stone laughed. "Oh, she guards my body, all right."

I just stared at him, embarrassment flooding through me in waves. He said that, in front of my *mother*.

"We've only started dating. We met through her work. In fact, I'm helping her with an investigation."

"Oh." Mom raised her eyebrows, giving him the once-over, taking in his total hotness and handsome features. Her eyes sparkled with curiosity and a little awe. "That's wonderful." She leaned in to me, barely lowering her voice. "I'll bet he's a good kisser."

"Mom! Jeez."

"What?" She straightened, smiling at Stone. "You need some happiness in your life. I'm glad you found someone, especially after all you've been through. And don't get me started about Brandon. That man can rot in hell, for all I care." She leaned in again. "So, was it good?"

A blush stained my cheeks. "Mom! He's standing right there."

Her eyes narrowed, and a sly smile spread over her lips, but she shrugged like I was an idiot and muttered, "Well... if you haven't kissed him, then something's wrong with you."

"Okay, everybody," Felicity said, saving me from further embarrassment. "Let's get this party started."

Felicity explained where the food was, and how to proceed. While everyone hurried outside to the deck, and the grilled hamburgers and hot-dogs, I darted a glance at Stone.

He caught me looking and grinned. "I like your mom."

I rolled my eyes. "I guess you heard all that?"

He snorted. "Of course. And she's right." Grinning, he leaned close to me. "But luckily, I know there's nothing wrong with you."

"Well, *that's* a relief." I shook my head. "You want a hamburger?"

"Sure. And I want some of that chip dip you made. Is it a special recipe?"

"Yes... it's actually a family favorite. My Grandma used to make it."

He took my hand again, his touch sending little butterflies through my stomach, and I didn't even fight him as we followed everyone outside like we were a real couple. Warmth spread over me, filling a big hole in my heart. But was this all an act? Just a fun way to tease me? Or was that sparkle in his eyes just for me?

Soon our plates were full of food. I was hoping to sit somewhere safe, preferably with the kids at their table, but my sister motioned for us to take the spots beside her, and we sat down to eat.

We'd only taken a couple of bites before the questions started.

"So, Nate," my father began. "What do you do for a living?"

I'd never known a boisterous group of people could get so quiet. All of the adults glanced toward Stone, waiting with bated breath.

"I'm the security specialist for a large corporation."

"Oh. You mean like cybersecurity?"

Stone smiled. "I've got a tech specialist for that. My main concern is the security of the building and grounds, as well as the personnel."

"Wow. Must be a high-class corporation."

Stone nodded, but didn't give my dad the company name he was fishing for. "I keep threats at bay, but if they come in, I'm the guy who handles them."

My dad's brows rose. "Oh... that's interesting. What kind of degree do you need for that?"

Stone shrugged. "I got my training in the military. Now I work in the civilian sector. It's less messy, and there's no politics involved, so it's a win-win."

That shut everyone up, but it also begged for more information.

"So tell us how you two met." My mom motioned between us. "Serenity's kept you a secret. I didn't even know she was dating."

Stone met my gaze, a twinkle in his eyes. I opened my mouth to answer, but he beat me to it. "We met on the job. I guess you all know about Serenity's business?" He waited for their nods. "My boss hired her and introduced us." He met my gaze again. "What she does is quite remarkable."

He placed his hand over mine, and a sudden lump got stuck in my throat.

"That was all my idea," Dad crowed.

"No it wasn't," Mom said.

"Sure it was. After we found out what she could do, it only made sense to start her own business, especially when she said she wanted to help people. I told her it wouldn't hurt to make a little money at the same time. And I was right."

"You always think you're right," Mom said. "But as I remember it, I think Serenity came up with that herself. She has a lot of initiative." She glanced at Stone, pride shining in her eyes.

"Are all of you seriously forgetting Serenity's childhood dream of being Sherlock Holmes?" Felicity asked, her eyes wide. "If it wasn't for Bran— uh... her ex... she would have been a PI a long time ago."

"Sure, but don't forget her new psychic ability," my brother Will said. "That sealed the deal. Of course it's not all fun and games." He met Stone's gaze. "Just make sure you're not hiding any secrets when you hug her."

"You mean like the time you were eating my homemade chocolates out of the pantry?" Mom glared at Will, then turned to Stone. "I was saving those for Christmas, and I had to get Sen to tell me what had happened to them."

Will's eyes widened. "You're the one who told her?"

"Yeah. She paid me in chocolates." I shrugged. "What else was I supposed to do?"

"So, Nate." Felicity jumped in. "Where did you find the stone you gave Gracie?"

"You mean the dragon egg?" Stone glanced at Gracie, who sat at the smaller table with her brother and cousins. She looked up at him and smiled. He winked before continuing. "I've always liked rocks." He shrugged. "It might have something to do with my name."

Everyone laughed and gave him their undivided attention. "I didn't know my grand-dad well, but he was always showing me his rock collection. Naturally, I started one of my own. When I was in the Middle East, I came across a few that I brought home. Gracie's was one of them. It's a black onyx, and I had it polished; that's why it's so smooth."

"Wow. That's so cool." Felicity set down her fork. "So what's your favorite type of stone?"

"That's a tricky question. There are three types of stones: igneous, sedimentary, and metamorphic. I tend to like gemstones the most because they're pretty and have the most value. Gemstones are usually igneous rocks that are mostly found in areas where magma cools and crystallizes, deep in the Earth's crust."

My brows rose. Wow. He really did know his rocks.

Felicity nodded. "Gemstones. Like diamonds. Yeah. I like those the best too. What's the most unusual stone you have in your collection?"

Stone shrugged. "The most unusual? I don't know. I like black stones the most because they're so rare. With that in mind, I have one that's called a Shungite. But I'd really like to get my hands on a black opal. They're rare... and extremely expensive."

"I have an opal my brother gave me," Mom said. "He brought it home from Australia."

A squeal came from the kid's table, and Will's wife, Emma, told her kids they had to finish their food if they wanted any cake. A few minutes later, the kids scattered to play in the yard, and my mom left to get the cake, while we cleaned up the table.

As we threw our paper plates in the garbage, I caught Stone's arm. "Sorry about all the questions."

He grinned. "I enjoyed it. Not too many people like to hear about rocks."

"That's true, but I don't think you're off the hook yet. If I know my brother, he'll corner you for sure. If you want, we can leave right after Gracie opens her presents."

"And miss the cake?"

"Well... no. But after that."

Stone placed his hands on my shoulders. "I'm fine, Sen. Don't worry about me. We can stay as long as you want."

My lips twisted at his use of my nickname. "If you say so, Nate. But don't tell me I didn't warn you."

He chuckled and put his arm around me before we stepped back to the table. I didn't even try to stop him. It was hard not to believe he meant it. Could my heart get any bigger without bursting out of my chest? I couldn't stop a goofy grin from spreading over my face. I caught Felicity watching me and tried to wipe it off, but she sent me a raised brow and a knowing dip of her head.

Mom brought out the cake, and we all sang to Gracie. She had to compete with the other kids to blow out her candles, but managed to get them out with the first try.

After eating our cake and ice cream, the presents came next, followed by all the kids running off to play. I went inside to help Felicity clean up. As I washed the plates, I glanced out the window and noticed that my brother had cornered Stone. "Ugh." I rolled my eyes. "Can't they just lay off him?"

Felicity glanced up to see them talking and shrugged. "You can't blame Will after what Brandon pulled. But I wouldn't worry. Your man is like testosterone in a bottle. I'm a little surprised that Will would even dare."

I glared at her. "He's not my man."

Her brows rose. "Yeah. Right." Her gaze moved to the window. "Uh-oh."

"What?" I glanced up to find my dad joining Will.

"They've ganged up on him."

I closed my eyes. "I didn't want Stone to come, but he insisted."

"Your text said he was a client." Her brows dipped. "Is that true? He made it sound like you've been dating for at least a little while."

My shoulders slumped and I let out a sigh. "Yeah, he's the twenty-four-seven client."

"Oh." Her eyes widened, and she gazed out at him again. "I don't think I'd complain about that situation." She paused. "You two have some serious chemistry though. Have you...?" She raised her eyebrows at me.

"No."

"You've at least kissed him though, right? He seems like he really likes you."

I squeezed my eyes shut, a blush heating my face.

"Oh, you have!" She gave a small squeal.

"Shut up." I widened my eyes at her. "It was... I wasn't thinking." I didn't want to tell her about the vision, about how much danger he was in. Or how much danger I was in because of this job. "We just, sort of... kissed."

"Oh, I get it. It was an accident. You both just turned around at the same time and your lips touched, huh? Kind of like Tommy in second grade?"

"Shut up!" I flicked water at her.

She laughed and flicked me back. After our mini water fight, we finally settled down and got back to the dishes.

"Well, either way, it's been fun having him here. And that gift was really thoughtful."

I sighed. "Yeah, I guess. But, did you hear what mom said?"

She chuckled. "Yeah... I did. She obviously sees the same thing that I do."

My lips twisted. "I think you're imagining it."

"Girl... you can't deny the attraction between the two of you. It's off the charts. We can all see it, even if you won't accept it."

My stomach dropped. This was not helping. "Sure... I admit we're attracted to each other, but he's off-limits."

"Why?"

"I already told you, he's a client."

"So what did he do that he needs you twenty-four-seven?"

I pursed my lips. "I can't talk about it."

She glanced out the window. "So he's not who he said he was?"

"He's exactly what he said. It's all true. There's just something he needs help solving, and his boss thought that, with my special skills, I could figure it out."

"So... his boss is the one who hired you?" She raised an eyebrow at me.

"Yes," I answered reluctantly. What was with the look?

"Well, if that's the case, then Nate isn't your client."

"What? Yes he is."

She grinned. "He's not the one paying you."

I groaned. "Stop."

"So, who's his boss, then?"

Shit. I did not want to tell her it was Quentin Vanetti. She'd had a fit when I told her about the last job I'd done for him. "I can't tell you that either."

She folded her arms and gave me a pointed stare. "It better not be who I think it is."

"And what if it is?" I threw my hands up. "What matters is that it's a job, and once it's over... I'll get paid, and then I can pay my lawyer and finally get divorced. So back off."

Felicity stared at me for a few seconds before she let out a breath, her eyes softening. "I'm sorry, Sen. I just want to make sure you're safe, that's all."

"I know."

She rubbed my arm before glancing out the window. "You know you could actually date him once the job's done."

"Ha! I don't know. I mean... I don't even know why he's pretending to be my boyfriend. He probably won't even want anything more to do with me after this. Besides, he's not the type to settle down."

She studied Stone, who had somehow managed to make Will and my dad laugh. "Okay, I get what you're saying... but seriously? Have you seen the way he looks at you? I mean..." She fanned herself. "It's pretty obvious you have feelings for each other, and with a guy like him... I think it would be worth it, even for one night. I mean... look at him. How could you regret that?"

"Oh. My. Hell!"

She laughed. "Don't tell my husband I said that."

I shook my head. "I can't believe you're telling me to have sex with someone I hardly know. What if he breaks my heart?"

"Okay, look. I'm not telling you to sleep with him, but I am telling you to give him a chance." She pulled me around and looked me in the eyes. "Serenity. From everything I've seen of him, he truly cares about you. I don't know what will come of it. Hell... nothing is guaranteed in this life. But you can't live without taking risks. At least a broken heart means you're still alive."

She turned away. "Besides, you and Brandon would have been divorced a long time ago if he'd just signed the damn papers. Seriously, don't let that asshole have any more control over your life than he already has. He just keeps taking from you. What I'm telling you to do is live for yourself."

She lifted her chin in Stone's direction, then let out a dramatic sigh and shook her head. "I'll be disappointed if you miss out and nothing happens between you two." She caught my gaze. "And it's not the sex I'm talking about; though... I mean, come on. He cares about you."

"But you don't—"

She raised her hand. "Sen. Stop. You haven't seen how he looks at you while you're talking to someone else. He seems like a hard man, but his eyes get all soft. When Will accused you of telling on him, Nate bristled, like he was ready to beat Will up. Just look at him out there."

She motioned toward the yard. Stone held Gracie in his arms, and they were laughing. He set her down, and she dragged him over to her playhouse. He was too big to go inside, but he crouched down while she showed him her kitchen.

Felicity shook her head. "It's your life. But, if you ask me, he might be worth the risk."

I swallowed past the lump in my throat. If only she was right. But she didn't know that Stone worked for a mob boss, and I was beginning to understand that he didn't just take care of security.

He'd basically confessed to shooting someone, even though it was self-defense. Then there was his reputation, and the way he'd fought Joint. All of that pointed to a lot more that I didn't know about. Did I want to be involved with someone like that?

Still, a deep yearning filled my heart. I was falling for him. And she was right, it wasn't just physical. This went much deeper. He could break my heart. After Brandon, I wasn't sure I could be that vulnerable again. Was I ready to take a chance with Stone? Even if it was just one night?

It was starting to get dark, and we needed to leave. I wasn't sure about the plan to draw Johnny out, but we needed to plant all the security cameras tonight if it had a chance of succeeding. I hoped my psychometry kicked in, so we'd know if it would work before we went through with it.

"We need to go." I turned to Felicity. "Thanks for the talk. I'll think about everything you said."

"I love you, Sis." She pulled me into a quick hug. "You know that saying from our favorite movie. *A life lived in fear—*"

"*—is a life half-lived.* I know. I love you, too." I grabbed my jacket and stepped toward the patio.

"Before you go, I've got some leftovers for you."

Glancing at Stone, I nodded her way before stepping onto the patio. I caught his eye with a wave. He nodded and brought Gracie with him so I could give her a hug. As we told everyone goodbye, Gracie gave Stone a big hug and kissed him on the cheek, raving about her cool dragon egg. Sheesh! Even a seven-year-old wasn't immune to his charms.

We made it to the car before Felicity yelled at me from the front door. "You forgot your leftovers!"

I turned to Stone. "I'll be right back." I left him standing beside the car and hurried back to the porch. "Sorry."

"Don't worry about it. If I was leaving with him, I'd be a little scatter-brained too."

I shook my head and took the plate of food.

"If you get a minute, please call me. I need details."

"You're the worst." I playfully swatted her arm before turning to leave. With a wave, I hurried across the lawn to the street.

Before stepping onto the road, I noticed a car coming down the street. I wasn't sure they could see me, so I stopped to wait for them to pass. The car came to a stop about fifty yards away, and their high-beam lights flashed on. I waited a couple more seconds to make sure they could see me before starting across.

The sound of rolling tires on the pavement confused me. I jerked my gaze to the car and terror seized my heart. It was picking up speed and heading straight for me.

Chapter 21

Serenity

Before I could scream, Stone tackled me, hurtling us out of the way. The momentum threw us to the ground, where Stone took the brunt of the fall. I rolled with him until we came to a stop in the gutter.

Stone shifted off of me. "You okay?"

"I think so."

"Serenity!" Felicity shrieked from the house. "Oh my God!" She ran down the lawn towards us.

Stone jumped to his feet, but the car was long gone. Bending down, he helped me stand. I clung to him, my legs shaking. "What the hell was that?"

Stone's hold tightened. "Someone just tried to kill you."

Felicity reached us, her gaze traveling over my body. "Holy hell! Are you okay?"

"Yeah. I'm all right."

"That car nearly hit you! I thought..." She covered her mouth with her hand. "If Nate hadn't—"

"What's going on!" Mom rushed to my side.

"What happened?" Dad yelled, coming up behind her, followed by Ryan and Will.

Felicity turned to them. "A car almost hit Serenity! I saw the whole thing! It was waiting for her to cross, but it sped up while she was in the road. It would have hit her if Nate hadn't tackled her out of the way."

"Did anyone see the car?" Will asked.

"The brights were on." I shook my head. "I didn't see a thing."

"Should we call the police?" Mom asked. "You could have been killed!" Mom jerked me into her arms. "Are you sure you're okay?"

"I'm fine. Just a little shook up." She held me tight, rocking me back and forth like I was a child. I pulled back from her smothering embrace, and Dad grabbed me next, then Felicity joined him. I held them both for a few seconds before pulling away. "I'm okay. It's fine."

"I'm calling the police." Will pulled out his phone.

I glanced at Stone. He stepped beside me, and I leaned into his arms. "Is that a problem?" I whispered.

"No. It's fine." He glanced at the others. "We should file a report with the police, but you need to be prepared that they won't be able to do much. I didn't even see what kind of car it was." He motioned to my sister. "Do you have a security camera on your house?"

Her shoulders fell. "No. I've been wanting to get one, but—"

"It's okay. Maybe one of your neighbors has one."

"I don't understand," Mom said. "They were waiting for you to cross? But then they sped up? Were they trying to hit you? Are you sure that's what happened?" Her voice got louder and more hysterical as she spoke.

"Yes!" Felicity said. "I saw the whole thing. Someone just tried to kill her! If not for Nate, she'd be dead."

"We don't know that for sure." I shook my head. A shiver ran down my spine, and I couldn't seem to stop shaking.

"Let's go inside." Stone held me close. "We're all a little shaken up, and it's going to be a while before the police show up."

I sank against him, grateful he was taking charge. As we filed into the house, Will finished his phone call to the police. "They said it would be about half an hour before anyone could get here."

Stone took me to the couch and pulled me down beside him while my mom left to get us some water to drink. Emma had kept the kids in the back yard, away from all the excitement.

Felicity sat beside me, and I turned to her. "Don't let the kids know what happened, okay? When the police get here, let's meet them outside. I don't want to ruin Gracie's birthday."

Her eyes held worry, but she pressed her lips together and nodded. "That's a good idea."

We hardly spoke before the police arrived, all of us in a state of shock. Stone and I hurried out to meet them, along with Felicity and my parents. It didn't take long to tell them everything we knew. The fact that no one saw a license plate, or the make and model of the car, didn't give them much to go on.

One of the officers pulled me aside. "I don't want to upset your family, but do you know why someone would want to kill you?"

I swallowed. "No. I have no idea."

"No husband, boyfriend, co-worker, or ex-lover?"

"My husband and I are going through a divorce, but I can't believe he'd want me dead."

The officer's brows drew together, and she glanced at Stone. "Is that him?"

"No... that's... he's a friend."

"Okay. So what's the name of your ex?"

"Brandon Jones."

"You have an address and phone number for him?"

"Sure." I gave it to her, and she added it to her notes.

"Okay. Anyone else?"

I shook my head. "Not that I can think of."

"I'll file a report and see if one of our detectives can look into it. In the meantime, I'd suggest you be extra careful, and let us know if anything else happens." I nodded and she put her pad away. "We'll be in touch."

"Thank you."

As they drove away, Stone came to my side. He'd had to give them his name as a witness, and I worried it would be bad for him. "I'm sorry you had to talk to them."

He raised a brow. "Don't be. It's not a problem." He sighed. "Can we go now? Not that I don't like your family, but they're a little much, and we need to talk."

A smile crossed my lips. "No kidding." We stepped to where my parents and Felicity stood. "We're going home now."

My mom's brows rose. "But someone just tried to kill you. I don't want you in your house by yourself. You should stay here, where you'll be safe."

Oh crap. Now what?

"She won't be alone." Stone wrapped his arm around me. "I'll be staying with her."

"Oh." Mom glanced at Dad and Felicity, and then back at me. "Really?"

I nodded. "Yes. Nate told you he was in security, so he's been helping me. He already installed a security camera on my front porch and changed the locks."

"Why? Has someone been threatening you?"

"No. Nothing like that. I just don't want Brandon to get in the house when I'm not there. In case he made a copy of the key."

"Oh... right."

"I thought it was a good idea," Stone said. "And after this, I'm getting a security system set up as well." He glanced at my mom. "I'll make sure she's fine, and I'm going to find out who did this. They won't get away with it, I promise."

My mom's eyes widened, then she rushed forward and threw her arms around Stone. "Thank you, Nate. I don't know what's going on, but I'm so glad you and Serenity are together."

Caught by surprise, it took Stone a few seconds before he returned the hug and patted her on the back.

I did a mental head-slap. Did she just say we were together?

She stepped away, only to have Felicity throw her arms around him and thank him as well. After she was done, my dad stepped forward. Stone braced for another hug, but Dad held out his hand, instead.

As Stone shook his hand, Dad leaned toward him and lowered his voice. "I'm trusting you have the resources to take care of my daughter?"

"Yes, sir. I'll protect her. You have my word."

My dad gave him a nod before pulling me into his arms. "Sen. I love you, sweetie. I wouldn't let you go if I didn't think you'd be safe."

"Thanks Dad. I'll be fine, I promise." After I hugged my mom and Felicity, we hurried across the street to my car. I fumbled with the keys, and Stone took them from my hand.

"I'll drive."

I nodded and slipped into the passenger seat. My family watched as we drove away, and I sent them a wave before glancing at Stone. "Holy hell."

Stone snorted. "Yeah. That was... unexpected."

"The way my mom and Felicity threw themselves at you? Or the nearly-getting-killed part?"

He snorted. "The hugs were kind of nice. But... I don't get it. Why are you a target? Is there something I'm missing?"

"I know. It doesn't make any sense." I swallowed, still shocked that I'd nearly died. What the freak? It couldn't be real. Why would someone want to kill me?

The rest of the drive went by in a blur, and Stone pulled the car into the garage, shutting off the engine. I opened my car door, and Stone unlocked the door to the house and ushered me inside. I flipped on the kitchen lights and slipped off my jacket. "I need to sit down."

"Let's go in the living room." Stone took off his jacket and draped it over the chair with mine. I flipped the light switch, turning on the lamps and filling the room with golden light. Stone pulled the drapes shut and came to sit beside me on the couch.

I turned to face him. "What do we do now? Maybe it was all a mistake, and they just thought I was you?"

"Babe... I hate to break it to you, but you look nothing like me."

"Fine. But why would someone want me dead?" I blinked, surprised that my eyes had filled with tears.

Stone reached for me, and I gladly fell into his arms. He held me firmly against his chest, and I took comfort in hearing his heart pound beneath my ear in a soothing rhythm. I breathed in his scent, and felt his strength surround me. Slowly, the tightness in my throat began to loosen.

"Thanks for saving me. I... couldn't even move."

His hold tightened and he kissed the top of my head. "Yeah. It shocked me, too. I'm glad I was right there, but try not to get almost killed again, okay?"

I sighed. "I'll do my best."

"Good. Because I'm pretty sure you're the only person who would even consider saving my sorry ass." He shook his head. "We're quite the pair. But at least that makes us even now, right?"

I snorted. "No way. I've saved your life more than once, and I have wounds to prove it. You're not even close."

"Hmm... I suppose that's true." He shook his head. "I still don't get it. Who would want you dead? And why? Do you think it's because of me?"

"How could it be? The driver obviously knew I was at my sister's house and waited for me to come out. Who would even know about that?"

"The only person I told was Vanetti, and we know he doesn't want you dead."

I closed my eyes. "So, the only person who'd do this is Brandon, but he'd get nothing if I died. I changed my will, so all my assets go to Felicity, whether I'm married to Brandon or not."

"Does he know that?"

I shrugged. "Maybe not, but even then it's hardly worth the risk. I mean... maybe if I had millions... but I don't. So why would he do it?"

"Anger? Jealousy? Who knows?"

"I can't believe it's him, but I can't think of anyone else."

His lips twisted. "Have you done any other jobs where you've made an enemy or two?"

I tried not to laugh. "Hardly. I haven't done that many jobs. So. No." A car honked outside and I tensed. "Do you think we're safe here?"

"Yes. Although I'd feel better if you had an alarm system. I'll have to get one for you tomorrow. But we're good for now."

I shook my head. "I appreciate that, but alarm systems cost money, and I don't have enough for one. Besides, you have to keep paying them monthly for it to do any good."

"Babe. Let me do this for you. I'll put it in my name and pay the fee. It's the least I can do. Besides, I promised your Dad. You don't want to make me a liar, do you?"

"No... but..." He put a finger over my lips, and I raised my eyes to his.

"Please, Sen. Let me do this."

My heart squeezed. I didn't know if it was the concern in his eyes, or the use of my nickname, but something shifted inside of me. My breath caught and sudden tears filled my eyes.

I tried to hold my emotions in check, but I couldn't make them stop. I knew most men hated crying women, and Stone was probably horrified. "Sorry. I'm just a little overwhelmed. It's been kind of a crazy couple of days."

He wrapped both arms around me, and I laid my head against his chest.

"We'll figure this out. You didn't die, so we've got time to get to the bottom of it."

I sniffed. "But I'm supposed to be protecting you. Not the other way around. I'm even getting paid the big bucks for it."

"True." He leaned his cheek against the top of my head. "But, I want to protect you, and not just because you saved me. I want you, Sen."

"You do?" My mouth dropped open. "Are you saying..." I pulled away to meet his gaze, noticing the flecks of gold in his dark eyes. "...that you... really want...?"

His eyes darkened. "Do you?"

Swallowing, I nodded.

His lips were only inches from mine, and he waited a split second before lowering his mouth.

Right before his lips brushed mine, I raised my fingers to his lips. He hesitated, then pulled back. Lowering my hand, I swallowed. It took all my courage to say the words, but I needed him to know how I felt. Once he knew that this meant more to me than simply paying him back, he may never kiss me again.

"First of all, you need to know that this... what's happening between you and me... it isn't just lust for me."

He brushed his fingers across my cheek. "So... this *thing* between us, it's not just... a fling?"

I turned my cheek to rest in his cupped hand. "Not for me." I took a deep breath and met his gaze. "So... if you're not okay with that... tell me now."

His lips twitched and his gaze bored into mine. "Damn, you're so beautiful." He leaned in to kiss my forehead, then my cheeks, my nose, the side of my mouth. "I'm more than okay with it."

"Really?" My heart practically soared out of my body.

His lips moved to my neck, just below my ear, then he continued to rain kisses down the side of my neck. My breath caught, and I closed my eyes, twisting to give him better access.

"There's nowhere..." His lips moved up to my face. "I'd rather be. Than here..." He kissed the side of my mouth. "...with you."

My heart lurched, and I turned my face to meet his lips. His tender kiss sent my pulse racing. All my worry and fear evaporated, replaced by a haze of yearning desire. He was here, and I felt safe in his arms. I wanted this... oh, did I want it.

The kiss deepened, robbing me of thought. Desire rushed through my body, sending my pulse racing. Giving in, I climbed into his lap, pushing him down onto the couch. Lying on top of him, I pulled away to breathe, and his lips brushed against my arched neck.

Lowering my lips to his, I plastered my body against him. His arms came around me and his hands lifted my shirt, pulling it up to expose my back to the cool air. A small voice in the back of my mind sent a warning that if I didn't stop this now, I would regret it. Then I heard my sister's voice saying I would regret it all right, but only if I didn't give him a chance.

All at once, Stone pulled away, breaking the kiss. "Someone's at the door."

A loud knocking sounded, jolting my heart with panic. "Are you kidding me?"

"You want to ignore it?"

"Yes." The pounding kept up, and I held still, hoping whoever it was would go away.

"Serenity? You in there?"

Oh my gosh! It was Brandon. What the freak? Before I could move, the door knob jiggled but didn't open. I could hear keys jingling and his attempts to get the door unlocked. His loud muttering that I must have changed the locks came next. Then he used a few choice curses before trying the door again.

I pushed against Stone's chest and sat up, moving off his lap. Stone stepped silently to the window and lifted the curtain so he could see Brandon. I covered my mouth and watched Brandon's shadowy form through the marbled glass on the door panel. He tried the knob one more time before turning to leave.

Stone stayed where he was, watching until Brandon drove away. "He's gone."

I shook my head and put my face in my hands. Anger and frustration flooded my veins. Could anything else go wrong tonight? I couldn't even look at Stone. I had to face it, my life was a mess.

Here I was, worried about getting involved with a possible hitman for the mob, and Stone was probably thinking my life was a nightmare. If anything, he was grateful for the interruption.

Pulling my hands away from my face, I glanced his way. "I guess it's a good thing you changed the locks."

Stone came back to my side and sat down. "I kind of wished I hadn't. It would have been interesting to see his face when he walked in on us, don't you think?"

My eyes widened. "He would have gone ballistic." I shivered just thinking about it.

"Yeah, but then I could have beaten the shit out of him. It would have been totally worth it."

I lifted a brow, but couldn't stop the grin that twisted my lips. Just imagining Stone punching Brandon a few times lightened my heart. I shook my head. I was a terrible person for wishing that, but since it didn't actually happen, maybe I wasn't so bad.

"I like seeing you smile like that. The sadness is gone, and you look ready to take on the world."

My brows rose. "Really?"

"Yeah. It's sexy as hell."

My breath caught, and I grinned, turning toward him. "You know what's sexy?" I pushed him back on the couch and moved onto his lap again. "You... without a shirt."

I began to unbutton his shirt, running my fingers over his taut stomach muscles as I went. "You know... the first time I touched your skin, I felt an electric shock run through me."

I undid the last button and spread his shirt apart. Taking in his sculpted muscles and defined pecs, I swallowed before spreading my hands over his skin, exploring every inch of his hot perfection. A soft moan escaped my lips.

My gaze met his, and heat surged through me. His dark, hypnotic gaze swept over me, and he reached for my waist, his hands slipping under my shirt to gently expose my skin. His fingers roamed over my ribs and lower back, giving me time to accept or reject his touch. I raised my arms, and he tugged my shirt up to push it over my head. I pulled it from my arms, sending it to the floor.

Gazing at my chest, he swallowed. My black lacy bra showed the swell of my breasts, and he raised his hand toward my collarbone, tracing a line from my neck to my cleavage. My skin tingled beneath his fingers, and shivers ran down my spine. I watched his eyes darken, and my pulse raced in response to the erotic feel of his touch.

He sat up, pushing his shirt off his arms, and bringing his hands around to support my back. He leaned in to trail kisses down my neck, and I ran my fingers through his hair. As he kissed the swell of my breasts, he released the bra clasp, and pulled it away from my skin.

"Oh, baby, oh baby." Staring at my breasts, his husky voice sent my pulse racing. Then his fingers traced the long scar below my left breast and down my stomach. "From the accident?"

"Yes. It looks hideous—"

"No. It just means you survived something terrible." His fingers brushed along the scar before he lowered his mouth to kiss the puckered skin. "You're beautiful."

Tracing the scar with his lips back to my breast, he used his tongue to caress first one, and then the other. I'd never thought my small breasts were anything special, but the way he suckled them sent all my worries out the window.

His breathy declaration sent fire through my core, and my body responded to his slightest touch, humming with anticipation and desire. Never in my life had I experienced such deep yearning for fulfillment.

His lips left my breasts and met my lips, his kisses gentle at first and then becoming more demanding. Sucking and tugging on my lips and tongue soon became an erotic dance.

Pulling away to breathe, he gathered me in his arms, tugging me tight against his naked flesh. Feeling his hard muscles and soft skin rubbing my breasts sent ripples of desire down my spine.

His lips found my ear, and his soft breath and wet tongue sent jolts of pleasure through my core. I returned the favor and kissed his neck, breathing in his amazing scent and feeling his pulse begin to race.

Urgency throbbed through my blood. I couldn't wait any longer. I wanted to feel all of him. Sensing my readiness, Stone rose to his feet, still holding me in his arms, and kissed my lips. As my feet touched the ground, his hands moved to my jeans and he easily unclasped the button and pulled down the zipper.

He stepped away, breathing heavily while his gaze raked over my half-naked body. Feeling a sudden chill, I wanted to close the gap between us, but the way his eyes devoured me filled me with anticipation.

A smile tilted my lips, and I reached for the belt on his jeans. His left brow rose, but he did nothing to help me with the buckle. His breath caught as I undid his pants and pulled down the zipper.

That feeling of power only lasted a heartbeat before I glanced down at his flat stomach and the V between his hips. Holy hell. I wanted to shove his pants out of the way to see more, but I also wanted this moment to last.

The sexual tension between us was off the charts, and each second we waited made it more powerful. The desire in his eyes held a desperation that matched my own.

The last few days of keeping my distance from him was like holding back an avalanche. I didn't know what we had, but he'd become much more to me than a job. Maybe none of this made sense, and I'd never see him again once the job was done, but right now, I'd take this moment over never having it at all.

He reached for me, but I stepped back. Doubt flared in his eyes until I kicked my shoes off and tugged my jeans down my hips. As they fell around my feet, I stepped out of them, wearing only a black, lace thong. He took a step toward me, but I held up my hand again.

Stopping, he swallowed, his eyes darkening as he drank in the sight of my body. He closed them for a split second, signs of strain on his face. "Babe... I don't know how much more of this I can take. I want you so bad it hurts."

Feeling more powerful, I slowly pushed my underwear down my body, watching his chest catch while he held his breath. Fully exposed and vulnerable, I stepped closer to him, trailing my fingers across his chest. He quivered at my touch, and I glanced into his eyes with a saucy grin. "I kind of like you like this."

His lips twisted into that sexy grin of his, and it took all my will power to play this game I'd started. "Babe... you're killing me."

I glanced down at his jeans and my mouth went dry. I knew he was a big guy, but if that bulge was any indication, he wasn't kidding about it hurting. "Uh... we'd better get you out of those."

He bent down to take off his shoes and socks, before straightening. "You want to finish this?" He raised a brow, challenging me.

I chewed on my bottom lip, unsure if I could do it without causing him pain. "Uh... okay. I'll try and be careful, but no promises."

He snorted, but waited for me to get busy. Instead of pushing his jeans down, I ran my hands over his chest and down his stomach to the V of his groin. Using both hands, I turned them so my fingers were pointed down his thighs and began to move them lower. His earthy scent filled my nostrils, and I wondered why the hell I was taking so long.

Stone inhaled sharply, then tugged his jeans away from his body to finish the job.

"Whoa." My eyes widened, and I glanced over his body while he kicked his jeans away from his feet. Now it was my turn to drink my fill, and he held perfectly still while my gaze roamed over every perfect inch of him. He literally took my breath away. "Wow."

A satisfied grin split his lips before he moved toward me. I stepped his way at the same time, and our bodies crashed somewhere in the middle. I stood on my tiptoes and plastered my breasts against his chest. For some reason, I couldn't seem to get close enough.

Stone picked me up and carried me into my bedroom. Laying me on my bed, he followed, taking me with him to his side. Gently holding my head, his frantic kisses stole my breath until I could hardly breathe.

We both pulled apart. Breathing heavily, he met my gaze. "I need a condom."

Still breathless, I managed to speak. "I have some... right there. In my bedside table. Top drawer."

Relief filled his eyes, and he stepped from the bed and pulled the drawer open, only taking a moment to find one and open the foil.

"Let me." Scooting to the edge of the bed, I took it from him. Swallowing, my lips dropped open as I slid it over his erection. He groaned and I glanced up at him, an impish grin on my face. He narrowed his eyes, hesitating a moment before he began to tickle me.

I shrieked and tried to escape, moaning and laughing at the same time. We fell on the bed and our wrestling movements turned into passion. He claimed my lips, and his hands roamed over my body, rubbing expertly over my core and sending me into oblivion. Our movements changed into a frantic rhythm, only slowing for a few seconds while he paused to enter me.

I opened for him, and a shudder rushed through me to feel him inside. I groaned, wanting to take every inch of him into my core, and savoring each and every second of this moment in his embrace.

Our movements became a steady rhythm, climbing faster and faster and continuing until all thought left me and I soared into the stratosphere. Then his thrusts took me even higher into the dark sky where bright stars exploded like fireworks around me. The electric charge of pure pleasure burst through my body, and I let it all out, his name spilling from my lips.

Chapter 22

Stone

My chest heaved as I cradled Serenity against me, the last vestiges of pleasure shuddering through my body. Her ragged breathing brushed against my skin and I held her close, an unfamiliar tightness in my chest. I'd loved hearing my name pour from her lips as she'd climaxed. But it wasn't enough. I wanted to hear it again and again and again.

After all that had happened in the last couple of days, I suddenly realized that there was nothing I wouldn't do to keep Serenity safe. Nothing. I didn't know what that meant exactly, but the truth of it burned in my heart.

I didn't want to think about the car barreling toward her tonight. It had scared the shit out of me. But it wasn't just that. The last few days with her had changed me. Even though I'd balked at being saddled with her, I'd also enjoyed every minute of it.

I hadn't wanted to admit that I looked forward to her comments and reactions. The way she wouldn't put up with my bullshit, but still looked at me like I mattered. She added a new dimension to my life that I didn't know I was missing. She brought light and joy into my heart, those simple things I'd lost after my mom died.

To lose her would be like losing something unique and precious, and that scared me even more. I hated being vulnerable, but I'd come to trust her. I knew if she ever broke my heart, it would be because I deserved it, not because of anything she did. I'd just have to make sure that never happened.

Serenity snuggled closer, a shiver running over her cooling body. "Let's get you under the covers. I've got to clean up, but I'll be right back."

Her languid gaze met mine, and she nodded while I helped her pull the comforter back. After she climbed between the sheets, I tucked her in and hurried into the bathroom.

I came back a minute later and slipped in beside her. I thought she was asleep until she scooted close and flung her arm over my chest. Her deep breathing came a minute later, and I closed my eyes, enjoying the feel of her soft body against mine.

Sharing her bed felt right, and it wasn't long before my eyes drooped shut and I slept.

—◦+ ⬥⬦⬥ +◦—

The sound of a ringing phone invaded my sleep, and I stirred, opening my eyes to the dark room. A soft, warm body curled around my back, reminding me of where I was and all that had happened.

My phone quit ringing, and I relaxed until it started up again. Slipping out of bed, I stepped down the hall and into the living room where I'd left my clothes. Digging my phone from my pocket, I swiped to answer.

"What?"

"Hey man," Razor said. "Where are you?"

I checked my watch. "Shit. I'll be there soon." I didn't wait to hear his curses, and disconnected. It was four in the morning, and I was supposed to be at Razor's place twenty minutes ago.

Picking up my discarded clothes, I hurried into the guest bedroom and found the black clothes I'd brought. I debated waking Serenity, but she'd been through so much lately, I wasn't sure she needed to come. I'd be fine without her. Of course, she'd probably hate that, so I'd better wake her up after all.

I checked my gun and slipped it into my shoulder holster and looked for my leather jacket.

"Going somewhere?"

My breath caught, and I turned to find Serenity leaning against the door jam, a short, silky blue robe wrapped around her. With one brow cocked, and her lips pursed, I knew I was in trouble.

"Razor called. We need to go. How fast can you get ready?"

"Were you going to leave without me?"

I stepped toward her and she stiffened, so I got real close to her and lowered my voice. "I thought about it. But no. I was going to wake you up."

"Oh." Her shoulders relaxed, but only slightly. "You're not lying to me, are you?"

I folded my arms. "Babe... do you think I'm stupid?"

Her lips twitched. "You really want me to answer that?"

Growling, I reached for her, but she dodged my hand and scurried into her bedroom. I followed behind, but she slammed the door in my face. I didn't hear the lock turn, so I could have gone in, but I let it go instead.

If I went in there now to exact my revenge, it would be morning before we made it to Razor's shop. I'd just have to wait. Thinking about how I'd make her pay sent a smile across my lips. Oh, I'd get my revenge all right, and I looked forward to every minute of it.

Unsure how long she'd take, I ambled into the kitchen and warmed up the coffee, knowing it would be morning before we came back, and I needed a jolt of caffeine.

Just as I poured a cup, she hurried out, her hair pulled back into a ponytail, with a black cap on her head. She was dressed in a black, long-sleeved shirt, and some kind of black exercise leggings that hugged every inch of her long legs. Shit. How was I supposed to concentrate on work when she looked like that?

"Something wrong?"

"You should put on a coat. Or a sweater. It's probably cold."

Her brows rose. "I'll wear my leather jacket. It's right by yours."

"Fine. Let's go." I grabbed her keys and stepped to the door.

"What about your coffee?"

"It's fine."

"I have a thermos I can put it in. Give me a second." She pulled a gray bottle out of the cupboard and filled it with coffee. "You want it black?"

"Sure." While she screwed on the lid, I unlocked the door and stepped into the connecting garage. "You mind if I drive?"

She shrugged. "Not at all."

Soon, we were backing out of the garage. "We have to stop at the office for the camera equipment, but it shouldn't take too long."

"Yeah, that's right. Did Razor sound mad?"

"Yes. He'd been waiting for a while." I shook my head. "For some reason, I forgot all about our appointment." I glanced her way and she flushed.

"Yeah. Me too."

Twenty minutes later, we pulled into the parking garage and parked close to the elevators. My car and motorcycle were the only vehicles there, along with one other car I didn't recognize.

Before I opened the car door, Serenity grabbed my arm. "Wait. Give me your hand."

I held it out and she took it, closing her eyes and breathing slowly. A few seconds later, she shook her head. "I didn't get anything, so we must be good to go."

"Good. Let's hurry."

Using my pass-key, we made it to the twenty-sixth floor in short order. The equipment was in the security office in a large closet. I got three cameras and a controller, and locked everything back up.

Soon, we were on the road to Razor's shop. After arriving, instead of parking in front of the shop, I pulled around to the back entrance. The main garage door was open with a lone light in the back by the desk.

I couldn't see Razor anywhere, and tension flooded my shoulders. Where was he? From the shadows, Razor stepped to the door and waved at me to come in before disappearing back inside.

"One more time." Serenity held out her hand and I took it. This time her eyes widened and she stared blankly ahead. Damn. She must be seeing something. She gasped and blinked several times before coming back to herself.

Her brows drew together, and her gaze turned toward the building. "Razor's in trouble." I moved to open the door, but she stopped me. "Wait! You can't go in there. You'll die."

"What's going on?"

"It's a trap. We have to drive away. Now."

"But what about Razor?"

She lowered her gaze. "It's not good, no matter what we do."

"If we leave, will he die?"

She glanced at me, her eyes wide, and nodded.

"Shit. There has to be another way."

She closed her eyes. "This is what I saw. Razor's sitting in his office. The guy... Johnny... is sitting by Razor and holding a gun. As soon as you walk inside, he shoots you and then kills Razor."

"Okay. So he's waiting for me. That means I can still draw him out. I have a plan. I'm going in."

She grabbed my arm. "Nate."

"I can't leave Razor to die. I'll draw Johnny out and shoot him first. He doesn't know that I know he's there. It will work."

"Fine. Then I'm coming, too." She pulled her gun from her purse and loaded it.

"Sen... I don't know."

"I do. You need my help. I'm here, and I'm coming with you."

I let out a breath. "Okay. This is what we'll do. I'll go in through the garage, but I'll stop just inside the door. I'll drag a ladder or chair or something to make noise, and yell at Razor to come out and help me. That should draw Johnny out, and I'll be ready for him."

She nodded. "Okay. While you're doing that, I'll skirt around the car that's on the platform and take cover behind it. I'll be able to see everything from there. If anything goes wrong, I'll have a clear shot."

I raised a brow. Would she really shoot him? Her determined gaze settled it. "Fine. Let's go."

Leaving the keys in the ignition, I slipped out of the car, and we hurried to the entrance. Serenity quickly ducked the other way around the car and crouched behind it. I stepped further inside and found a ladder. Quickly taking it down from the wall, I pulled it across the floor.

"Razor! I know you're mad, but can you at least come out and help me?" Hearing nothing, I called to him again. "Razor. Come on man, are you really gonna make me do this by myself? It's gonna take twice as long."

Not getting a response, I realized Johnny wasn't falling for it. "Fine. I'll do it myself." I started dragging the ladder outside the entrance and set it up in front of the garage door.

Just as I got it open, Razor stepped from the back room. He didn't move past the doorway, so Johnny had to be holding a gun to his back.

"I need to show you something, first," he called. "Why don't you come on back, we can get the cameras set up after that."

"If it's about Joint, I'm not interested." I twisted to pull my gun from my holster.

"It's not. But I think I figured out who set you up."

"You mean it wasn't Cash?"

"Oh, Cash was involved, but you're gonna want to see this."

"Fine. But can you grab that drill for me? It's right there, next to that car."

Razor didn't hesitate and dropped to his stomach. He rolled under the car beside him, exposing a man with a ball cap crouching behind. The man rose to his full height and fired at me.

I'd been expecting it, and had already taken cover behind the car. I took a shot at Johnny, and he jerked back, grabbing his arm. He roared with anger and quickly ducked back into Razor's office.

I started toward the office, but another shot came from Serenity's position. He must have been waiting for me, and she shot at him to scare him off. It must have worked, because the sound of breaking glass reached me. Had he gone out the office window?

Rushing back to the garage entrance, I ran to the side of the building, hoping to catch him. He'd already sprinted down the alley to the front of the shop. I started to follow, and he turned to face me. As I took another step toward him, he lobbed a small object that looked like a grenade my way.

"Shit!" I pivoted back the way I'd come and took a flying leap, hoping to make it out of the way before it exploded. The blast sent me flying, and pain lanced through my left calf and lower thigh muscles. I rolled on the ground, coming to rest behind the relative safety of the building.

The brick wall where I'd been standing began to crumble and fell in a heap, just inches from my body. Coughing from the dust, I quickly rolled to my stomach and shoved to my feet.

Pain lanced through my leg, and I went down on one knee. Somewhere along the way, I'd lost my gun. As I scrambled to look for it, footsteps sounded on the broken bricks. Was he coming to finish the job? Where was my gun?

As I rolled back behind the remains of the wall, Serenity reached me. Before she could say a word, we both heard footsteps closing in on us. Her eyes narrowed, and she stepped closer to the edge of the wall. Raising her gun, she crouched low and swiveled around the corner, taking a quick shot before taking cover again. The footsteps made a hasty retreat, and she moved into position for another shot. Rising to her feet, she took aim, but held back.

"He's getting away." In the distance, a car door slammed, and the car took off down the street. "I missed." She turned to me, noticing that I hadn't moved. "You're hurt." Dropping beside me, her hands roamed over my chest. "Where?"

"My leg. It's not too bad." I groaned. "Just some shrapnel."

"What should I do?"

Before I could answer, Razor rushed to stand beside us. "Shit. He was gonna kill me."

Serenity turned to him. "Nate's hurt. Do you have a first aid kit? I need to stop the bleeding."

"Sure. I'll be right back."

Serenity's brows drew together. "Show me where you're hurt."

"It's in the back of my thigh and my calf. Just help me up, and get me to Dix. He can take care of it." I managed to stand, keeping my weight on one leg, and holding onto the side of the building.

"Sure, but let me at least wrap it."

Razor returned, opening the pack. Serenity grabbed a pad and placed it over the wound on my thigh. "I can still see the shrapnel, so it's not too deep, but I'm leaving it there." Using some stretch tape, she wound it around the pad. Next, she did the same thing for the wound on my calf.

"That should hold it," Serenity said.

"Good." I turned to Razor. "What happened?"

Razor shook his head. "I have no idea. One minute I'm alone, and the next, he's standing there with a gun in my face. I never said a word about it, I swear."

Sirens sounded in the distance. "We need to go." I draped my arm over Serenity's shoulders and limped toward her car. "Don't tell them I was here."

"I won't. I know what to do."

"Oh... and find my gun before they get here. It's in the rubble somewhere."

Razor started in that direction, and Serenity opened the passenger door. I slipped inside, hissing at the sharp pain. She hurried around to the driver's side and drove out of the lot. "Where am I going?"

"There's an all-night urgent care on Third West and Main. I'll call Dix, and he'll meet us there."

"Okay."

I found my phone and put the call through. Dix picked up right away and said he'd be there in about fifteen minutes. Whatever Vanetti paid him was totally worth it. I let out a sigh and disconnected, grateful Vanetti had a doctor on call.

Closing my eyes, I laid my head back. "How did he know? No one knew we were going to be there except Vanetti and Razor."

"Maybe there's a bug in Razor's office? Cash could have hidden it. We've been there enough times that Johnny would know what was going on. And you've called Razor while he was in his office, too. That has to be how he found out."

I shook my head. "I should have checked."

"Hey. You didn't know. Besides, I think you may have hit him with your shot. He jerked to the side, so he's probably wounded. That should slow him down."

"Yeah. But it wasn't enough to stop him from throwing that grenade."

"Is that what it was? Where would you get something like that?"

I shifted in my seat and grimaced. "I know a few places. Maybe we can get a lead on him from them."

Serenity nodded. "There's the urgent care."

"Good. Pull around to the back, and we'll wait for the doc."

"Okay."

We were only there for a few minutes before Dix pulled in. He used his key and opened the back entrance. After slipping inside, he held the door open for us. Leading us to a curtained area, he stopped beside an exam table. "What have we got?"

"There's shrapnel in my leg from a grenade."

Dix's brows rose. "Okay. Let's get the bandages off." He glanced at Serenity while he went to work. "How's the head?"

Her eyes widened. "Good. I forgot all about it."

He chuffed. "I'll bet." He motioned to me. "You're going to have to drop your pants and get on the table. There's a drape you can cover yourself with. I'll be back in a minute with what I need." He left, and Serenity took his place.

"Here, let me help." She unlaced my boots and helped me slip them off. I took off my jacket and handed it to her. Unbuckling my belt, I carefully lowered my pants over my wounds. I wasn't a novice when it came to shrapnel, but I'd forgotten how painful it could be.

Serenity helped me finish taking them off, and her face went pale. She took a deep breath and frowned. "That looks like it hurts."

I slipped onto the table to lay on my stomach, and Serenity put the drape over my ass.

"You're not wrong."

Dix came back in, took a long look at my leg, and shook his head. "I don't know how you do it, but you're one lucky son-of-a-bitch. Only a couple places that need stitches, and I can pluck out the rest."

He glanced at Serenity. "I'll be done in about half an hour. You can sit over there if you want, or wait in the waiting room."

She swallowed, and I remembered how much she hated the sight of blood. I fully expected her to leave, but she stepped over to the chair and took out her phone. "I'll stay."

The doc got to work numbing each wound. If I didn't know better, I'd think he enjoyed stabbing me with that needle. At least I couldn't feel it when he started digging out the shrapnel.

He was right. Considering how close that grenade had come, I was lucky to have found cover in time. Lucky Stone... and I didn't even have that rock in my pocket.

Shit! So much for my plan to draw Johnny out. I had a feeling that I knew him from somewhere, but I couldn't put it together, and it had been too dark to see his face.

Good thing Serenity had scared him off. Too bad her shot hadn't hit him, but I'd take what I could get. She thought I'd hit his arm, so it wasn't a total loss; still, it frustrated me to no end that he'd nearly succeeded... again. What the hell? Was I losing my touch? Without Serenity, I'd be dead.

So far, nothing had worked. Even his tattoos had been a dead end. If things didn't change soon, my luck just might run out. But that wasn't the worst of it. Just like my days in the army, people around me tended to die. Razor had gotten lucky because of Serenity. But now I had to worry that, because of me, she could be next.

Chapter 23

Serenity

It seemed to take forever before Dix was done with Nate's leg. I'd finally gotten used to hearing bits of metal hitting the pan on the stainless steel tray. He'd said Nate was lucky that it wasn't worse, but it looked pretty bad to me.

Finally, Dix said he was done with Nate's wounds. "Before you go, how long has it been since you had a tetanus shot?"

Nate shook his head. "I don't know."

"Okay. Stay put. I'll be right back."

After he left, I ventured to Nate's side to see the damage.

He lifted his head to look, but couldn't see much. "How does it look?"

"Not too bad. There're stitches in only a couple of places, and a bunch of bandages on the rest. Does it hurt much?"

"Not yet. I'm sure once the numbness wears off, it will." Nate swiveled off the table, and got to his feet.

Dix returned with two syringes. "One is for tetanus, and the other's an antibiotic. Hold still." He stuck one in Nate's arm, and the other in his backside. "Okay. You're good to go. I'll take the stitches out in a week. In the meantime, try not to tear them."

"Thanks."

After Dix left, I helped steady Nate while he got dressed. Once his boots and jacket were on, we stepped out of the clinic. The sun was coming up, and it promised to be another beautiful day.

I took Nate's arm. "Dix didn't seem to mind getting called in to work. He must make the big bucks."

"Vanetti's generous when it comes to things like that. He takes care of his own."

"Yes. I'm finding that out." I unlocked the car and we both got in. After buckling my seatbelt, I turned his way. "Do you have another pair of pants at my house?"

"Yes."

"Okay. I'll head home then."

"Sounds good." He shook his head and let out a sigh. "So... how many times has that bastard tried to kill me now?"

"Let's see... five or six?"

"This has got to stop."

"Yeah, for sure. We need a lucky break. I wish I'd helped more. I mean... yeah, I saw the vision of Johnny holding a gun on Razor, but I wish I'd seen it sooner, so we could have warned him and avoided the whole thing."

"Hey. It kept me and Razor alive, so don't be too hard on yourself. You know, for a brief moment, right before he threw the grenade, there was something familiar about Johnny. I can't place it, but I must know him from somewhere."

"That's encouraging. Maybe it'll come to you."

"Yeah. Maybe."

A few minutes later, I pulled into the garage, and we hurried into the house. Stone left to change out of his bloody pants and clean up. I decided to cook some breakfast. He'd left his phone on the counter, and it began to buzz. I glanced at it and found the name, Aubree, on the caller ID. Wasn't that his ex-girlfriend?

A spike of jealousy hit me in the chest, and I contemplated answering it to tell her to get lost. It stopped ringing before I could decide, which was probably for the best. Still, she needed to leave him alone and move on.

I began whipping up eggs and milk for French toast, and had two pieces in the pan when Stone limped out. He'd washed all the grime off his face, but he hadn't shaved, which gave him that totally hot, dangerous, and sexy vibe.

Would I ever get tired of looking at him? Swallowing, I dished the toast onto a plate, and put two more in before glancing his way. "You want to make the coffee?"

"Sure."

While he got to work, I motioned to his phone. "You missed a call from Aubree."

He raised a brow. "Oh. I should have called her back by now, but I keep forgetting."

"What for?"

He shrugged. "I was on the phone with her in the apartment right before you saved my ass."

My brows dipped. "Oh?"

"Yeah. She and I have been done for several months now, but she keeps calling me."

"About what?"

He shrugged. "Um, that day it was about a pair of earrings that she thought she'd left in the living room. I was looking for them when you knocked me down."

"Earrings she'd left there several months ago? That you never noticed before?" I shook my head. "I'm not buying it."

His eyes narrowed. "So... what? You think she's in on it?"

"Did she hear what happened? The gunshots and everything?"

"Probably. I dropped the phone when it happened, so she would've been on the line. When I found it later, there were several missed calls from her. I was going to let her know I was okay, but I forgot."

I grimaced. "It's got to be her. She must be the link... she must have set you up. *She* got you in the living room at the right time so Johnny could take a shot at you. She knows where you go to the gym, she knows what kind of motorcycle you ride, your schedule. All of it. It makes perfect sense now. Didn't you wonder how the shooter knew where you'd be standing?"

He closed his eyes and rubbed the bridge of his nose. "Shit." He shook his head. "It makes sense, but I'm having a hard time believing it." His mouth twisted as he met my gaze. "She... well, she said she was in love with me. If that's true, then why would she want me dead?"

I raised an eyebrow. Really? "You should call her back."

"And say what?"

"Tell her you've been busy and you're sorry you didn't get back to her sooner. Maybe you could tell her you found her earrings, and you'd be happy to drop them by her place. If she's in on it, she'll jump at the chance. Either way, I can touch her and find out."

His lips turned down. "If you're right, this changes everything." After letting out a breath, he nodded. "Fine. I'll call her and put it on speaker, so you can hear what she says."

I nodded just as the phone clicked and she picked up. "Nate? Is that you? I've been so worried. Are you okay?"

"Yeah. I'm fine. Sorry I didn't call you back. I forgot."

She sucked in a breath. "Oh, sure. I get it, but last time we spoke, it sounded like something terrible was going on. You must have dropped your phone. So what was it? What happened?"

"Oh... that. It wasn't a big deal. I accidentally knocked a painting off my wall, and the glass broke. I was looking for your earrings when it happened."

"Really? That's all it was? It sounded worse."

"Yeah, but I found your earrings. Want me to drop them by your place later?"

She gasped. "You did?"

"Yup."

"Okay... you can come over. Um... let me check my schedule for the best time, and I'll call you back."

"Sure. Talk to you then." Stone disconnected and met my gaze. "Well, she definitely sounded a little nervous. You might be right." He rubbed the back of his neck. "And if she's in on it, that means she knows Johnny. But how?"

"Good question. I know that the darkness and anger I picked up in the building where he took the shot was from Johnny. So whatever he's got going with Aubree, it's benefiting him, not her. He's got to be the one behind it."

"And if you touch her, we can find out for sure. Then we can use her to get to him."

"As long as she doesn't tell him we're coming. Maybe we should surprise her? Show up at her work or something? That way she can't set a trap for you."

Nate let out a breath. "That's a good idea. But she's a real estate agent, so her office hours aren't set. I guess we could still stop by and see if we get lucky?"

I sent him a grin. "Well, that is your nickname, so it's worth a try."

"I definitely got lucky with you." He laced his fingers with mine. "But I'm a little worried."

He began kissing each of my knuckles, sending a shiver down my spine and warmth through my heart. "About what?"

"The part where I'm lucky... the lucky one. It means I always get out alive, but no-one else does. It puts you in danger, and I don't want to lose you."

"But I'm different." I pulled his hand toward my lips and kissed his knuckles. "I'm a psychic."

My phone began to ring, and I sighed. "Guess I'd better get that." I found my phone and quickly answered. "Hi Mom."

"Hey. I just wanted to call and see how you're doing."

"Everything's good."

"Is Nate there?"

I glanced his way. "Yes, he is." She didn't say anything. "Uh... why?"

"Can I talk to him?"

"What? No. I mean, you can just talk to me."

She hesitated. "Just let me talk to him for a minute. I promise I won't embarrass you."

"Mom. You already are."

"Please, Serenity. Let me talk to him."

I huffed out a breath and glanced at Stone. "She wants to talk to you."

His brows rose, but he held out his hand for the phone. "Hey, Kristin. What's up?" He listened and began to nod. "Yes. I can put it in today... no, that's not necessary. I've got it covered... no... I don't need you to pay for it." Another pause. "Yes, I'm sure... okay... yes... I'll make sure she's safe... right... okay, here she is..." He handed the phone back to me with a cocky grin on his face.

"Hey, Mom. Have a nice chat?"

"Yes. Is he... uh... sticking around for a while?"

"As far as I know."

"So... things are going okay?"

"Well, I haven't scared him off yet, if that's what you mean."

She sputtered. "I'm just worried about you. Someone nearly ran you over last night. Did you forget?"

Since that was right before the best thing that ever happened to me, I had actually forgotten all about it. "Of course not. Nate and I are working on that right now. You don't need to worry."

"That's a relief. Well, call me if you figure it out. And keep that man close."

"I'll do my best." She said that last part loud enough that I was sure Nate heard every word. We disconnected, and I closed my eyes. "Sorry about that." I opened them to find him grinning at me. "What?"

"Nothing. It's just nice that your mom cares, that's all. Since she reminded me about installing a home security system, I guess I'd better get to work."

"Sure, but what about Aubree and Johnny? And your leg? And figuring out who tried to kill me?"

He nodded. "It is a lot. As far as who's after you, it wouldn't hurt to talk to your ex in person and touch him, right?"

He had a point, but did I want to talk to Brandon? No way. "Okay. Maybe while we're out delivering earrings to Aubree, we could stop by his office. It'll be the day of exes."

A corner of his mouth quirked. "Works for me, but I might have to borrow a pair of earrings from you."

My lips twisted. "I can't wait to see her face when she realizes they're not hers."

"My thoughts exactly." Nate's phone began to ring, and my heart quickened. Was it Aubree again? He glanced at me. "It's Razor." He answered and listened while Razor filled him in on the aftermath of the explosion.

"Did you find my gun in time? ... good ... yeah, I got a few stitches, but I'm fine otherwise." Nate paused, then glanced my way. "No... *she's* the one who saved your life. You should be thanking her."

His lips flattened. "No. I'm not coming over there for a while. You can have one of your boys deliver it to me." He paused to listen. "I don't know, but we think your office might be bugged."

He pulled the phone away from his ear while Razor said a few choice swear words. "Yeah, that's too bad, but at least you have insurance, right? ... sure. We'll talk later." He ended the call.

"I take it he's not happy?"

"Nope."

"You can't blame him. How bad was the damage?"

Nate shrugged. "It only got that side of the garage, so it wasn't a total loss. Razor's checking his office for a bug, along with the rest of his place. I sure hope he finds one, otherwise it means someone's playing us both."

"Would Joint do that? Don't forget that you humiliated him yesterday."

"No. He's a hot head, but he's loyal to Razor."

His phone rang again. "It's her." He swiped to answer. "Hi Aubree." He paused to listen. "At noon?" He met my gaze and nodded. "Yeah. I know the place. Sure. See you then."

He disconnected, and my lips turned down. "A lunch date?"

"Yeah. It's a public place, so I'm not real worried it's a trap. I can introduce you as my girlfriend. She'll love that."

"Yeah... no doubt. And then even *more* people will be trying to kill me." I began to clean up the dishes and put things away. "Do you need something for the pain?"

"Yeah. I'm glad the stitches are low enough that I can still sit down, but they're starting to hurt."

"Now you know how I felt." I smirked, handing him the pills. I put the dishes in the dishwasher. "I'm going to take a shower. Will you be okay?"

"Only if I can join you."

My brows rose. "Sorry, but the Doc told you not to get the stitches wet for twenty-four hours, remember?"

"Damn." He reached for me, pulling me into his arms. "I'd like to thank you properly for saving my ass back there."

I closed my eyes, luxuriating in his embrace. Would I ever get enough of him? "You scared me, going after him like that."

"But you held him off... even if you missed." His lips twisted into that sexy half smile of his, turning my insides to mush. Still, I struggled to get away, but his hold only tightened around me.

His head dipped, bringing his lips to gently brush over mine. He nipped on my lower lip before kissing the sides of my mouth, then taking my lips in a searing kiss. My heart began to race, and everything but him faded away.

His phone began to ring. Swearing softly, he broke the kiss and glanced at it. "It's Vanetti."

I nodded and stepped away. While he answered, I headed toward my bedroom, knowing this was my best chance to get in a shower. Nate watched me go, his eyes hungry with desire. He blinked and turned away to talk, and I made my escape. As much as I wanted it, now was not the time for a repeat of last night. We had a job to do, and we were getting closer to figuring everything out.

Aubree had to be involved. It couldn't be a coincidence. And talking to Brandon was a good move for me as well. Maybe we'd have this whole thing figured out by tonight?

My heart stuttered. What did that mean for us? Would Nate go back to his place, leaving me here alone? If he didn't need me to protect him, would he forget all about me? Just the thought of being without him sent a crushing wave of pressure through my chest.

What had I done? Was one night with him all I'd get? I swallowed, knowing deep inside it would never be enough. But the last thing I wanted was to be like Aubree, clinging to something that wasn't returned. He'd said he couldn't lose me, and that gave me hope. As long as I had that, even if it didn't last, I wouldn't regret one minute of our time together.

After showering, I got ready for the day. With not a lot of sleep, I spent a few extra minutes making sure I looked and smelled good. I found Nate in my office, working on my computer. I leaned against the door jamb and drank in the sight of him. Even in my office, he looked like he belonged.

He glanced up and his eyes darkened. "Hey, beautiful. Hope you don't mind that I'm using your computer."

"Not at all. What are you looking for?"

He shook his head. "I thought I'd check out Aubree's social media posts and see if she mentions anything that would connect her to Johnny."

"Good idea. Any luck?"

"No. But I found a photo of her and me at a bar. I told her to keep me off her social feeds, so she must have posted it behind my back." He shook his head. "No wonder I ended it with her."

"Yeah... that makes sense. It's almost time to meet her, but I'm still a little worried that she's setting you up. Why don't we go to her office first? I'd rather take her by surprise."

He nodded. "That's a good idea. Before we go in, you can kiss me and see if you pick up anything that she's planning."

I smirked. "Kiss you? Yeah... that won't work."

"Why not?"

"If I'm kissing you, do you think I'll be thinking about her?"

"I hope not."

"Exactly."

He frowned. "Okay. So you have to be thinking of her when you touch me. That's how it works?"

"Yes. I'm learning as I go, but that's the way it works when I'm with you."

"Makes sense. Okay. Let's get going." Nate rose to his feet, trying not to grimace.

"How's the leg?"

"I've had worse. I'll be fine."

He grabbed his jacket and we left the house. I drove while he gave me directions to Aubree's office. Soon, we pulled into the parking lot outside her building, and I held my hand out for his.

Taking it, I concentrated on Aubree, but got absolutely nothing. I let out a breath and turned my focus to Johnny, coming up empty as well. "Maybe she's not in there."

"That's a possibility. Let's check it out."

We strode inside, and the receptionist told us she wasn't there, just like I'd thought. "Sorry. She's with a client and won't be back until this afternoon."

"Can I leave a note on her desk?" If I could get into her office, I could touch something that might give me a vision. "It's that one, right?" I started toward the door with Aubree's name on it before she could tell me not to.

"Wait. You can't—"

"Cindy, right? I'm Nate Stone. Didn't Aubree introduce us a while ago?"

With the full weight of his handsome face focused on her, she forgot all about me. "Oh... no, we never met, but she told me all about you. You're the one... I mean... yeah... she talked about you a lot. Didn't you guys break up?"

"Yeah, but we're still friends. I was hoping to catch her before lunch—"

I slipped into the office and let the door click shut behind me. While Nate did his thing, I stepped to her desk and looked for something personal that might speak to me.

It didn't look like she spent a lot of time in her small office, because there were no pictures on her desk, or other personal items. Even the walls held only the usual office prints. The only thing that looked promising was the pencil holder. If she'd touched any of them recently, I might get something.

Picking one up, I waited for a vision, but nothing came. I carefully slid open the top drawer of her desk and found a picture frame turned upside down. I picked it up and turned it over, finding the glass shattered, and a photo of her and Nate. It was the same one she'd posted on her media page.

A vision hit me, and I saw her standing in a dark parking lot with a shadowy figure. After glancing around, she handed him a wad of cash. I caught a glimpse of his hands and gasped. The tattoos on his fingers were the same as those I'd seen before. It had to be Johnny, but why would she give him money?

The vision ended, leaving me slightly disoriented. After shaking my head, I slipped the frame back into her desk and hurried back to the door. Pulling it open, I quietly slipped out, hoping the receptionist wouldn't notice how long I'd been in there. Nate had her full attention, so she barely noticed when I joined them.

He finished his story and glanced my way. I gave him a slight nod, and he smiled at the receptionist. "Guess we'll be going. But it was nice to meet you."

"You too. I'll tell Aubree you stopped by."

"Thanks."

We strode out of the building, straight to my car. After sitting down, Nate turned to me. "You were in there a while. Good thing I'm so charming. Did you get anything?"

"Yes. She had a framed photo of you and her in her top drawer. The glass had a big crack in it, and it was upside down, like she'd broken it on purpose. I picked it up and saw her giving money to a man with tattooed fingers."

"Johnny."

"Yeah. I couldn't see his features, but it has to be him. But why would she pay him to set you up the other day?"

"Shit. I can't believe she'd do that."

"Yeah. She must have a reason, and it's gotta be more than the fact that you broke up with her, right? At least we can assume she has a way to contact him, so that's good."

Nate nodded. "We just need to talk to her. Then we'll know what's going on." He checked his watch. "We're a little early to head to the restaurant, but that might be best since I can take a look around and make sure it's not a trap."

"Okay. Let's go." I'd been to that restaurant before, so I knew how to get there. It wasn't far, and we soon pulled into the parking lot. "Do you see her car anywhere?"

Nate shook his head. "No, but she could be driving something else by now."

I held out my hand for his.

"Don't you want to try a kiss first? Just as an experiment?"

I huffed, but then leaned toward him and captured his lips in mine. He reached for me, cupping my face with his hands. I grasped his shoulder, then moved my fingers up to run them through his dark, wavy hair. So soft. His masculine scent filled my senses, and all I wanted to do was put his seat back and climb onto his lap.

A blaring honk startled us, and we jerked apart. A car had stopped right in front of us, and Aubree stared daggers at us from the driver's seat. Her contorted face held anger and hatred. Her lips parted, and a low scream sounded through the glass. Whoa. If looks could kill, we'd be dead.

"Shit." Nate hurried to open the door. As he stepped out, the car sped off. Coming back, he slipped inside and closed the door. "Well, damn. That was bad timing."

"Should I follow her?"

"Yes." He twisted to catch a glimpse of her car leaving the parking lot.

I pulled out of our parking space and drove through the parking lot to the street. "Do you see her car anywhere?"

"No. She probably turned right, so go that way."

"Okay." I had to wait for several cars before I could pull out. I kept driving, but with all the traffic, it was a lost cause. "I don't think we'll find her now. Should we go back to her office?"

He sighed. "I don't think she'll talk to me now." He glanced my way. "We'll have to corner her somehow."

"Yeah. That was kind of scary. She looked mad enough to kill you without Johnny's help. You're lucky she didn't try to run you over."

"I had no idea she was so... unhinged."

"Well... they say a woman scorned and all that... but there's got to be more to it, right?"

He shrugged, unconvinced. "I have no idea. We'll have to track her down somehow."

"Yeah. In the meantime, do you want to head to Brandon's office? We could try the same thing there and see what happens."

He chuckled. "With my luck, he'd see it and probably try to kill us both."

I laughed. "He could try, but he's no match for you." I turned on the next street and made my way toward Brandon's office on the south side of town.

"What does Brandon do, anyway?"

"He works for a plumbing company. He's an accountant and does the payroll."

"Does he usually go out for lunch?"

I shrugged. "I don't know. If he does, we're early enough that we can catch him."

A few minutes later, I pulled into the parking lot in front of his building. Part of me did not want to go inside, but, this time, Nate was with me, and that gave me the courage to get out of my car.

I still found it hard to believe that Brandon would try to kill me, but who else could it be? I stepped inside, with Nate right behind me.

The receptionist glanced up, and her eyes widened. "Serenity?"

"Hi, Katie."

"It's been a while. How are you?"

"I'm good. Is Brandon around?"

"Let me see." She picked up her phone and glanced at Nate. If anything, her eyes got even bigger. She punched in Brandon's extension and waited for him to pick up. "Hey, Brandon, you have some visitors. Can you come down?" She listened before replying. "Yeah... it's Serenity... and... some guy." She glanced my way and nodded. "Sure... I'll tell her."

She put the receiver down and gave me a fake smile. "He's not available right now, but he's happy to talk to you after work."

"Oh. Okay. Thanks." My phone buzzed with a notification. I took a quick glance and found it was from Brandon. *Sorry babe, but I'm busy. Let's meet up after work. I'll come to the house. I'm keeping my fingers crossed that this is the news I'm hoping for. TTYL.*

I shook my head and motioned to Nate. "Let's go." He followed me out the door and into the parking lot. "Guess he's too busy to talk right now, but he sent me a text saying that he wants to come over to the house after work. Should I tell him to come?"

"Yes."

"Really?"

Nate nodded. "If I wasn't going to be there, I would say no, but since I am, we can do things our way."

"Okay." I sent the text, and Brandon responded with a thumbs up. "Hey... there's his car. Does it look like the same one that tried to run me down last night?"

"It's a sedan, so it could be."

"Maybe I should touch it."

"Good idea."

I wandered over to the car, not expecting anything to happen. Still, it was worth a try. Concentrating on Brandon, I touched the door handle and closed my eyes. Nothing happened at first. Then the darkness changed to a green lawn with trees and headstones. Brandon stood in front of a headstone, and I realized it was the same one I'd seen several months ago when he'd freaked out.

This time, I concentrated on the headstone, and my heart stopped. It read, "Serenity Jones, Beloved Wife." Gasping, I jerked my hand away and stepped back. Nate's arms circled me, keeping me from falling.

"What?"

"It was me. The headstone..." I met Nate's gaze. "Remember the vision that freaked him out? It wasn't his great-aunt; it was me."

Nate glanced at Brandon's building. "Come on. Let's talk about this in the car." He wrapped his arm around my waist and led me to my car.

After we were both inside, I could breathe again. "I guess that answers who tried to kill me last night."

"Yeah... no kidding."

I shook my head. "But why? It makes no sense."

He let out a breath. "Well, since he's coming to the house after work, we can make him tell us."

"How do we do that?"

His lips twisted. "We take control. Just think about it... in the comfort of your own home, we can tie him up and torture him for a while until he spills his guts."

I snorted. "Oh... now I get it. I like it."

He waggled his brows. "I figured you would."

I set my lips. "As long as I get to do the torturing. We could invite Aubree and make it a party."

He chuckled. "Bloodthirsty little thing, aren't you?"

"Yup. I just need some torture tools. Do you have any handy?"

"I've got it covered."

My eyes widened. "Wow. You're a handy man to have around."

"Oh yeah?"

"Yes. Definitely."

He raised a brow. "How handy, exactly?"

I twisted my lips. "Well... for one thing, you're really handy at neck massages. For another... you're pretty good at dodging grenades." I nodded. "You're definitely good with kids... and parents. You're also handy with changing locks

and installing security cameras." I rubbed my chin. "Hmm...
I know there's something else, but I just can't put my finger
on it."

He raised a brow. "Is that right? Maybe this will refresh
your memory." Cupping my cheek, he leaned in and
brushed my lips with his. Just as I was beginning to enjoy
it, he sat back in his seat.

I leaned toward him. "That's it? I think I might need
more before I know for sure."

He sent me a grin, but his gaze shifted to the front door
of Brandon's building. "Well... look who's suddenly free."

Brandon strode to his car, not even noticing that I was
parked a few cars away. He jumped inside and backed out. I
started my car and backed out to follow him. "Where do
you think he's going?"

"Let's find out."

I kept a couple of cars between us, just like I'd learned in
my PI course, and Brandon never had a clue. He pulled into
the hardware store down the street and hurried inside.

"Should we go in?"

"No. I don't want to risk getting spotted."

"Sure. I just wish I knew what he was buying. Do you
think it might have something to do with our meeting
tonight?"

"That would be my guess."

A few minutes later, he came out carrying two shopping
bags. He opened his trunk and put them inside before
getting into his car.

"I couldn't see what was in the bags, could you?"

"No."

I started the car as he pulled out of his parking space,
and managed to keep my distance. Disappointment washed
over me to see him pull right back into his office parking
lot. "Damn. That didn't tell us anything."

"Yes it did. He's planning something. Once you touch him, you'll know exactly what it is."

I frowned. "Yeah. Most likely my death."

"Don't worry. We'll be ready for anything." A buzzing sound came from Nate's phone and he picked it up. "It's Keola." He swiped to answer. "This is Stone." He listened for a minute before nodding. "Sure. We can come right now. See you in a few."

"What's up?"

"Keola might know who Johnny is."

Chapter 24

Stone

Serenity pulled the car into the parking lot of the Tiki Tabu Bar and we hurried out. "Keola said to come in the back way."

Serenity froze. "Wait. Do you think it could be a trap?"

"No. I trust Keola. But you can test the door if you want."

She nodded. "I will." She placed her hand on the knob and closed her eyes. "I'm not getting anything. It must be okay."

"Good." I pulled it open and we headed inside, following the hall to the back offices where Keola did his bookkeeping.

He sat at his desk and raised his hand in greeting. "Hey, bro. You made it. Come on in."

"I brought Serenity."

He sent her a wave. "Nice. I was hoping to see you again."

She smiled. "Thanks."

Glancing at me, Keola's brows dipped. "You okay, bro? You're moving a little slow."

I sighed before sitting in the chair in front of Keola's desk. "I had a run-in with a grenade earlier, but I made it out with just a few stitches, so I can't complain."

"Shit, bro. What happened?"

"It's why I'm trying to find Johnny. He almost killed me last night. So what have you got?"

Keola shook his head. "I didn't realize it was that bad. Hopefully this will help. After you came in the other day, it got me thinking about our days in the service. Remember Johnny-Two-Legs?"

My brows dipped. "Johnny-Two-Legs? What the hell kind of name is that?"

Keola's lips turned down. "You don't remember Johnny-Two-Legs? Huh. Maybe he got that nickname after you left? But I could have sworn he was there when you were."

"I think I'd remember a name like that."

Keola rubbed his chin and stared off into the distance. "Huh... now that I think of it, I think he earned his nickname because his legs were badly burned from an explosion that he walked away from. Everyone started calling him Johnny-Two-Legs, since he walked away with both legs. You know how it can be."

A face popped into my mind, and my stomach tightened. "Shit. It's JB. John Bowles." I could hardly believe it. I'd spent the last ten years trying to forget what had happened that day.

Keola snapped his fingers. "That's right! We all called him JB. That must be why the name Johnny didn't ring a bell. You won't believe this, but he was here. He came in last week."

"What did he want?"

"I thought it was just a coincidence that he came in, but now I'm not so sure. He didn't ask about you, so I didn't put it together until today."

Serenity placed her hand on my arm. "You think it's him?"

I closed my eyes. "Yeah." Taking a breath, I met her gaze. "And he has good reason to want me dead. The blast that nearly killed him was my last mission. It was a nightmare. We had bad intel, and he and I were the only ones who made it back alive. But it's worse than that. I carried another soldier out and left JB behind, but only because I thought he was dead."

Her brows drew together. "I can see why that might upset him, but hardly enough to kill you for it."

"There's more." I shook my head. "That was my mission. I knew the intel might be bad, but I decided to chance it anyway. I risked all our lives, thinking it was worth it." My jaw tightened. "I was wrong, and my men paid the price." I stared down at my hands. "After the explosion, I found Cooper gasping for breath. He begged me to help him. I didn't even think about anyone else; there wasn't time, and they were all down, so I just grabbed him and ran."

I shook my head. That day would haunt me for the rest of my life. "Cooper still died. I should have checked everyone, but we were under fire and I had to get out of there. I'm sure JB blames me for everything that happened to him, and for the friends we both lost."

"So you never saw him again?"

"No. I got transferred and left the service a couple of months later." I glanced at Keola. "But why come after me now? After all this time? What did he say to you?"

Keola shook his head. "It was easy to see he had a big chip on his shoulder. He was complaining about all the time he'd spent in rehab because of his addiction to pain killers. Probably from his injuries. He told me he'd just lost his job and was looking for work."

"Damn." I shook my head. "No wonder he wants me dead. He probably thinks I ruined his life."

"But you didn't." Serenity's earnest gaze met mine. "He just wants to blame someone for what happened to him."

Keola nodded. "I told him he could work here for a while until something else came up, but he said he had other plans."

I closed my eyes and nodded. Serenity may not agree, but I knew I shared some of the blame for what happened to him. Still, there was nothing I could do about it now. But how had he met up with Aubree? "Was he with anyone when you saw him?"

"No."

"Did he say where he was staying?"

Keola shrugged. "He said he had a friend he was staying with. But he didn't say who it was."

"Did he say anything about a trailer court?"

Keola's brows drew together. "You know what? Yeah, he said he was living in his friend's 'mobile manor'."

I nodded. "Makes sense. It all fits. His friend was probably Cash, and JB used him to get close to me. When Cash told JB I was asking questions about someone named Johnny, he killed Cash. I don't really get it, though. He hates me enough to kill a friend? And the other thing I just can't figure out is how he got together with Aubree."

"Aubree?" Keola's brows rose. "Didn't you end things with her a few months ago?"

"Yeah, but she's been hanging on. Now we think she may have been helping JB... Johnny."

"Bro. This whole thing is messed up."

"Yeah... tell me about it."

Serenity sighed. "We're hoping Aubree will lead us to Johnny if we can talk to her. I say we track her down and try again."

"I don't think that's gonna fly now." I shook my head. "I really wish she hadn't..."

"Hadn't what? What happened?" Keola asked.

"We were supposed to meet her for lunch today, but she got a little upset over something she saw."

Serenity's eyes widened, and she shook her head.

Keola noticed and leaned forward. He glanced between us, his eyes lighting up. "Sounds juicy... what was it?"

Serenity licked her lips, and I could hardly take my eyes off them. Memories of her in my arms last night flooded my senses, and all I wanted to do was take her out of here and run off to a private island somewhere. Just the two of us.

"Wait. Are you two together?" When neither of us answered, he slapped his desktop. "I knew it. I saw sparks flying when you came in a few days ago. It's like... off the charts. So what did you do? Did she catch you kissing or something?"

"Yes," I said. "We were sitting in Serenity's car in the parking lot. She wasn't even supposed to be there yet."

Keola shook his head. "Oh man... if she didn't want you dead before, she will now." He glanced between us. "Both of you."

"She'll have to get in line." I stood. "We need to take off, but thanks for your help. At least we know who we're dealing with now."

Keola stood as well. "Wish I could do more, but I'll let you know if he comes in again. And if you need me, let me know. In the meantime, have you got your lucky stone on you?"

"No."

"Maybe you'd better get it, cause a little more luck might come in handy about now."

"You have a point."

Keola met my gaze. "I remember how dangerous he is. Watch your six."

"I will."

We said our goodbyes and left. As we walked out, Serenity bumped her shoulder against me. "Don't worry. I'm here to watch your six, and we'll figure this out."

I took her hand, more grateful than ever to have her at my side. "Thanks Babe... just... I don't want you to get hurt either."

She squeezed my hand. "I won't. You've got my back, too. We can do this because we'll do it together."

My heart swelled. I'd been alone for so long, I'd forgotten what it was like to have someone who really cared about me. Dropping her hand, I took her face in my hands and planted a kiss on her lips, wanting to burn this moment into my heart, so it would be there forever.

She kissed me back like her life depended on it, and it was hard to pull away. Breathless, I rested my forehead against hers. "That's right, and I'll always have your back, Sen. Always." I almost added, *even if that means leaving you behind*, but I kept my mouth shut.

A car pulled into the lot, and I grabbed her hand to walk back to the car. "Now that we've got a name, let's check the database for information. It might tell us more about John Bowles. It also wouldn't hurt to talk to Dino and see what he can find out."

She raised a brow. "You think the detective will help?"

"That's what he gets paid for... off the record, of course."

"Of course."

While Serenity drove back to her house, I scanned the roads to make sure no one followed us. I'd been taken by surprise too many times now, and it wasn't going to happen again.

I hadn't told Serenity that JB was one of the best sharpshooters around, or that he was an expert on bombs, since it was pretty obvious. But that wasn't the only thing that worried me. The JB I knew wouldn't stop or give up until he'd accomplished his goal. If that meant killing me, it meant one of us would die.

After all of his attempts on my life, I could see why he'd gone to such extreme measures last night. He was getting frustrated and reckless which meant things were bound to escalate. But it also meant he could make a mistake that I could capitalize on.

Still, at this point, he'd be coming for me, and he probably wouldn't care who was in his way. That meant Serenity's life was in more danger than she knew. Maybe it was time to leave her behind. She'd hate me, but if it saved her life, I had to consider it. Thoughts of her dying because of me sent cold chills down my spine.

Chapter 25

Serenity

I drove into my garage and we hurried inside. Nate had been quiet for most of the ride, and I worried that he was still blaming himself for Johnny's sorry state.

His emotions were usually hidden behind a stoic mask, but I'd learned how to read him better now, and it was easy to see that finding out about Johnny had brought back all those deep wounds he'd kept buried for so long.

As we entered the kitchen, I reached for his hand and wiggled my eyebrows. "Why don't you get started on a search for Johnny-Two-Legs, and I'll make us a sandwich."

His lips twisted, and he tugged me against his chest. Closing his eyes, he inhaled. "How do you always smell so good?"

"It's part of my natural charm." I smirked, wrapping my arms around his neck and meeting his gaze. "Is it working? Do you find me irresistible?"

He lowered his lips for a tender kiss. "Definitely. I'd say, if it wasn't for this mess, I'd cart you back to bed for a week or two. But since this mess is what brought us together, I guess we'll just have to figure it out first."

"That's probably best. But look at it this way—now we have something to look forward to once we're done, right?"

He groaned. "Do I have to wait that long?"

"Hey! Maybe we'll figure it out today? You never know."

"You're always putting a positive spin on things, aren't you?" He stepped away, taking my hands in his. "In that case, I'd better get started." He held my hands for a moment longer before heading to the office.

My heart fluttered, and I stood there like a love-sick dummy, watching him until he disappeared down the hall. Did I have it bad, or what? At least he wanted me as much as I wanted him. Still, what the hell was I doing? Sure, my body craved his touch, but now my heart was involved. If he walked away when this was over, would I have the strength to let him go?

Not wanting to think that far ahead, I got busy making a couple of ham and cheese sandwiches. I didn't know what he liked on his, so I just made them the way I normally did, and took the plate and some potato chips into my office.

I set the plate down beside him, and he dove in, grabbing a sandwich and taking a bite. "Thanks. This is great."

"You're welcome. So how's it going? Find anything?"

"There's not much here, but I found a photo of Johnny." He pointed to the monitor. "Is that the guy from your visions?"

I glanced at the screen, and my breath caught. "Yeah. That's him all right." He wasn't wearing a hat, but there was no doubt it was the same guy. "What does it say about him?"

"His address is listed in Kansas." He shook his head. "So that's no help. It also mentions his service in the army and his honorable discharge, but that's about it. I couldn't find him on any of the regular social media accounts either, but that doesn't mean he's not using a fake name."

I smirked. "Like Johnny-Two-Legs?" He snickered, and my brow furrowed. "So I guess he looked you up and found you here?"

"That's probably right, but I still can't figure out how he hooked up with Aubree."

"Didn't she post a picture of you and her together? If she used your name, that might have done it."

He finished his sandwich and opened a new tab to check her posts. Finding the one with his photo, he swore. "Looks like she added my name."

"Maybe that's how Johnny found you."

"It must be, but I still feel like I'm missing something. I'm going to give Dino a call and see what he comes up with. I'll even throw Aubree's name into the mix. Maybe that will do it."

He put the call through and told Dino all about Johnny, as well as mentioning the grenade at Razor's place. I left to get us both a soda while he told him about Aubree.

After opening the blinds, I glanced out the living room window. A man was walking his dog down the sidewalk, but otherwise, nothing was happening. Still, a chill ran down my spine.

Oh a whim, I stepped to the front door and touched the handle. Nothing came to me, and I dropped my hand, but I couldn't shake the feeling that something bad was coming.

Heaving out a breath, I rolled my eyes and shook my head. Well, duh... of course something bad was coming. It was Brandon. I checked the time, knowing he got off work at four-thirty. That gave us a couple of hours to figure out what to do about him.

Nate came out of the office and caught me standing in front of the door. "Something wrong?"

"Just a bad feeling about Brandon showing up in a couple of hours. That weasel. I don't know if I'll be able to play along without going for his throat and strangling him. You know?"

"No kidding, but you can do it. Just invite him inside so he can't run off before you touch him. I'll take care of the rest."

I let out a deep breath and nodded. "Okay. So what did Dino have to say?"

"He's looking into both Johnny and Aubree's names, but it will take a while. He'll call me back if he finds anything. He mostly chewed me out for causing another explosion, even though he knows it wasn't my fault."

I nodded. "You know, if Aubree tells Johnny we tried to talk to her, do you think he'll want to use her to set you up? She'd probably jump at the chance to get you killed again, right?"

"If she did it once, I suppose so. It's still hard for me to believe that she's so cold-hearted though. I mean... sure, I may have broken her heart, but killing me for it? How crazy is that?"

As if on cue, Nate's phone began to ring. He checked it and glanced my way. "It's Vanetti." He swiped to answer, and, from their conversation, I picked up enough to know that Vanetti wanted to be filled in on everything that had happened since their last phone call.

After Nate explained our visit to the Tiki Tabu Bar, and Johnny's identity, he stopped speaking to listen. A minute later, he glanced my way and his brows rose. "Is that right? Well, if you need her, we can come—"

His breath caught and he shook his head. "But you said we needed to stick together—" His lips flattened. "I know, but he can't be everywhere at once... yes, that could work... okay, we'll do that first. If anything's off, I'll let you know."

He put his phone away and sat down on the couch, pulling me down beside him. He laid his head back and let out a sigh. "Vanetti needs your help at the office, but he doesn't want me to come. He's worried about another sniper attack."

"Oh." My stomach twisted just thinking about Stone getting shot. "That... makes sense. So what's going on?"

"He thinks someone's been in his office because he noticed a few things were out of place. He thought if you touched them, you'd know who was in there."

"Does he think it has something to do with Johnny?"

"Not necessarily. But you never know."

"That's true." I snuggled against him, wanting to soften his disappointment about not coming with me. "But Vanetti's got a point about you staying here."

His lips turned down. "I know, but I don't like you going without me."

"Because you like being stuck with me?"

He snorted. "You're an acquired taste... but yeah."

I smacked him. "Yeah, because when we first met, you couldn't take your eyes off me."

"I think it was the other way around."

"Ha! You wish."

He pulled me closer and sighed. "I still don't want you to go without me."

His confession melted my heart. "I don't either, but you'll be safer here. I shouldn't be more than an hour, tops, and just think... you could take a nap. I can tell you're tired."

He bristled. "I'm not that tired."

I shrugged. "I guess I could try getting a vision to see what's coming—"

Before I could say another word, Nate gathered me in his arms and crushed me against him. His lips pressed against mine, tugging and teasing them apart.

Soon, my heart was racing and I melted into his chest, giving as good as I got. He deepened the kiss, stealing my breath.

Pulling away, he met my gaze. "Did you see anything?"

Breathless, my brows drew together. "Huh? Is that why you kissed me?"

"Of course. Why else?"

I pushed against him. "Yeah... right. Guess I'd better get going."

"So you didn't see anything?"

I shook my head. "Honestly, when I'm kissing you, a vision is the last thing on my mind."

He sent me that sexy half-grin of his that turned me into a puddle of goo. I rolled my eyes and pushed to my feet. "Stay here. I'll be back before you know it." I hurried into the kitchen and grabbed my car keys before I could change my mind. Sending him a little wave, I stepped into the garage and climbed into my car.

As I drove out of my garage, I realized this was the first time we'd been apart for days. An unexpected shiver ran down my spine. Was he safe at my house? Johnny couldn't know about me. Even if Aubree told him that she saw Nate with a woman, she didn't know who I was.

Nate had to be safer there than coming with me, and he couldn't leave, since I had the car. Knowing he was stuck there relieved the tension in the pit of my stomach, and I relaxed. He was fine, and this little errand wouldn't take long.

I arrived at Vitality Solutions and pulled into the parking garage. The elevator took me to the twenty-sixth floor, and I stepped through the doors. Striding through the high-class lobby, I hurried straight to Vanetti's office.

Julia sat at her desk and glanced up. "Hey, Serenity. How's it going? Is Stone okay?" She glanced behind me, expecting to see him.

"Yes. He's good, but I left him at..." Not sure I could trust her, I fumbled on. "...anyway, Mr. Vanetti wanted me to come in and take a look at something."

She shrugged. "Oh... he didn't tell me, but you can go down to his office if he's expecting you."

"Okay. Thanks." I hurried down the hall and knocked on his door before sticking my head inside. "Hey there. I'm here. Nate said you needed me?"

Vanetti waved me inside. "Yes. Come in." He glanced behind me, and his brows drew together. "Nate didn't come?"

"No. I convinced him that it was safer to stay away."

He blinked. "I'm impressed. He's usually not so pliable, but I'm glad he's not here." Vanetti sighed and shook his head. "I'll feel better when this is all over. At least you know who this fellow is now."

"Yes. We're closing in on him, so that's good." That wasn't exactly the truth, but at least we were making progress.

"Good. Thanks for keeping Nate safe." He pushed his chair back and stood. "I didn't tell Nate, but I'm pretty sure someone broke into my safe. I wouldn't have known except for this." He pointed to a gold coin on his desk. "I found it on the floor, right before I called him. I keep this coin in my safe, so the only way it could have fallen on the floor is if someone opened it. I thought if you touched the safe before I did, you'd get a vision of who it was."

"Oh, wow. I hope they didn't take anything important."

"I guess we'll find out soon enough." Vanetti opened the lower cabinet door, revealing a black safe. "Go ahead." He stepped away to give me some room.

I closed my eyes and touched the handle, taking a moment to feel the smooth texture before gripping it with my palm. I got a faint impression of a gloved hand, which didn't tell me anything.

Letting out a sigh, I glanced at Vanetti. "I saw a gloved hand. Maybe if you opened the safe, I could touch whatever's inside and find out more."

Vanetti's lips turned down and he nodded. I moved out of the way, and he made quick work of opening the door. After taking a look inside, he shook his head. "It looks like everything's there."

He moved aside and I knelt in front of the small safe. There were several stacks of paper currency on one side. A couple of folders, along with a few black binders, and a small leather notebook on the other.

Figuring the money had been left alone, I reached in for the small leather notebook. As I tugged it out, I immediately felt the beginning of a vision. My hand turned into someone else's, and I watched as both hands flipped through the notebook to a table of numbers and dates inside. Holding it flat, they took a photo before slipping it back inside and closing the safe.

My vision cleared, and I focused on the notebook. "This was what they were after." I opened the book and found the page with the table. "They took a photo of this page." I handed the book to Vanetti.

"Shit."

"What is it?"

"Delivery dates and shipments." He sighed. "I'm glad you caught this. It gives me time to make some changes." He pursed his lips. "Knowing this schedule would put Stone in danger, since he's usually involved. But this hints at something bigger." He raised a brow. "I think someone's trying to move in on my territory. Did you see anything else?"

"Yes. The person's hands had tattoos on the fingers. Just like the ones I saw on Johnny's hands. But it wasn't him, because they were smaller and more delicate... like a woman's."

Vanetti narrowed his gaze. "The only people with after-hours access to my office are the cleaning crew. I don't have a camera in here, but surveillance video might show us more."

He picked up his phone and pushed a button. "Slater. We need to see the surveillance video from last night... yes... now." He set the phone down. "Slater's on Nate's security team. He can access the video on my computer, so he's on his way. While we check it out, do you think you could sketch the tattoos you saw? I'd like to know what they look like."

I shrugged. "I can try. But honestly, I didn't see them all that well."

Vanetti nodded. "That's okay. Anything would be helpful."

I sat at the round table in Vanetti's office with a pencil and piece of paper while Vanetti and Slater watched the video. I closed my eyes and concentrated on the vision. I'd thought the tattoos were symbols, but maybe they were letters or numbers in an Old English style font.

"There she is." Vanetti pointed at his screen, and I hurried over to take a look. The cleaning woman wore light blue overalls and a ball cap. She pushed a cart into Vanetti's office, but kept her face turned away from the cameras, and all we could see was the top of her hat.

Vanetti turned to Slater. "Call the cleaning service. I want to know who was here last night." Slater hurried out of the office, and Vanetti picked up his phone. "I'm calling Nate."

While he explained what we'd found, I went back to the table and closed my eyes. Concentrating on the vision, I managed to draw a couple of symbols, but they just looked like circles with lines drawn through them. They weren't right, and frustration tightened my jaw.

Vanetti ended the call and glanced my way. "Get anything?"

"Not really. I'm sorry. I might recognize them if I saw them somewhere, but it's not real clear what they looked like."

"That's fine. I told Nate I'd send you home, so you might as well get going. He's probably more familiar with those kinds of tattoos than I am, so maybe he can help you figure it out."

"True. But at least we know it's got something to do with a gang, right?" I jumped to my feet, suddenly anxious to get home.

"Yes. But which one? Didn't you check them out all ready?"

"Yeah. It wasn't any of them."

He sighed. "If you can figure the tattoos out, it might tell us what we need to know. Let me know what Nate thinks." Vanetti stepped to the door and held it open for me. "And Serenity... keep Nate alive, all right?"

I met his gaze and nodded. "I will."

His eyes narrowed, seeming to take in more than I wanted him to see. Before he could comment, I blurted, "see ya," and hurried down the hall. After a quick wave to Julia, I stepped through the lobby to the elevators.

With growing unease, I took the elevator to the parking garage and stepped out, glancing toward the corner where Nate kept his motorcycle. A sudden desire to take a ride with him washed over me. His sleek, black, shiny bike looked lonely, so I took a detour to admire it.

Running my fingers across the fuel tank and leather seat, I could almost smell Nate's amazing scent. My lips twisted into a smile before my vision changed and Nate's face swam into view. My heart lurched to see blood running down the side of his face.

He sat in a chair and his hands were tied behind his back. I heard a gun go off, and a bullet slammed into his chest, sending him backwards to crash onto the floor. "No!"

The vision cleared and I gasped. That was my kitchen! Yanking out my phone, I called Nate, praying that he'd answer.

"Hey Babe, what's up?"

"Nate! You're in danger! Get out of there! Now!" He didn't answer right away, and my heart sped up. "Nate?"

"I'm going. What did you see?"

"You were tied up in my kitchen and you got shot in the chest. Please don't let that happen!"

"I won't. I'll call you when I'm someplace safe."

He disconnected, and I leaned over to catch my breath. My head swam with dizziness, and I leaned against the bike so I wouldn't fall on my face. I breathed in through my nose and slowly let it out. After another deep breath, I was steady enough to head to my car.

Before I could take a step, I caught movement from the corner of my eye. Alarm raced across my chest. Was that Johnny? Was he waiting for me? Is that how he finds Nate?

Not about to let that happen, I dashed to my car, hitting the unlock button. As I opened the door, I heard talking and glanced across the lot to see a couple of people heading toward the elevators. They were right where I'd caught the movement, so it was probably them and not Johnny. Still, I got into my car and locked the doors before starting the engine.

I drove out of the lot and began the drive home, my heart finally slowing down. Driving through town instead of taking the freeway gave me time to think about the best course of action. I also took a round-about way so I could spot a tail.

I wasn't sure going home was a good idea, but Nate couldn't get far without a car, so I kept heading in that direction while I waited for his phone call. There was no sign of anyone following me, so at least that was in my favor.

As I turned into my neighborhood, I slowed and pulled to the side of the road. Why hadn't Nate called me back? I grabbed my phone and pushed his number. It rang several times before going to voice mail. What the freak? Did he make it out or not?

Shit! If he hadn't, I had to stop Johnny from shooting him. In a panic, I pulled my gun from my purse and got it loaded. There was still time... there had to be!

I drove straight to my house, pushing the button to open the garage door. Leaving my car where it was, I grabbed my gun and rushed through the door into my kitchen, ready to shoot Johnny.

Finding it empty, I froze. He wasn't there. Relieved, I continued through the house, but found no sign of him. Knowing I had no time to lose, I rushed out the door, determined to get out of there.

As I stepped into the garage, a man grabbed me, knocking the gun from my hand. "No!" Before I could scream, his grip tightened and his gun jabbed me in the side.

"Stay quiet, or you're dead." I tried to move, but he pressed the gun harder. "Inside." He started toward the door, dragging me along with him.

No. No. No. This wasn't supposed to happen!

He shoved me into a kitchen chair... the same one I'd seen Nate tied to in my vision. Was this some kind of sick joke for saving Nate's life? Was I going to take his place? What had I done? I was totally screwed, and he would be too, if he came back.

"Good timing." Aubree stepped into the kitchen, a pleased smirk on her face. Johnny slipped his gun into the waist of his jeans and pulled my hands behind me, fastening a zip tie around my wrists.

"What's she doing here?"

"Aubree?" He snickered. "You still don't know, do you?"

"Know what?"

Aubree shook her head, then pulled out a gun and took a tour of my house. A minute later, she came back to stand in front of me.

"Where's Stone?"

I met her gaze. "I don't know. He must have left."

She held out a hand. "Where's your phone?" I didn't answer, and she motioned to Johnny. "Find it."

He stepped toward me, raising his hands to pat me down.

"It's in my jacket pocket."

Stepping close, he found my phone and handed it to Aubree. She turned it on and frowned. "I need her thumb-print."

Handing it back to Johnny, he grabbed my thumb and pressed it to my phone. "Ow."

It opened and he handed it back to her. She found Nate's number and put the call through. He didn't answer, so she tried again and still got nothing. Frustrated, she threw my phone onto the kitchen table and leaned toward me. "He's not answering. Where did he go?"

"I... I'm not sure."

"Better go move the car," Johnny said. "He won't come back if he sees it in the driveway."

Aubree grabbed her keys and left.

"How did you find me?"

"You didn't think I'd have someone watching Vanetti's office?" He shook his head. "You fit the description Aubree gave me, so it was easy enough."

Johnny stepped to the window, watching Aubree park down the street. "I don't know why you'd help Stone. He's a worthless piece of shit."

"Then you don't know him very well."

He stepped close to loom over me, narrowing his eyes, with his lips curled. "I'd expect that from a woman. But that's because you're only looking at the goods. Deep down, he's a selfish bastard. Aubree thinks he'll come for you, but I'm not counting on it."

Aubree came back inside, setting her keys on the counter. "Let's try Stone again." She put the call through, but he didn't pick up.

It gave me hope that Nate might know what was going on, and that's why he didn't answer. If he'd been close, he might have taken Aubree out while she was outside, so that meant he was further away than I thought.

"We might as well take her to the warehouse," Johnny said. "We're too exposed here."

"Let's give it a few more minutes."

"Why? I don't think he'll come back."

"I don't want to upset Larry. A few more minutes isn't going to hurt."

He sneered. "He's a dick. I can't wait to see the look on his face when we're done."

"Yeah... the guy has no balls, but we have to follow what Needles told us."

"Fine. Ten more minutes... that's it."

She opened her mouth to answer, but the doorbell rang. They both froze. With a huff of annoyance, Aubree stepped away to glance into the living room. The doorbell rang again, followed by loud knocking.

"Serenity! Your car's in the driveway. I know you're in there. Come on. Let me in. You promised to talk to me." Brandon waited another few seconds before shouting. "I'm not leaving until you open this door."

"Who's that?" Aubree asked.

I swallowed. "That's my ex... uh... my husband. I told him to stop by for a chat."

"Shit." Johnny glanced at Aubree. "What should we do."

Aubree turned to me. "You need to get rid of him. But don't try anything, or we'll kill you both. I don't need you alive to lure in Stone."

I stood and motioned to my hands. "You'd better get this off me first."

Johnny pulled a knife from his pocket and cut through the zip-tie.

Rubbing my wrists, I slowly made my way to the door. Johnny followed close behind, but stayed out of sight. I opened the door a few inches and tried to smile. "Hey Brandon. Now's not a good time after all. Can you come back later?"

"What? No. We need to settle this, now." His eyes narrowed, and he glanced at the door. "What's going on? Is that guy here?"

"No. But... something's come up. You need to go."

He put his hand on the door, and his eyes turned dark. "I'm not leaving. We have unfinished business, and I'm tired of waiting." At my widened gaze, he shoved the door open, and I jerked out of the way.

He rushed inside and came face-to-face with Johnny. Lurching back, he nearly fell. "Who the hell are you?"

Johnny sneered and punched him hard in the stomach. Brandon doubled over, going down on one knee. Johnny slammed the door shut, turning the lock for good measure, and hauled Brandon up before punching him in the face.

Brandon's head jerked to the side, and he went down again. As Johnny leaned in to grab Brandon's arm, Brandon pulled a gun on him. Before he could shoot, Johnny kicked the gun out of Brandon's hand and followed through with a punch to the jaw, knocking him flat. This time, Brandon stayed down.

Johnny picked up the gun before I could go for it, and stuck it in the pocket of his jacket. He glanced my way, his gaze narrow and filled with accusation. "Did you know he had a gun?"

My shoulders rose. "No. I had no idea." I glanced at Brandon. Dazed, he shook his head and blinked a few times. As he pushed into a sitting position, I stepped toward him. "What did you bring a gun for?"

He growled. "To kill you! But you just won't die." He rubbed his face and swore. "Dammit, Serenity. You should be dead by now." He lunged for me, going for my neck, but I danced out of his way.

Johnny grabbed his arms and pulled them behind his back. "Maybe, if you cooperate, I'll let you kill her; but for now, you need to take a seat."

He dragged Brandon into the kitchen while I stood there in shock. Just as they reached the doorway, I gathered my wits and turned to escape out the front door. Turning the lock, I grabbed the knob.

"Don't, or you're dead."

I glanced up to find Aubree aiming a gun at my head. I stiffened, and tried to rein in my terror.

"Get back into the kitchen." I hesitated, and her voice hardened. "Now."

Out of options, I stepped toward her. She moved aside, nodding for me to go ahead of her into the kitchen.

Johnny had shoved Brandon into my chair and zip-tied his hands behind his back.

"Sit down." Aubree motioned toward another chair, and I sat. She slipped the gun into the back of her pants and pulled my hands behind my back, fastening them with another zip-tie.

While she got to work, I let my fingers graze her skin, praying for a vision. I closed my eyes and caught a glimpse of her in a dark room. She stood facing a wall, with a photo of Nate and Vanetti. Raising her hand, she smudged out Nate's eyes with a black marker. Then she moved to Vanetti's photo. "I'm coming for you, next."

The vision cleared, and I gasped. Holy hell! This was so much worse than I thought. I had to stop her, but how?

Brandon groaned, blood dripping down his chin from a cut on his lip. He glanced at me with accusation, his face hard as granite. Lifting his chin, he looked at Aubree. "I don't know what's going on here, but I'm on your side. I want her dead. Just let me go, and I'll do it for you."

Aubree shook her head, her gaze moving between Brandon and me. "You guys are so screwed up. And I thought my life was a mess." She snorted before meeting my gaze. "Does Stone know about him?" Shaking her head, her lips turned down. "You'd better hope he doesn't find out he's with you, or he won't come to save you."

Johnny stepped to the kitchen window, motioning for Aubree to follow. "You ready to go now?"

"Just another few minutes. Sooner or later, Stone will call her. Once he knows we have her, he'll come. We can finish them off here."

"You sure about that? He's not the type to save anyone but himself."

"You didn't see them kissing. He'll come."

He shook his head. "I've got it all set up. I say we go."

"Look." She motioned toward Brandon. "If we do it here, the husband can take the fall for all of them. It could be a murder-suicide-love-triangle thing. We just need to get Stone to show up."

"We've waited long enough. We're leaving."

"But—"

He got in her face, his voice low and menacing. "I call the shots, or did you forget?"

Her breath hitched. "Fine. But I want to call Stone again." She glanced at me. "Only this time, Serenity's leaving him a message that he can't ignore. If he doesn't call back after that, we'll do it your way."

Chapter 26

Stone

My phone rang, and I sat back on my heels, not sure what to do. It was from Serenity, but I knew it wasn't her. I clenched my teeth and did my best to keep it together until help came, but with Serenity in danger, it was a hard-fought battle.

After her call to warn me, I'd crossed through her backyard and into the yard behind hers. It was a huge mistake, since I'd run into trouble with a dog. The brute didn't like me in his yard, and I'd had to run like hell to get away. He'd even managed to jump over the fence to chase me. By the time I got away, I'd run several blocks and had finally climbed into a tree-house. Of course, the dog was still there, so I couldn't climb down.

At least the cameras in her house were up and running, so I knew what was going on. I'd barely managed to get the one in the kitchen set up before she'd called to warn me. I'd been too busy saving my ass to call her back, but that didn't explain why she'd gone home.

I only knew she was there because of the cameras. Dammit. Where was my luck when I needed it? One missed phone call was all it took to screw up everything.

Then Brandon showed up with a gun. At first, I thought he meant to help Serenity, but when he lunged at her, I knew she was his target, and red-hot rage still pounded in my veins. It was all I could do not to rush in there and beat him to a bloody pulp.

Too bad I didn't have audio along with the camera feed. I could tell they were working out a way to lure me in, and I worried that it would involve explosives. I could handle most anything, as long as they didn't make Serenity wear an explosive vest. I wouldn't put it past Johnny, which meant that I needed to get her out of there before they even thought about it.

A car pulled up in front of the house, and I let out a breath. I'd warned Ricky about the dog, and he had a nice juicy steak to lure the dog away. With the steak in his mouth, the dog happily trotted off, and I climbed down from my perch.

I slid inside the car, thanking Ricky for getting there so fast. Slater sat in the passenger seat and told me they'd brought guns, bullet-proof vests, and flash grenades, everything I'd asked for. Now we could get down to business.

"Where's the house?" Ricky asked.

"Not far. A couple blocks. I have a visual of the kitchen where they're holding Serenity and her ex."

"Her ex?"

"Yeah. I guess he showed up to kill her."

"What? That's messed up."

"Yeah, and I don't even know why he wants her dead, so I'd like to keep him alive if possible." I shook my head. It would be nice to kill him myself, but I didn't think Serenity would approve unless it was self-defense. But I could totally make that happen.

Ricky motioned to the bag at my feet. "Put the vest on while we figure this out. There's an extra gun in there. I guess you lost yours."

I slipped off my shirt and pulled the vest around me, tightening the straps before tugging my shirt back on.

"Maybe Slater and I could draw them out while you go in and free Serenity."

I picked up the gun and loaded it. "No. Johnny's too smart for that. The only thing I can come up with, is surrendering like they want, and then you guys breaking us out."

"I don't like it." Slater held out his hand for my phone. "Let me see what we're dealing with."

I passed the phone over, showing him the video feed. He studied all the angles, including the camera on the front porch. "The garage door is open. That's a plus. Is there a door from the back?"

"There's a patio door just outside the kitchen, right there." I pointed to the area. "You can barely see it. Unfortunately, they'd see us coming. I think going through the front door or a bedroom window might be our best options."

"Wait. Something's happening." Slater held the phone so I could see it. Aubree stepped to Serenity and held a phone to her face. My phone began to ring, but I let it go to voice mail. Serenity began to speak, but Aubree jerked the phone away and slapped Serenity across the face.

My jaw clenched, and I grabbed the door handle.

"No. Not yet." Slater grabbed my arm. "She's fine. Aubree's yelling, but she's not hitting her again."

"I need to call Serenity, or Aubree will lose it. It's time we go in. Get geared up."

"We're ready. But think a minute." Ricky's measured tones calmed me down. "She's not going to let Serenity go if you show up. You know that, right?"

"I don't know shit, but if I call, I'll find out what Aubree wants. If we know that, it will help us figure out what to do."

"Sure, but first, listen to the message from Serenity."

"Fine." I hated that my emotions were making me irrational. I was usually the calm, cool, collected one. Sighing, I called my voice mail, setting it on the console and putting it on speaker so all of us could hear.

Serenity didn't waste any time. "Nate! It's a trap. Whatever you do, don't come!"

Aubree's slap came through loud and clear. Before ending the call, she spoke into the phone. "If you don't come, I'll do to her what you did to Seth."

The line went dead, and a chill ran down my spine. "What the hell?"

"Who's Seth?" Ricky asked.

"I have no idea." I wracked my brain, but couldn't come up with a thing. Running my hands through my hair, I went back to the beginning. I'd gone over all this with Serenity, and nothing had come up. So who was Seth? "It must have something to do with the tattoos and a gang."

I quickly explained the tats Serenity had seen in her vision. "Oh, yeah," Ricky nodded. "We talked about that after the shooting. Johnny had them, right? We thought they were gang-related. This might sound strange, but could Aubree be part of the same gang? Did you notice any tattoos on her?"

My eyes narrowed. "She had one on her shoulder, but it wasn't a gang tattoo." I shrugged. "Or maybe it was, and I just didn't put it together."

"What was it?"

I closed my eyes to remember. "It was like a banner of some kind with flowers twined around it. There were words on it... something like... *love never dies.* I thought it was weird because the edge of the banner had a point... like a sharp pencil."

"Or a weapon? Like a dagger?" Ricky said.

My breath caught. "No. A spike. That's it. Spike. Seth's moniker was Spike. I remember him now. It was two years ago, but yeah... he and his brother tried to kill me."

Ricky raised a brow. "Let me guess... you killed him first?"

I swallowed. "Yeah. His brother went by Needles. He's in jail, so I didn't think he was behind this... but if Aubree and Spike..." I closed my eyes. "They must have been together, and this whole time she's been using me. Most of Needles' gang is in jail, but there must be enough of them to do his bidding... and Aubree's behind it."

"But how does Johnny fit into it?"

"I don't know... but since he wants me dead, too, they must have joined forces."

"Guys!" Slater held up the phone. "It looks like they're leaving the house."

The video feed showed Johnny grabbing Brandon's arm and pulling him toward the door. "Shit!" I pushed Serenity's number and hoped that would slow them down. They all stopped while Aubree answered the phone.

"It's about time you called your girlfriend." Aubree's sarcastic voice grated on my ears. "I was beginning to think you were ghosting her."

"What do you want, Aubree?"

"I want you dead. You killed the love of my life, and now I'm going to kill Serenity. But at least I'll give you a choice. You can trade your life for your girlfriend's, and she might live, or you can both die. Johnny doesn't think you'll do it. He's convinced you'll leave her to die, just like you left him. So what's it going to be?"

"I don't want anyone to die. Let's work something out."

"No. You either come, or I kill her. You have five seconds."

"Fine. I'll come, but you have to let her go—alive."

"Oh... she'll be alive."

I heard rustling before Johnny came on the line, his voice low and menacing. "But first you have to come out and play. For old time's sake."

"Give me that!" Aubree took the phone, and I held my breath, hearing a muffled argument between her and Johnny. Finally, she came back on the line.

"I'll text you the address. Be there in one hour, or she's dead." The phone disconnected, and a text came through with an address I wasn't familiar with.

"Are they leaving?"

"Yes. We're too late to stop them now, but she sent me the address." I shook my head. "I think we can beat them to it."

"Nice. Let's roll."

My stomach knotted. This was too easy. "Wait a sec. Johnny's sent me into too many traps to believe this isn't one of them. He doesn't know how close we are, so we might be better off if we follow them."

"Okay. Your call." Ricky shook his head. "I just hope you're right."

"So do I."

Chapter 27

Serenity

Aubree forced me into the back seat of her car, so I was sitting beside Brandon. For the first time, he seemed to realize this was serious, and he might not make it out alive.

"What the hell are you into?" he hissed.

"I told you to leave." I arched my brow at him. "Were you really going to kill me?"

He shook his head. "I should have just waited and let them do it."

I sniffed. "Yeah... right. You're just having a bad day, all the way around."

"Shut up."

Not about to do that, I continued. "But why kill me? That makes no sense. You'd get nothing."

"You're wrong about that. I took out a hefty life-insurance policy when we got married. Once you're dead,

I'll be set for life. But it has to be sickness, murder, or an accident. And the accidents don't seem to work."

"Oh, so you were going to make it look like murder?"

Aubree and Johnny got into the car, and Brandon clamped his lips together. Johnny drove, and Aubree glanced back at us. "Having a little spat, are we?"

"I want her dead," Brandon began. "Like I said, we're on the same side. I don't care how you do it, just let me go, and I won't breathe a word of this to anyone."

"We'll see." Aubree faced forward again. "If you cooperate, we might let you go."

"I'll do whatever you want."

She glanced over her shoulder, and a satisfied smile twisted her lips. "That's just what I wanted to hear. I think we can work something out."

Brandon let out a breath. "Thank God."

I shook my head. Didn't he see how ridiculous this was? What an idiot. "What happened to you? A life-insurance policy? That's what this is all about?"

"Of course not. But you changed into this... this... freak."

Aubree glanced my way, then at Brandon. "What are you talking about?"

My breath caught. "Shut up, Brandon. You already sound crazy. Don't make it worse." I bit my lip, praying he'd keep his mouth shut. Would they keep me from touching them if they knew?

"Oh..." Aubree grinned. "Now I really want to know." She lifted her brow in an invitation for Brandon to confide in her.

He glanced my way before settling on her. "Serenity can see things after she touches you. Like where you've been, or where you're going. It's like she steals your thoughts. She's a psycho."

I shook my head. "And you're delusional."

He pursed his lips together. "Trust me, we'd all be better off if you were dead."

"Ouch." Aubree's brows rose. "And you're still married to each other?"

Brandon sighed. "I need the insurance money. If we're divorced, I won't get it."

She shook her head, glancing at me with pity in her eyes before turning around.

"We're almost there," Johnny said. "Do you think he took the bait?"

"Let's hope so."

My heart lurched. What bait? Was this another trap? Oh hell. Now what?

We'd driven out toward the dump and a bunch of warehouses and old buildings. Johnny pulled off the road onto a side street that took us behind a row of buildings.

He stopped beside the back entrance of a large warehouse and turned off the car. "Stay here with them. I've got a few things to finish up before everything's ready." He stepped to the door and hurried inside.

Aubree got out of the car and leaned back against it, watching both ends of the side street for signs of trouble. After a few minutes, she locked the car doors and stepped inside the building.

Now was my chance. With my hands behind my back, it was hard to move, but at least I didn't have a seat belt on. I twisted to unlock the door and managed to push the right button, but nothing happened. "Damn! She must have the child lock on."

Brandon had tried the same thing, with the same results. Now what? I could try getting into the front seat, but maybe I should touch Brandon first. Since he was involved, that might help me know what was coming and how to get out of this.

I scooted toward him, and his eyes got big. "You are not touching me!"

He used his shoulder to push me away, but I slid closer. Before I knew what was happening, I lost my balance and tipped over, my face falling into his lap. "Ugh! Oh my gosh! Get me out of here!"

Brandon wiggled under me. "What the hell, Serenity. Get off me."

"I can't. You're going to have to help me up."

"How?"

"I don't know. Figure it out."

With his hands tied behind him, the only thing he could do was lift up his pelvis. As he did this, I tried to get some leverage to pull away, but without my arms it wasn't enough. He tried it again, but it wasn't working. Frustrated, he began lifting his hips up and down like he was trying to buck me off.

As my face came down in his lap over and over, I could feel him getting hard. Holy hell! How was I ever going to get off him?

The front passenger door flew open, and Aubree stuck her head inside. "What the hell is going on back there?"

Brandon froze, and I turned my face to get some air, positive my cheeks were red from rubbing against his jeans so violently. "I fell over and now I'm stuck. Can you pull me up?"

She froze for a moment before slamming the door. A few seconds later, my door opened. Aubree reached in and grabbed my upper arm, pulling me upright with a grunt.

"Uh... thanks. Can I get out now? It's getting hot in here." I glanced at Brandon, but he wouldn't look at me. If things weren't so dire, I would have burst out laughing.

Aubree stepped back and propped the door open. I took that as a yes, and scooted around until my body faced the door. I kept scooting to the edge until I could get my feet out, but, from this angle, I couldn't stand without my arms.

I squinted up at Aubree. "Will you help me up?"

"Oh, for the love of God." She rolled her eyes before grabbing my upper arm, and pulled.

I got my feet under me, but managed to sway into her. She braced me up, and my fingers brushed against her arm. As a vision rushed over me, I staggered a bit, then froze in place until I caught my balance.

"Come on." Keeping hold of my arm, Aubree led me toward the building. Knowing I'd die if I went inside, I waited until the last moment, then wrenched my arm out of her grip. I ran like hell, grateful I'd kept up with my exercises.

"Stop, or I'll shoot!"

I kept going, willing to chance it. A shot rang out, and a sharp pain in my thigh sent me tumbling to the ground. I tried to get back up, but the pain was too much.

Footsteps pounded on the pavement, and I glanced up to find Aubree looming over me. "You had to run, didn't you. Well, guess what? Stone's already in the building. Johnny's got him, so I don't need you anymore."

She raised her gun to shoot me, and my breath caught. This was it. I was going to die. A shot rang out, but I didn't feel any pain. Then I noticed a dark red stain blossoming on her chest. The gun slipped from her fingers, and she went down in a heap.

A few seconds later, her ragged breathing stopped.

More footsteps sounded, and I glanced up to find Ricky beside me. "I've got you. You're safe." He cut through my zip-tie with a knife.

"Where's Nate? Aubree said Johnny had him."

"We need to wrap your leg."

I grabbed the front of his shirt. "Where is he?"

Ricky finally met my gaze. "He's inside, but I don't know more than that."

"Shit. We have to get him out."

"I know. We will."

"No. You don't understand. Johnny's planning to blow up the building, and he doesn't care if he goes up with it."

Chapter 28

Stone

I entered the dark building, standing just inside the door and keeping my senses alert. The place was dingy and had a musty smell. The only light came from skylights in the ceiling. There were mounds of junk, old machine parts, and crates, stacked here and there throughout the building, leaving plenty of places to hide.

Movement came from the back end of the building, and I drew my weapon. Johnny stepped into view, his hands raised high. "Stone."

"Where's Serenity? Tell me, or I'll shoot."

"She's waiting for you, but you're going to have to use some of that luck of yours to find her before her time runs out."

"What do you mean?"

"Just a little exercise. Remember our last mission? Where you left me for dead?"

My nostrils flared, but I didn't argue.

"Well... this is your chance to redeem yourself. Your girlfriend's here, somewhere. All you have to do is find her and get her out before the bomb goes off."

My heart raced, but I kept calm. "What's the catch?"

He grinned. "There may be a few booby-traps along the way. But don't worry. If you're careful, you should be able to avoid them." He turned his hand so I could see the device in his palm and the numbers flashing red as they counted down. "I just set the timer. You have seven minutes before the place blows up."

A shot sounded from outside the building. Johnny flinched, and I knew it had taken him by surprise.

"What was that?"

He schooled his features. "I told Aubree to take care of the ex who tagged along with us. I guess he didn't want to cooperate. You'd better hurry. I left you a clue, but you only have six minutes now." He turned to leave.

"Where are you going?"

"I'd prefer not to get blown up this time." Another shot sounded from outside, and he quickly disappeared behind some crates.

"Shit." I believed that he'd set an explosive, but was Serenity really in here? What was going on outside? Whatever it was, I had to trust that Ricky or Slater would deal with it, and I needed to concentrate on finding Serenity.

With my time limited, I set my watch timer for five minutes and headed toward the largest stack of junk, deciding to climb up to get a better look at the layout. If Johnny had left me a clue, I had no idea what it was.

I climbed on top of a couple of rusted filing cabinets and took a few precious seconds to glance around. Nothing made sense. It was just an old building stacked with junk. I'd have to search from one end of the building to the other as fast as I could. Before I climbed down, a flash of light caught my eye.

It came from the northeast corner. Was it the clue? It flashed again, and I jumped to the ground and hurried in that direction. The hiss of a canister came from behind me, skittering along the concrete floor. I ducked behind an old desk and instinctively covered my ears and eyes. A flash-bang temporarily disoriented me.

I darted from my spot, depending on my memory to get me away from the smoke. Johnny must have thrown the device. Which meant he was still here. Reason told me that he couldn't have set this up very elaborately. Not after planning my death last night. So, instead of booby traps, the only thing I had to worry about was him.

I rushed around another row of filing cabinets and found an uncluttered path. Using that to guide me, I hurried toward the back of the building. The sound of a door opening and closing came from up ahead. Was that Johnny leaving before the building exploded?

"Nate! Where are you?"

"Serenity?"

"Hurry! I'm at the back of the building. We need to get out of here!"

I rounded the corner and dodged around some pipes and metal bars. Emerging from the stacks, I found Serenity standing just inside the building, about fifty feet away.

"Serenity, get out of here!"

She turned toward me. "Not without you. Hurry!"

As I closed the distance, Johnny stepped into my path. "No! I won't let you leave." He pointed a gun at my chest and fired.

Pain lanced through my ribs, throwing me on my back. I gasped like a fish out of water and couldn't catch my breath. Another shot went off, and I found the strength to push into a sitting position. Johnny lay on his back, blood pouring from his chest.

"Nate! No!" Serenity hobbled to my side, reaching for me.

"I'm fine. Bullet-proof vest."

"Oh my God. We have to run. The bomb!"

I lurched to my feet, seeing Ricky holding the door open and yelling at us to hurry. I pushed Serenity in front of me, and we stepped over Johnny's prone form. A hand grabbed my ankle, and I fell to my knees.

"You're not... leaving... not again..."

For a dying man, his grip was strong, but I twisted my ankle out of his hold and got to my feet.

"No!" Reaching for me, he caught nothing but air.

Without sparing him a glance, I rushed out the door, not far behind the others. A car was parked right outside the building, with the front passenger door wide open. Serenity had jumped into the back seat, and Ricky sat in the driver's seat. "Get in!! Quick!"

I jumped inside and he took off before I'd shut the door. Ricky floored it, driving to the end of the alley. Before we made it out, the building exploded, sending a wall of plaster and mortar towards us.

Ricky kept going, but something crashed into the car, spinning it around before we hit the side of the other building. Debris rained down on the roof and crushed it in toward our heads. "Get down!"

Glass shattered under the weight, and the back window blew out. A muffled yelp came from the back seat as more debris rained down on us. Dust filled the car, but the rumbling finally stopped, leaving us pinned inside.

Squished into the small space, it was hard to move, but I wasn't hurt. Ricky blinked his eyes open, blood running from a cut on his head. He shifted his weight, straining to get out from under the steering wheel.

A groan came from the back seat.

"Serenity? Are you okay?"

"I think so." She coughed. "I might need help getting out, though. It's pretty cramped back here."

"Yeah... we're cramped up here, too."

"Don't worry. We'll be okay. It's going to take a few minutes to get help, but we'll all walk out of here."

I licked my lips. "How do you know that?"

"Brandon's back here. I... saw it when I got in and touched him. He's kind of... pinned beneath me."

"Shit." Imagining her lying on top of that bastard curdled my stomach. I found the door handle and pushed against the door. It opened but hardly budged. I kept working at it, grateful that some light came in through the windshield, proving that we weren't completely buried. Shouting sounded from outside, and my heart jumped.

"Stone! Ricky? Where are you?"

"We're here." I yelled. "We're okay, but we need help getting out."

Slater stepped into view. "I see you. Give me a minute." He began clearing a space to the door, but it was slow going. He finally got the rubble cleared away from my side of the door, and I shoved it open enough to slither out.

As I stood, I took in the rest of the car, finding the whole back end totally smashed, the rear window gone, and the car roof dented inward. The damage ended abruptly at the back door, and I quickly cleared the debris away and wrenched it open. "Sen?"

She lay on the floor, level with the seat, her legs and feet close to the door. "I'm going to have to pull you out."

She rose onto her elbows, and a sharp yelp came from Brandon beneath her. "Yeah, that's a good idea."

Crouching, I tugged her toward me, my hand coming to a blood-soaked bandage around her thigh. "You're hurt." I pulled her close enough that I could wrap my arm around her waist and finish pulling her out.

As she gained her freedom, her arms snaked around my neck, and she leaned her head on my shoulder. I rose, gently gathering her in my arms to carry her away from the car.

"What happened to your leg?"

"Aubree shot me. But it's not bad. Just a nick."

From all the blood, it looked a lot worse than that.

"Hey... don't leave me here!" Brandon's voice was muffled. "Help! I can't move."

Serenity met my gaze. "Oh... Brandon's still tied up, so he can't get out."

I arched a brow. "Too bad for him, but I'm not lifting a finger for that bastard."

Her lips twisted. "I get it, but we can't leave him there."

"Yes we can. Someone else will have to do it."

She let out a sigh and dropped her face against my neck. "You made it. I wasn't sure, for a minute there... you got shot... right in the chest. Thank God you had on a vest."

Out of the blast zone, I set her down before claiming her lips. It had scared me, too, and relief spread over me in a powerful wave. Relief and something deeper I hadn't expected to feel... love. I loved her. It had happened so fast, it was hard to believe. But I'd never felt this way. Not for anyone else in all my life. "Sen... I think I... I..."

I closed my eyes. Why was it so hard to say the words? My mom and I used to say them to each other all the time, but it had been so long. I wasn't sure I knew how to say them anymore. Opening my eyes, I met her gaze, finding tenderness in the blue depths of her soul. Her smile broke my heart wide open. "I love you."

"I love you, too. I was so scared I'd never get to tell you."

My lips twisted into a lop-sided grin, and I kissed her again and again. Our world narrowed down to just the two of us, and I couldn't get enough of her.

"Uh... you guys? Sorry to interrupt, but the police are on their way."

The sound of sirens pulled me back to reality, and I reluctantly ended the kiss, but kept her firmly in my arms. Slater stood in front of his car, with Ricky and Brandon already inside.

"There's room for you both in the back next to Brandon."

I did not want to be anywhere near the guy, but what choice did I have? "Fine. Let's get out of here."

I slid in first, and Serenity slid in beside me. Slater wasted no time and peeled out of there. He drove to the end of the lot, turning in the opposite direction of the sirens. I didn't know what kind of trouble we'd all be in, but we'd figure it out later.

Slater glanced at me in the rear-view mirror. "Where do you want to go?"

"Serenity's wound needs to be looked at, so head the to the urgent care."

"Good call," Ricky said. "I'll call the Doc to meet us there." Ricky pulled out his phone and put the call through.

"What about him?" Slater motioned to Brandon.

"He's coming with us. Once Serenity's patched up, we'll take him back to her house." I glanced at Brandon. "We have some unfinished business."

His face drained of color, and he hunched over in his seat. His hands were still bound behind him, and it gave me a perverse pleasure to see him so miserable.

Lucky for us, Dix was already there, so it didn't take long to get Serenity stitched up. Still, it was starting to get dark by the time we headed back to Serenity's house, and I could hardly wait to get rid of Brandon.

I didn't think she'd let me kill him, but she might be persuaded into something else. With so many possibilities, I could hardly wait to see which one I could get away with.

Chapter 29

Serenity

We arrived home in the dark, which was a good thing, since we had to drag Brandon into the house through the front door. He didn't put up much of a fuss, but I had no idea what we were going to do with him.

Half his face was swollen, and the anger coming off Nate promised even more damage. Still, I just didn't have it in me to see Nate beat him up, even if he deserved it.

There had to be something else we could do.

Nate led him into the kitchen and pushed him into a chair. Brandon glanced at Nate and quickly turned his gaze to me. "Look. I don't know what you're involved in, or what's going on here, but I don't want anything to do with it. Just let me go, and I'll forget any of this ever happened."

Nate folded his arms and raised a brow. "Sorry, Dude, but it doesn't work that way. First you have to tell me why you wanted Serenity dead."

While Brandon sputtered out a denial, I pulled out a chair and sat down. "He took out a life insurance policy on me... I need to be dead for him to collect."

Brandon flinched and lowered his head. "It was a mistake. I don't want you dead... not anymore. Just let me go, and you'll never see me again."

"I wish I could believe that." Nate pulled out another chair, moving it in front of Brandon's, and sat down. He leaned forward into Brandon's space. "But this is what I'm going to do. I'm going to leave it up to Serenity. What happens to you is up to her."

He glanced at me, and sat back in his chair. "But I strongly recommend ending his miserable life. He shouldn't get away with attempted murder. How can you trust that he won't try again? I know how to make him disappear, and you won't have to worry about him ever again."

Brandon's gaze jerked to mine. "Serenity! No. You can't go along with him. That's murder. Can you live with that? I'll do whatever you want. Just let me go."

I met Nate's gaze, trying to decide if he was serious or just toying with Brandon. His hard edge never wavered, but would he really do whatever I wanted? Even if it meant killing Brandon? "You'd really kill him for me?"

His eyes crinkled a little, like he was happy to play along. "Of course I would. There's nothing I wouldn't do for you." His gaze flicked to Brandon. "And this asshole tried to kill you, so... yeah. I would."

My lips tilted up, and warmth tightened my chest. "Wow... you really love me, don't you?" I waited for his sexy-smile and nod before glancing at Brandon. "Well... in that case—"

"No! Serenity! You can't be serious?" Brandon's eyes widened. "Look. I'll sign the divorce papers right now. You'll never have to see me again. I promise. Just... you can't let him kill me."

"Yeah... but there's more to it now. What about everything that happened today? Can you keep your mouth shut about Johnny and Aubree and what happened to them?"

He swallowed. "Absolutely. Already forgotten."

"And the divorce papers?"

"I'll sign them first thing in the morning."

"Just to make sure you're telling me the truth..." I slowly reached over to touch his arm. He flinched, but couldn't move away from my touch. He closed his eyes like it would be painful, and I shook my head.

Concentrating on him, I took a deep breath and slowly let it out. I caught a glimpse of him arguing with the woman from the club. Her face was scrunched up in anger, and she was telling him it was over.

Hmm... did that mean he'd signed the papers and had none of the millions he'd promised her? I tried not to smile and glanced at Nate. "I think he'll go through with it. I don't love it, but I guess I'm good with it... unless he changes his mind."

Nate's lips twisted. "Are you sure that's what you want?"

I sized Brandon up, like I wasn't sure, before turning back to Nate. "It is."

He shook his head, like he was disgusted, and turned to Brandon. "As much as I don't want to do it, I guess that means that I have to cut you loose." He pulled out his knife. "Go ahead. Stand up."

Brandon lurched to his feet, but before he could turn around, Nate grabbed his shoulder and held the knife to his throat. "But know this, sleazebag. If you don't do everything you agreed to, your life is over. I will come for you. Understand?"

Brandon swallowed, and his throat bobbed before he nodded.

"Good." Nate lowered his knife. "Now turn around." He cut through the zip-tie, and Brandon quickly backed away. Rubbing his wrists, he hurried toward the front door. Pulling it open, he rushed out of the house like his pants were on fire.

I glanced at Nate. "That was oddly satisfying. Thank you." His smile melted my heart, and he pulled me into his arms.

"Anyone else you want me to threaten?"

"Um... not right now."

"Good, because I'm beat. What a day."

"No kidding. When Johnny shot you..." I shook my head. "Every time I shut my eyes, I still see it happening." I couldn't help the shudder that ran through me. "I thought I'd lost you."

"Babe... I was afraid of losing you, too. If it wasn't for that stupid dog—"

"What dog?"

He explained his adventure through the neighbors' back yard and how he'd ended up in a tree house and missed my call.

"Oh my gosh!" I shook my head. "From now on, you're carrying your lucky stone *everywhere* you go. And if you won't, I will."

"Sounds good to me." His lips lowered to mine in a tender kiss. Pulling away, he tugged me toward my room. "Come on. I want to savor every inch of you."

Before he could take a step, his phone rang. "Dammit!" Pulling it out of his pocket, he sighed. "It's Detective Scardino. I'd better answer." He swiped his phone. "Hey, Dino, what's up?"

Nate held the phone away from his ear, and I could hear Dino yelling about an explosion. Nate shook his head and waited for him to stop before responding. "Yeah. I got that, do you want me to tell you anything, or are you going to keep yelling at me?"

Listening, he closed his eyes. "Arrest me? What for? I didn't do anything..." Nate sighed and rubbed his forehead. "The owner of the property? Who is it?... Is that right?... good to know..." He let out a breath. "Yeah. I may know something about that, but I'm not telling you unless you can guarantee my anonymity... Sure... okay... yeah, yeah... I know the drill." He hung up and sighed.

"What was that about? He's not coming to arrest you, is he?"

"No, but he asked if I knew who the bodies belonged to. Then he said that the owner of the property dropped my name to them... telling them that I might have had something to do with it."

"What? Who is it?"

"Vanetti's competition. His name is Bruce Lawrence."

My brows drew together. "Aubree mentioned someone named Larry. Wait... I know that name... but I don't know from where."

"While you think about it, I need to call Vanetti."

"Yeah... that's a good idea."

I stepped to the refrigerator and pulled out a diet soda. I held the can up and Nate nodded, so I popped the lid and handed it to him. He closed his eyes and took a swig while waiting for Vanetti to pick up. "It's me. Did Ricky tell you what happened?"

He listened for a few more seconds before explaining his phone call from Dino. I held my can to my forehead, feeling drained and tired. All I wanted was to fall into bed with Nate, but from his conversation, I wasn't sure that would happen.

"She's okay, but she got shot." Nate met my gaze. "You want to talk to her? She's right here." He held out the phone and I took it, setting my soda on the counter.

"Hey there."

"I can't believe what happened, but I'm not real clear on how Johnny got you." I stifled a yawn and limped over to the couch, tugging Nate along with me. We sat down, and I explained the whole thing. Nate listened in, since he didn't know that part either.

"Good work. You've earned every bit of that money. In fact, you should come in tomorrow and I'll cut you a check."

"Thanks. I'll do that."

"I guess, with the job over, Nate can go home now."

I glanced at Nate. "Uh... yeah... I guess he could. Did you want to talk to him again?"

"Sure."

I handed the phone over. "Your turn."

Nate held the phone to his ear, and glanced my way. "Yeah?" He gently rubbed the dirt from my forehead and brushed his thumb across my lips. "Uh... sure. No. I'm staying here tonight." He shook his head. "Don't give me that ... Yeah? ... Whatever. See you tomorrow."

He put his phone away. "He wants us in his office first thing in the morning."

"Did you just tell him you were staying the night?"

He chuckled. "Yeah... he said he'd known something was going on between us, and we hadn't fooled him. But I think he just likes to act like he knows everything."

My brows rose. "Well, he kind of does."

Nate stood and tugged me to my feet. "Look at us. We're a mess."

I smiled. "Maybe we should take a shower?"

He pulled his shirt out and began to unbutton it, revealing his bullet-proof vest.

"Need some help getting it off?"

He nodded. "I'd appreciate it. My chest is a little sore."

We got the vest off, along with the t-shirt underneath, and I got a good look at the purple bruise where the bullet had hit him. "Ouch. That looks painful."

"It is."

"Should I kiss it better?" I stepped close and gently kissed his bruise. "Anyplace else that needs a kiss?"

"Yeah. Lots of them. But let's shower first."

That was all it took for us to head into my bathroom. There were a lot of bruises on both of us, but that didn't limit the amount of places that needed kissing.

By the time we were done, the water was running cold, but it was easily the best shower I'd ever taken in my life.

———•◦⊰⊱◦•———

I woke the next morning, cradled against Nate's chest. My heart expanded, knowing something special was happening between us. It was the start of something new and more exciting than I could have imagined.

"Sen?"

"Hey."

He inhaled deeply. "I don't want to get up."

I chuckled. "Me neither. Will Vanetti be okay if we wait until tomorrow? After yesterday, I think we deserve a day off, right?"

"Ha. If only. No. We'd better get going."

"I guess so." I slid out from under him, but he tugged me back down and nuzzled his face against my neck.

"I just need one more kiss... then you can get up."

That one kiss lasted a little longer than it should have, and it was another half hour before we finally got out of bed.

"Do you think Vanetti will yell at us for being late?" I asked, tugging on my boots.

Nate shrugged. "He can yell all he wants. It was totally worth it." He sent me that sexy, lop-sided grin that always made my heart flutter, and I had to agree.

I didn't think I could ever get enough of him. Was I an idiot for falling for a hitman? Maybe... but he was a good guy... not like a real hitman, right? Still, whatever this was, I wouldn't change it for anything.

Before we left, my phone rang. The caller ID said it was my lawyer, so I quickly answered. "Hello?"

"Serenity! I have some great news for you. Brandon just dropped off the divorce papers. And get this: he signed off on everything. I knew you'd be thrilled, so I had to call."

"Wow! That's great. Thanks for letting me know."

"Of course. I wonder why he changed his mind."

"Yeah... no kidding. I guess he had a change of heart. So, what's next?"

"I'll file with the judge today. That means the divorce should be final in the next couple of weeks."

I let out a breath. "That's the best news ever. Thanks." I disconnected and glanced up at Nate. His brow rose, and I tried to suppress my enthusiasm. "Dang. I guess you don't get to kill Brandon... sorry."

He snickered and pulled me into a hug. "I'll just have to get over it. But at least he's out of our lives."

My heart swelled. "I like the sound of that."

He gave me a sweet kiss, full of promise, and I couldn't hold back the love I felt for him. Pulling away, I sighed. "We'd better get going before Vanetti fires you."

We stepped off the elevator onto the twenty-sixth floor and went right to Vanetti's office, passing Julia. "There you are. I was just about to call you." Julia glanced between us, and a sly smile curved her lips. "Go on down. He's waiting for you."

Nate gave her a chin nod, and continued down the hall with me beside him. He didn't waste any time knocking, and opened the door.

Vanetti glanced up from his desk. "It's about time."

Nate raised a brow. "We had a rough day, yesterday." He glanced at me. "Didn't we?"

I wanted to add that the night was pretty rough too, only in a much better way. Instead, I cleared my throat and glanced at Vanetti. "Yes. But don't blame Nate. I had a hard time getting out of bed this morning." My eyes widened. Did I just say that out loud?

Vanetti rolled his eyes. "Well... since you're both so worn out, you'd better sit down."

As we took our seats, Nate grinned at me, and I couldn't help smiling back.

Vanetti let out a small huff before getting down to business. "We need to pay Bruce Lawrence a visit. I have a feeling he's more involved with this than we know."

He met my gaze. "Remember that first job you did for me? Finding the letter that got lost?"

"Oh my gosh! That's right. It was from him. Bruce Lawrence. That's where I've heard that name before."

"Exactly. He's been encroaching on my business for a while, and I think he decided to make his move. At least that's what it looks like, since he owns the property that Johnny blew up. We need to pay him a visit and find out what he's up to."

He met my gaze. "And I'd like you to come with us. You might be the key to uncovering his secrets. Will you come?"

"Sure. If it's tied to Nate, I'd like to finish the job."

"Good. Let me get Ricky and Slater. They're coming with us."

A few minutes later, we were all headed down to the parking garage. As we passed Nate's motorcycle, I slowed to glance at it and let out a sigh. I'd made sure to wear my leather jacket, just in case I could get a ride.

"Hold up," Nate said, calling to the others. "We'll meet you there." Without waiting for a response from them, he pulled me over to the bike.

Barely able to hold in my excitement, I grinned up at him. "How did you know?"

"Babe... it's what made you fall in love with me. Right?"

I raised a brow. "Maybe. I mean... it definitely helped."

"Yeah? What else?"

"Well... it could have been seeing you without your shirt for the first time..." I sent him a saucy smile. "Then there's the way you kiss me... and you really are quite handy—"

A car honked, and I practically jumped out of my skin.

With a chuckle, Nate pulled our helmets from the trunk of his car, handing mine over. "As much as I'm enjoying this, I guess we'll have to finish the conversation later."

I pushed my helmet on and fastened it like a pro. At least I'd learned how to do that right. We quickly mounted the bike and followed behind the black SUV.

I wrapped my arms around Nate, giving in to the enjoyment of the moment. I didn't think I'd ever get tired of this, either. And just thinking about all the rides ahead of us sent sunshine right into my heart.

Before I was ready, we pulled into the parking lot of an office building in a plaza on the other side of town.

With Vanetti taking the lead, we followed him into the building. We passed the receptionist's desk, ignoring her cries that we couldn't go into Lawrence's office.

Vanetti opened the door and we followed him in, flanking his position and surrounding the man sitting at his desk. He was a big guy, but a little on the pudgy side. "What the—what is the meaning of this?"

"Hello, Lawrence." Vanetti motioned to Ricky, who stepped back to lock the door. "I think we need to have a chat."

Lawrence stiffened, then he moved to open his desk drawer.

Nate pulled his gun. "I wouldn't do that if I were you." He motioned with his gun. "Hands on the desk."

Letting out a huff, Lawrence placed his hands where we could see them. "I have no idea why you'd barge in here like this. What is this about?"

"I'd like you to explain why you told the police that Stone was involved in the explosion at your property yesterday."

"How did you—" He swallowed. "That was confidential information."

"And yet... you did. So, what's your plan? Trying to move in on my business?"

"No. Absolutely not. I know better than that."

Vanetti glanced my way, then back at him. "Could Serenity borrow that pen you're holding?"

I stepped forward and held out my hand.

"I guess." He shrugged before handing it to me.

"And that notepad, too?"

Picking it up, he gave it to me.

A couple of seconds later, I quickly wrote down what I'd picked up, tore off the paper, and handed it to Vanetti.

He read it, then folded the paper and put it in his pocket. "It looks like you've been trying to undermine my business for a while, now. It was you who paid someone to break into my safe. Was it your idea to kill Stone, too?"

"What? Absolutely not. I don't know what you're talking about."

"Right. Well... I have some news for you. Both Aubree and Johnny are dead. Your plans have failed."

Lawrence's eyes widened. "They're dead?"

Vanetti nodded. "You have a lot to learn, Lawrence, but the most important thing you should know is to stay out of my way. I'll give you a warning, and I'll say it only once. If anything even remotely close to this ever happens again, you'll pay a heavy price. Even if you survive, you'll wish you were dead."

Lawrence pursed his lips, then glanced away and nodded. "Fine. Are you done?"

Vanetti smiled, but it didn't reach his eyes. "For now, but you should know that I'm just getting started. You owe me. Expect to hear from me soon."

With that, Vanetti turned toward the door. Ricky opened it and followed him out, Slater went next. Nate motioned for me to follow, and turned for a parting glance at Lawrence. "You tried to have me killed. I don't care what Vanetti said, it's not something I'm going to forget."

Lawrence swallowed. "It wasn't my idea. I swear."

Nate nodded. "Maybe not, but I wouldn't get too comfortable in this town if I were you. In fact, a change of scenery might be the best thing for your continued good health."

If anything, Lawrence seemed more afraid of Nate than he had of Vanetti.

"I'll be seeing you." Nate stepped into the hall and pulled the door closed behind him.

As we followed the others out, I lifted a brow. "Damn, you're scary."

He tried not to grin. "Why, thank you."

We congregated in the parking lot, and Vanetti rubbed his hands together. "That went well. Thanks for the tip, Serenity."

"Of course."

"While I've got you, there's something I'd like you to consider. Now that I've seen what you can accomplish, I'd like to hire you on a permanent basis."

My eyes widened. "Really?"

He smiled. "Yes. It could be on a job-by-job arrangement, if that's best for your business, but I'm sure we can work something out. You can think about it first, if you need to."

I glanced at Nate to gauge his response, and caught a flare of excitement in his eyes. Sending him a saucy grin, I turned to Vanetti. "I'd like that."

"Wonderful." Vanetti turned to Nate. "And Stone... take the rest of the day off. You deserve it."

Vanetti grinned at both of us before turning to the car and getting inside with the others. As they drove off, Nate shook his head and handed me my helmet. "You're sure you want to work for a mob boss?"

"Would you be okay with that?"

He chuckled. "Hmm... well it might mean I'd have to haul you around on my bike, and make sure you don't get killed, but... I guess I'd be okay with it. There's only one stipulation."

"What's that?"

"Keeping us both alive is your number one priority, so I expect you to touch me as much as possible to make sure that happens."

I grinned up at him. "I think I can handle that."

He caught me under my arms and pulled me against his chest. As he lowered me back down, his lips met mine in a searing kiss. "Ready to ride?"

"You know it."

Thank you for reading *The Hitman and the Psychic*. If you enjoyed this book, please leave a review on Amazon or anywhere you post them! It's a great way to thank an author and keep her writing!!

ABOUT THE AUTHOR

Jocelyn Drake is the pen name for Jackie Manetto, a character in the Shelby Nichols Adventure Series. She writes steamy romance novels, and admits that she gets most of her ideas from her job at Thrasher Development working for Joe E. Manetto, a prominent businessman who is often accused of being a mob boss.

Connect with Jocelyn at www.manettobooks.com

ABOUT THE AUTHOR

USA TODAY AND WALL STREET JOURNAL BESTSLLING AUTHOR

Colleen Helme is the author of the bestselling Shelby Nichols Adventure Series, a wildly entertaining and highly humorous series about Shelby Nichols, a woman with the ability to read minds.

When not writing, Colleen spends most of her time thinking about new ways to get her characters in and out of trouble. She loves to connect with readers and admits that fans of her books keep her writing.

Connect with Colleen at www.colleenhelme.com

NEWSLETTER SIGNUP

For news, updates, and special offers, please sign up for my newsletter at www.colleenhelme.com.
To thank you for subscribing you will receive a FREE ebook: *Behind Blue Eyes: A Shelby Nichols Novella.*

www.ingramcontent.com/pod-product-compliance
Lightning Source LLC
Chambersburg PA
CBHW030551260626
47157CB00006B/2277